Hold You
Down

ALSO BY TRACY BROWN

Single Black Female

Criminal Minded

White Lines

Twisted

Snapped

Aftermath

White Lines II: Sunny

White Lines III: All Falls Down

Boss

ANTHOLOGIES

Flirt

Hold You Down

TRACY BROWN

ST. MARTIN'S
GRIFFIN
NEW YORK

First published in the United States by St. Martin's Griffin, an imprint of St. Martin's Publishing Group

HOLD YOU DOWN. Copyright © 2022 by Tracy Brown. All rights reserved. Printed in the United States of America. For information, address St. Martin's Publishing Group, 120 Broadway, New York, NY 10271.

www.stmartins.com

Designed by Omar Chapa

Library of Congress Cataloging-in-Publication Data

Names: Brown, Tracy, 1974- author.
Title: Hold you down / Tracy Brown.
Description: First Edition. | New York : St. Martin's Griffin, 2022.
Identifiers: LCCN 2022023075 | ISBN 9781250834935 (trade paperback) | ISBN 9781250834942 (ebook)
Subjects: LCGFT: Novels.
Classification: LCC PS3602.R723 H65 2022 | DDC 813/.6—dc23
LC record available at https://lccn.loc.gov/2022023075

Our books may be purchased in bulk for promotional, educational, or business use. Please contact your local bookseller or the Macmillan Corporate and Premium Sales Department at 1-800-221-7945, extension 5442, or by email at MacmillanSpecialMarkets@macmillan.com.

First published in the United States by St. Martin's Griffin, St. Martin's Publishing Group

First Edition: 2022

10   9   8   7   6   5   4   3   2   1

*This book is for the little boys who became
men without the benefit of a father figure or mentor.
And for the women who love them.*

Part One

MERCY & LENOX

Harlem, 1984

Standing at their mother's gravesite, the sisters locked eyes and had a silent conversation.

Mercy shivered against the brutal February cold and hugged her coat tighter around her body. Her sister, Lenox, appeared to be freezing, too, as she blew deep breaths into her hands in a futile attempt to warm them. Frustrated, Lenox finally shoved her hands into the pockets of her wool coat and glanced at Mercy, helplessly.

Mercy looked around. The handful of mourners who had gathered with them at their mother's burial seemed just as frustrated by the preacher's long-windedness as they were. The icy winter air sliced through them. The minister seemed indifferent as he continued his lengthy prayer for their mother's departed soul. With his eyes shut and his shearling coat shrouding him in warmth, he kept right on stringing big words together in the name of Jesus.

"We ask you to welcome Sharon into your kingdom with open arms, Lord. Notwithstanding the sins of her youth or the snares the enemy laid in her path throughout her lifetime. Welcome her into Heaven. Wrap your loving arms around her, Lord. Wash her in the blood of the lamb and forgive her transgressions."

"Reverend Bell," Lenox interrupted.

The minister's eyes flew open and landed on her scowling face. He stared at her, stunned by her audacity in interrupting his grand finale.

"You preached already at the service. And now you said a real good prayer. We're gonna need you to say 'amen' and let us get up out of here. We made peace with our Mama. If God ain't done the same by now, it ain't meant to be."

Several mourners reacted audibly, some chuckling and others gasping.

Mercy closed her eyes and pressed her lips together.

Reverend Bell cleared his throat. He had only met Sharon's daughters in the final weeks of her life. Even with that brief amount of experience with Lenox, he knew that it was smart not to argue with her.

"Amen," he said.

"Amen," the small crowd said in unison before quickly dispersing.

Mercy scampered over to her sister's side. Both of them walked quickly back toward the row of cars.

"Len, something is wrong with you. You know that, right?"

Lenox sucked her teeth.

"Shit, we were *all* thinking it."

They hustled over to Mercy's Buick Century parked nearby. Mercy climbed into the driver's seat and turned the heat up higher. Lenox climbed in, shut the passenger door behind her, and rubbed her cold hands over the vents as the heat poured forth.

"Leave it to our mother to go to hell on the coldest day of the year!"

"Lenox!" Mercy chided. She glared at her sister before she turned around to the backseat where their sons, Judah and Deon, sat together innocently. "Watch your mouth. The boys are in here."

"And?" Lenox asked. "They know she's dead."

"They're little kids, dummy. They don't need to hear you talking about it like that."

Lenox waved her off.

Mercy offered a weak smile to the boys. "Y'all alright?"

Her son, Judah, nodded.

"Are *you* alright, Ma?" His voice held genuine concern. Even at eight years old, he understood that death was something very sad and very final, that his mother had just buried her own mother. He expected her to be breaking down. Instead, she hadn't shed a tear all day.

Mercy smiled at him again, more sincerely this time. "Yes, baby. I'm alright." She turned around, put the car in gear, and drove off.

Deon sat forward in the backseat and looked at Lenox.

"How 'bout you, Ma? You okay?" He was a year younger than his cousin, but was usually the more outspoken of the two.

Lenox laughed.

"Yes, boy! I keep telling you that losing Mama doesn't make me sad."

Mercy cut a side-eye at Lenox.

"What she means is that it's complicated," Mercy explained. "Our mother wasn't around much. Not since we were little girls. That's why you only met her for the first time a few weeks ago when we brought you to see her."

Lenox turned around and faced her son and nephew.

"Mama disappeared on us when our daddy died."

Deon's eyes went wide. Judah listened intently as his Aunt Lenox continued.

"We were all one big happy family until Daddy died from a heart attack. After that, Mama met a new man and said she fell in love. Her new husband didn't want a 'ready-made family.' So, Mama left us behind and went and lived her life without us."

Lenox turned around in her seat and lit a cigarette. "The only

Mama we know is Lula Mae. That was our grandmother. We called
her Mama Lula."

Judah and Deon both listened carefully to this rare moment
of candidness. Neither of their mothers had spoken much within
their earshot about their extended family. Attending their grandmother's funeral today—even though they only met her once before
she died—and hearing a little family history was fascinating for
both of them.

"What's a ready-made family?" Deon asked, innocently.

Mercy groaned.

"He didn't want a woman who had kids," Lenox clarified.
"That's what that means."

Deon gave it a moment's thought. "So, she just left you?"

"Just like that." Lenox exhaled some cigarette smoke and
cracked her window a bit.

Mercy frowned at her.

"You were just so cold you had to interrupt the preacher. Now
you got the window open, letting all the warm air out."

Lenox shrugged. "I feel a little better now," she said, honestly.
"I just needed to get out of there. We all did. Mama's gone. Ain't no
bringing her back. No matter how hard Reverend Hallelujah prays."

Mercy laughed, despite herself. "You need help."

Lenox took another puff of her cigarette and smiled. "I know."

Hours later, after their mother's small gathering of friends and
family had joined them for the repast, Mercy and Lenox Howard left
Harlem. It was a place that held so many bittersweet memories for
both of them. Harlem was where they grew up. Their grandmother
had sought refuge there after fleeing the Jim Crow South. Grandma
Lula Mae had moved to New York, working in factories and taking
odd jobs to make ends meet. She had settled on 123rd Street and
raised her daughter, Sharon, single-handedly, doing her best to provide her with a good life. Her efforts had not been in vain. Sharon
had not been wealthy, but was certainly not raised in poverty. As a

result of her mother's hard work, Sharon wore pretty new dresses all the time and had a recurring weekly appointment at the neighborhood hair salon. Lula Mae had ensured that her daughter grew up knowing that she was loved.

When Sharon came of age and married, she struggled to conceive at first. After several failed attempts, she had her daughters back-to-back. First Mercy—aptly named after her mother suffered several miscarriages—then Lenox—named for the block they lived on. Mercy and Lenox had fond memories of being little girls in pigtails playing double Dutch on the sidewalk in front of their row house. Their parents in love, their grandmother only blocks away. Those had been the good days.

When their father suffered a heart attack and passed away, their mother didn't mourn for very long before leaving them with their grandmother Lula Mae. That arrangement was supposed to be temporary, but it quickly became apparent that she wasn't coming back.

Harlem became the only world Mercy and Lenox knew, the only place they felt like they belonged. Growing up there had been exciting and treacherous at the same time. A never-ending whirlwind of delightful sights, sounds, and colors with danger lurking around every corner. Pimps and prostitutes, preachers and panhandlers always present.

After she remarried, their mother, Sharon, sent money for them each month. She dropped by Harlem every couple of years for a one-week visit then disappeared back into the new life she had made for herself with her new husband—a jazz musician who moved around a lot. For the most part, Mercy and Lenox had been on their own. Their grandmother had worked long hours as a home health aide, leaving the girls to navigate the gritty streets of Harlem largely by themselves.

It was clear early on that Lenox was the spunkier one. She was tougher than Mercy was, willing to fight her own battles as well as her sister's. Mercy had always been eager to please their grandmother, so she steered clear of trouble and kept her focus on school. When problems came her way from jealous girls in school, Mercy rarely fought back. But when those beefs spilled over to dismissal, things changed. Lenox would step in cussing and break a bottle, backing all the bullies off her sister. Lenox had been fearless from the start.

They had a small friend circle, mostly keeping to themselves. They grew up as confidantes, friendly competitors, and as flip sides of the same coin.

Fresh out of high school, Mercy had fallen in love and gotten pregnant by a guy from the neighborhood who abandoned her the moment he found out that she was pregnant. Alone and ashamed, she felt like a burden to her grandmother. So, she got a welfare case and put her name on the waiting list for the projects. The first housing development that selected her application was one all the way out in Staten Island. It seemed like a world away from Harlem. But Mercy decided that might not be such a bad thing. She wanted a fresh start for her and her son. She packed up the little she had and moved to the city's fifth borough in 1977.

Lenox had been miserable without her sister at first. As close as they were, she felt a void where Mercy had been. They usually rose early each morning and Lenox played with her nephew, Judah, while Mercy and their grandmother made breakfast. With Mercy gone, the mood in the apartment had changed. Life felt boring and for the first time in Lenox's life, she was lonely without her sister. But she soon found a welcome distraction in an older man she met while she was shopping on 125th Street. He wined and dined her, seduced her, and Lenox fell in love. She found out she was pregnant and was worried that he would react the same way that Mercy's man had. Instead, he told her to pack her things. He was getting an apartment for them and he would take care of her. Lenox had rushed home and told her grandmother, and happily packed her things. She waited expectantly, but he never showed up. Devastated, Lenox assumed that she had been played. But she soon discovered that he hadn't abandoned her after all. He had been killed over a dice game, shot in the head and left to die alone on the cold city street.

Grieving, Lenox had followed her sister out to Staten Island. She slept on Mercy's couch at first. Then eventually she got her own place—a Section 8 apartment in a private home a few minutes away from Mercy. Now the two of them were as inseparable as they had ever been, and their sons were growing up side by side.

Lenox stood barefoot now in the kitchen of Mercy's apartment. The kids were playing noisily together in Judah's bedroom. Lenox snapped her fingers to the music playing from the boombox sitting on the kitchen counter. She twirled around, winding her hips with a smile spread across her face.

"I know you remember this song, Mercy! Mama Lula used to play this all the time."

"Chain of fools . . ."

Lenox sang along with Aretha Franklin.

Mercy smiled at the memory. Smiled wider at the sight of her sister dancing dramatically around the room. Lenox twirled herself in a circle, winding her voluptuous body like a seasoned pro.

"Mama Lula loved this song. Sang it every weekend while she was cleaning the apartment."

Lenox laughed.

"Dancing around with the mop like it was a man."

The sisters giggled together at the thought.

"I miss her so much," Lenox said. "I wish she was here to see how big the boys are. She would be spoiling them rotten."

"She sure would," Mercy agreed. She opened the refrigerator and pulled out a soda. "I can't believe it's been five years since she passed. Seems like just yesterday I was calling her for advice."

"She gave the best advice." Lenox said it dreamily, with her eyes closed. She opened them again and looked at her sister.

"Like right after Deon's father was killed. I wanted to curl up in a ball and die, too. Mama Lula wasn't having it. She said, 'LENOX!

Get yo' butt up and LIVE! You're a fighter. You don't need no man to save you. Don't need no man to rescue you and your baby. God gave you everything you need to survive. It's in *you*! All you gotta do is dig down deep and find your strength. Then you get up and you do what you gotta do for that baby and for yourself.'" Lenox smiled at the memory. "That shit snapped me out of the fog I was in. Mama Lula never played that damsel in distress shit. She let me know I had to be my own hero."

Mercy nodded.

"She was one tough lady. Never took no mess. She passed that down to us."

Lenox laughed.

"And thank God she did. Otherwise, we might have ended up just like Mama. Dick-matized by some no-good, trifling bastard."

Mercy laughed, too. "You have a way with words."

Lenox shook her head. "You know it's true. Mama was only good as long as a man was around. Never could stand on her own two feet the way we've been doing."

Mercy scoffed. "I'm not on solid ground yet. I'm a single mother on welfare." Mercy looked around her modest apartment and longed for a breakthrough. "I told myself it was only gonna be for a little while. But I can't find a decent job to save my life."

"Don't be negative," Lenox chided her sister. "I'm not doing that great either. Not right now anyway. Things might not be perfect for us. But at least we're trying. We're raising our own kids and being better mothers to them than Mama ever was to us. That's a start."

She squeezed Mercy's hand, reassuringly.

"Besides, Mama might not have been shit. But she left us a little change behind at least."

Mercy snickered.

"After all the funeral expenses, we'll have about ten thousand dollars to split. That ain't life changing."

"*Shiiiit.* It's enough to get me some new furniture, a new hairstyle, and, hopefully, a new man." Lenox laughed. "And that's just what I'm gonna do!"

Mercy laughed, too. She loved her sister and all of their differences. They balanced each other out and drove each other crazy at the same time.

"What you gonna do with your half?" Lenox asked.

Mercy looked at her sister, skeptically. She worried that Lenox would dismiss her idea as a crazy one.

"I think I want to open a restaurant. Like the ones uptown. A soul food spot like the kind they got on every corner in Harlem. Staten Island doesn't have anything like that. At least not a good one."

Lenox stared at Mercy silently for a time. She tilted her head as if the thought was literally shifting through her mind.

"I think that's a great idea," she said at last.

Mercy beamed.

"Yeah? You don't think it's crazy?"

Lenox shook her head. "Nope! With all the recipes Mama Lula taught you and the way you love to cook . . . it's brilliant."

Mercy clapped her hands, gleefully. "I thought you would say it sounded unrealistic."

"Nope," Lenox said. "No risk, no reward. I'm down for anything that will help us level up and make some real money."

Mercy nodded.

"I'm sick of being broke," Lenox continued. "Seems like we've been struggling to make ends meet since we were born. Mama Lula did the best she could. Now Mama left us a little something. But there's real money to be made out there. Did you see all those fancy cars and white women in fur coats while we were uptown today? I want *that* life."

Mercy chuckled. "You should be my partner, then."

Lenox shrugged. "It's your dream. I think you should do it on your own. I'll help, of course! I'll even invest some of my share. But you don't need me. You can do this for you and Judah. Make Mama Lula proud."

Mercy sighed.

"Thank you, Len. I was worried you would laugh at me."

Lenox smiled.

"I was worried you were gonna play it safe for the rest of your life. Sweet Mercy. Always coloring inside the lines. Never breaking the rules or taking too many chances. This is brave. I like seeing this side of you."

Mercy sat down at her small kitchen table and glanced out the window at a handful of young men huddled together near the front of her building. It was dark outside and the group seemed immune to the brutal cold wind blowing.

"I used to dream about going to culinary school, but I got pregnant. Had to put my plans on the back burner for a while. I'm a mama bear first. You know how it is."

Lenox nodded. "Yeah. But it's the eighties now. Women are raising kids and living their dreams at the same time. So, don't forget that, mama bear."

Mercy smiled. "You've always been the risk-taker, Len. Not me. Since we were kids it's been that way."

Lenox agreed. "That's true. But I wished I could be more like you."

Mercy was surprised. "Really?"

"Hell yeah. You think about something, plan it out, and make it happen. In school you were like that. Focused and prepared. I graduated by the skin of my teeth." Lenox chuckled. "Then you tackled motherhood the same way. I know you were hurt when Judah's sperm donor disappeared. But you fought past the pain and focused on preparing yourself for your new role. I watched you making lists, comparing prices, setting up his little nursery in our bedroom. Reading books about what to expect and shit. I was impressed! By the time Judah took his first breath, you were READY! And you haven't changed. You're still the thinker, the planner, the mama bear. I'm more like Goldilocks wandering around looking for sum'n to steal."

Mercy laughed. "On that note, I'm about to get Judah ready for bed. Make him take his bath and all of that."

"You mind watching Deon tonight?" Lenox asked softly.

Mercy looked at her.

"Again?"

"I know. You watched him last weekend, too. And I'll return the favor. I promise."

"Where you going this time?"

Lenox grinned, sweetly.

"G wants to take me out again. Said he got a party uptown he wants to show me off at."

"Okay. So, tell 'G' to find you a babysitter."

Mercy pretended not to notice when Lenox pouted like a kid who wasn't getting her way.

"Come on. Don't be like that."

Mercy sucked her teeth.

"Since when did you two start spending so much time together? For years, GERARD has been strutting around here saying and doing whatever he could to get your attention. All of a sudden he's driving a Mercedes and got everybody calling him 'G.' Now you need a babysitter every weekend."

Lenox smirked, guiltily.

"He seemed corny before. All those polyester pants and high-water jeans." She shuddered at the memory.

Mercy laughed despite herself. Style had always been of the utmost importance to Lenox. Even on a tight budget, Lenox kept up with the latest fashion trends no matter what.

"But now he seems to be getting his shit together. He moved his mama out the hood and got some respect about himself. Last week he took me to the movies and I realized he's got a sweet personality. He's growing on me. Plus he didn't skimp on the *good* snacks!"

Lenox walked over to the counter and picked up her pack of cigarettes. She sighed, realizing there was only one left.

Mercy watched her, then rolled her eyes and turned her attention back to the men huddled outside. Some of them had scattered now, but two remained in position in front of her building. Finally, she sighed.

"Be careful out there, Lenox. And don't think I'm gonna be your babysitter every weekend. One of these days you're gonna watch the boys while I go out for a change."

Lenox laughed. "When?"

Mercy narrowed her eyes.

"Soon, bitch! Just know that. And I need you to pick Deon up before noon tomorrow. I have my eye on a place I might be able to rent on Castleton Avenue for my restaurant. I wanna go check it out. I would take Deon with me, but you know how wild he gets when you're not around for too long. I don't feel like fussing with him in public."

Lenox smiled sweetly, grabbed her purse, and headed for the door.

"No problem. I'll pick him up early. Tell Deon I love him!" she called out over her shoulder as she rushed to the elevator.

Mercy braced herself for the bang of the door slamming shut. When it did, she shook her head, turned the music up on the radio, and sat back. She took a deep breath and thought about their mother. For Lenox it may have been no big deal. But Mercy was feeling a bit melancholy. Her mother wasn't around much. But when she did show up, Mercy had always lit up with excitement. Seeing her was like seeing an angel in the flesh. One with broken wings, but an angel nonetheless.

Glancing out her window, she watched her sister floating down the block yelling greetings to all the people she knew. Mercy smiled, thinking that Lenox was probably more like their mother than she cared to admit.

FUNHOUSE

"Oh shit!"

G stepped back from the melee.

Lenox gasped as the bouncer tossed a drunken partygoer out the front door of the Funhouse nightclub in midtown Manhattan. A long line of clubgoers stood on the slowly progressing line outside. But G had walked her right past all of those hopeful people and marched her right up to the door. There two burly bouncers stood guard searching each person and denying entry to several. Some were told that they weren't dressed appropriately, others had apparently suffered run-ins with the bouncers on previous occasions. A slim woman in a skintight bodysuit stood at the door with a list of VIPs.

G stepped up and gave his name.

"I'm with Benny and them."

Seemingly unconvinced, the woman scanned the list, then looked him up and down. She nodded slightly, and the bouncers parted the velvet rope without so much as a pat down. Lenox, impressed, held G's hand as they stepped inside the nightclub. Hip-hop music boomed from the speakers and a spectacular light show made Lenox's eyes widen with delight. While she stood in awe of the colorful psychedelic projections, G scanned the crowded club looking for his crew. Dancers were letting loose all around them and Lenox started dancing, too, caught up in the rapture of it all.

G looked at her and smiled.

"I can tell you like it here."

"This place is crazy!" she shouted back over the music and laughter. She pointed excitedly at the DJ booth, which was inside the mouth of a huge clown's head. Partiers crowded the bar, packed the dance floor, and a few entertained themselves playing a bunch of arcade games at the other end of the vast nightclub.

G smiled, pleased with himself for impressing her so much already.

"You ain't seen nothing yet. Come let me introduce you to my man Benny. I see him over there."

He took Lenox by the hand and led her through the crowd. As they neared the end of the bar clouded by cigarette smoke, she saw a short and stocky Puerto Rican guy gesture to G and smile in their direction. When they got close to the man, G spread his arms wide and the two embraced like old friends. G turned and immediately greeted a bunch of the man's friends, including a group of women wearing miniskirts and skimpy tops despite the frigid winter cold outside.

G introduced Lenox to his friends.

"This is my man Benny from uptown. We do business together."

Benny hugged Lenox tightly like they were long-lost acquaintances who hadn't seen each other in ages. She stiffened a bit at first, but relaxed as she noticed his warmth and charm.

"She's fuckin' beautiful, G. You don't deserve her. What's your name, gorgeous?"

"Lenox," she replied, smiling.

"You from Harlem?"

"That's where I was born and raised."

"I could tell by your name. No wonder I like you! I'm from the Bronx. Practically neighbors and shit."

He stroked her cheek, quickly, and smiled again.

"What you drinking?"

G pulled her closer to him.

"I got her covered. Don't worry."

Benny frowned, though his lips still curled a bit at the edges.

"Get the fuck outta here. It's on me tonight. Everything!" He gestured to the bartender and she rushed right over. "Give my friend and his lady whatever they want to drink. Keep that shit coming, too. I don't want to see their glasses empty!"

He winked at Lenox, slapped G five, and hustled off to the dance floor with one of the scantily clad ladies.

Lenox and G ordered their drinks and joined the crowd. Young and old, black and white, straight and gay people all danced together. The DJ played a mix of disco, rap, funk, and dance music that made the crowd go wild. Lenox had never seen anything like it. She and G swayed together to Blondie's "Rapture," her arm wrapped tenderly around his neck.

"You having fun?" he asked.

She nodded, beaming.

"If I knew hanging out with you was gonna be like this, I would have said 'yes' a long time ago."

He laughed.

"I tried to tell you. Can't always judge a book by its cover. I know I didn't look like I had much. *Shit . . .* I didn't for a long time. But then I got plugged in. Now everything is different. Life is good."

"Plugged into what?" she couldn't help asking. "Where did you get all this money from? All these new friends?"

"I got a tip. Like them white boys on Wall Street."

She frowned as she tried to understand.

"Like stocks and bonds and all of that?"

He nodded.

"Yeah. Sum'n like that. My cousin Mark lives in the Bronx. He started working with Benny. Made a bunch of money overnight. I kid you not. Went from living in a rat-infested tenement building to owning a house on Long Island. Within months. Mark put me on. Now I'm working with Benny, too."

"Doing what?"

He grinned, then kissed her tenderly on the lips.

"Making sure people have fun," he said. "You said you're having fun, right?"

She nodded, and squealed a little as he spun her around. He pulled her close to him, holding her tightly around her slim waist.

"Good. I like that."

The DJ switched songs and Lenox took a sip of her drink.

"So, what kind of 'fun' are we talking about? Does Benny know the owner here?"

"He knows everybody."

"How? What kind of work does he do?"

G tapped her on the tip of her nose, playfully.

"You ask too many questions."

Before she could press him further, Benny was back at their side.

"Come on. Let's take a picture!"

Within seconds, they were part of a large group of people posing in hip-hop stances against a graffiti backdrop. Lenox had only met these people moments ago, but she laughed and mingled with them now, all doing choreographed poses as the photographer clicked away. Benny took on the role of photo shoot director, instructing each person on how to stand. He made jokes as he stood in the center of them all, making everyone laugh. Soon, Lenox pushed all of her questions to the back of her mind and allowed herself to get swept up in the thrill of the moment. She was in the IN crowd for once, partying the night away with a little money to her name for once and a decent man on her arm. She threw her hands in the air, thrust her booty out, and blew a kiss to the camera as the lights flashed all around her.

Hours later, Lenox sat across from G in a booth at a diner on Broadway. They had shut the club down along with Benny and all his friends. All of them were feeling the effects of a long night of hard partying, including Lenox. Benny and his crew had piled into expensive cars and gone back uptown where they lived. Now she and G were alone together sipping strong coffee and eating breakfast as the sun rose.

This meal was an attempt at sobering up a bit before making the drive back to Staten Island. G had slickly suggested that they stay overnight at a luxury hotel in Manhattan.

"VIP all the way," he'd promised. "We can drive back to the island in the morning."

Lenox had turned him down gently. Even with all his obvious signs of success, she wasn't about to give the pussy up so soon. She was interested in playing the long game. All night she had been mesmerized by the opulence she was witnessing. Benny had spared no expense ordering bottles and captivating his audience all while dripping in thick gold jewelry and designer labels. It was a life Lenox had always fantasized about. Having the freedom to spend money without worrying about the cost of things. With the money Benny had tipped the waitress alone, Lenox could have bought groceries for a month. She knew what G wanted. A good time and some arm candy to impress his new friends. But Lenox had greater aspirations than that.

"I had a good time tonight. Thank you for taking me out," she said now, smiling at him across the table.

G nodded.

"Thank you for saying 'yes.' I been wanting to take you out for a while. I would see you all the time, dropping your son off or picking him up from your sister's place. Always looking so serious. Never giving me the time of day no matter how hard I tried."

"I wasn't trying to be bitchy. I just don't have time to waste. I want to give my son a good life."

"I can understand that. You remind me of my moms. It was just me and her. Just like you and Deon. She raised me in the projects and worked hard to give me what I needed. But there was never enough left over for us to get the things we wanted. Like nice clothes and sneakers. Name brands and shit like that were luxuries for us. And it wasn't because she wasn't trying. She worked at a nursing home, babysat part-time for people in our building. Still, it was never enough."

He sipped his orange juice before continuing.

"So, I understand how you feel about your son. Like it's just you and him against the world."

She chewed her toast and thought about that.

"When I was living in Harlem, I fell in love with Deon's father. He didn't have much, but he was ambitious, you know. So, I gave him a chance. He was good to me. Spoiled me. We were gonna get married. But he got killed before our son was born. That's why I moved to Staten Island with my sister. Since I moved out there, guys try to get with me all the time. But I can't pay attention to everyone that tries to waste my time. I got bigger things to worry about."

"Bigger things, huh?" He caught her gaze.

"Yeah. Last time I got distracted by smooth talking and shiny things, I wound up a single mother. Fool me once . . . and all that shit." She shrugged. "I'm just being careful, that's all. It had nothing to do with you personally."

G nodded. A cute smirk graced his lips.

"So, you shutting me down all those times had nothing to do with my cheap kicks and highwaters?"

She laughed.

"Maybe a little," she admitted.

They both laughed.

"But look at you now! Shining!"

He smiled at her.

"I like you. I always noticed the way you strut through the hood with that sexy little walk of yours. Always dressed nice. Your son, too. I can tell you're a good mother. And I'm sorry to hear about his father. Sounds like he was a good man."

He looked at her meaningfully.

"I hear what you're saying about not having time to waste. And you don't have to worry about that with me. I'm not like all them other guys. What you see is what you get. I just want to show you a good time. Get to know you a little better. Maybe get to know your son. But I won't waste your time. I promise you that."

She sipped her coffee, set the mug back down, and looked at him.

"So, how do you and Benny make money?" she asked.

He sat back and opened his mouth to respond, but she cut him off.

"You said you like honesty. So do I. So, keep it real."

He chuckled a bit and wiped his mouth with his napkin. He looked her in the eyes, shrugged, and dove in.

"We got our hands on some shit that's about to change the game."

Lenox's eyes narrowed.

"What kind of shit?"

"Cocaine," he said, leaning forward in his seat.

Lenox let it register in her brain, eyeing him skeptically. "Cocaine ain't new, G."

"*Crack* cocaine," he whispered. "Trust me. It's different."

Lenox was all ears.

"I got family in the Bronx like I told you. I would go uptown to visit them and my cousin Mark put me on to selling nickel and dime bags of weed. He's a little older than me, so he took me under his wing. I would get it from him, bring it back to Staten Island, and sell it. I made a little money. But just enough to buy some sneakers and jeans, bullshit like that. Then one weekend I went uptown and Mark brought me with him to see Benny. Before we got there, Mark told me to give him the money I was planning to spend and let him do the talking. I gave him $100. We get in there and Benny and a bunch of other guys are in a room and I realize that Mark ain't there to get weed this time, though. He was getting some shit in little bottles and they calling it crack cocaine.

"At that point I was nervous and pissed off. I felt like Mark was playing with my money. We got outside in the parking lot and I was HOT. We damn near came to blows. But Mark was like, 'Trust me!' So, he came back to Staten Island with me. He gave me ten of the little bottles and he had whatever amount he had. We hung around the block late at night and the prostitutes was out. You know nasty Keisha?"

Lenox nodded. "Yeah. She lives in my sister's building."

"Right. She was out there that night. She walked up to us and said, 'Who got it?' Mark pointed to me and said, 'G got them jumbos.' Keisha got hype. She was like, 'Word?' And Mark gave me the head nod. I held my hand out and there was three little bottles of that crack in my hand. Keisha snatched all of them shits and gave me sixty dollars."

Lenox's eyes widened.

"I was open! By the end of the night, I sold all ten of them shits and I had $200. A clean flip. The bottles we got from Benny were bigger than the ones the other hustlers on the island had. And remember like I told you before, there's not a lot of us that had it at the time. I don't know where everybody else was getting their shit from. But what I was getting from Benny had the hood jumping! I went back uptown with Mark the next day and did it again."

Lenox was so engrossed in his story that she didn't notice her food getting cold. G shoved a forkful of eggs in his mouth and kept talking as he chewed. Lenox didn't mind one bit. She was fascinated by what she was hearing.

"I started stacking my money. Saving it up." He smirked. "Well, I spent a little. Bought my car, hit my moms off with some dough, shit like that. But for the most part I stacked my paper. Until it was time to take the next step up the ladder."

"What was the next step?" Lenox asked eagerly. "Building a team?"

G chewed his food and thought about why he was speaking so freely. He had a sense that he could trust Lenox. She seemed genuinely interested in his story. And the truth was it felt good to have someone to talk to about it.

"Nah. I roll solo. Can't trust nobody. Especially in Staten Island. I learned that when I was hustling weed and stickup kids out there tried to rob me for the little money I was making. I don't want to build a team with guys like that. I take all the risk, keep all the reward."

He belched and excused himself before continuing.

"Mark's girlfriend has a little coke habit," G explained. "At least it started out little. Now the shit is a full-blown crisis. At the time, though, she had it under control. She told Mark we could make a bigger profit if we got a brick of cocaine from Benny on consignment and cooked it up ourselves. She knew how to do it, so she became our little scientist in the lab turning the powder into rocks."

"That's smart," Lenox said. "Now your profit is bigger. How much do you pay her to cook it?"

G scoffed.

"She's so fucked up at this point that all we do is pay her rent and keep food in the fridge so her kids don't go hungry. She was stupid enough to start using the shit. Selling crack is one thing. But the worst thing you could ever do is smoke that shit. Makes people turn into zombies. I never seen nothing like it."

Lenox tried to recall the last time she'd seen the prostitute Keisha he had mentioned. Now that she thought about it, Keisha was looking worse than ever lately.

"So, how long before all the hustlers in Staten Island catch on and give you some competition?" she asked.

G smiled, impressed that she was already thinking ahead. It was clear that Lenox was smart. He nodded.

"You're right. It's already happening. But thankfully Staten Island is slow to catch on. I already got a head start. Muthafackas is just figuring out how to go uptown and buy prepackaged shit. What me and Mark got going with Benny is already ten steps ahead of them. We got a whole network set up. Mark got his crew clicking uptown and I got my little slice of the pie on the island."

He sat back and wiped his mouth with his napkin.

"But I guess good things don't last too long. Shit was going smooth for a while. Then Mark got locked up on a gun charge."

"Damn," Lenox said sadly. "I'm sorry."

"Yeah. He's gonna be gone for a minute. In the meantime, I've been keeping shit going with Benny. And Mark's girl is still cooking the rock up for me. But she's an addict now. So, I can't trust her. She's stealing, got all types of people hanging out over there. I already had to move my stash and shit. But soon I'm gonna have to cut her off completely and figure this all out on my own."

He stared at his plate, concern etched on his face.

Lenox sat forward with her elbows resting firmly on the table and flashed her most brilliant smile.

"Nah. You don't have to do it on your own. I think you just found yourself a new partner."

WILDFLOWER

"You're late."

Mercy stood in her doorway and said the words flatly before turning and storming back inside her apartment.

Guiltily, Lenox followed suit, peeling slowly out of her coat.

"I'm sorry, Mercy. I overslept. We partied late and by the time I got home this morning, the sun was up. I told myself I would just close my eyes real quick and then come and pick up Deon. But I slept longer than I meant to. Don't be mad at me."

Mercy sucked her teeth. It was nearly two o'clock in the afternoon and she was sick of Lenox's excuses.

"I told you I needed you to be here *early*. I needed to meet the man this morning about the restaurant space like I told you. Instead, you stroll in here in the middle of the afternoon. The next time Mr. Wonderful takes you out, pay a babysitter."

"I'd rather pay *you*," Lenox said, softly.

Mercy scoffed.

Lenox pulled a stack of cash out of her purse and set it on the coffee table. Mercy scanned the bills out of the corner of her eye, reluctant to seem so easily appeased. But her eyes widened when she counted five $100 bills spread out on her coffee table like a fan.

Lenox smiled brightly, turning on the charm.

"This should be enough to cover last night. Maybe tonight, too, if I'm lucky."

Mercy took a good look at the money on the table and then at her sister.

"Where did you get all this money, Len? Mama's insurance check didn't even clear yet."

"I found it at the party last night." Lenox sat down on the couch.

Mercy looked at her skeptically. Lenox sucked her teeth.

"G gave it to me," she admitted.

"For what?"

"I think he likes me." Lenox batted her eyelashes coyly.

"So, he's moving his mother out the projects, driving around in a fancy car, and giving you money all of a sudden?" Mercy was frowning. "How?"

Lenox shrugged.

"I didn't ask all that." She was lying, but hoped her facial expression and tone were convincing.

"You're full of shit," Mercy said. "You always ask questions. So, spill it."

Before Lenox could answer, the kids came bouncing into the room. Deon made a beeline for his mother, throwing his arms around her in a bear hug.

Lenox hugged him back, but protested at the intensity.

"Boy, you're hugging me like you haven't seen me in days!"

Mercy resisted the urge to point out that she was spending more time apart from him lately.

Deon finally let his mother go.

"I beat Judah at Hangman so many times that he quit!"

Judah sucked his teeth and plopped down on the couch next to his mother.

"Shut up, Deon!"

Lenox laughed.

"Y'all been in the house too long. Come on. I'm gonna take you to McDonald's."

Both boys erupted in cheers and ran to get their sneakers.

Mercy glared at her sister the second they were out of earshot.

"Where did you get all this money from? And don't lie to me."

Lenox shrugged.

"I told you already. It's no big deal. G just gave me some money to go shopping, that's all."

She picked up her purse, pulled a pack of cigarettes out of it, and lit one.

"I'm sorry I came to pick up Deon so late. I didn't mean it, I swear. And I know I've been asking for a lot of favors lately. But could you babysit again for me tonight, please? This will be the last time for a while. I promise."

Mercy let out a deep sigh.

"Where are you running off to this time, Len?"

Lenox grabbed an empty bottle cap nearby to use as an ashtray and grinned.

"We're gonna cook together. At his place."

"Cook? *You*? Please! Since when?"

Judah and Deon came running back into the room, and Lenox was relieved for the interruption. She knew Mercy was too smart to fall for her act. Sooner or later, she would have to tell her exactly what she had gotten herself into.

"I'm gonna take the boys to McDonald's. Then I'll take them home with me for a while. Give you a little break. I'll drop them off back here later on. You need me to bring you anything?"

Mercy stared at Lenox silently, suspicion written all over her face. Then she shook her head.

"No. Just be careful out there."

Thirty minutes later, Lenox strolled down her block with the boys trotting behind her. She was oblivious to the men stopping to stare at her hips swaying to a rhythm all their own. Even with a long coat draped around her frame, it was clear that she had *body*!

Judah and Deon were clueless as well. As they walked along, they played with the action figures they had gotten inside their Happy Meals.

Lenox ignored the catcalls and stares and didn't break stride as she sauntered up to her door with her keys in hand. Judah and Deon followed her inside and scampered into the living room. They peeled out of their coats and tossed them on the couch. They sprawled out on the floor with their toys and busied themselves noisily.

Lenox chuckled at the sight of them, then she retrieved their coats and hung them on the hook near the door. She did the same with her own and then turned back to her son and nephew.

"Y'all watch TV and play while I go get ready for tonight."

Deon sat up.

"Where are you going, Ma?"

"My friend G is gonna help me start a business. If I do it right, I can make a lot of money. And, if you two are good, I'm gonna spend a lot of it on you."

Judah and Deon exchanged delighted glances and cheered.

Lenox stepped out of her shoes and strolled down the hall toward her bedroom. She walked over to the radio and turned on KISS FM. She snapped her fingers and danced along to "Forget Me Nots" by Patrice Rushen. Smiling widely, she twirled around her room with a million happy thoughts running through her mind.

For a moment it occurred to her that she should feel sad at this point in her life. Her mother had just passed away after all. But Lenox felt no sadness whatsoever. There was no time for that. Her mother had been a ghost in her life, making cameo appearances from time to time. The loss of her felt like a blip on the radar, another speed bump. Lenox had mourned her mother long before she died. When she was a little girl longing for her, crying herself to sleep when she didn't show up for birthdays and holidays, Lenox had decided that she had to mother herself. Sharon wasn't coming back to save her daughters, so it was up to them to save themselves. Lenox pushed thoughts of the woman to the back of her mind.

She had bigger things to worry about. As Mercy had pointed out earlier, Lenox had always been the bolder one. If the adults told her to avoid something or someone, she rushed toward the forbidden fruit as eagerly as Eve did in the Garden of Eden. Part of what drove her was curiosity about what type of excitement might await her. The other driving force was pure rebellion and blind ambition. She knew that if their family was ever going to elevate out of poverty, it would be up to her to lead the way.

She took a long, hot shower and changed into a pair of jeans and a caramel-colored turtleneck that matched her skin tone. She sprayed on some of the perfume Mercy gave her for Christmas and put her hair in a neat French braid. She admired herself in the mirror. Her smooth brown skin and pretty face. She stared into her own doe-shaped eyes and saw the hint of mischief reflected in them. She knew it was her body that got all the men's attention. G included. But what none of them had discovered yet was how intelligent she was, how shrewd. She smirked and applied a little lip gloss.

She thought about everything she and G had spoken about last night. She hadn't told Mercy about it because she knew her sister would never approve. Mercy wasn't a risk-taker. Her plan for taking her share of their mother's money and opening a restaurant was a noble one. But Lenox had bigger dreams. She wanted to be a boss wearing fur coats, diamonds, and designer clothes. She wanted to drive an expensive car and live in a lavish home. She wanted Deon to have everything he wanted, everything she didn't have when she was growing up. The arrangement she and G had worked out at the diner had given her hope. All the things she ever wanted felt within her reach for the first time in years.

Her phone rang and she only let it ring twice before she picked it up.

"Hello?"

"Hey, beautiful."

She could hear the smile on G's face.

"Hey," she said. "I just finished getting dressed. I just need to pack Deon's bag for the night and I'll be ready."

"Good," he said. "I'm on my way. I'll honk the horn when I'm outside."

Lenox hung up, turned the radio off, and headed back to the living room where the boys were watching TV. She overheard their conversation as she drew closer.

"I'm gonna ask Mommy for a new bike," Deon said proudly. "We can share it."

"Aunt Len said she ain't buying you nothing else until you stop wetting the bed," Judah reminded him.

"Shut up!" Deon shot back.

Lenox chuckled as she stepped into the room.

"Y'all stop fussing. Deon, come help me get your stuff together so I can bring you back to Aunt Mercy's."

She led the way to Deon's room and the boys followed her closely.

"Ma, when you start making money, I want a lot of stuff," Deon said.

"Well, for now just focus on the stuff you have already. Get a pair of pajamas and some play clothes out of your drawer."

Deon did as he was told while Lenox looked around for his backpack. She found it in the corner of the room and began packing his things.

Judah plopped down on his bed and felt the springs in the mattress poking him a little. He shifted over an inch or two to a spot on the bed where it was more comfortable and sat cross-legged.

Lenox stole a glance at her nephew.

"Judah, your mother was talking to me about starting a new business, too. She wants to open a restaurant. What you think about that?"

Judah smiled. "She should do it. She cooks really good. Sometimes she tries to make extra so we can have leftovers the next day. But everything tastes so good that I eat it all up."

Deon agreed.

"Aunt Mercy cooks better than anybody!"

"Aye!" Lenox pretended to be offended.

Deon shrugged and Lenox laughed.

"It's true," she admitted. "Mercy's a great cook. She used to watch our grandmother like a hawk whenever she was in the kitchen. Always had a passion for it."

She looked at Judah.

"You should watch her. Learn all her recipes. Girls like boys that know how to cook."

Judah grimaced.

"Who cares about girls?"

Lenox laughed. "You say that now, but come back and talk to me in a few years."

A car horn honked outside and Lenox grabbed Deon's backpack and nudged both boys toward the door. She got them into their coats and made sure they had all their things.

"Take your time. Don't forget anything."

Lenox realized that she was talking more to herself than to the boys.

She shuffled them out the front door and smiled at G sitting proudly in the driver's seat of his car. She sauntered over to the car and ushered the boys into the backseat. She climbed into the passenger seat and turned around to face them.

"Say hi to G."

"Hi," both boys said.

"How y'all doing?" G glanced at the two of them quickly. He looked at Lenox and licked his lips. "Looking good as always."

"Thanks. I can't wait to get started." She rubbed her hands together in excitement.

G laughed. "I'll show you everything you need to know." He pulled up to a red light, looked over at her, and smiled.

Deon watched closely from the backseat. He leaned forward slightly to get a closer look at the guy. G was a big guy with broad shoulders and a thick neck. Deon frowned as he sized him up.

"How come your name only has one letter in it?"

Lenox sucked her teeth, turned around, and faced Deon.

"Sit back in the seat, smarty."

G glanced at Deon's reflection in the rearview mirror and laughed.

"My name is Gerard. Everybody calls me 'G' for short."

Deon locked eyes with Gerard in the mirror but didn't return his smile.

"How old are you?"

"Seven," Deon answered flatly.

"Okay. Seven is a good number. This is your lucky year."

Deon eyed him, warily. He thought about all the things he wanted and wondered if this guy was gonna help his mother get it.

They pulled up in front of Mercy's building at the tip of Richmond Terrace. Lenox and the boys climbed out and were surprised to see Mercy approaching them as she returned home from a quick run to the corner store.

Mercy held up her shopping bag and smiled.

"Got y'all some candy!"

The boys cheered.

Mercy looked at Gerard's Benz gleaming in the sunshine. Her sister stood next to it smiling just as brightly.

G craned his neck out the window and waved at Mercy.

"How you doing?"

"Nice ride," Mercy offered weakly.

Lenox kissed the boys goodbye.

"I'll see y'all tomorrow. Be good!"

Mercy waved to her as Lenox climbed back inside the car and sped off with her new friend.

G pulled up in front of the stash spot at the corner of a dead-end block in the Tremont section of the Bronx and turned the car off. He looked over at Lenox and saw her glancing cautiously out of the passenger window. The house was run-down and gloomy looking. He could sense her apprehension though she said nothing.

"You sure you want to do this?" He asked the question seriously. "This ain't the glitz-and-glamour side I've been showing you. This shit is raw. It's ugly."

Lenox tore her eyes away from the ominous-looking house and met G's gaze.

"I told you. I want in."

He nodded.

She looked at the house again. "Your cousin's girl lives here? With her kids?"

G shook his head.

"Nah. She has an apartment in the projects. Leaves the kids there with neighbors and family while she stays here most of the time. Her job is to cook up the work and I bag it up. I used to drop the shit off to her and she would work through the night cooking and I came to pick it up in the morning. But now she's using the shit. So, when I bring it here like I'm doing tonight I have to stay with her and watch her every move. Then I gotta take the shit home and bag it up on my own. I hit her off with some for herself and she's happy with that."

He looked at Lenox.

"You need to watch her tonight. Learn the process. Then we'll see if your little plan works out like you think it will."

Lenox smiled.

"It's gonna work. You'll see."

They climbed out of the car and walked up to the house. G used a key to open the front door and they were immediately struck by the noxious odor of burning plastic or nail salon chemicals. G seemed oblivious to it, but Lenox held her breath to block out the stench.

The place was filthy and sparsely furnished. The floors were dusty and cluttered. G headed straight to the kitchen and Lenox followed him. Music was playing from a small radio on the counter. Lenox recognized the song by the Eurythmics. She looked around, still bothered by the odor in the house. A woman was seated at a small wooden round table with a dirty tablecloth on top of it. She was thin and frail wearing a sweater two sizes too big for her little frame.

"Hey, G!" she said, excitedly as he walked toward her. "I was waiting for you. You brought the stuff?"

G ignored her and started pulling out the tools of the trade. From the cabinet he retrieved a mesh strainer and a Pyrex pot. He set them down on the countertop next to a box of Arm & Hammer baking soda and a triple beam scale. He poured water into an old pot he grabbed from the top of the stove and then set it to boil. Finally, he turned back to the woman at the table.

"Tatiana, this is Lenox. I'm gonna hit you off like I always do. But first I want you to show her how to do what you do."

Tatiana seemed hesitant. She looked Lenox up and down, frowning.

"Why do I have to show *her*?"

He shrugged. "Cuz I'm asking you to. I know the basics, but you're a pro. You got a real talent for that shit. I'm trying to see if I can maximize it."

Tatiana frowned.

"What, you trying to replace me or some shit, G? Did Mark tell you to do this? He said to cut me off?"

G shook his head.

"Mark didn't tell me to do nothing. And nobody's trying to replace you either. I'm just asking you to do me a favor since I don't always have time to come all the way uptown to see you. I'm gonna split the work up and double my production. And I'll make sure you keep getting your piece."

Lenox could tell that he was lying and wondered if Tatiana could sense it as well. Lenox knew that as soon as she mastered this process, G was going to cut Tatiana off without looking back.

G set a Ziploc bag full of crack vials on the table in front of him. Lenox saw Tatiana practically drooling at the sight of it.

"Cook one batch and show her how to do it. Then I want you to let her cook a batch while you supervise. You give her pointers and shit. Teach her everything she needs to know. If you help me out with this, I'll make sure I leave you with enough to party for the rest of the weekend."

Tatiana nodded. She wiped her nose.

"What about after that? You still gonna keep me in the mix, right? You're not cutting me off?"

He scoffed as if the thought was absurd.

"Never that, T. We're family."

She looked at the bag again and nodded.

"Okay."

Lenox looked around the room. "Is that smell in here from the cooking process?" she asked.

Tatiana stared at her without answering. She had been doing this shit for so long that she couldn't smell anything.

Lenox took off her coat and removed her scarf from around her neck. She tied it around her nose and mouth in preparation. She looked at Tatiana and noticed her staring longingly at the bag of crack.

"Okay," Lenox said. "Let's do it."

Tatiana's eyes darted in Lenox's direction.

"You get high?"

Lenox shook her head.

"No. I get money."

G smiled. Any lingering doubts he had about her readiness for the game dissipated in that instant.

"That's what I'm talking about. Let's get it!"

PLANET ROCK

"They're just little magic off-white nuggets that help people ease their pain for a little while."

That was how Tatiana had described the crack cocaine as she eagerly filled her pipe up and sucked on it like a glass dick the moment they had finished cooking the batch. Lenox had watched her, pityingly, and promised herself that she would never use that shit no matter what. Seeing the grip the drug had on Tatiana was enough to convince Lenox that the drug was far from magical.

She went home that night and could barely sleep. Excitement and anticipation coursed through every vein. She could tell that Tatiana had approached the situation all wrong. She got hooked on the wrong side of the game. While she was busy getting high, G and Benny were busy getting rich. Lenox intended to play with the boys.

She repeated the formula in her head so much that she could recite it by heart. She thought about ways she could shield it from Deon—and more importantly, from Mercy. And she devised a plan to make it all work.

Three days later while Deon was in school, Lenox stood over the stove in her apartment swirling baking soda and cocaine into a crystal-ish concoction and watching the water around it bubbling.

She was fascinated by this process, the way just the right amount of this mixed with the perfect amount of that formed the intoxicating substance G had introduced her to.

He stood nearby watching her closely.

"Don't stir it too much," he coached her. "Let it bubble up. But not for too long."

She nodded. They had gone through the process together several times. Plus, she had gone over it with Tatiana so many times that she knew every step by heart. By now she understood that it took the right amount of finesse to get the batch just right.

"Why do you sell it so cheap?" she asked. "If you got something no one else has, why wouldn't you make it expensive? Make them pay top dollar for this new shit."

G laughed.

"I said the same thing the first time I got put on to it. But Benny taught me the game. Gotta keep it affordable. That way the average guy can afford it. Keep 'em coming back."

She thought about it, then nodded.

"Keep that money coming in."

"Exactly," G agreed. He turned off the flame beneath the pot. "That's it. Let it sit for a while. Then we'll chop it up."

Lenox stepped away from the stove and took off the handkerchief that had been tied around her nose and mouth. Incense burned throughout the apartment in an effort to combat the smell and the windows were ajar even though the winter wind was relentless outside.

She exhaled and smiled, pleased with the arrangement she had made with G. A thousand dollars a week to cook up his work. Plus, he paid her rent, which wasn't much since she was on Section 8. Still, the money would mean a drastic improvement from the life she and Deon had been living. She was overjoyed at the thought of it.

G stepped closer to her, pinning her against the counter where she stood. He leaned in and kissed her lips, bit her neck and licked it.

"We been talking all business for the past few days. I don't want you to forget the fact that I'm feeling you."

She smiled and didn't protest when his hands roamed her body. He kissed her again, this time more aggressively. She let him unbuckle her pants and stick his hand inside her panties. She didn't protest as he groaned, touching and sucking on her as he tugged her clothes away. They tumbled to the floor together and he anxiously peeled out of his jeans.

Lenox lay beneath him as he had his way with her. She moaned a little as he entered her and he seemed encouraged by that. Soon he was pounding away as she grinded beneath him. Her mind was filled with images of what would be her new normal. Shopping sprees, new furniture, a new car. The thought of it excited her and she opened her legs wider. She felt G deep inside of her and couldn't tell if it was the way he was hitting her spot or the thoughts of her new life that made her scream in ecstasy as she came.

Days later, Mercy sat on her couch watching TV. The scent of the chicken and potatoes she was roasting made her stomach growl. She heard a knock on her apartment door and slid her feet into her fuzzy slippers. She walked to the door and looked through the peephole to find Lenox and Deon smiling brightly at her. Mercy unlocked the door and opened it.

"Hey!" Lenox rushed in and hugged her tightly. Deon followed closely behind her and greeted his aunt.

"Hey, Deon." Mercy hugged him. "Judah's in his room doing his science project."

Lenox peeled out of her coat and frowned.

"Schoolwork on a Friday night?"

"Yes," Mercy said. "He's not complaining."

Lenox shrugged, helped Deon out of his coat, and sat down on the sofa.

"Deon, why don't you go help him? He's doing something about the solar system. He keeps trying to explain it to me, but I don't understand it," Mercy said.

Deon laughed and ran down the hall to his cousin's room.

"Where you been?" Mercy asked, wasting no time. She sat on the sofa next to Lenox. "I haven't seen you all week."

"Deon had a doctor's appointment. Then I had to do a bunch of running around, you know?"

"With G?"

"Yeah, so?" Lenox sat back and crossed her legs.

Mercy stared at her silently. Finally, she shrugged.

"I don't know. Something don't feel right about it to me. Gerard starts riding around here flashing money around. And all of a sudden you're giving me hundreds of dollars and waltzing in here like I don't notice your new coat and your hair smelling like you just came from the salon. Judah told me that Deon didn't take the school bus all week because you and G chauffeur him in his Benz every day. Deon got new sneakers, furniture for his room, a new game system. He told Judah all about it at school. And it ain't the money from Mama's insurance policy because you haven't even stopped by to pick up the check. It got here on Wednesday, by the way."

Mercy set the check for $4,800 down on the coffee table and sat back.

Lenox chuckled, feeling attacked.

"G took me shopping. He gave me money to get my hair done. So, what? You're jealous?"

Mercy looked offended.

"Nah, bitch. I'm worried about you. What the fuck is he into? What's he getting you into?"

Lenox sighed. She wished Mercy was cool enough to handle the truth, but she knew she would never understand.

"G does some work with a guy who owns nightclubs," she lied. "He meets important people, makes good money, and he's generous. It's as simple as that. He's not my man. It's nothing serious.

I'm just having fun, giving the guy a chance. I don't see what the big deal is."

Mercy tried to read her sister to see if she was telling the truth. But Lenox always had an excellent poker face.

"I got everything under control, sis. Trust me."

Lenox leaned forward and picked up the check on the table. She tucked it into her purse and winked at Mercy.

"I think I found the perfect spot for your restaurant," she said, grinning at Mercy. "It's on Richmond Terrace. It's vacant and the rent is cheap. I can help you pay it if you think it's too much. The owner said we can go and look at it on Monday."

Mercy's eyes narrowed.

"How did you find it?"

"If I tell you that G knows the owner of the building and he told me about it, are you gonna roll your eyes and start asking a whole bunch of questions?"

"No."

Mercy rolled her eyes anyway.

Lenox laughed. "The spot is on Richmond Terrace. I'll take you there to check it out whenever you want. G already introduced me to the guy."

"So, G's not your man?" Mercy asked.

Lenox shook her head.

"Nope. He's cool, though. I fool around with him a little. Let him spend his money on me if he wants to. But I ain't looking for love. That shit hurts too bad."

Mercy decided to let it go and just prayed that her baby sister was being as careful as she claimed she was.

"What did you make for dinner?" Lenox asked. "It smells good in here."

Mercy smiled, proudly. "A whole bunch of everything! Come in the kitchen and get a plate."

Lenox didn't need to be asked twice. She rushed into the kitchen ahead of Mercy and started pulling out plates and flatware. Mercy giggled and retrieved the chicken from the oven.

"What's up with *your* love life?" Lenox asked. "Since you're all up in my business."

Mercy smiled coyly. "Love life? What's that?"

Lenox sucked her teeth. "See? That's your problem. You keep focusing on being a mother so hard that you forget that you're a woman first. You gotta take care of that puss, sis!"

Mercy laughed. "You're stupid."

"No. I'm serious."

"I don't need a coach in that department, Lenox. Trust me."

"You sure? Cuz I'll hook you up in a heartbeat!"

Mercy groaned. "With a nigga like G? I'll pass." She leaned into the hallway and called the boys in to eat.

Lenox sat down at the table and grabbed the hot sauce. "You gotta loosen up a little, Mercy. Just get you a little friend to come by at night when Judah's asleep and . . . you know . . . eat up all your leftovers."

Mercy laughed as the boys rushed into the kitchen and sat down for dinner.

"I'll keep that in mind," she said.

Lenox winked at her and dug into her meal like she hadn't eaten all day.

As promised, Lenox brought Mercy to see the property she had told her about. The owner was a slim white man with a skittish and frantic disposition. He seemed eager to rent the place, and his eyes lit up when Lenox mentioned paying the first two months in cash up front.

"It's a great place for a restaurant. A lot of foot traffic in the summertime. Winter, too. You'll do good business here."

Lenox half listened, focused instead on her sister as she walked around the place eyeing every detail.

"What you think?" Lenox called out to her.

Mercy turned to face her and smiled. "I can see the potential. I feel like I could make it work."

Lenox smiled back and nodded. She looked at the owner. "We'll take it."

Days later, Deon sat at the new dining room table his mother had purchased for their apartment. He was scarfing down a bowl of Alpha-Bits cereal like it was his last meal. Judah sat across from him, taking the time to carefully spell out words with the letters in his cereal.

"Look! I spelled *box*."

Deon laughed with his mouth full.

"So, stupid?"

"You're stupid," Judah responded, though he was laughing, too.

They were cousins, but more like brothers and their playful banter masked the affection they truly felt for each other.

Lenox entered the kitchen draped in a floor-length black bathrobe. Her hair was slicked back in a ponytail and her high cheekbones were even more visible as she smiled at them.

"Good morning, gentlemen. Y'all ready to go on an adventure today?"

School was closed for Memorial Day and she had promised the boys that she would take them to the zoo.

Judah couldn't contain his excitement.

"Aunt Len, I can't *wait* to get there! I wanna see the elephants and the tigers and all that."

Lenox leaned against the counter and exhaled. It had been three months since her arrangement with G began. The money was rolling in and things were going smoothly. He was even hitting her off with extras—clothes, cash, jewelry—as a bonus for the good pussy she was doling out to him in spurts. Her entire apartment was newly furnished. Her closet was bursting with designer labels, and her pockets were swollen.

Today she had set aside time to take the boys to the zoo. It was a dual-purpose trip. She would get to spend time with them and get them out of the house for the day while G came in to bag up his work. As if on cue, the doorbell rang. Lenox walked over to open it, expecting to find him standing there ready to get to work. Instead, she found Mercy on the other side of the threshold.

"Oh! Hey. What are you doing here? I thought you were going to work on setting up your new restaurant today. Judah said you were going over to clean up the place."

Mercy winked.

"Surprise! I decided to do it tomorrow instead. Judah seemed so excited when I spoke to him on the phone this morning that I figured I couldn't miss it."

Lenox was aware that her heart rate had sped up. Mercy hadn't been to her home in weeks.

"You gonna let me in?" Mercy asked, frowning.

Lenox laughed nervously and stepped aside.

From the second she walked in Mercy knew something was up. Her eyes scanned the room and landed on the leather sectional, the large floor lamps, plush rugs, new furnishings, and the floor model TV in the corner. The scent of Egyptian musk wafted through the apartment from incense burning somewhere—part of Lenox's system for getting the stench of the cooking process out of her home.

Mercy looked at her sister, her gaze thick with suspicion.

"So, this is what you been up to lately, huh?"

She gestured around the apartment dramatically.

"What's all this stuff, Len?"

"Don't start your shit. I just did a little redecorating. That's all."

Mercy scoffed. She noticed the large diamond studs in her sister's ears and shook her head.

"I been wondering why I hardly see you anymore."

"What are you talking about? I just saw you the other day."

Lenox was deflecting and she knew it.

"Yeah. You do a quick drive-by every now and then just to drop off Deon or pick him up. You barely stick around anymore because your new friend G is always waiting for you downstairs. Stop acting like this is something casual and tell me what's really happening with y'all. All this ain't the result of no friendship."

Lenox sighed.

"Hi, Mom."

Judah walked innocently into the room and hugged his mother. "Are you coming with us?"

Mercy looked at her sister, and Lenox stared back guiltily.

The doorbell interrupted their standoff. Lenox went to answer it. Mercy looked down at her son.

"Yes, baby. I'm coming with you."

Judah smiled happily, then ran back to the kitchen to tell his cousin the good news.

Lenox returned with G in tow. He smiled at Mercy and waved his hand.

"Hey! Good to see you, Mercy."

Mercy stared back at him, noting his costly leather jacket and heavy gold chain. She wasn't dumb. In her gut, she knew what this was.

"Hey," she managed.

Lenox looked at G, helplessly.

"She surprised me, so I'm gonna go throw something on real quick and get ready."

He nodded, set his backpack down in the corner, and got comfortable in the recliner close to the TV. He sat back like he owned the place.

Mercy watched him, watched Lenox, too, scrambling to make the boys get dressed so they could all get out of this awkward situation.

Once Lenox had shuffled out of the room to get ready, Mercy sat down on her sister's new sofa and looked at Gerard.

"You live here now?" she asked.

He smiled. Truthfully, he wished he did. He had feelings for Lenox and had suggested it on several occasions. But she barely let him spend the night a couple of times a week.

"Nah. I got my own place. I just hang around here with Lenox sometimes, you know?"

"Hang around for what?"

He seemed caught off guard by the question.

"She's a beautiful woman. I like her company. And Deon is cool. We just kick it."

Mercy nodded.

"Did you buy her all this stuff?"

She looked around again at all of her sister's new things. She wondered why Lenox hadn't mentioned the extravagant turn her life had taken.

"Some of it," he admitted. "But mostly she bought it for herself."

"How can she afford all this by herself?" Mercy asked flatly.

G stared back at her in silence. Finally, he licked his lips and chuckled.

"I think that's a conversation you should have with your sister."

"Hmm," Mercy muttered.

Lenox reemerged with the boys at last.

"On that note," she said. "Let's go."

It didn't take long before Mercy lit into her with questions. The moment they were in the car, she turned to Lenox and barraged her.

"Is this car stolen?"

"No."

"Did he buy it for you?" Mercy's own car had broken down months ago, so she had brought it to the junkyard and started taking the bus everywhere.

"This is a rental, Mercy."

"Since when did you start driving around in rental cars? What the fuck is going on with this guy, Lenox? I walk into your apartment after months of playing peekaboo with your ass, and all I see is money. Even now, you look like one of them bitches on *Dynasty*!"

Lenox started the car and laughed despite herself.

"I do not, Mercy, calm down! What happened to all that shit you talk about watching our mouths in front of the kids and all that?"

"Don't change the subject, bitch. I asked you a question."

"You asked me like a dozen questions. And I'll answer every one of them. But you gotta promise me two things."

Lenox looked at her seriously.

"Number one, you gotta promise that you'll hear me out completely before you jump to conclusions. Number two, you gotta remember that we have an audience. So, let's watch what we say."

Lenox nodded her head toward the boys in the backseat. Both were hanging on every word.

Mercy exhaled.

"Fine. We'll speak in pig Latin like we used to do when we were kids."

Lenox smiled at the memory and nodded. She put the car in drive and headed for the Bronx Zoo.

"Okay. Here's what's been happening."

While Lenox launched into her story, the boys sat confused in the backseat trying to understand the twisted language their mothers were speaking. They looked at each other and shrugged, neither of them able to make sense of what they were hearing. Finally, they turned their attention to the Rubik's Cubes Lenox had given them the night before.

Mercy listened in amazement as her sister discreetly relayed the events of the past few months. She had been cooking up crack cocaine in her apartment for G, had been getting paid large sums of money to do so. She wasn't selling it. G had that part taken care of. All Lenox did was turn powder into rock and provide G with a place to bag it all up every couple of days.

Mercy was floored.

"You're crazy. This is dangerous, Len. If the cops find out—"

"They won't. How would they find out? Nobody's coming to the door buying anything. It's just me and G. That's it."

"And you trust him?"

"I trust myself," Lenox corrected her. "I know what I'm doing. One of the reasons I didn't tell you was because I knew you would have a million questions. I needed to make sure the shit was gonna work before I told you anything. And it *is* working, Mercy. I'm telling you. Three months with no glitches. I'm making a lot of money. You could make some, too, if you want in."

Mercy shook her head.

"No thanks. I'm doing alright."

Lenox drove quietly for a while. Mercy broke the silence.

"I don't want to open the restaurant after all. You can tell Mr. Miller I changed my mind and get your money back."

Lenox sucked her teeth. "Why?"

"Because the more I think about it, the more I realize it's a gamble I can't make right now."

"That's a lie. You can handle it. You need to bet on yourself, Mercy."

Mercy shook her head. "I'm gonna use the money from Mama's insurance to put Judah in that private school I told you about. Right now, I can't afford a restaurant."

Lenox looked at her sidelong.

"You know I'll help you."

Mercy didn't respond.

"What if we became partners? I'll put up the money. You'll run the whole shit." Lenox looked at her, seriously. "What if we do it together?"

The question lingered in the air between them for the rest of the day. Mercy hadn't answered it in the car. Now that they were roaming around the zoo taking their time to enjoy each exhibit, it remained unanswered. As they laughed and talked with the boys about all the animals, Mercy stole glances at the diamond studs dancing in the light each time the sun shined on Lenox's earlobes. She told herself it wasn't jealousy she was feeling but caution instead. None of this felt right.

Still, it was hard not to feel relief each time Judah asked for a souvenir and Lenox offered to pay for it. She paid for lunch and for cotton candy afterwards. Mercy's funds were perpetually tight. Her low-level temp job at the hospital was barely enough to get by, leaving little room for extra indulgences. Even with the small windfall they had gotten from their mother's insurance policy, Mercy knew she was in no position to spend recklessly. She had always been the type of person who thought several steps ahead. She knew that Judah was a special child. His teachers thought so, too, suggesting that she get him out of public school as soon as possible in order to give him the best options for his future.

Still, Mercy had to admit that seeing Lenox spending money with reckless abandon was nice. It wasn't until the ride home that she finally responded to the question that had haunted them all day.

"I don't want any part of what you and Gerard are doing. I think it's dangerous and I think it's dumb."

Lenox nodded.

"I'm not surprised, Mercy. I love you. But me and you are like night and day. You're too scared to take a risk. Like your restaurant. You won't open it because you're scared. You tell yourself you can't afford it, but you'll spend all that money for Judah to go to that tight-ass Catholic school."

"He's gonna learn a lot at that tight-ass school."

"He's a smart kid. He's gonna learn a lot no matter where he goes. You just feel more comfortable gambling on your son than you do gambling on yourself. You're afraid to fail. I'm not."

"Maybe you should be."

Lenox shrugged.

"Maybe you're right. But I'm still gonna take the chance. So far it's paying off. I trust myself to be smart enough to know when it's time to get out. I wish you trusted me, too."

They rode in silence all the way back to Staten Island.

INFERNO

Unspoken words burned like a flame of hushed resentment. For the first time, the sisters' bond felt truly tested. Both held firmly to their positions, and the silence between them felt deafening.

A week passed before Lenox came around again. She knocked on Mercy's apartment door one Tuesday morning and stood there facing her sister, neither of them smiling.

"Come take a ride with me." Lenox's tone was flat.

Mercy was tempted to argue. Instead, she grabbed her keys, locked up her apartment, and followed Lenox to the elevator. They rode downstairs in silence, then walked to Lenox's car parked at the curb. They climbed inside and Mercy carefully buckled her seat belt, purposely avoiding her sister's gaze.

Lenox started the car and cleared her throat.

"Listen, Mercy. I know you don't approve of what I'm doing."

"I'm worried about you," Mercy said.

"I know," Lenox assured her. "And no matter what I say, you're gonna continue to worry. That's just who you are. So, I'm not gonna try to convince you that I got this all under control. I understand that to you it sounds crazy. But to me it's easy money. So, let's just agree to disagree."

Mercy stared out the window as Lenox drove down Richmond Terrace.

"You're not just my sister, Mercy. You're my best friend. Since we were kids, we always looked out for each other. That's not gonna change now just because you don't approve of how I'm making money."

Lenox glanced at Mercy, her expression serious.

"I know how much the tuition costs at that school you enrolled Judah in. And I know that you ain't making any real money down at that little temp job you got. So, I spent the past few days making some investments. On your behalf."

Mercy looked at Lenox, confused. Lenox nodded toward a storefront as they pulled up in front of it. Reading the sign above the door, Mercy gasped.

"MERCY'S SOUL FOOD SPOT!" she yelled. She looked at Lenox, wide-eyed. "What did you do?"

Lenox smiled proudly. "Come and see!"

Mercy realized her hands were shaking as she bolted out of the car and rushed inside behind her sister.

"Oh, Len! Why did you do this?"

Mercy's eyes glimmered as she looked around the room. The place was small, but it was exactly as Mercy had envisioned it. New flooring, fresh paint, tables, and chairs. The kitchen was furnished with all new appliances. Spice racks, pots, pans, and all the tools of the trade were on hand. Mercy spun around and beamed at Lenox.

"Lenox, this is too much!" She shook her head, suddenly reminded of Lenox's lifestyle. "I can't accept it."

Even as the words left her lips, Mercy knew it wasn't true. There was no way she could say no. It was a dream come true.

"You don't have a choice," Lenox said. "I didn't do all this work for nothing!"

Mercy shook her head. "Don't I need a license or permits or something like that? I can't just open up for business."

Lenox waved her hand dismissively. "Don't worry about all that.

Me and the landlord, Mr. Miller, will work all of that out. Just set up shop and get busy making this place come alive."

Mercy could barely contain herself. She held her hands up over her mouth in an effort to keep from squealing with delight. She looked around at everything, all of it perfect. Lenox had tended to every detail.

"This is yours," Lenox said. "I set it up and everything, but this is your place. Your own business. You decorate it, decide on the menu. I'll help you out when I can. Judah and Deon can help after school. Eventually when you start making money you can hire a staff." She looked at Mercy seriously. "I know you don't approve of what I'm doing. So, this is *your* thing. Think of it as my investment in you."

Mercy's eyes flooded with tears as she rushed toward Lenox. She threw her arms around her shoulders and squeezed her tightly.

"Thank you!" she managed, through sobs.

Lenox fought back her own tears as she hugged Mercy.

"You deserve it. All these years you've been putting Judah first. As you should. But this is something that's for you."

Mercy wiped her eyes. She looked at Lenox and sighed.

"I still don't think you should be hustling, Len."

"I know you don't. And like I said earlier, we're gonna agree to disagree. But what I do has nothing to do with this. You got it from here. I'm just another one of your customers. This is *MERCY'S* Soul Food Spot. In here, you're the boss."

Mercy grinned. She liked the sound of that.

Lenox handed her the keys. "Now let's go celebrate before the boys get out of school!"

Mercy busied herself with her new restaurant and pretended not to notice that Lenox was involved in the drug game. Lenox was careful to keep her occupation from interfering with their bond. She had a system. She dropped Deon off at school each morning and went to work with G. By now, crack had caught on like wildfire and she could barely cook the batches fast enough to keep up with demand.

G had been forced to reconsider his stance against hiring workers. Now he had a small team of young, hungry hustlers working for him. Lenox insisted that the workers never came to her house. Instead, G made drop-offs all day while she worked her magic.

On Fridays, she picked Deon and Judah up after school and dropped them off with Mercy at her restaurant. Always the sensible one, Mercy had opted to keep her job at the hospital. She wanted to keep a safety net in case things didn't go as well as she hoped. She opened her soul food spot for business on weekends. The boys spent the afternoons doing their homework and helping Mercy out around the kitchen. They swept and cleaned tables and put cutlery in the bags for the increasing number of customers frequenting the business. Each night the place was open, Lenox drove there and picked up her sister and the kids. Mercy was unaware that Lenox was strapped with a .38 Special these days. G had given it to her for protection and she always kept it with her. Even without knowing that Lenox was strapped, Mercy felt safer with her sister around. As much as she hated to admit it, Lenox seemed to have it all under control.

Mercy was happier than ever. Not only was the restaurant thriving with rave reviews from her customers, but for the first time in years, she was beginning to feel like she had hit a flow. Her life had a rhythm to it that felt right. Judah was thriving in his new school and Mercy had begun making new friends. One in particular, a man named Xavier who lived next door to the restaurant, proved to be a special one.

He came in one Thursday afternoon in June and ordered a plate of stewed chicken, rice, and cornbread. Mercy noticed him the moment he walked through the door. He had a nice smile, a smooth walk, and a deep voice that made her blush. He placed his order and welcomed her to the neighborhood. She put extra cornbread in his order and smiled at him as she handed him his change.

"My name is Xavier," he said. "I live next door and I've been meaning to come in here and check you out." He gestured at the bag in his hand. "If it's good, I'll be back all the time."

Mercy laughed. "Then I'll see you soon, Xavier."

He had been back every weekend since then. The atmosphere was cozy and people tended to hang around for a while. Thanks to Lenox, the place had a state-of-the-art stereo system, and Mercy kept hip-hop and R&B music playing. The patrons loved the food and Mercy's hospitality. Xavier was no exception.

He had a favorite table in the back of the spot. He sat there for hours at a time enjoying Mercy's soul food and talking to her about his job as a delivery driver for a local beverage company. He and Mercy formed a friendship that slowly began to grow into something more.

"You really ain't gonna tell me the secret to your chicken and waffles?" he asked each time he ate it.

Mercy would giggle and refuse to divulge her recipe.

"Nope."

"What if I promise not to tell anybody?"

"If I tell you, I have to kill you," she joked.

Xavier liked her instantly. Not only was her cooking spectacular, but she was pretty, soft spoken, and funny. She usually wore her hair in a ponytail, accentuating her deep cocoa eyes and her shy smile. She seemed to be a caring and attentive mother. Judah was always close by her side with his nose in a book. Mercy had a quiet confidence about her that Xavier admired.

One Friday in late June, he sat at his usual table slurping the bones of the oxtail Mercy served him. The place was empty except for them, and Mercy decided to sit down and join him. She took off her apron and slid into a seat across from him. Xavier smiled at her.

"Wow. I feel special. The only person I've ever seen you take off your apron and chill with is your sister."

Mercy laughed. It was true. Whenever Lenox came in and things weren't too busy, Mercy would often sit with her at a table close to the entrance laughing and talking.

"So, you've been watching me I guess."

Xavier nodded. "Guilty." He wiped his hands with a napkin. "Seems like you two are really close. That's nice to see."

"We balance each other out. She reminds me to let loose sometimes, and I remind her to play it smart."

"Judah said the same thing about you. He said his aunt is the fun one."

Mercy scoffed, offended. "I'm fun, too."

Xavier grinned. "He told me you're the smart one. I asked him where he gets his intelligence from and he said he gets it from you."

Mercy brightened hearing that.

"What about you?" she asked. "You have any family close by? I noticed you always come in here alone."

He smirked. "So, you've been watching me, too?"

She fidgeted shyly, and Xavier laughed.

"Moms passed a couple years ago. My brother got married and lives in Baltimore. Now it's just me here."

"Ever get lonely?" The words were out of Mercy's mouth before she realized it.

Xavier didn't hesitate to answer. "Hell yeah. But I work a lot. That keeps me busy." He smiled proudly. "I just got my CDL license. So, now hopefully I can get a better job with a bigger company. The guy I work for right now is the worst. I might have to quit before he makes me put hands on him."

Mercy frowned. "What's up with him?"

"Crack," Xavier said flatly. "He started getting high and now payroll ain't right, drivers are leaving. I've been picking up their shifts, trying to make some extra money. But now he's high all the time and the whole business is falling apart. Customers are getting shorted, creditors are chasing him. I'm about to jump ship before the shit gets worse."

Mercy recalled Lenox telling her how addictive crack was. It sounded like Xavier's boss was far gone already.

Xavier sipped his water and set the glass back down on the table. "Your landlord—Mr. Miller, the guy who owns this place—he's on that rock, too, you know?"

He could tell from the expression on Mercy's face that she hadn't known.

She shook her head, all the dots connecting for her now. Mr. Miller was an associate of Gerard's.

"He's my landlord, too. So, I can tell you in advance that if you need any repairs done around here, you're on your own. He only comes around to collect the rent and then he disappears."

Mercy's head was spinning.

"It's like that shit took over and now it's everywhere," she said, almost to herself.

Xavier agreed.

"Some people are making a lot of money off it. Other people are getting strung out on it. Not just here, either. My brother told me the same thing is happening down in Maryland where he's at."

Mercy sighed, trying to ignore the nagging voice in her head reminding her that Lenox was playing a dangerous game. "Well, congratulations on getting your CDL license. Hopefully you can quit that job soon and get something better."

Xavier smiled.

"Thanks. You should let me take you out so you can help me celebrate."

Mercy was visibly caught off guard. She recovered quickly, though, nodding.

"Okay. That sounds nice. When?"

"How 'bout tomorrow night after you close up for the night?"

Mercy deflated a little. "It's gonna be late by then."

Xavier laughed. "You've been on Staten Island too long. This is NYC! The city that never sleeps. We'll go to Manhattan where everything is open all night. Hang out in Times Square and get off this boring island for a while. Seems like you could use a change of scenery."

Mercy smiled, marveling at how right he was. She nodded. "Okay, cool. I can get my sister to babysit. She owes me."

Xavier nodded. "Perfect."

Lenox was thrilled!

"FINALLY, BITCH! Yes, of course I'll watch Judah. Pack him a bag and I'll pick him up tonight. Matter of fact . . ." Lenox looked Mercy up and down. "I'm gonna bring over some clothes for you to choose from. You can't go out with that man wearing your school-teacher wardrobe."

Mercy sucked her teeth, looking down self-consciously at her denim skirt and white V-neck shirt.

"What's wrong with my clothes?"

"Nothing," Lenox lied. "But you want to look special. So, let me spice you up a little for the night."

Mercy looked Lenox over, skeptically. Lenox wore a curve-hugging dress, her neck dripping in gold chains and door knocker earrings dangling from her ears.

"I want to look like myself, Len."

Lenox smiled and waved her hand. "You will. Only better!"

She loaned her a black T-shirt dress that was shorter than Mercy was typically comfortable with.

"You can't go to Forty Deuce looking average. Trust me!" Lenox insisted.

She loaned Mercy a pair of earrings and a simple gold necklace.

"You can wear your Reeboks if you want. Or some flats. That way you'll be comfortable. If it was me, I'd be wearing a pair of heels. But that ain't you."

Mercy agreed. "Sure ain't. I'll wear my flats."

Lenox shoved her new Fendi bag in Mercy's direction. Mercy shook her head.

"I'm not trying to get robbed on our first date."

Lenox thought about it and laughed. "Could you imagine that shit?"

Mercy laughed, too. "I'm nervous enough as it is. The last thing I need is to be worried about the stickup kids on 42nd Street."

"Don't be nervous," Lenox said. "Xavier seems like a nice guy. He's lucky to be spending time with you. And ain't nobody gonna try to stick y'all up. Stop thinking the worst."

"I hear you. But I'm still not borrowing your fancy bag. Thank you for all the rest of this though." Mercy winked at her sister.

Lenox narrowed her eyes.

"Just make sure you have fun, Mercy. Don't be calling every five minutes checking on Judah. I got him. You go enjoy yourself."

Mercy promised to do just that.

Xavier picked her up in his burgundy Chevy Cavalier. He smiled when he saw her, realizing it was the first time he had ever seen her outside of the restaurant. She had been feeding him so well for the past few weeks that it felt like he had known her for years.

"Hey," he greeted her as she climbed into his car. "You look nice."

"So do you," she said, looking him over. He wore a Kangol bucket hat, a Giants jacket with a white tee underneath, and a pair of track pants. His car smelled good, too. Mercy got cozy, buckled her seat belt, and tried to slow her speeding heart rate. She talked a good one when she was around Lenox. It was bad enough that everyone viewed her as the boring one. In an effort to seem more carefree, she pretended sometimes like she had a life outside of Judah. But the truth was Mercy hadn't been with a man in years.

Xavier broke the ice.

"I get the feeling you don't get out much. Between being a mother, your job at the hospital, and the restaurant, you're pretty busy. So, tonight I'm gonna do my best to show you a good time."

He kept his promise. During the drive they spoke about their history. Mercy learned that Xavier had been born and raised on Staten Island and that he had a four-year-old daughter from a relationship that didn't work out.

"Me and her mother get along alright. But she's still mad at me for cheating on her. So, we're not exactly friends."

Mercy looked at him. "She must have really loved you if she's still mad."

He caught her gaze. "She did. I loved her, too. I was just dumb enough to think I could creep around and get away with it. Have my cake and eat it, too." He shrugged. "My mother used to say, 'A fool has to get burned before he believes that fire is hot.' I was that fool back then."

"And now?" Mercy asked.

"Now I don't play with fire anymore."

They talked about Mercy's childhood in Harlem, her move to Staten Island, and all that had transpired since. She left out the part about Lenox's new profession. But it seemed that Xavier had figured it out for himself.

"Gerard comes around your restaurant a lot," he said. "I went to school with him."

"Oh yeah?" Mercy looked at him, curiously.

Xavier nodded. "He got picked on a lot back in the day. He was kinda corny." He chuckled a bit at the memory. "Kept to himself mostly, but me and my brother were always cool with him. We would let him play ball with us when the other kids wouldn't. Shit like that."

Mercy nodded.

"He's making a lot of money these days," Xavier continued. "Now he's a lot more popular. I see Lenox spends a lot of time with him."

Mercy avoided his gaze and waited for him to continue.

"She should be careful. He changed his name to 'G' now, so he feels like he reinvented himself. From what I hear, he's out there making some big moves in the streets. Trying to gain his respect as a man. Rewrite history. But to me he's still the same old cornball he always was."

After a moment or two he looked at Mercy apologetically. "I'm sorry. That's just how I feel about the guy. I apologize if that sounded foul."

Mercy looked at him and scoffed. "I can't stand him. I hate that my sister hangs around with him. I can tell he's nothing but trouble. But the more I try to get her to see it, the more we fight."

Xavier shook his head, sympathetically.

"In some ways, I think she identifies with him," Mercy said. "The way you described Gerard growing up. Getting picked on, not having a lot. We grew up like that, too. It didn't bother me too much. I was happy just being at home with my grandmother making do with what we had. But it was never enough for Lenox. She always wanted more. The fancy cars, lots of clothes, and all that superficial shit. It matters to her. I think that's what she sees in him. That same longing."

"That makes sense," Xavier admitted.

Mercy sighed. "I just want her to be careful. Everything that glitters ain't gold."

Xavier nodded. "If she's half as smart as you are, she'll figure that out."

They parked the car and walked around together, instantly swept up in the music and energy of Manhattan. The smell of the roasted nuts, pretzels, and hot dogs from the street vendors, the flashing lights of the theater signs and marquees, the sound of men playing percussion on overturned buckets while hip-hop music blared from boomboxes mounted on the shoulders of people walking by. Girls in neon clothing and bamboo earrings, guys in Cazal glasses and tracksuits. Mercy felt exhilarated by all of it, such a welcome distraction from her normal routine.

Xavier held her hand as they navigated the crowd. They stopped at a hot dog cart and argued over toppings.

"You put ketchup, mustard, relish, and onions on it?" Mercy asked in amazement. "All of that doesn't mess your stomach up?"

He shook his head, smiling. "Nah. This is a little taste of heaven right here."

Mercy scrunched up her nose and pretended to be repulsed.

They stopped to watch a group of break-dancers battling while a large crowd cheered them on. Xavier began to show Mercy a few of his amateur moves and she laughed. Then she shocked him by busting out a perfect pop lock.

"Ohhhhh shit!" He covered his mouth in amazement.

Mercy laughed.

"Nah. I knew I was right about you. You're the quiet storm. All calm and serene, but you got some tricks up your sleeve!"

They kept walking and came upon a very talented artist who drew sketches of subjects as they sat curbside in lawn chairs. Xavier paid the man to draw them and they sat side by side while the artist did his thing. Xavier admired Mercy's toned legs as she sat down in her short dress. She noticed him looking and didn't mind one bit.

They talked about their plans for the future. Mercy was hoping her restaurant continued to thrive and that she could eventually run it full-time. Xavier wanted to own his own trucking company with a fleet that made deliveries up and down the East Coast and a crew of drivers he could employ. Under the stars and bright lights in Manhattan it all felt possible.

The artist's rendition of them was masterful. He had captured the sparkle in Mercy's smile and the gleam of mischief in Xavier's eyes perfectly. It was so good that Xavier tipped him extra. Smiling, he handed the sketch bound in a black border to Mercy.

"Here you go, Quiet Storm." By the end of the night, Mercy knew that sketch would be a souvenir she would treasure forever.

"SO?" Lenox barked into the phone early the next morning. "How did the night end? Did he spend the night? Is he still there?"

Mercy laughed.

"No, tramp! I don't give it up on the first date. We went to a bar and had a couple drinks. Well, I had a couple. Maybe three." Mercy muttered the last part.

"Scandalous!" Lenox teased.

"He only had a beer since he was driving. We talked some more and laughed. And I forgot how long it's been since I drank like that. I was a little tipsy on the way home. Started rapping along with Slick Rick on the radio."

"Oh, God . . ." Lenox sighed. She closed her eyes in exasperation. "You showed him your drunken alter ego?"

"The rapper!" Mercy said, laughing. "Yes! He thought I didn't have skills. But I showed him."

"Mercy . . ."

"He joined in! We went verse for verse." Mercy laughed at the memory.

Lenox shook her head. "Well, at least he has a sense of humor."

"I pop locked for him, too."

"Jesus!" Lenox threw herself back against the pillows on her bed.

"He liked it," Mercy insisted. "I think he was impressed. Anyway, he drove me home and made sure I got to my door. We kissed goodnight and he left."

"How was the kiss?" Lenox asked.

"It was nice." Mercy smiled as she replayed it in her mind. "He's sweet."

"If he's so sweet, you should have invited him inside."

"I will," Mercy said. "When the time is right. If it's meant to be, he'll be patient."

Xavier proved to be patient indeed. He continued coming into the restaurant, sneaking kisses and hugs when Judah wasn't around. Mercy appreciated his discretion and his willingness to take things slowly. They spoke on the phone each day, and soon she invited him to her apartment for dinner on a weeknight. It was the first time Judah had ever seen his mother with a man and Mercy worried at first that it would be awkward. But Judah was excited to have him there. He was familiar with Xavier from his constant presence at the restaurant and he liked him. Despite their efforts to be discreet,

Judah had noticed the way they smiled at each other and how their hands lingered together whenever they exchanged money at the register. He was glad to see his mother happy, and it was clear that she enjoyed Xavier's company. They ate red snapper with rice and cabbage and Mercy smiled as Judah and Xavier both asked for seconds.

Soon, Xavier was around all the time. He came after work and helped Judah with his homework. He fixed things around the apartment and watched TV with them until it was Judah's bedtime. Then Mercy would dim the lights and spend the night wrapped in Xavier's arms making sweet love until they both were spent. They lay together afterwards making plans for a future together. As the summer months rolled on, the heat between them intensified. And for the first time in years, Mercy began to believe that she could have it all.

When she woke that fateful August morning, she felt an unexplainable sense of dread in the pit of her stomach. Later she would reflect that she should have known then that her blissful days were over.

It was a Monday morning and Mercy was exhausted. Xavier had spent the night and both of them had risen early as was their usual routine. They were always careful to at least be awake and dressed before Judah rose for the day. Xavier had work that morning, so he woke up extra early and made love to Mercy one more time before he left. They had lingered in the doorway kissing for long moments before tearing themselves away. Mercy had gone back to bed and had just fallen back asleep when her phone began to ring, blaringly.

With trepidation, she rolled to her bedside and answered the phone.

"MERCY! The whole place is on fire!"

She felt her heart racing in her chest. Her brain scrambled trying to compute what she was hearing. Xavier was yelling over the sound of fire engines blaring in the background. Mercy could hear people shouting behind him.

"What? What happened?"

"Your restaurant. My apartment. All of it. The whole building is on fire! You gotta get down here."

She was on her feet, rushing around the room frantically. She grabbed a bunch of clothes out of the dresser drawers and then stopped, realizing that she was trembling.

"It's on fire?"

"Yeah," Xavier yelled into the pay phone. "I got home and the street was blocked off with fire trucks. They're still putting the flames out. I can't get too close. But from what I can see, the whole building is on fire."

Mercy stopped hearing what Xavier was saying. She stretched the phone cord as far as she could while throwing on a pair of shorts and a T-shirt. She told him she was on her way and hung up, hurriedly sliding her feet into some flip-flops.

"JUDAH!" she called out to him, desperately. She rushed into his bedroom and pulled him out of bed.

"Wake up! We gotta go!"

FANTASY

Mercy wanted justice.

Tears filled her eyes as she watched the firemen tromping over broken glass and debris in the gutted restaurant. Everything she had worked so hard for had literally gone up in smoke. She watched helplessly as the firemen walked nonchalantly past all the charred remnants and overturned furniture soaked in water from their hoses.

Judah stared at his mother as she sat on the hood of a blue and white police car parked at the curb. The fire had been out for hours, all the fire engines gone. All that lingered were a couple of police cars, a fire marshal's vehicle, and the stench of burnt air among the scorched remains.

The fire had started in the back of the restaurant, gutting the place and spreading to the residential units next door. The first level had been eviscerated. Xavier's apartment upstairs had suffered damage also, though he was able to salvage most of his belongings. The fire department had deemed the property uninhabitable. So, Mercy sat on the police car waiting for Xavier to gather what he could from his apartment. She stared into the blackened restaurant, the windows shattered, debris strewn all over the floors. And Mercy cried.

Judah watched her, realizing that her heart was broken at the realization that she had lost it all. He went to her and hugged her tightly, choking back tears of his own.

"It's okay, Ma. I swear. One day I'll get you another one."

Mercy chuckled, wiped her eyes, and hugged him back tightly.

"I love you, baby. We're gonna be okay."

She only half believed it.

Lenox came rushing toward her with Deon in tow. She saw the gutted building and gasped. She looked at her sister, helplessly.

"What the fuck happened?"

Mercy shook her head. "They said it started in the back of the restaurant. Something about an accelerant being used." Mercy glanced over at the fire marshal nervously. "They're asking a lot of questions about Mr. Miller—when I saw him last and if I have a copy of my lease for this place. They're asking for licenses and shit."

Lenox groaned. She could hear Mercy's voice trembling, and she gripped her arm reassuringly.

"It's okay. What did you tell them?"

"I said that the license is in Mr. Miller's name, and he has all the paperwork for the lease and all of that. But he's nowhere to be found. Xavier said he hasn't seen him in weeks. He hasn't come around for the rent money or nothing."

"Okay. Let's get you out of here," Lenox said. She hugged Judah, aware that he was upset, too.

Xavier came out with two duffel bags in his hands. He greeted Lenox glumly, then looked at Mercy.

"You sure you don't mind me crashing with you? I can stay at—"

"It's fine," Mercy said, staring at the burnt awning above the restaurant. *Mercy's Soul Food Spot* now looked damaged and distorted. She shrugged and looked at Lenox. "So much for taking a risk."

Lenox opened her mouth to speak, but Mercy was already walking away.

"Meet you back at my place," she called out over her shoulder.

Judah trotted after her and Xavier followed. Lenox stared after them, speechlessly. She looked down at Deon and sighed.

"Let me tell you something, D. No good deed goes unpunished. Trust me."

Minutes later, Lenox walked into Mercy's apartment and noted the sullen expression on her sister's face. Mercy looked defeated with her shoulders slumped as she sat at the kitchen table. Xavier sat nearby looking just as crestfallen.

Deon and Judah exchanged glances. Reading the room, they quietly retreated to Judah's room, leaving the adults alone.

"Hey," Lenox said. "I would ask how y'all are doing. But I can tell already."

Mercy glared at her.

"You know Mr. Miller's cracked-out ass burned that place down for the insurance money, right?"

Lenox leaned against the wall and sighed. She stuck her hands in the pockets of her acid-wash jeans.

"We don't know that yet. Don't start jumping to conclusions. It's an old building. Could have been the wiring or something."

Mercy balked. "Lenox, cut the bullshit. This is the last straw. I tried to pretend like what's happening hasn't been happening. But THIS . . ." Mercy closed her eyes and took a deep breath before continuing. "Lenox, G introduced you to this man. This fuckin' crackhead who owns some storefront. And I let you convince me to open up a business there, only for this son of a bitch to burn the shit to the ground leaving me with nothing!"

Lenox pulled a cigarette from her purse and lit it. She exhaled the smoke and looked at her sister.

"We'll get you a new spot, Mercy. Set you up someplace else."

"Are you crazy? Seriously. Have you lost your mind? You think I would do this shit all over again?"

Lenox rolled her eyes. "Shit happens, Mercy. I'm sorry about this. But you're acting like this is my fault. I didn't light the match!"

"You can't seriously think this is normal. Living life like this. Doing business with sketchy people, cutting corners, breaking all the rules. That shit has consequences, Lenox. I had to sit down there and answer questions from those people. The fire marshal, the cops, all of them looking at me for answers. They're gonna go to the Housing Authority and report my miscellaneous income. Probably raise my rent. Xavier had his property destroyed. He lost his home. This shit ain't a game, Len. You're getting tangled up with the wrong people."

Lenox frowned. "So, I'm a bad judge of character because I convinced you to rent the spot from Mr. Miller? Does that mean Xavier was bugging when he rented an apartment from him? The guy seemed legit!"

"He used to be," Xavier said. "I've been living there for three years. He was cool in the beginning. But once he got strung out on that shit, he started wilding."

Mercy locked eyes with her sister. "That crack shit is destroying everything and everybody in its path."

Lenox laughed. "Oh, so that's what this is about?"

Xavier rose from his seat.

"I'm gonna go out for a while. Let y'all talk."

Mercy stopped him.

"Tell her what you told me about Gerard."

Lenox groaned. "What does G have to do with this?"

"He's the reason you're in this life!" Mercy shouted. She looked at Xavier pleadingly.

Xavier sighed.

"I was just saying it seems to me like Gerard is trying to be somebody he's not. Hustling and all of that . . . that shit ain't him. I would just be careful getting caught up with him. Fast money don't last forever."

Lenox looked at him for a long while without responding. Then she plastered on a convincing smile and nodded.

"Thank you, Xavier."

He nodded back, looked at Mercy, and said, "I'll be back in a while."

When he was gone, Lenox lit into her sister immediately.

"What the fuck was that, Mercy? You're talking to this mutha-fucka about what I'm doing? You trying to get me locked up?"

Mercy laughed. "Xavier's not a cop. Calm down."

"This shit I'm doing ain't appropriate for pillow talk. Why the fuck would you tell him about what I'm doing with G?"

"Because Xavier knows Gerard. Since they were kids. Unlike you who barely knows anything about him."

"I keep telling you that me and G are not in a relationship. I'm doing business with him. That's it!"

"And the business you're doing with him is dangerous. People are becoming zombies. Businesses are getting destroyed. I'm fuckin' worried about you, Lenox. You heard what Xavier said. Gerard is not cut out for this shit he's into. He's trying to be somebody he's not. He could get you hurt."

"I'm fine," Lenox insisted. "And I'd appreciate it if you stop talking about my business to Xavier. Or anybody else for that matter." She called Deon's name, and slid her purse onto her shoulder, prepar-ing to leave. "I apologize for getting you involved with Mr. Miller. All I was trying to do was help you live out your dreams. I won't do that again. Go back to your job at the hospital and struggle to make ends meet. Stay out of my business and I'll stay out of yours."

Lenox and Deon left, and Mercy stared out the window watch-ing them walk away.

Weeks passed with the sisters stubbornly holding firmly to their convictions. Xavier crashed at Mercy's place for ten days be-fore he found a small studio apartment on Union Avenue. Even in that short timeframe, his bond with Mercy and Judah deep-ened. They cooked together, listened to music, played board games. Their relationship became more solid, and Xavier began to earn Mercy's trust and her love. He also found a new job and was grateful to feel some relief from the troubles that had plagued his old boss and landlord.

Crack had New York City in a chokehold. It seemed that every neighborhood was feeling the paralyzing effects of the drug. The addicts were swept up in a world they couldn't easily escape. And the hustlers were making millions.

Lenox kept working with G and the money kept pouring in. Mercy was able to secure a permanent job at the hospital processing insurance claims. The investigators had confirmed that the fire at the restaurant had been arson. Mr. Miller had set the fire in an attempt to collect on the insurance money and leave town. Instead, he was arrested and charged with reckless endangerment as well as a slew of other charges. Mercy gave up her dream of running a restaurant after that, focusing on her administrative job at the hospital instead. The pay was decent enough for her to pay her rent, Judah's tuition, and a few other necessities. But Mercy was still struggling in contrast to her sister. Every time she saw Lenox, she was fresh out of the hair and nail salons. Her wardrobe was so extensive that people stopped her on the street to gush over what she wore.

Judah noticed, too.

"Ma, how come Deon has a different pair of sneakers for every day of the week?" he asked one Saturday while they folded clothes together at the laundromat.

Mercy tried to downplay it. "He doesn't have that many sneakers."

"He does!" Judah persisted. "He has two new pairs of Pumas, a pair of Reeboks, and he just got a pair of shell-toe Adidas."

Mercy shrugged, avoiding his gaze. "Well, even if I could afford it, having all those sneakers would be a waste of money. You can't wear sneakers at your school. It's not part of the uniform."

Judah thought about it. "But it's summertime. I'm not even in school right now. I could just wear them around the neighborhood like Deon does."

Mercy shrugged. "It wouldn't make sense to me."

"Why not?" Judah pressed.

Mercy tried to think on her feet. "Well . . . you're a better basketball player than Deon is. All those sneakers he has aren't made
for playing ball in. If you had a pair of Adidas right now, you would
scuff them up out there on the courts."

Judah considered that.

"I would be careful," he said.

"Believe me, the sneakers you have are good enough." She
winked at him. "Clothes and shoes are temporary. You're getting
a good education. Knowledge is something nobody can take away
from you."

They folded clothes in silence for a while.

"You really think I'm better at basketball than Deon is?" Judah
asked.

Mercy's eyes widened. "Way better!"

Judah smiled and seemed to be content with that. For now. But
Mercy knew it was just a matter of time before the vast difference
between her lifestyle and her sister's drew a permanent wedge between the cousins.

When the boys were with Lenox, they always came back with
stories about the wonderful things they had done and places they
had been. Judah didn't bat an eye when Lenox whipped out wads of
cash to pay for all their tickets at the movie theater, roller-skating
rink, or the mall. But Mercy felt small and complicit each time she
accepted Lenox's handouts. When Lenox invited Mercy and Judah
to join her and Deon at Six Flags amusement park, Mercy declined.
She began to distance herself from her sister. On her days off, Mercy
took Judah to libraries in Brooklyn and Manhattan and museums
with low admission fees. She and Xavier took him to the park, and
Mercy sat on the bench while they played basketball. She began to
carve out a life of her own for the first time. One that didn't involve
Lenox as heavily as it used to.

Mercy seldom visited her sister's home and never let Judah

spend the night anymore. She had thoughts of the police kicking in the door while her son was over there and it terrified her. Instead, she never protested when Lenox asked her to babysit Deon. It gave her comfort knowing that her nephew was safe with her. It also provided her with opportunities to ask him questions.

While the boys watched karate flicks on Saturday mornings, Mercy prodded him with questions. Deon told her that G came over all the time. That he had clothes there, and a toothbrush.

"He doesn't live there. But he's there every day. Even if it's just for a few minutes."

Mercy had nodded when Deon told her that, though in her mind she knew it made no sense.

"Does anyone else come over all the time?" Mercy asked.

"Not really," Deon had answered innocently. "Just G."

When she did see Lenox these days it was always in passing. She was driving a newer car now. No more rentals. Now she drove around in a blue Mazda RX-7 with vanity plates that read LENOX7. Mercy had turned down her sister's offers to go for a spin in it. Her pocketful of bus and subway tokens was sufficient for her. She felt that Lenox was living dangerously and taking it all too lightly. But there was no getting through to her. To Lenox, the money rolling in was proof that she was right about this. Crack was gonna make her rich.

Mercy wanted nice things, too. She would have given anything to have the ability to provide Judah with all the material things he desired. Judah worked hard to get straight A's in school and deserved to be rewarded. But Mercy's greatest fear was not being there for her son. Going to prison or having him taken away by child services was a nightmare she couldn't survive. The absence of her own mother had affected her deeply. Mercy was determined to be nothing like her. She would continue to work her menial job as long as it meant that she could provide a stable homelife for Judah.

Her relationship with Xavier was a welcome distraction. When he wasn't working or visiting with his daughter, he spent most of his time with Mercy. Their time together was full of laughter and bliss. Both were aware that a sweet love was beginning to blossom between them.

Mercy began to bond with a neighbor down the hall named Barbara. Barbara had a daughter Judah's age named Chanel, and the kids often played together. Barbara babysat for Mercy whenever Xavier took her out on dates. On weekends when Mercy wasn't working, she and Barbara often sat together on the bench in front of their building while all the neighborhood kids played in the water pouring forth from a fire hydrant nearby. They formed a friendship that Mercy was grateful for in the absence of her sister.

On Labor Day in early September as Mercy and Barbara sat on the bench sipping Riunite on Ice out of red Solo cups, Lenox pulled up in her car. Mercy was laughing at a story Barbara had just told her and didn't notice her sister approaching with Deon in tow.

The summer sun was blaring, and Lenox fanned herself as she approached. The men in the vicinity all paused to watch her ass as it bounced with each sway of her hips as she sauntered up the pathway. She wore a pair of denim shorts and a tight T-shirt with her name on it.

Lenox cleared her throat as she drew near. Finally, Mercy looked at her and smiled.

"Oh! Hey, Len. I didn't see you."

Lenox frowned. "I know. You were too busy kee-keeing with . . . who's this?"

Barbara's smile faded as she introduced herself.

Mercy shot Lenox a warning look.

"This is my sister, Lenox."

Barbara nodded.

"Anyway," Lenox said. "Today's my twenty-fifth birthday, in case you forgot. Happy birthday to me!"

Her tone dripped with sarcasm and her facial expression was anything but celebratory. She stood towering over her sister in an aggressive stance.

"I know we haven't been talking lately, but damn. You could have at least called me. Today of all days!"

Mercy sucked her teeth.

"I did call you. Twice as a matter of fact. Didn't G tell you? I guess he's your personal secretary now, because he always seems to be the one answering the phone."

Lenox laughed.

"So, that's you calling and hanging up like a kid? You need to grow up, Mercy."

Barbara sensed the tension building, and quickly rose from her seat on the bench. She looked at Mercy and smiled.

"I'll see you later, girl. I'm about to do Chanel's hair."

Mercy said goodbye to her friend and watched her walk over to the fire hydrant to get her daughter. She saw Judah's disappointment that his friend was leaving. But his face quickly brightened when he saw Deon approaching. The boys ran to each other and hugged before running off together toward the makeshift sprinklers.

Lenox sat down next to Mercy.

"Who's that chick supposed to be? My replacement?"

Mercy laughed. "That's Barbara. She lives down the hall from me."

Lenox waved her hand as if it didn't matter.

"You were really gonna let my birthday pass without coming to see me?"

She glared at Mercy. Her pain was evident as she asked the question.

Mercy looked at her sadly.

"I miss you, Len. I wanted to come over there with a bottle of wine and a pack of cigarettes and play some music and laugh like we used to. But everything is different now. *You're* different now. I can't act like it's cool that you're out here selling crack and risking everything for a dollar. I'm worried about you. I think G is bad news. And I don't want me and Judah getting caught up in that bullshit."

Lenox shook her head as she listened to her sister voice her fears.

"So, you call my house and hang up when he answers the phone. On my birthday? I mean, that's cold, Mercy. When are you gonna put your pride aside and stop grandstanding? I get it. You don't like G. You don't approve of what I'm doing. But I'm still your sister. And it's my fuckin' birthday."

Mercy looked down guiltily. She gripped the cup in her hand and offered it to Lenox, half-heartedly.

"Cheers?" She smiled, hoping to break the ice.

Lenox rolled her eyes and snickered before pushing the cup away roughly.

"Get that cheap shit out of here! I got some good champagne in my car."

Mercy looked at the car shining in the summer sun.

"I baked you a cake. It's upstairs. I was gonna come by eventually. I just needed to swallow my pride first."

Lenox crossed her legs and rested her arm on the top of the bench.

"I know you're afraid. I was, too, at first. I won't even lie. Cocaine? That alone is risky. But this shit is even more potent than just the average powder shit. Crack has these people out here spending money. Consistently. In fact, it's hard to keep up sometimes. The demand for it is so high that I'm busting my ass in that kitchen every day. I could use some help, but there's nobody I can trust."

Mercy shook her head. Hearing Lenox speak about drugs so casually was unsettling for her. It was clear that Lenox had immersed herself in a world that Mercy had never imagined.

"I'm not asking you to help me," Lenox said. "I understand that you can't wrap your head around the shit. Fine. But I need you to help me with Deon. I can't keep having him around all of it . . . I don't want him to know what's going on. And he's starting to ask questions."

"Like what?"

"Like why the house smells like that when I make the shit. Or why he has to stay outside while G's in there bagging up for hours at a time."

"So, it sounds like you're in over your head, Len. You already made a bunch of money. Why don't you get out now?"

Lenox wished she could explain the high she got from the life she was living. The parties she went to, the friends she was making, the money. So much money. She shook her head.

"I'm almost at my goal. I got a bunch of money saved up. I'm gonna buy a house out in Todt Hill where all the fancy mansions are. Me, you, and the boys will live there. And you can reopen your restaurant. I'll buy the building this time. You can pay me back if your pride insists on it. But once it's successful and everything is going the way I'm envisioning it, you'll see why I did this. You'll see that it was all worth it."

Mercy wanted to argue that what Lenox described sounded like a childish fairy tale. But she saw the glint of hope in Lenox's eyes and reminded herself that today was her sister's birthday. So, she plastered on a phony smile and nodded.

"Let's forget all that for now. You're twenty-five today! Let's celebrate!"

They drove out to Midland Beach in Lenox's new car. It was Mercy's first time riding in it and she felt a bit uncomfortable. She did her best to hide it, though. She forced visions of being pulled over by DEA on the side of the highway out of her mind. She spent most of the ride talking about her relationship with Xavier, her new job at the hospital, and her new friend Barbara. She pretended that she wasn't wondering whether her sister had a gun stashed in the glove compartment like all the hustlers in the movies they watched.

Lenox could sense Mercy's tension, no matter how hard she tried to disguise it. Her nervous chattering gave her away. She had barely shut up since they got in the car, and Lenox knew that Mercy was yapping in an effort to drown out her fears. Lenox let her talk as much as she needed to. She was just happy to be back in her sister's presence again.

When they got to the beach, they found a spot close to the water and spread their beach blankets out. The boys splashed playfully in the water nearby while Mercy and Lenox sat on the sand sipping champagne out of plastic cups. Mercy sat with her one-piece swimsuit on and a pair of sunglasses while she smoothed some sunscreen over her body. Lenox watched her, smiling. Sweet Mercy, always so cautious.

"You covered Judah in so much of that shit that he's light skinned now. We're black folk, sis. We don't get sunburn."

Mercy scoffed. "Tell that to Bob Marley." She kept right on applying her SPF.

Lenox wore a two-piece black bikini and a pair of Gucci shades G had given her for her birthday. The matching Gucci slides lay beside her beach towel as she reclined and closed her eyes. She had purchased a pricey diamond tennis bracelet as a gift to herself for "twenty-five trips around the sun" as she put it. It glittered in the sunshine as she lay there sunbathing.

Mercy stared at her in awe for a while. She didn't agree with how she was going about it. But there was no doubt that Lenox looked happier, healthier, and wealthier than she had ever seen her look before.

"Lenox . . ." Mercy wasn't sure where to even begin.

Lenox turned over onto her side and propped herself up on one elbow.

"What's up?"

"I'm not sure why. But I just can't shake this feeling that this new life of yours is going to cost you. Big time. I know today is your birthday. It's the first time we've hung out in a while, and you don't feel like going over this again. But I have to say what's on my mind."

"I want to hear it," Lenox said.

Mercy nodded.

"When we took the boys to the zoo that time, you said that I'm not a risk-taker. And you're right about that. I'm not. I never liked breaking the rules or doing anything that would get me in trouble. You were never that way. You like to push boundaries, gamble, and all of that. You're a wild one and I always admired that about you. I thought we balanced each other out. Me all level-headed and you all . . . not."

Lenox laughed at the truth in that summation.

"We each had something the other one didn't. It made us compatible. Ever since you started doing this crack thing . . . this just seems way more dangerous than all the other risks you've taken before. I worry all the time."

"About what?" Lenox asked. "Specifically."

"About you trying it out and getting addicted to the shit; about some jealous muthafucka in the street kicking in your door to get to the money or telling the cops what you're doing and having them kick in your door instead."

Lenox sat up.

"Well, let me put your fears to rest. I would never use that shit. Not in a million years. I have no curiosity to try it out at all, trust me! I've seen what it does to people who use it. Makes them into zombies who can only focus on getting that next hit."

"That's the other part of it that bothers me, Len. The shit is poison. So, good, *you're* not using it. But somebody is. Your neighbors, mine. That shit is lethal. You don't feel bad for being a part of it?"

Lenox shrugged. "If G wasn't selling it, some other nigga would be. In fact, he's not the only one out here hustling it anymore. The shit caught on like wildfire. So, I'm just trying to get in and make as much money as I can before the streets get saturated with it." She gestured excitedly with her hands. "G compared it to the stock market. The sooner you get in, the more money you make. The key to this is knowing when to get out. And I swear, Mercy, I'm not gonna stay in this game forever. I just want to get a leg up on everything. Then I'll go get a job and live a normal life. You'll see."

Even as the words left her mouth, Lenox knew she didn't mean a word of it. She had managed to avoid falling in love with G. He was just a means to an end for her. But she hadn't been able to resist falling in love with the crack game. She was enraptured by it. Understood all aspects of the business from production to supply and demand to packaging and distribution. She had the profit margins down pat, had the projected sales for the next fiscal year and the movements of their competitors all figured out. The crack game felt like a legitimate business to Lenox, and she had no intentions of walking away from it anytime soon.

She sighed.

"Mercy, I wish I could make you understand. I'm good at this. Like . . . really good at it. You remember the way I was in school. My two best subjects were science and math. That's all this is. The science of turning powder into rock and the addition and multiplication of my finances."

Mercy chuckled involuntarily.

"I swear on everything," Lenox continued. "I wouldn't do this if I didn't know that I could handle it. I'm not out there interacting with the fiends one on one. I just cook up the shit, help G bag it up, and get my cut. I keep his money in a safe at my house and that's why he's there every day. We're not together. Not like that. He does his thing and I do mine. It's just a business arrangement. And in that arrangement, G is the one taking most of the risk. He's the one who goes uptown to buy the cocaine, travels with it, brings it to me. All I'm doing is cooking it up. Then he's the one out there moving it, him and his workers. And he only has a few of them. None of them comes to my house. Nobody but G. So, it's safe. We've been working this way for a while now. Not one single problem. Except not having you around. That's the only part of my life that's fucked up right now."

Mercy felt bad hearing that. She didn't want to be apart from her sister.

"I've started to come by your place a million times," Mercy said, honestly. "But I don't even know what to expect anymore. Is crack being cooked in the kitchen while you and Deon are watching TV?"

Lenox laughed. "No, smart-ass. It's only cooking at night when he's sleeping or during the day when he's outside playing with his friends. I don't do none of that shit around him. He has no idea what's going on."

Again, Mercy scoffed.

"He knows something is going on. Kids ain't stupid, Lenox. He sees all the money, the clothes, jewelry, furniture, video games, leathers, and furs coming through there. He asked me the other day if you hit the lotto or something, because you never say you don't have 'McDonald's money' anymore."

Lenox laughed a bit uneasily. Maybe she had underestimated how perceptive her son was. She looked at Mercy curiously.

"How have you been doing with money?" she asked. "That little settlement we got from Mama's insurance must have ran out by now, with all that expensive tuition you're paying them white folks for Judah's education."

Mercy wished Lenox wasn't right.

"I'm doing alright," she lied. "Between my salary at the hospital and the little food stamps I get each month, we're managing."

Lenox knew her well enough to hear the part she wasn't saying. That each month when the food stamps ran out, there were times when Mercy had to try to make a dollar out of fifteen cents.

"Okay," Lenox said. She clapped her hands together as if she had some great solution to all their problems. "Here's the plan. I'm gonna put an end date on this little hustle of mine. Give me one year. On my birthday next year, I'm out. In the meantime I'll stack as much money as I can and make all the moves I need to make. And you will let me help you. You don't have to like it. You don't even have to acknowledge it. But just put your pride aside and your fear about what could happen to me. And let's get back to being sisters. The kind who look out for each other and have each other's back. And the kind that don't let birthdays pass without spending them together."

Mercy smiled and nodded eagerly.

"Okay. That's a deal."

Lenox beamed with joy. "GOOD!" she said, smiling widely. She snatched off her sunglasses, stood up, and got into a sprinter's stance. "Last one in the water drives us home!"

Lenox took off running toward the water before Mercy had the chance to scramble to her feet. She hurriedly did so now.

"Dammit! You cheater!" she called out as she darted after her.

Lenox plunged into the water with Mercy chasing after her.

FOOL'S PARADISE

The trouble with ignoring the elephant in the room is that it takes up a ton of space.

Though they didn't discuss the obvious turn Lenox's life had taken, it still impacted their relationship. Mercy knew that her sister was making a load of money in the drug game. But it was impossible to avoid noticing the grip the crack epidemic had on the city. Once thriving communities were now lined with crack houses. Vials with multicolored tops littered school playgrounds that doubled as outdoor brothels at night. Property values declined, families were torn apart, robberies and violent crimes were increasing, and neighborhoods that had once been tight-knit were now divided.

Weeks turned into months in what seemed like the blink of an eye. In the fall, Mercy and Lenox took the boys to a pumpkin patch in New Jersey. By now, the sisters had developed a habit of not talking about work. They avoided discussing Mercy's decision not to pursue cooking as a profession and Lenox's choice to continue in the drug game. Instead, they talked about the TV shows they liked, the latest hip-hop music, current events, and their love lives.

"I see you and Xavier are getting serious," Lenox said. "I like him. Your face lights up when he's around."

Mercy smiled, watching Judah and Deon running ahead. "He's good to me," she said. "And Judah likes him."

"You think you'll settle down with him? Get married? Maybe have another kid?" Lenox's eyes flashed as she said it, excited at the very thought.

"Calm down, Speedy! I like him."

"You love him."

"I love him," Mercy admitted. "But nobody's talking marriage or kids right now. I'm not in a rush for all of that. I just want to enjoy the moment."

Lenox considered that. "I guess you're right. It's good to take your time. But life is so short, you know? I'm afraid that if I wait too long to live it up, time will run out. Before you know it, we'll be old ladies with wrinkled skin, gray hair, and sagging titties."

Mercy frowned. "Come on now! Don't do us like that. We got that black that don't crack, healthy hair, and good, perky titties. That ain't gonna change."

Lenox laughed. "You're right. I'm tripping!"

"Exactly!"

When they got back to Mercy's apartment, she invited her neighbor Barbara over with her daughter, Chanel, to help them carve jack-o'-lanterns. By now, Barbara had grown on Lenox. She had envied the close relationship Mercy had with her new friend in the beginning. But the more Lenox hung around her, the more she could see that Barbara was cool. Like Mercy, she was a caring and devoted mother who was doing her best to keep her kids out of trouble.

Lenox watched as Chanel carved her pumpkin into a perfect cat face.

"You're good at this! Those whiskers are perfect. Deon, come look."

Deon glanced over at it and sucked his teeth. "That's nothing! Look at mine." He held up the monstrosity he had carved.

Chanel laughed. "It looks stupid."

Judah laughed, too. "What's it supposed to be?"

Deon shrugged. He had no plan in mind when he started hacking away at the thing. "Scary, dummy! That's what it's supposed to be."

Lenox, Mercy, and Barbara laughed.

"That's right, baby," Lenox encouraged him. "Tell them!"

While the kids kept at it, the women retreated to the living room and got comfortable.

"I like Chanel," Lenox said. "She gives Deon and Judah a run for their money."

Barbara smiled, proudly. "She's a little firecracker, that one."

"Good for her!" Lenox sipped her wine cooler. "She's not afraid to speak her mind."

"Chanel is focused," Barbara said. "She knows what she wants in life."

"What's that?" Lenox asked.

"She wants to get as far away from here as she can," Barbara said. "She wants to go to college, travel, and live out her dreams. Most of all, she wants to get out of here. And I don't blame her for that. This city is scary nowadays. The shootings, robberies, the drugs. It's too much."

Lenox took another sip and avoided Mercy's incriminating gaze.

"Yeah. Chanel is on the right path. My son, Dallas, is another story," Barbara shared. "He's in high school and he's got a chip on his shoulder that I want to knock the fuck off!"

Mercy laughed.

"He's not that bad."

"He's been experimenting with reefer lately. I'm starting to think he's doing more than that. Coming in all late, his eyes looking crazy. His basketball coach is on his case trying to get him back on track. But it's not easy with these kids nowadays."

The kids came in from the kitchen, covered in pumpkin guts.

"We're finished," Deon said. "Can we play video games now?"

Lenox huffed. "That's all you ever want to do these days. Let's have a dance party instead!"

Chanel cheered. She looked at Deon. "I love your mom!"

Lenox sauntered over to Mercy's boombox and inserted Michael Jackson's *Thriller* cassette tape. She turned the volume up and got the party started.

Chanel, Judah, and a reluctant Deon joined in the fun. Mercy and Barbara did, too. They danced so hard that Mercy's downstairs neighbor banged a broom on the ceiling to stop them.

Lenox turned the music up louder and used a spoon as a make-shift microphone. And her audience applauded on cue.

By the time winter descended on the city, Lenox had the crack game down to a science. Despite her promises to Mercy, Lenox hadn't slowed down at all. Things were going so well that G was going up-town to re-up more regularly. His connect, Benny, was so impressed that he took a trip out to Staten Island to see for himself.

Lenox was excited the day Benny came by. It was December and frigid temperatures had the city in a chokehold. Despite the cold, all of the windows in Lenox's place were cracked open as she cooked up the work G had brought over. Like Tatiana before her, Lenox was used to the smell of it now. She no longer needed a face covering and didn't recoil from the stench anymore. To her, it was just another part of her work environment. She burned incense and candles while she sang along to an Mtume song on the radio. She set the strainer down on the counter and began dancing while she snapped her fingers to the beat.

G watched her, smiling.

"Why you always winding your waist like that in front of me and then telling me 'no' when I try to get close to you?"

Lenox laughed and waved him off.

"Because you gotta learn to look without touching."

"That's not easy with you," he said, licking his lips. "For real, Lenox. What's up with you? We had a good thing going. Nowadays you're all business."

Her smile faded. "How many times we gotta have this conversation? We had fun. But I'm not trying to be on some Bonnie and Clyde shit with you. When Tatiana was cooking up your batches, there were no strings attached. Just money. That's how I want it between us. No more fuckin' and suckin'. Let's just get money. It's better that way. Smarter."

G stared at her while she nonchalantly went back to work.

"Why?" he pressed. "Because you're scared of getting your little feelings hurt or something?"

She chuckled. "I ain't scared of nothing but being broke again."

She turned the stove off and took a step back. Her heart nearly leapt out of her chest when she heard Deon's small voice behind her.

"Ma, what's that smell?" He stood in the kitchen's entryway with both hands covering his nose and mouth. He looked around and saw packages of white powder, colorful vials, and G standing near the window with a shocked expression on his face.

Lenox turned to Deon with her mouth agape. She stammered, lost for words at first. Then she picked up a dish towel and began fanning the air in a ridiculous attempt to ward the smell off. Realizing it was futile, she tossed the rag and grabbed Deon, pushing him down the hallway toward his bedroom.

"What are you doing home from school?" she asked, still shocked that he was there.

"We had a half day at school today. You didn't come and get me, so I walked home."

Lenox's heart sank. She recalled the notice she had gotten, the reminder that the last day before holiday break would be an early dismissal. She groaned and apologized to Deon for forgetting.

"What's that smell?" he asked again. "It's disgusting."

"I'm making some . . . um . . ." She struggled to formulate a lie.

"Is it poison?"

Lenox shook her head, though she knew she was lying. She brought him into his bedroom and shut the door behind them.

"I didn't expect you to be here," she said, honestly. She sighed, looking at his young, innocent face. He was only a baby. Far too young to understand what was going on. Or so she thought."

"Is it drugs?" he asked, looking her dead in the eyes.

She frowned. "Why would you ask me that?"

"Jason told me you sell drugs."

Her frown deepened. "Jason who's in your class?" She shook her head. They were in the second grade. "Why would he say that?"

"He said his mother told him that. And that's the reason why I have more stuff than everybody else."

Lenox felt her worlds colliding and swore to herself that she would confront Jason's mother the next time she saw the bitch.

"Jason's just jealous," she said. "His mother is, too."

"So, what's that smell?" Deon pressed. His expression was serious.

"LENOX!" G called to her from the kitchen.

"WHAT?" she shouted back, impatiently. She had too much going on right now.

"Benny is here!"

Deon noticed his mother's expression shift. She took a deep breath and looked at him. "We'll talk about this later on."

She rushed from the room. Deon could hear chatter down the hall as his mother greeted someone who sounded unfamiliar. His curiosity piqued, Deon held his breath to ward off the stench and walked down the hall.

"Yo! Y'all got this shit rockin' up in here!" Benny stood in the center of the living room looking down at the coffee table covered in crack vials and a round dinner plate full of little crystal flakes that hadn't been bagged yet. Benny held one of the vials up to the light, examining it the way a jeweler appraises a jewel. "No wonder y'all got this island buzzing!"

He slapped hands with G and they embraced. Lenox beamed proudly as Benny turned to her.

"You got the fucking Midas touch, Lenox! Where the fuck did he find you?"

Lenox laughed as Benny grabbed her around the waist and danced her around the room.

"We're making a lot of FUCKING MONEY!" Benny yelled, laughing, as he twirled Lenox like a ballerina.

Benny's gaze settled on the kid in the corner of the room, and he stopped mid-dance. For a moment, it felt like déjà vu. It was as if he were seeing himself at eight years old wearing that same confused and forlorn expression. In his mind, he went back to that moment as a child when he stood in the doorway of his living room and watched his mother tie a belt around her arm and inject a needle into her vein. He recalled the sinking feeling he had in the pit of his stomach then, learning the truth about his mother for the first time. That same expression was present now on Deon's face as he watched the scene unfolding in front of him. Benny cleared his throat.

"Hey," he said. "How you doing? My name is Benny."

Deon waved, half-heartedly.

Lenox stepped forward. "This is my son. He had a half day at school today and it slipped my mind." She looked at Benny meaningfully. "Normally, he's not here when I work. I was just talking to him about all of this when you got here."

Benny nodded, understanding the reason the kid looked like he had just seen a ghost. He smiled at Deon.

"It smells funny in here, right?"

Deon nodded.

"When we work it smells like that. Fumes from the factory." He smiled. "Go get your jacket. I'll take you for a ride in my car. We'll get something to eat." He looked at Lenox. "You want to take a ride with us?"

Lenox nodded. "Yeah." She rushed to get her and Deon's coats.

Benny turned to G and whispered. "Clean this up before we get back. Kid don't need to see this shit."

G nodded. "No doubt."

Deon stared at Benny, his big shearling coat, thick rope chain, gold teeth, and three-finger ring. This man seemed important. He noticed the way his mother and G both seemed to revere him. As they exited the house and walked toward the gleaming Jaguar parked at the curb, Deon knew Benny had to be somebody special to drive a car like that. They climbed inside.

"So, you never told me your name," Benny said.

"Deon."

Benny turned to face him in the backseat. "Nice to meet you, Deon. I'm a good friend of your mom's. She's a really smart lady. If you're her son, that must mean you're a really smart kid."

Deon nodded. "I am," he asserted proudly.

Benny laughed and started the car. Lenox gave him directions to the nearest McDonald's and they proceeded.

"If you're so smart, what's fifty plus fifty?" Benny asked, glancing at Deon in the rearview.

"A hundred!" Deon shouted without hesitating.

"Oh snap! You *are* smart!" Benny shouted.

Deon smiled, proudly. "That was easy!"

"Oh, yeah?" Benny said. "So, what's one hundred plus two hundred?"

Deon thought a moment. "Three hundred!"

"OHHHH!" Benny hollered. "This kid is a genius!"

Deon laughed.

Benny kept challenging him all the way to McDonald's. When they arrived, he let Deon order everything he wanted. Then they headed back to Lenox's place.

Benny didn't normally allow anyone to eat in his beloved car. But he didn't object as Deon dug into his food and chewed happily. He grinned at the sight of the kid who somehow reminded him of his younger self. Benny looked at Lenox and could sense that she was tense about the situation. He spoke to her softly.

"When I was a kid, my moms was in the game. But she was on the other side of it. The side Tatiana found herself on."

Lenox nodded, catching his drift.

"I knew what she was doing way before anybody told me outright. Kids ain't dumb. And no matter how hard we try, we can't hide this shit from them forever. Eventually—one way or another—they find out. You're a smart lady. I could tell that from the second I met you." Benny nodded in Deon's direction. "He's just like you. I think you gotta level with him. But give it to him in doses he can digest. A little at a time."

Lenox sighed and nodded. Her heart broke a little knowing that Benny spoke the truth.

Deon leaned forward as he chewed on a French fry. He was fascinated by Benny's clothes, jewelry, and the luxury car he drove.

"Are you rich?" Deon asked.

Lenox shot him a warning look. "Don't be rude!"

Benny chuckled. "That's not rude at all. Little man can ask me anything." He looked at Deon. "YES!" he shouted.

Lenox laughed despite the uneasiness she still felt after being busted by her son cooking crack.

"Yes, I am rich," Benny said. "And someday you will be, too."

"How? What do you do?"

Benny smiled. "I'm in the import/export business," he said. "Basically, that means I move products around the country, and I turn natural resources into profits."

Deon had no idea what any of that meant. But it sounded important.

"Wow," he said, trying to make sense of it.

Benny looked at Lenox, gingerly, and patted her hand as he said the next part.

"Your mom works with me. She's just getting started. But I

can already tell that she's got what it takes to be successful in this business." He looked at Lenox and nodded. "She's smart, she's tough, and she puts in work. That's the formula right there."

Benny glanced at Deon again. "Sometimes the work she does for me involves a lot of chemicals. It's a messy business. But she's not stupid. She knows how to keep the mess away from you. I know you came home early today, and you had to see and smell some bad things. But I want you to trust your mother. If you do what she says, and you pay attention to her, you'll be rich, too, someday. I promise."

Deon nodded. "I will." He sat back in his seat and kept eating his meal.

Lenox exhaled and assured herself that she still had everything under control.

Benny became a constant presence after that visit. At least once a month he pulled up in his flashy car, dazzling everyone with his big personality and his booming laughter. Deon was too young to understand that Benny was the plug, the faucet that kept the cocaine flowing through G's hands. In turn, Benny was the one keeping money raining down on Lenox, and Benny became someone she admired and respected.

Lenox and Benny were a lot alike. Benny was fearless, unapologetic, calculated, and always thinking three steps ahead. Like Lenox, he was strategic and trusted his own instincts over any logic. When they laughed together it was contagious even if no one else was in on the joke. They were both magnetic, loud, and fun-loving. In business, they found an easy rhythm. Benny grew to trust Lenox and the feeling was mutual. She took guidance from him when it came to Deon and allowed him to forge a close bond with her son.

"Uncle Benny" was how Deon referred to him. Benny always gave him money when he saw him. Whatever cash he had in his pocket, he'd wad it up and hand it all to Deon in a ball.

"DEEE-ON! My little man! Come here and let Uncle Benny line your pockets real quick."

Deon would thank him and rush over to a corner where he sat and counted it carefully. Uncle Benny had a jovial spirit and the flashiest style Deon had ever seen. He noticed the way his mother changed around Benny. She was seldom willing to do stereotypical "woman's work." She didn't cook or clean much. And when she did it wasn't with much joy or enthusiasm. She certainly never bent over backwards to make G comfortable. But when Benny came around, Lenox softened a little. She would make him a plate of food and pour him a drink. She paid attention when he spoke and complimented what he wore. Deon noticed these things, and he decided that Benny was the type of man his mother wanted him to be. Benny always had money. He had respect, wore his wealth and status loudly, and was unapologetic and bold. Deon adopted those characteristics as well.

Lenox noticed the change in her son, and she was proud of it. Deon had a tremendous amount of confidence. Some of his teachers called it cockiness. But Lenox loved it. When he asked for the hottest sneakers, she got them regardless of the price. She took him shopping uptown and sent him to school wearing labels by designers his peers had never heard of. She gave him a gold chain for his eighth birthday in February. It wasn't as big and thick as Benny's chain. But Deon felt like the man. Benny showed up for the birthday party at the roller skating rink with a leather bomber jacket with a fox fur hood for Deon. All the kids were excited when Deon's "Uncle Benny" walked in with cupcakes for everybody and the flyest jacket on the market for his "nephew."

Young Deon didn't have the words to express all of the things he was thinking and feeling. So, he kept them mostly to himself. He was experiencing a wide range of emotions that he kept bottled up within himself. Fear was chief among them. By now he understood that his mother was selling drugs. He worried about the dangers that came along with that, but he never told anyone about those concerns. Instead, he put on a cocky mask and set out into the world each day. He misbehaved in school in an attempt to get his mother's attention, whether negative or positive. And he kept his longing, fears, and loneliness to himself.

He wanted to sit alone with his mother and curl up next to her on the couch and express all the trepidation he had inside. But Lenox was always so busy. She had pickups and drops to make, people to meet with, parties to go to. And most nights, Deon was being dropped off at his aunt's house while Lenox hit the town. When she was around, she seemed proudest of him when he was pretending to be more self-assured than he truly was.

Deon began to equate love with material things. What Lenox wasn't giving him in time, she more than made up for in gifts and shopping sprees. The value of items mattered to him. Especially when all the kids in school came to equate him with the latest brands. He treated every piece of his wardrobe like a work of art. The only person he shared it all freely with was his cousin Judah.

The two were like night and day. Deon rambunctious and loud, Judah the quiet and studious one. But they shared an unbreakable bond forged over many weekends spent together in Mercy's cozy apartment while Lenox hit the town and put in work.

Since the day he had arrived home from school unexpectedly, things had changed. Now, after school, Deon walked the few blocks to Judah's apartment in the projects and hung out there until his mother called and told him to come home. He enjoyed his Aunt Mercy's cooking and his cousin's friendship and company. Being an only child was lonely, but it was less so for both of them when they were together.

Deon began to confide in his cousin.

"Sometimes I wish I was you."

They were chilling in Judah's room playing with one of Deon's video game systems. He spent so much time at Mercy's place that he started leaving toys and clothes there so that he wouldn't have to keep trekking them back and forth.

Judah looked at Deon like he was crazy.

"Why? You have everything." Judah meant it. Deon had all the things a kid their age desired.

"I have toys and clothes and stuff like that. You have your mother. Xavier is like your step-pops. You got friends who live in your building and y'all hang out. Sometimes I feel like I'm by myself."

Deon realized it was his first time telling anybody this.

Judah pressed the buttons on the joystick and shrugged.

"Aunt Len works a lot. But that's just so she can give you all the things you want."

Deon looked at his cousin. "What kind of work you think she does?"

Judah stopped playing the game and caught Deon's gaze. Judah sighed. He had heard the whispered conversations between his mother and Xavier late at night.

"I don't know," Judah said. "But, whatever it is, she's making a lot of money at it."

Deon hung his head. "She's selling crack."

"What's that?"

Deon shrugged. "I don't know. But it smells like shit."

"You ever seen it?"

Deon nodded. "Sometimes. G leaves it laying around sometimes in Ziploc bags."

"Just don't touch it," Judah warned. "My mother said drugs make you crazy."

"You think Aunt Mercy knows what my mother's doing?"

Judah hesitated, then answered honestly. "Yeah. She's worried about her."

Deon nodded. "Me, too."

Judah searched his young mind for words of reassurance but came up empty. "Why don't you tell her?" he asked at last.

Deon shrugged. "Cuz she's already dealing with a lot. If I tell her that, she'll just have another thing to worry about." He picked up the joystick. "I'm just saying you're lucky. That's all." He looked at his cousin and forced a smile. "But that luck is about to run out when I whoop yo ass at this game!"

Judah sucked his teeth and focused his eyes on the screen. "Let's go!"

Children always hear and see more than adults give them credit for. Deon and Judah were no different. They watched as Lenox up-graded cars constantly, dripping in glistening diamonds and thick gold jewelry, saw her turning heads in expensive clothes and keeping Deon clad in all the latest fashions. She was generous to her sister and nephew, too, despite Mercy's protests.

When Lenox overheard Judah telling Deon that he might have to leave his prestigious private school because his mother was behind on tuition, Lenox went down there and paid Judah's tuition for the rest of the school year.

"My name is Lenox Howard," she told the principal. "Judah is my nephew. If there's any issues with his tuition or any of the other fees y'all charge around here, you call me. I'll settle it." She paid the tuition in cash, much to the surprise and delight of the principal.

She didn't mention it to Mercy. Instead, she kept her mouth shut and waited it out. Mercy didn't find out about it until she went to the principal with the money and was told Judah's debt had been paid in full.

"Lenox Howard came in and took care of it," Sister Genevieve told her.

Mercy saw red, and all hell broke loose. She stormed over to Lenox's apartment and banged on the door. When Lenox let her in, Judah rushed into Deon's room to duck the storm he knew was coming. The sisters argued while the boys listened from the safety of Deon's bedroom.

"Who asked you to go down there and pay his tuition?"

"What were you gonna do, Mercy? How else were you gonna get the money?"

"That's for ME to worry about. Not you!"

"Your fuckin' foolish pride is gonna keep you stuck in one place for the rest of your life. If that's the way you want to live, then fine. But Judah shouldn't have to suffer just because you're too proud to ask for help."

"It's not about pride, Lenox! You said you were getting out of this shit. You're only getting in deeper."

"It's not as easy as you think it is," Lenox countered. "I can't just pack up and close shop. I'm getting out, Mercy. You just have to give me time."

"Time for what? You're not even working toward a goal!"

"I *would* be if you would stop being stubborn and let me finance a restaurant for you. Just because that shit happened with Mr. Miller doesn't mean that we can't make it work if we try it again. You could help me put this money to good use," Lenox shot back.

"I don't want your crack money."

Lenox recoiled a bit at the weight of that.

"You're better than this shit," Mercy said. "You're smart. You helped G turn his little hustle into this big-ass enterprise. Got all these little soldiers out here working for him. Thousands of dollars pouring in on a daily basis. You could stop all this drug shit and apply that same business sense to something legit. But you'd rather follow G's ass around playing games."

Lenox glared at her sister. "I don't follow G around. I don't even need him anymore, quiet as it's kept. I can do it on my own because I'm smart. Just like you said. Smart enough to know that if my son is gonna have a life that's better than the one we had growing up, I have to be the one to make that happen. Ain't no knight in shining armor coming to rescue us, Mercy. Not G or Xavier or any of these niggas out here. WE gotta be the ones to do it."

Lenox shook her head, frustrated by Mercy's refusal to see her side of things.

"You go into that hospital every day and sit at that desk and sort through those files like it's gonna elevate you out of poverty. But you're barely making enough to pay your rent and keep food on the table. I paid Judah's tuition. Big fuckin' deal! I made that money back in two hours."

"But what is it really costing you?" Mercy asked, rhetorically. "Your son is growing up in a crack house."

"Watch your mouth!" Lenox shot back, defensively. "I stopped doing it there. I have a separate spot for that now."

"And if you go to jail? You got a plan for that, too? If the place gets robbed? Some muthafuckas bust in there and put a gun to Deon's head, you ready for that shit?"

Lenox sucked her teeth. "Stop watching the news! It's making you paranoid."

"Maybe you should *start* watching it and take your fucking blinders off." Mercy tossed the money she had intended to give to Judah's principal on Lenox's table. "Here's the first payment. I'll give you the rest next month." She stepped closer to her sister with her gaze unwavering. "Understand me. I don't like what you're doing. And you promised me you were gonna stop. Until you do, I don't want your help."

Mercy stormed down the hall, grabbed Judah, and left.

Weeks went by before the sisters spoke again. When they did, it was with no acknowledgment of the explosive argument they had had. Lenox came by to pick up Deon, and Mercy invited her to sit down and have some dinner. They ate spaghetti and meatballs and talked about music and the kids and critiqued celebrity outfits in the latest magazines. The topic of Lenox's continued involvement in the crack game remained unspoken between them like an invisible line in the sand.

LOST ONES

1986

New York City felt electric. Hip-hop had emerged as a culture all its own, affecting everything from fashion to slang. Judah and Deon grew into adolescence against the backdrop of fluorescent colors, boomboxes hoisted on shoulders, thick gold rope chains, Kangol hats, Cazal glasses, and sneakers with fat laces. The girls around the way wore bangs, door knocker earrings, and belts with their names on them. The walls of buildings and bodega gates served as canvases for graffiti artists. Music, vibrance, excitement, and the threat of danger were ever present.

The basketball court became the boys' constant meeting place.

Deon stared straight ahead at Judah's neighbor Chanel as she dribbled the basketball across the court and made an easy layup. She was practicing alone now while both boys watched.

"She's a better ballplayer than you are." Judah looked at Deon with a smirk on his face as he said it.

They sat together on a graffiti-covered bench in the Big Park. Someone on the second floor of an adjacent building had put their stereo speaker in the window, blasting music across the projects. Dirty sneakers swung from telephone poles, tossed up there by neighborhood kids as a ghetto rite of passage. Teenagers sat huddled together in packs smoking cigarettes and sipping malt liquor from bottles wrapped in brown paper bags.

Deon shrugged. "She's better than you, too."

Judah laughed. "I just beat her. So, what are you talking about?"

"You only won 'cause she got distracted when her brother called her name."

Chanel often challenged the boys to one-on-one games. And although he wouldn't admit it to his cousin now, Deon knew that Judah was telling the truth. Chanel was usually victorious in those games.

"Her brother's the one who taught her how to play," Judah said. "He's on the team at McKee High School. I see him out here practicing with her all the time."

"You should ask him to show you sum'n. 'Cause you need a little help with your ballhandling."

Deon smirked as he said it, and shoved his cousin playfully.

At nine and ten years old, Deon and Judah had a bond that made them seem more like brothers than cousins. Deon spent more time at Judah's house than at his own. Despite her promises to the contrary, Lenox hadn't slowed down one bit.

She had made a few changes, though. After Deon came home early from school and caught her in the process, she had stopped cooking the product in her own home. Now G had gotten them a subleased apartment in the projects where Lenox cooked up crack while G bagged it up. They had a system now, and workers, too. G had been hesitant to hire local guys to help him sell his work. He worried that they would make mistakes and garner unwanted attention. Or worse, that they might get ambitious and try to rob him. But the demand for the crack Lenox was cooking up was so high that he had to change course. He had a few trusted workers who he handled with kid gloves.

Mercy worked the early shift at the hospital, which allowed her to get home from work at around four o'clock on weekday afternoons. By then Judah was typically at home already engrossed in his homework or whatever book his literature teacher had assigned him. He loved to read and would pour his heart out to his mother over dinner in their modest apartment. Mercy loved to see the way his eyes lit up as he spoke delightedly about books by Tolstoy, Alexandre Dumas, and other literary greats. She spent countless evenings laughing as she watched Judah consume soulful homecooked meals and the things he was learning with equal enthusiasm.

Deon was receiving an entirely different education. He had always been a curious child, alert and attentive even when it appeared that he was distracted by television or a toy he was playing with. He had mastered the art of listening without seeming to. In that way he learned a great deal about his mother. Despite the money she obviously had now, she didn't send him to the private school that his cousin, Judah, attended. Not that Deon wanted to go there. The thought of wearing uniforms and being herded around by a bunch of nuns seemed horrifying to him. But he did wonder why his mother didn't have the same passion for education that Aunt Mercy possessed. Whenever Deon spent nights—and lately entire weekends—at his aunt's house, she and Xavier were always helping him with some report or project. Mercy was always asking if his homework was turned in, what score he had gotten on a recent test. His mother never asked those types of questions. Not unless a teacher called to complain about Deon's outbursts in class, failed tests, or missed assignments. Even then, she seemed more bothered by the thought of school administrators poking around in her business than she was by the fact that Deon might be drifting off course.

When they were at home alone together—a seldom occurrence since G was always nearby—Lenox and Deon talked about her expectations of her only child.

"I want you to be a real man. Not a coward like a lot of these guys out there in them streets. You walk tall and hold your own. Just like I taught you."

Lenox did her best to demonstrate exactly what she meant by those words. In her view, she had stepped into the footprints of Deon's father. A man who died chasing a dream of prominence that proved elusive for him. But Lenox had achieved it. She had money, cars, jewelry, clothes, and every material thing she desired. But, more importantly to her, she had the respect of men who were revered by their counterparts. She walked into rooms and they fell silent. All eyes on her. People knew that she was *that bitch*.

And that was how she wanted Deon to be when he grew up. A man who commanded respect because he deserved it. Because he was brave enough to take risks and smart enough not to get caught. Just like his mother.

Lenox was deliberate about the men she brought around her son. G was a constant presence, of course. Somehow Deon could sense that his mother didn't love G. They seemed to be more than friends. Deon got the sense that G really cared for Lenox. But the feeling didn't appear to be mutual. Lenox had fallen in love with the money they were making. Nothing more, nothing less.

Mercy and Xavier's relationship had deepened in the year since they first got together. He spent the night regularly, and on some rare occasions when Judah stayed at Lenox's place, Mercy spent nights nestled with him in the full-sized bed in his modest basement apartment. It wasn't much, but when she was there with him it felt like their own blissful world. One night like that in late September, Mercy lay naked beside Xavier trailing an imaginary line across his chest. He took her hand in his and turned to face her.

"I'm leaving," he said, softly.

She frowned, hoping she heard him wrong. "Leaving?"

He nodded. "Bruce—the guy I work for—he has a brother down in DC. The guy started a trucking company. Big rigs. He needs help and they asked me if I would move down there and work for him. Driving an eighteen-wheeler cross-country, just like I always talked about."

"Wow," Mercy managed. "What about your daughter?"

"I'll come and visit her when I get time off. And once I get settled in, she can come down and stay with me sometimes." He saw the unsure expression on Mercy's face. Some of the excitement left his voice. "I told him I would do it. The money is right and it's the chance to learn the ropes from the ground up. I could have my own operation someday." He caught himself getting excited and toned it down. "My brother and his wife live in that area, too. So, I won't be all on my own down there."

He saw Mercy's face falling, and he cut to the chase.

"I want you to come with me. You and Judah."

She was shocked and it showed. "Wh-what? We can't do that."

"Yes, you can. Just pack your bags and come on." His eyes twinkled in the moonlight as he smiled.

"What are you saying, Xavier?"

"I'm saying we should get out of here." He sat up in bed. "Ever since the fire, I've been seeing how this place is turning into a war zone. Not just Staten Island. The whole city is worse than I've ever seen it, and I've lived here all my life. I feel like if I don't get out of here now, I'll be stuck here forever. This is the job I've been praying for. So, I'm gonna take it."

Mercy let it sink in. She nodded. "I'm happy for you," she said, emotionlessly.

"I guess you didn't hear me when I said that I want you to come with me."

Mercy shook her head. "I can't leave here, Xavier. Not now."

"Why not? It's not like we'll be living out of my car. The guy I'll be working for—Phillip—he's gonna help me find a place before I move down there. Somewhere in Maryland or Virginia with less crime and better schools. We could get Judah into a school just as good as the one he's in now. Except down there it won't cost you an arm and a leg. The public schools there are better than the ones up here. You could get a job at a hospital when we get settled in.

Or you could get back to your real love—cooking. You could do it right this time. Start over." He smiled at her. "We could have a kid of our own."

Mercy wanted to smile so badly. She wanted to throw her arms around his neck and say "yes" to all of it. But she couldn't, no matter how hard she tried.

"I can't leave here," she said again. "Not right now." She shook her head. "My sister . . . if I leave now . . . I don't know . . ."

Xavier kissed her, preventing her from stammering further. She felt unexpected tears fall from her eyes, and he wiped them away, gently.

"Your sister is a big girl," he said. "She's gonna do what she wants to do, whether you're here or not."

Mercy knew it was true. "My nephew," she said, weakly. "If I leave, who will he have?"

"His mother," Xavier said. "Mercy, you don't have to hold everybody together. Lenox can stand on her own. Deon is *her* son. She has the right to raise him the way she wants to. But when we lay in bed at night and talk about the future, the one you see for Judah doesn't look like where Deon is headed."

"Deon is a kid," Mercy said, defensively. "You can't tell where he's headed yet."

Xavier didn't argue that. "All I'm trying to say is that you talk about seeing Judah go to college and have a big life. Maybe the way to make that happen is to get him away from here. This gives all of us a chance to start fresh."

She sighed. "It sounds nice," she said. "But I think you should go on your own. At least for now. For me to quit my job, pull Judah out of school, and try to figure out how to start over in a new place . . . that's a lot to digest at once. I know this is the job you've been praying for, like you said. And you should take it. When you get settled in, then maybe we can see about the rest of it."

She forced a smile then, finally.

Xavier knew it was fake. Somewhere inside of him he knew this was the end for them. But he had made up his mind, and he was going.

"I love you," he said. "When I think about my future, I see you in it. If you won't come with me now, I understand. I don't like it, but I can wait for you to feel comfortable with it. Just don't wait too long. Don't stay around here waiting for permission to live your own life, Mercy."

"I love you," she said back to him. She touched his face tenderly.

She closed her eyes as he kissed her and held on to him with all her might as he made love to her until the morning.

Two weeks later, Xavier packed up and prepared for his big move. The day he left, Mercy rose early and made him a full breakfast feast. She fought back tears as he and Judah sat at her kitchen table battling over biscuits while she packed Tupperware full of food she had prepared for Xavier's journey.

"Will you teach me how to drive an eighteen-wheeler one day?" Judah asked.

Xavier laughed. "Hell yeah!"

"You think I can ride with you to California or somewhere like that in your truck?"

Xavier chewed his pancakes and shrugged. "If you can convince your mom to bring you down there, I'll take you wherever you want to go."

Mercy pretended not to hear as their conversation continued. She was shuffling through a million different thoughts in her mind. On one hand she felt foolish for letting Xavier go. They loved each other and had built something special. She knew that if she lingered too long, another woman could swoop in and steal his heart while she was planting her feet in Staten Island. But on the other hand she worried that if she left, Lenox would be all on her own. She could get hurt, and if that happened, Mercy would never forgive herself.

As Xavier prepared to leave, he hugged Judah and gave him

a handshake goodbye. "Keep listening to your mother, and I'll see you soon."

Xavier turned to Mercy next. She handed him a big shopping bag of food she had prepared for him.

"There's some sandwiches and snacks in there for the drive. And I packed some turkey wings for when you get there. Put the rest of it in the freezer so you'll have something to eat for a few days—"

"When are you coming to visit me?" he asked, pulling her into his arms.

She swallowed past the lump in her throat. "Soon."

He kissed her goodbye, long and passionately. Then he walked out the door, boarded the elevator, and left Mercy standing in her apartment doorway feeling more alone than she had in her life.

On a sunny Saturday afternoon, Lenox walked through her apartment, surveying the space she had just cleaned from top to bottom. Her stereo was blasting, and she smiled with contentment as she inhaled the freshness. Her doorbell rang, and she went to answer it. She muttered under her breath when she saw G standing outside.

"This muthafucka."

She opened the door and he stepped inside.

"Good afternoon." He bopped his head to the beat of the music playing and grinned at her. "Looks like I interrupted a good time. If you didn't change the locks, I could've just let myself in." He looked her over, always looked forward to seeing what she had on. Today she wore her hair in a perfect doobie wrap. A gold nameplate graced her delicate neck, and she wore a curve-hugging bodysuit. "You expecting company?"

"I changed the locks because this ain't the cook-up spot no more. No need for you to have a key. Me and Deon need our privacy."

He drank her in as she walked away. Her body was incredible, and her walk was even sexier.

"You didn't answer my question. You expecting company?"

"What's up, G? What you need? I know you didn't come over here just to find out if I'm expecting company."

He stared at her without answering. She shrugged her shoulders and looked at him, confused.

"What's up?" Lenox could tell something was wrong. She felt an uneasiness inside herself that she couldn't explain. G was acting sketchier than usual.

He stuck his hands in his pockets. "My cousin Mark got out of jail. My plan was for me and him to link back up. I was gonna take him back to see Benny, help him get on his feet, and we would get back to work like we did in the beginning. But Mark came home, and he didn't like the condition he found his family in."

Lenox listened carefully, piecing it all together.

"Tatiana got worse after I stopped bringing her the work to cook up. She started doing all kinds of shit for money, lost the kids."

"Lost them?"

"They're in foster care. She fucked everything up. And Mark blames me. He's telling my family that I abandoned her, that the shit is all my fault. He's upset. And he's talking kinda reckless." G rubbed his hand across his face in exasperation. "He went to Benny without me. Benny called me a little while ago. He wants to meet here. He's on his way."

Lenox sat down on her couch, slowly, her mind reeling.

"What does he want to meet for?" she asked nervously.

"We'll find out when he gets here," G said. He sat down on the couch beside Lenox.

He looked at her and could sense her tension.

"Don't get all worked up. Mark ain't gonna do shit."

"He knows where you live," she reminded him. "Y'all are family. If he wants to get to you, it ain't hard. You gotta talk to him."

"I tried," G said. "He got on the phone with me and said a lot of foul shit. Then he hung up on me. I spoke to my aunt, tried to get her to hear me out. But she's pissed off at me, too. Like I was supposed to keep the kids out of foster care. Why the fuck didn't she step up and take them?"

Lenox wrung her hands together nervously. "Does he know where I live?"

G shook his head. "Mark don't know shit."

The doorbell rang, and Lenox felt her heart jump. She caught her breath and went to answer it. Benny stood there wearing an 8 Ball jacket and sunglasses, grinning.

"Lenox Avenue!" He opened his arms and she hugged him. "How you doing, beautiful?" He stepped inside.

"I'm alright. Surprised to see you today."

He looked around, fishing around in his pockets for cash. "Where's my man Deon at?"

"He's with my sister."

Benny nodded. "Cool. Let's talk."

Lenox noticed that he wasn't his usual upbeat self. His tone was much more serious than it normally was in her presence.

She led him into the living room. He greeted G and he sat down in the leather recliner.

"Did you tell Lenox what's been going on?" he asked G.

G shrugged, and Lenox knew right away that he hadn't told her everything.

"Basically," G said.

Benny shook his head in disgust. "You know your cousin ain't playing with a full deck. Always been a loose cannon, that one. He's pretty pissed off that you left him hanging while he was away."

Lenox looked at G and saw him shifting a bit in his seat.

"I did what I could. I'm out here putting in work. Trying to make sure that me and my moms have what we need and shit. This muthafucka acts like I'm supposed to drop everything and run up north every five minutes to visit him."

"No, no, no," Benny said, shaking his head. "He said you didn't put money on his books, didn't hit his mother off with money or nothing while he was away." Benny frowned, disapprovingly. "That's your family. I don't care how busy you are, you could send some money, G. And then to make it worse you left Tati high and dry out there in the Bronx. She was selling her body, neglecting the kids, got evicted from the projects. Listen . . ." Benny held his hands up. "How you treat your family is none of my business. But Mark is very upset. When he came to see me, he asked me to cut you off."

Lenox groaned.

G sat forward in his seat. "Why?"

Benny sat back. "He reminded me that we go way back, and he's the one who brought you uptown in the first place. He talked a lot of shit about how he's the reason I'm getting so much money with you out here on this island. And he gave me a bunch of money and copped a lot of product from me. He got a crew already, and he said there'll be more where that came from. But he asked me to stop fucking with you. And he said he's gonna kill you, even if it means going back to jail." Benny looked at G seriously. "I believed him."

Lenox sat in silence. Benny looked at her.

"He got Tati in a rehab and shit. But he blames you for taking her spot. He's really mad at G, but he's directing a lot of his anger at you. And I always liked you, Lenox. I tried to reason with Mark, but . . ." Benny threw up his hands in frustration. "Some mutha-fuckas you can't reason with."

"So, you're saying he's after me, too?"

"Yeah," Benny answered honestly. "He's saying a lot of crazy shit right now. I think it's smart for both of you to lay low for a while."

Lenox saw the concern in Benny's eyes, and for the first time since she had gotten into the crack game, she was scared.

"Nah," G said, defiantly. "I ain't going nowhere. And now's not the time to stop getting this money out here."

Benny looked at G and felt sorry for him. He had seen guys like him a dozen times before. Young, ambitious, and stubborn. Most of the time, it got them locked up or killed. He shifted his gaze. Lenox was different, though. He saw her sitting there weighing the brevity of the situation, silently. He had always liked her, could sense that she was smarter and more capable than G. Benny had a soft spot for her and he smiled at her reassuringly.

"I can't make you do anything. But I came out here to suggest to you very strongly that you both lay low for a little while. Especially since you have Deon to think about."

He looked at G and tried to reason with him once again. "Let me see if I can calm your cousin down. Make him listen to reason. In the meantime, y'all should get ghost."

Lenox zoned out, thinking of where she could go, and how she would explain this all to Mercy. She could hear G arguing that now wasn't the time to slow down production since he had just tapped into a connect on the white side of the island. After a few minutes, Benny rose to leave. Lenox stood, too.

"Benny, thank you for coming out here to let me know what's going on. I had no idea this was happening."

Benny nodded. "You do what you gotta do to keep you and Deon out of harm's way." He shot a look at G. "You be safe, too. I'll be in touch."

Lenox walked Benny to the door, and he gave her a light hug as he left.

"You're smart, Harlem girl. You know what to do."

Lenox watched him leave, then shut the door and returned to G, still seated on the couch.

"You gotta go," she said. "And don't come back here until you fix this shit with your cousin."

"Calm down," G said. "I'm gonna talk to him."

"I knew you cut Tatiana off. But I thought you were smart enough to keep the peace with your family so the shit wouldn't come back to bite us in the ass."

"I don't owe nobody shit," G replied.

Lenox sucked her teeth. "Neither do I. Including you. So, like I said, you gotta go." She gestured toward the door. "I'll call you."

He stared at her for a moment, considering protesting. But he could tell there was no reasoning with her. She had that expression on her face that let him know she was done talking. Reluctantly, he rose to leave.

"This is no big deal," he said as he left. "Trust me."

Lenox locked the door behind him. She scoffed. Trusting him was the last thing she would ever do.

In New York City, seasons change in a flash. Warm fall days quickly morph into brisk winter ones without warning. It was October, and that was the case on this Friday afternoon. The boys had convened in the park behind Judah's building to challenge Chanel once again. But as they shivered against the cold together on the park bench, they faced the facts.

"It's too cold out here to be playing," Deon said.

Judah quickly agreed. They both rose to leave.

"Y'all done getting beat?" Chanel asked, laughing. She dribbled the ball as she walked in their direction. Her hair was in a messy ponytail, and her long lashes fluttered as she looked at them.

Deon groaned.

"You're lucky I wore shorts today. If I had pants on and long sleeves, I would stay out here all night and beat you."

Chanel laughed. She was a slim, cocoa-toned beauty with a smile that sparkled like sunshine.

"You and your cousin are the same size," she noted. "Just go upstairs and put on some of his clothes. Then come back out here and talk all that."

Judah laughed. He knew Deon would never call her bluff.

Deon shrugged it off.

"I don't wear other people's clothes. So, like I said . . . you're lucky."

Chanel rolled her eyes and Judah took the opportunity to steal the ball from her. He dribbled it toward the basketball hoop and she ran off after him once she got her bearings. Deon watched as Judah easily made the basket and Chanel protested as he ran off.

"CHEATER!" She ran to get her ball.

Judah joined his cousin, still laughing, and they walked together toward the building.

"Thank you!" Deon said. "I thought she was never gonna shut up."

Judah laughed and looked around at the neighborhood. The Mariners Harbor projects was a close-knit community on one hand and a cold world on the other. Judah knew most of the kids in the area, having grown up alongside them. But he didn't go to the same schools they attended. Not anymore. So, a gulf had grown between him and many of the guys he once hung around all the time. Instead, he spent most of his time with his cousin, Deon, his neighbor Chanel, and a handful of boys in the neighborhood who he was still cool with. He didn't have any beef. He just wasn't the most popular kid in the projects. And he definitely didn't have the flashy wardrobe his aunt and cousin sported.

Judah nudged his cousin and gestured toward the curb as they approached his building.

"Aunt Len's Benz is here. I didn't know she was coming over."

"Neither did I," Deon said.

When they got to Judah's apartment door, they knew right away that something was up. They could hear their mothers' raised voices on the other side of the door.

"Shh," Deon said. "Let me hear what they're saying."

He and Judah pressed their ears to the door and listened carefully.

"I don't fuckin' understand, Lenox! What are you saying?"

"Listen! I'm trying to tell you. G has a cousin. This guy named Mark. He lives uptown and he's the one who put G on. He introduced G to Benny, and Benny is the one who's been supplying us with all the shit."

Mercy grumbled something inaudible, but Lenox pressed on, ignoring her.

"Mark and G had a system going. But then Mark got locked up. G kept getting money with Benny. I think that's where the problem started. Mark didn't like that too much. But he didn't complain because G was hitting Mark's girl off with money. This bitch named Tatiana. She was cooking the crack up for him in the beginning."

"She was doing what you're doing," Mercy clarified.

"Exactly. Except she was *using* the shit and fucking up the money. I came in and started working with G and the whole thing has been going much better."

"So, what's the problem?"

"Mark's home from jail now. And he's pissed off that G cut Tatiana off. Now she's all fiended out, and her kids are in foster care. It's a mess. And now Mark thinks G is to blame for that. And me."

Lenox said the last part in almost a whisper. But Mercy heard her loud and clear. She exhaled loudly.

"Now what?"

"Benny came over today. He said that Mark is running around uptown talking a lot of shit about G. And Benny thinks we should lay low for a minute."

Mercy choked back tears hearing her worst fears coming to life.

"Calm down," Lenox coaxed her. "It's not that serious."

"NOT THAT FUCKING SERIOUS, LEN? There's mutha-fuckas from uptown talking about coming after you."

"That's why I want you to let Deon stay here for a while. Just let me lay low and get off the radar until this shit blows over."

"Why don't you stay here with us?"

"I think it's safer if I get off the island. Out of the city. Just for a little while. I'm gonna go to Pennsylvania."

"What? Who do you know in Pennsylvania?" Mercy felt like she was having a nightmare. She wished she was, in fact.

"Nobody. And that's the point. It's far from here, but not *too* far.

I'm gonna lay low. Just for a week or two. I'm not telling anybody where I'm going except you. Not even G knows I'm leaving."

Mercy was relieved to hear that.

"I'll call you every couple of hours so you know I'm safe. Just keep an eye on Deon for me, and make sure he goes to school. I don't need them truant officers coming to my house asking questions."

"Lenox . . . this is crazy. Do you hear yourself? You're about to leave your son behind to go on the run. Over some beef G got you involved in, over *crack cocaine,* Lenox. What the fuck are you doing with your life?"

"Mercy! Damn, I don't need this shit right now. You know what I'm trying to do with my life? I'm trying to fuckin' save it!"

Lenox leaned against the door and sighed. She shook her head and locked eyes with her sister.

"You were right. Okay? I got in too deep, stayed in it for too long, and I never should have got in the drug game in the first place. But I'm *not* sorry. I was sick of being broke, having nothing, running down there to the welfare office spilling my guts to some caseworker for a few dollars. I got tired of seeing my son's disappointed face on Christmases and birthdays when I couldn't afford the shit he wanted. And I got sick of waiting for buses, walking everywhere. I wanted more out of my *life.* So, I did something about it."

"You happy now?" Mercy asked, sarcastically.

"Yes," Lenox said, honestly. "The past couple of years have been more exciting than my whole life up to this point. I just got too distracted by the fun I was having to notice that it couldn't last forever. If it wasn't Mark, it would have been something else. We had a good run. But now I can admit that I need to get out. I just need to do it the right way so nobody gets hurt."

Lenox was crying, too, now. Tears slid softly and silently down her cheeks as she looked at her sister, pleadingly.

Mercy nodded.

"Deon can stay here as long as you need him to."

Lenox walked over to Mercy and threw her arms around her shoulders. The sisters hugged tightly in silence.

They were startled by the sound of Judah's keys turning the lock on the door. They quickly separated and wiped their eyes as the boys entered the apartment.

"Hey, Ma. What's wrong?" Deon was at his mother's side in no time.

Lenox put her game face on and smiled at him, reassuringly.

"Nothing's wrong, Papa. Come here."

She hugged him.

"I just came by to tell Aunt Mercy that I have to go out of town for a few days. I brought your clothes over so you can stay here with her and Judah until I get back."

"I want to go with you," Deon protested.

Lenox could see the fear in his young eyes as he looked up at her.

"I can't take you with me. Not this time, Deon. You're staying here with Aunt Mercy until I get back. I'll call you every single day to check on you. You be good and go to school just like normal. And when I get back, things will be better. I promise."

Deon wasn't sure what was happening, but he nodded his head and watched sadly as his mother thanked Mercy and made a beeline for the door. He didn't see the tears in her eyes as she rushed down the hallway and the apartment door slammed shut behind her.

Mercy stood speechlessly after Lenox left. She watched as Deon walked over to the window and stared out of it looking for his mother. Mercy locked eyes with Judah and offered a weak smile to her son. Judah rushed forward and hugged her. Like his cousin, he wasn't sure what was going on. All he knew was that the tension in the apartment felt thick enough to slice. Mercy hugged him back tightly and looked over at her nephew.

Deon watched his mother exit the building and rush toward her car at the curb. She got into it quickly and sped off. He thought about everything he had overheard between his mother and his aunt. He could sense that his mother was in serious danger. As her car disappeared out of sight, Deon felt tears fall from his eyes and thought to himself that this might be the last time he'd see her. He let out a soft sob.

Mercy was at his side before he realized it. She pulled him close to her and rubbed his back reassuringly.

"It's okay, baby. She'll be back."

Mercy said a silent prayer that Lenox wouldn't make her a liar.

THE TRAP

Lenox hit the highway and headed for I-95 with a bag full of cash and all her most prized possessions loaded into the trunk of her car. She found a nice hotel in Philadelphia and stayed there for three weeks instead of two, just to be sure that the coast was clear. While she was there, she sold her car and bought a much less conspicuous black Chevy Celebrity. She wore sunglasses and ordered room service and talked to Deon on the phone every night before bed.

"Did you brush your teeth and wash your face like you're supposed to?"

"Yeah. Aunt Mercy makes me and Judah do all that stuff. Are you okay?"

"I'm fine, baby. I'm sitting in bed watching *Golden Girls* and missing you."

Deon tried to imagine her in her hotel room.

"Is your door locked? What if somebody comes there?" Deon kept his voice low so that Judah wouldn't know how scared he really was. When they spoke about it in the darkness of Judah's bedroom at night, Deon pretended that he wasn't too concerned. But he worried about his mother constantly.

"My door is locked. I got the dead bolt on. There's security downstairs. I'm safe. I promise. Don't worry about me. Just listen to Aunt Mercy and don't give her a hard time. And pay attention in school. I'm counting on you."

Deon gripped the phone. "I will," he promised. "I'm counting on you, too."

Deon looked forward to those calls desperately. Hearing his mother's voice was confirmation that she was still alive and that his nightmares weren't real. He had terrible visions at night of what might happen to her if G's enemies got their hands on her. Deon heard his Aunt Mercy praying often and he began to do so, too, each night before bed. Whispered prayers that he offered up to God each evening in the darkness of Judah's room. He waited until he heard the sound of his cousin's rhythmic snoring. Then he closed his eyes and pleaded for protection.

"God, please protect my mother. Keep her safe from everybody who wants to hurt her. Please keep me safe, too. And my cousin Judah and Aunt Mercy. Watch over us and protect us, God. Amen."

Mercy overheard Deon's prayers a few times as she lingered in the bedroom doorway late at night. She was just as concerned for Lenox's safety, and she shared those feelings with Xavier. It had been three weeks since he moved to DC. He had gotten an apartment in PG County, and all of the necessary licenses and certifications to do business as an interstate truck driver. He called Mercy at night when he figured the boys were asleep, and they talked until they both were yawning.

"I miss you," she said one night.

"I miss you, too. You would like it here. It's not New York, but it's dope. Got a nice little vibe to it. They call DC 'Chocolate City.'"

Mercy smiled. "Once all this dies down and Lenox gets back, me and Judah will come and visit you."

"How's she doing?" Xavier asked.

"She says she's fine. It sounds like she's done with G for good this time. So, that's reassuring."

Xavier opened the refrigerator to grab some juice. "Why don't you try to convince her to move down here with you and Judah? This could be the perfect chance for y'all to start over. Away from all the beef and the bullshit."

Mercy thought about it. "I don't know if she would go for it."

"Can't hurt to try," Xavier said. He looked around the kitchen for a snack and sighed. "On another note, I really miss your cooking."

Mercy laughed. "Don't worry. I'll be there as soon as I can. And I'll cook you all your favorites."

He smiled. "You're my favorite. Just get here."

Each day, Mercy made sure the boys were taken care of and tried not to think too much about the threat of impending danger surrounding Lenox and her life choices. She felt like her life was in turmoil and she was powerless to change it.

Those three weeks felt like an eternity for Lenox. Not only was she missing her family, but she had left the hustle behind. And the truth was she missed that, too. She decided that she couldn't work with G anymore. What little desire had existed between them in the beginning was long gone now. At least for her it was. It hadn't taken long for Lenox to realize that she was a better hustler than G would ever be. She kept working with him against her better judgment and had found herself in a hornet's nest with him. Now G's beef with Mark had disrupted her life. It was something she could never allow to happen again.

She ignored him each time he paged her on her beeper. Ignored every number except for Mercy's. For the first time in years, she was far enough from New York City to hear her own thoughts.

She thought long and hard about getting out of the game completely. But the notion terrified her. Working a normal job, living an average life. The idea of those things petrified Lenox. She had tasted the fast life and liked it.

She called Benny while she was in Philly.

"Lenox Ave!" his voice boomed through the phone. "Good to hear your voice."

"How's it going, Benny? How's the temperature uptown?"

Benny knew she wasn't talking about the weather.

"It's better than it was," he said. "G came uptown yesterday. He said he brought his mother with him to visit his aunt. At the end of the day, it's a family dispute. That shit got nothing to do with you. I let Mark know that I'll cut him off completely if he touches you. So, it's safe for you to come home."

Lenox breathed a long sigh of relief.

"As far as G is concerned, I think Mark is gonna harbor some resentment for a long time. Hopefully, they work that shit out and we can all get back to getting money."

"I'm done with G," she said. "For good. This whole situation showed me that if I keep fucking with him it'll cost me everything."

"So, what now? You getting out the game?" Benny's tone was somewhere between shock and disappointment.

"No. I want you to work with me solo. I'm a big girl. I learned the ropes of the game, and I'm ready to get in the ring with the big dogs all by myself."

"I can't do that."

"Why not?"

"There's already a problem with these two muthafuckas fighting. Now you want me to cut you in. You know that's gonna piss G off."

"Fuck G!" Lenox was done letting him drag her down. "I guarantee you'll make more money with me than you are with him. All I need is for you to say 'yes' and back me up. If G gets mad, tell him the same thing you told Mark. Let him know that I have your protection."

Benny laughed. "I gotta admire your balls. I already did you one favor. Now you're calling me asking for an even bigger one."

"I'll repay the favor, Benny. You know I'm thorough. You can count on me. All I need is to know that I can count on you, too." She took Benny's hesitation as a sign that he was considering it. She pressed on. "Start me out the same way you did with G. Let me get a brick on consignment. I'll flip that shit just like I been doing. And me and you can get this money on our own."

"You'll be competing in a market that's already getting crowded. Staten Island is a small borough," he warned.

"Let me worry about that. Just give me the shot."

Benny was silent while he considered it. He had always felt that Lenox had a spark. He believed that without G and all his family drama, Lenox could make it on her own. Reluctantly he agreed.

"Okay. Come and see me when you get back to New York."

Lenox set her plans in motion. She knew a couple of G's workers that would happily break ranks with him and hustle for her instead. She knew that it wouldn't be easy, but she was determined to become one of the few female contenders in the crack game.

She waited until Benny confirmed that things had finally settled down between G and his cousin Mark. Within a week, Benny said that the two had come to some type of peace treaty that involved G giving Mark a lump sum of money. They were family, after all. So, in the end their beef had simmered without bloodshed. At least for now.

Lenox came back to Staten Island the week before Thanksgiving. Deon was relieved to have his mother back home. He had enjoyed his time with Aunt Mercy and his cousin Judah, though. His grades had gone up and his behavior in school had improved. Lenox was impressed.

She brought it up as they ate Thanksgiving dinner at Mercy's place.

"So, maybe me and you should move in here with Mercy. It seems like you know how to act when your aunt is around. I left town for a few weeks and came back to find a little Einstein."

Deon smiled shyly.

Judah beamed proudly. He had finally gotten Deon to admit that being smart wasn't corny after all.

"Deon's smarter than me," Judah said. "He just likes to act dumb for attention."

Mercy put some more macaroni and cheese on her plate.

"Deon came home every night and sat there doing his homework with Judah. Even helped Judah with some history project he had about the state of Oregon and the explorers Lewis and Clark."

Deon nodded, his eyes wide with excitement.

"Them fools were crazy. They had a Native American slave named Sacagawea. And they almost died when it got cold and they wasn't prepared for it."

Lenox couldn't believe her ears. She looked at Mercy in amazement.

"Maybe I should put him in Judah's school after all!"

Mercy gave her a look that said "told you so" and shoved some stuffing in her mouth.

Deon scoffed.

"Not unless I can wear my regular clothes. That uniform Judah wears looks like something Pee-wee Herman designed."

Judah sucked his teeth as they all laughed. Mercy caught herself and grinned at him sympathetically.

"My baby don't look like no Pee-wee Herman!"

"Don't let him make fun of your uniform, Judah. Someday you're gonna be a big executive. Mark my words. Guys who dress like that are the successful ones." Lenox winked at her nephew.

Judah smiled.

Deon thought about that as he chewed his turkey.

"So, why don't Benny dress like that?" he asked innocently.

Mercy and Lenox locked eyes across the table. Finally, Mercy subtly shook her head, looked down, and pushed her fork around her plate absently.

Lenox looked at her son.

"What made you bring up Benny?"

Deon shrugged.

"He's successful. Every time I see him he gives me money. He drives a nice car, has all that jewelry and everything. And he don't dress in a shirt and tie."

Mercy sat back and sipped her apple cider while she watched Lenox scramble for an answer.

"Deon, I never told you that Benny or G or any of them guys are successful. And don't assume that just because you see a few shiny things that means everything is sweet. Those guys are living a certain type of life."

"What do you mean? Cuz they hustle?"

Mercy groaned.

Lenox shot a look at her before refocusing on her son.

"What you know about hustling, Deon?"

He shrugged. "I hear you saying that all the time. That you get your money by hustling. You, G, Benny, all of y'all."

"And what do you think it means?" Lenox pressed him.

"Selling . . . selling drugs," Deon said, matter-of-factly.

Judah watched everyone closely. He saw the look of simultaneous outrage and amusement on his mother's face; the flash of regret in Aunt Lenox's eyes as she stared at Deon speechlessly; and the expression of innocent curiosity on Deon's face as he stared back at her.

"That's what you think I do, Deon?" Lenox asked, softly.

Deon nodded slowly, aware suddenly that this conversation was breaking his mother's heart. Now he wished he had kept his mouth shut.

Mercy seemed to sense the emotions Deon was feeling in that moment and spoke up.

"Lenox, he ain't wrong. That *is* what you do. It's what you been doing for years. You, G, Benny, and God knows who else you been parading past Deon on a regular basis. And what? You thought he wasn't smart enough to figure it out?"

Lenox side-eyed Mercy, but Mercy was unfazed.

"It's Thanksgiving. I'm grateful for a lot this year, especially the fact that you're home safe. That all of us are here together. But I'm done pretending, Len. I'm not gonna walk around acting like what's happening ain't real. I'm not keeping my mouth shut anymore. Deon has questions. I'm sure Judah has some, too."

Judah nodded his head for emphasis.

"I'm always telling you to watch what you say in front of the kids," Mercy continued. "But when you left a few weeks ago to go on the run, I realized that if we keep all these secrets . . . and something happens to you . . ."

Mercy's voice cracked and she paused for a moment to gather herself.

"I realized that I'll be the one who has to explain that shit to your son. And where the hell would I begin?"

Lenox felt her heart sinking lower in her chest. Varied emotions fought for dominance inside of her. Anger, frustration, regret, fear, shame, defiance. She looked at her sister and found irony in the fact that her name was Mercy. At the moment, she seemed like she was fresh out of that shit.

Lenox sighed. "Deon, Judah . . . listen," she began. "Yes. I was hustling for a little while. But it's not how you think it is. I was never out there selling drugs to people. Taking money out of people's hands and risking arrest. The way I was doing it was safer and smarter than that. I won't get into the details about it because that's all behind me now. I'm not doing that anymore."

She knew as each word slipped from her lips that it was all a big lie. She was a drug dealer in every sense of the word. She was risking everything and making a ton of money in the process. And she had not stopped. In fact, before she even came home to Staten Island to see her family, she had stopped in the Bronx to get her first brick from Benny. Over the past week, she had set up her own new crack operation in a run-down apartment she had rented on Sharpe Avenue in Port Richmond. She looked at Mercy and saw her looking skeptically back at her.

"I had a close call," Lenox said. "I almost got into some trouble. And that was all I needed to put me back on track. I'm done with hustling," she lied. "From now on you won't be seeing G anymore. So, you don't have to worry. You hear me?"

Deon and Judah nodded.

"I don't want y'all looking at guys like G and Benny and thinking that's what success looks like. Look up to hardworking men like Xavier. He might not have fancy clothes, but he's got peace of mind. Everything that glitters ain't gold. Sometimes people seem like they're having a good time when really they're scared to death. Looking over their shoulders all the time, worrying constantly. No amount of money makes that easy to deal with."

Mercy felt so relieved as she listened to Lenox speaking. Like her prayers had been answered. Finally, Lenox sounded like she understood that in the streets the juice was seldom worth the squeeze. When their eyes met across the table, this time Mercy smiled at her sister. Lenox returned the gesture, though her heart still felt heavy.

Lenox knew the truth. And she knew that Mercy would never understand. But Lenox wasn't done with the game just yet. She wanted to do it on her own terms this time. She had promised herself that she would be more careful, that she would only do it until it got hot again. Then she would stop for good. But it was clear that she couldn't tell anyone. Not Mercy, and certainly not Deon or Judah. She knew that she would have to keep the truth to herself for as long as possible so that the people she loved—all seated around this Thanksgiving table, staring at her expectantly—wouldn't be disappointed in her.

In the days that followed, Deon was bolder with his questioning of his mother. Like Aunt Mercy, he was done skirting around the issues at hand.

"Why did we have to change our phone number?" Deon asked. "I had to give the new one to all my friends."

Lenox shrugged. "It was time to switch up. Change is good."

She was shielding Deon from the truth. From the moment she

got back to New York, G had been calling her house and beeping her nonstop, and she had been ignoring him. She put an extra lock on her door and kept her gun even closer to her than she usually did. She slept with it, fearful of how desperate G might get in his efforts to get to her. Although Benny had assured her that she was safe, she still worried about other competitors. She was on her own in every sense, and it was both liberating and terrifying.

It was also lonely. Aware that Deon was paying close attention to her, Lenox switched her routine up. She took him to school each day without fail and was there to pick him up each day. After school, she took him with her to Mercy's apartment and they spent the afternoon there. Deon and Judah would do their homework and play outside. Lenox and Mercy would cook dinner together (at least that was how Lenox described watching Mercy prepare meals each night) while talking and laughing the hours away. After dinner, Lenox and Deon drove home and got ready to do it all again the next day.

What no one knew was that while the boys were in school and Mercy was at work, Lenox wasn't out job hunting like she claimed. She was in her stash house cooking like her name was Betty Crocker.

She had two workers now—Andre and Theo—who had once worked for G. She knew that they were unhappy with the cut they were getting from G. So, she summoned them to her stash house and offered them a better deal than the one that G was doling out.

"G was giving you a flat one hundred fifty dollars a day. I want to offer you thirty dollars for every one hundred you sell. The more you sell, the more you make."

They didn't hesitate to accept her offer. Lenox only dealt with them at the stash house, never at her own apartment. She was being extra careful to keep the drug game as far away from her family as she could.

Everything was going smoothly except for one unrelenting problem. G was growing increasingly agitated.

BOOM! BOOM! BOOM!

"Yo, Lenox! Open the fuckin' door!"

He pounded on her apartment door late one night.

Deon rushed into his mother's bedroom, terrified. "Who is that?" he asked.

"It's G," Lenox said, pushing him back into his bedroom. "Stay in there and don't come out."

G banged harder on the door. "LENOX! Stop playing with me!"

"Ma, what's going on?" Deon asked, panicking. "Why's he yelling like that?"

Lenox gripped Deon tightly by the shoulders. "Listen to me! Stay in here. Don't come out until I tell you. You understand?"

Deon nodded, though he was scared to death.

Lenox rushed out and shut the door behind her. She ran to her bedroom and grabbed her gun from beneath the mountain of pillows on her bed.

G was jiggling the doorknob now, kicking the door, still shouting.

Lenox stood near the door in the dark, waiting. If he got through the door, she was prepared to blow his fucking brains out. She stood silently, her heart thundering in her chest, praying that Deon obeyed her and stayed in his room.

G gave another violent kick to the door that rocked the front of the house. Lenox planted her feet and raised the gun in preparation. Then she heard sirens outside of her house, and the pounding ceased. She rushed over to the window and discreetly pulled back a small part of the curtain. Peering out, she saw police cars, the flashing lights lighting up the block. She could see two uniformed officers approaching her house. G was obscured from her view, but she glimpsed the sleeve of his brown leather jacket as he stood facing the officers. She listened to the voices outside of her window.

"We got a complaint about a disturbance. Do you live here?"

"No, officer." G didn't sound like himself. He spoke properly, no slang. "I just came by to see my girlfriend. That's all."

Inside the house, Lenox scoffed.

"When we pulled up it looked like you were pretty upset."

"Not at all. Like I said, I just came over for a visit. I was knocking on the door a little hard, thinking she must be asleep."

"You couldn't call first?" the second officer asked.

"I tried, but she's mad at me. I think she might have changed her number."

Lenox was done hiding. Emboldened by the police presence, she rushed over and opened the door. "I'm not his girlfriend. I want him away from my door. Away from me and my son." Lenox glared at him. "I wasn't asleep. I changed my phone number for a reason. You need to get away from me."

G stared at her contemptuously. "You called the cops on me?"

"No," she said. "I was ready to handle you myself. My neighbors must've called because you were about to knock my door down."

"You don't got nothing to say to me? After all the shit I did for you?"

Lenox sucked her teeth and turned her attention to the police.

"It's late. My son is trying to sleep, and I want him off my property please."

"You want to file a complaint?" one of the cops asked.

Lenox stared at G, unblinking. "No. I just want him gone."

G held his hands up in front of him, a sinister smile on his face. "No problem. I'll be on my way."

He strutted down the stairs and walked to his car.

Lenox looked at the cops. "Thank you."

Their expressions were glum. "He's probably going to come back, ma'am. You should call our family counseling center. There's a domestic violence counselor who can help you deal with this."

Lenox nodded, thanked them, and shut the door, carefully securing all of the locks.

She turned and Deon stood facing her.

"Why's G so mad?" he asked.

"He's a hater, that's why. Come back to bed." She did her best to calm her son down, got him back into bed with promises that everything was over now, and they were safe. Then she rushed into her bedroom and called Benny.

He answered on the second ring.

"What's up, mami?"

"That son of a bitch was just here trying to kick my door down, Benny. I already changed my phone number, changed the locks, and I'm sleeping with a gun at my side every night! What the fuck, Benny. I thought you would look out for me."

Benny took his time responding. He took a puff of his blunt and blew out the smoke slowly. "I'm gonna give you a little tough love, Lenox. Cuz I always liked you. You remind me a lot of my mother. Sometimes I look at you and I see what she could have been like if she wasn't a dope fiend. If she was stronger like you. I see how you take care of your son, how you take care of business. I admire those things about you."

Lenox knew there was a "but" coming and steeled herself.

"You wanted this. You asked to learn Tati's process. You mastered that shit, got into business with G. That was your idea. At least that's the story you told me. You told him you wanted in. Now you're in. This game ain't for lightweights, mami."

"I ain't a lightweight." Lenox rolled her eyes defiantly.

"Then you gotta handle that muthafucka. I did my part. I told him and Mark that you're with me now. Under my protection. Mark don't have beef with you no more. But your problem with G is personal. He got feelings for you and shit. And there's only so much I can do to keep an emotional nigga from acting up."

Lenox sighed.

Benny softened his tone. "I'ma talk to him again. Still, you need to switch things up. You can't get too comfortable in one spot for too long. It might be time for you to move. Get you and Deon somewhere he can't touch you. Keep some soldiers around you. I can send you some if you want. But that's gonna cost, you feel me?"

She sat back against her headboard. "I hear you. Loud and clear. Let me put some things in motion." She thanked Benny, hung up, and started plotting her next move.

G's erratic behavior was the reason she spent the majority of her time with her sister these days. She was secretly afraid to be alone in case G popped up on her. He was taking this a lot harder than she expected. Being mad for a while was one thing. But his behavior had crossed the line into harassment. She got a lease to rent a ranch-style house in the West Brighton section of the borough, and began to pack in preparation for their move scheduled for the first week of the new year. She was looking forward to a clean start and she prayed that G would finally get over their split once he no longer knew where to find her.

While she had been on the lam in Philadelphia, Lenox had made it clear to him that she was not working with him anymore. The situation with Mark was too messy, and Lenox loved her son too much to put their lives in jeopardy that way over a beef that didn't even involve her. G said that he understood, but was quietly hopeful that when she came home she might change her mind.

Instead, Lenox had returned to Staten Island and established herself as his competition. She had the same supplier, had pilfered two of his workers, and was paying them more. He had to find someone new to cook up the work for him. Worse still, Lenox had her workers selling crack in the same areas she had once shared with G. And she was unapologetic about it.

It would have been one thing if she had done all of this while still letting him see her from time to time. He had deep feelings for Lenox, always had from the start. He had tried to take their relationship to the next level over the years. Offered her the world if they could make it official. He wanted Lenox to belong to him.

It hadn't taken him long to resign himself to the fact that Lenox wasn't the type of woman who could belong to anyone but herself. She had never loved him, never even pretended to. She let him have his way with her when she felt like it. Let him come around from time to time and spend the night grinding into her impeccable curves. But she wasn't interested in being any man's wife. Lenox was married to the game.

That arrangement had been digestible for G at first. But the situation with his cousin had spooked her. Suddenly she wanted nothing to do with him or his hustle. He thought it might take time for her to get over it. But now she was getting money without him and going out of her way to avoid him.

He was furious. Who the fuck did Lenox think she was?

They had never been exclusive. Never been more than glorified business partners with benefits. But there was something about the way that Lenox had left him without looking back that cut G to his core. He spoke to Benny about it, how he felt betrayed that Benny would get into bed with Lenox when it was G who introduced them in the first place.

"It's business," Benny had said. "And Staten Island is big enough for both of you. Let shorty get her money."

But G couldn't let it go.

He watched her from safe distances, always careful to avoid detection. Soon, he had her routine mapped out, on weekdays at least. Weekends she was harder to pinpoint. Always making moves early or staying out late. But Monday through Friday he had her schedule down pat. He could tell that she was living some type of double life. All family oriented after school but making trips to re-up and get her hustle on during business hours. G watched her closely and waited for his opportunity to strike.

Lenox dropped Deon off at the schoolyard gate one morning and leaned down to kiss him. He ducked out of the way just in time to avoid contact.

"Ma! I told you you can't be kissing me in front of my friends. They be making fun of me."

Lenox laughed. "I don't care about them. They just jealous I'm not kissing them, too." She grabbed Deon and smothered him in a slew of kisses despite his protests.

"Ugh!" he groaned, sounding more annoyed than he really was.

"I'll be here to get you after school. Make sure you write your homework assignment down this time, Deon. ALL OF IT!"

"Okay," he said. "I will."

"Love you," Lenox sang.

Deon thought she looked so pretty with the sun beaming down on her that cold December morning. Her smile shined just as brightly. She had just gotten her hair done, and her doobie wrap was so perfect that she looked like a model. He smiled back at her.

"I love you, too, Ma."

She pretended to be shocked.

"What if one of your little friends heard you say that?"

Deon laughed. "They just jealous. Like you said."

"EXACTLY!" Lenox said, proudly.

Deon waved at her and turned to walk into the school as the bell rang.

Lenox headed back to her car and climbed inside. It was cold that morning, and she could see her breath as she started the car. She drove straight to her stash house, singing along to a Whitney Houston song on KISS FM. She got there in minutes, parked her car, and stepped out. She walked quickly up to the front door, spurred forward by the icy air whistling around her.

The moment she stepped across the threshold she could sense that something was off. The house felt eerily still. She stuck her car keys in her coat pocket and walked into the kitchen.

G was standing near the stove staring back at her.

Lenox's heart skipped a beat.

"What are you doing in here?" she managed. She gripped the keys in her pocket a little tighter.

He raised his eyebrows and laughed a bit.

"Wow. That's how you greet me, Lenox?"

"What's up, G? How you been? Now what are you doing in here?"

Grinning, he shook his head.

"Damn. You're acting real cold for someone that I used to consider my friend."

"We're still friends, G. What's the problem?"

"I've been trying to get in touch with you. You know that. Calling the cops on me and shit—"

"I didn't call the cops on you. My neighbors did. And I don't blame them. You came to my house banging on my door in the middle of the night. Woke my son up out of his sleep and scared us both. What did you think I was gonna do?"

G looked genuinely hurt.

"'Your son,' like Deon doesn't know me. Like I wasn't over your house all the time and we wasn't like family."

Lenox laughed. His fists balled up involuntarily.

"Family, G. Really? We were getting money together."

"That's all we was doing?"

Lenox saw it then. The flash of crazy in his eyes. She had underestimated his feelings.

"No," she said, softly. "That's not all. But we were never . . . G, you know it wasn't that deep."

He could feel his adrenaline rushing. He took a deep breath.

"Okay, so cool. If you a ho and you just go around handing pussy out and it don't mean nothing, that's one thing. But you just cut me off completely? Then go and start working with Benny, getting money with him on your own? What, you fucking him, too?"

Lenox sucked her teeth.

"Why are you here, G? You never answered that question. How do you even know about this place? What, you been following me?"

"You fucking him?" he repeated.

Lenox laughed again. This time, G stepped closer to her, his voice so loud that it echoed through the room.

"LENOX, YOU THINK I WON'T HURT YOU?"

Fear coursed through every inch of her body. Lenox turned to rush out, but he was on her instantly. She felt a painful thud against the back of her head and tumbled forward into the next room. He didn't give her time to recover from that blow before he followed it up with another one. Rattled, she held her hands up to cover her head and face against the onslaught of blows raining down on her. G was hitting her repeatedly with something heavy. He cursed her as he beat her, spit flying from his mouth with each blow.

"G, STOP! I'M SORRY!" she yelled desperately.

Her arms hurt as she used them to shield her face and head from the force of the blows. She was crouched on the floor, crying. He got down there with her, straddling her as he beat her.

Lenox felt the weight of each blow. Each time, she prayed he was done. But he just kept going. He stopped suddenly and she could see the gun he was holding in his hand. She started crawling frantically toward the door. He pulled her back to him, roughly, and hit her hard with the gun again. She rolled around on the floor with an excruciating ringing in her ears. She felt him tearing her coat off, ripping her clothes from her body. Then she was pinned against the floor, unaware that the sobs she heard echoing in her ears were her own.

He pulled her leggings off and tore her panties as he held her down.

"G!" she yelled out. "STOP!"

But he didn't stop. He was inside of her now, pummeling her harder and faster, grunting with rage. Seeing her huddled helplessly on the floor gave him gratification. She cried out, begging him to let up. But her cries only fueled him more.

"You fuckin' bitch!" he cursed her over and over again. Lenox stopped crying, aware that it was pointless. She was looking for a way out. Her eyes scanned the area on the floor around them, frantically searching for the gun. She couldn't move her head because of the way he had her pinned down. She couldn't see the gun from her vantage point but kept looking around for any kind of weapon she could use. She prayed silently while G raped her mercilessly. She waited patiently until he came.

The moment he grunted with pleasure, Lenox squirmed with all her might until she wrested herself out from underneath him. Naked, she got to her feet quickly and made another desperate run for the door. She made it within inches of the front door before G snatched her back by her hair and dragged her back into the living room. He began pistol-whipping her again, and this time Lenox fought back.

He laughed at first at her audacity as she slapped him, clawed at him, swinging with all her might, kicking at him. He stopped laughing, though, when one of her punches connected with his jaw followed by a kick to his groin. Lenox fought him with all her might, ferally landing blows. He dropped the gun and she dove for it, desperate to blow his fucking head off.

He went for it, too, and they fought viciously just inches away from it. He punched her hard in the face, then stomped her in the stomach. Still, Lenox kept fighting. As she lunged desperately for the gun on the floor, he got to it first. G grabbed it, pointed it at her, and fired.

She felt the impact of it instantly, then a hot sensation began to spread through her chest, and down through her stomach. The pain was excruciating. It tore through her body as she lay on the floor in the fetal position, groaning in agony.

G was pacing now. Lenox watched his feet as they moved back and forth in front of her.

"YOU MADE ME DO THIS SHIT!" he kept yelling.

Lenox felt herself slipping in and out of consciousness and could sense death lurking nearby waiting to consume her; could almost *see* it in the form of a dark orb that appeared in her sight line as she lay in a heap on the floor. She stared at that blackness and thought of Deon, how worried he would be when she didn't show up to get him after school. She began to speak his name as if he might hear her somehow.

"Deon! Deon!"

She thought she was yelling, but her voice was barely a whisper.

She tried to move her hands in order to help hoist herself up. But each movement made the pain worse. She cried desperately, every nerve in her body feeling agony unlike anything she had experienced before. Her mouth felt dry. The sound in her ears faded in and out, but she could sense G moving frantically around the apartment. She tried again to get up, fighting past the pain, trying to drag herself toward the door. The black orb in her vision grew bigger, seeming to expand with each movement. She could hear G's voice closer now and she stopped moving. The room seemed to grow even darker.

With tears streaming down her face and her heart racing in her chest, Lenox became consumed by the darkness, closed her eyes, and stopped breathing.

Unaware of the devastation that awaited him, Deon ran out of school with all the other kids when the final bell rang that Thursday afternoon. He couldn't wait to tell his mother about the grade he'd gotten on his history test. It was a subject he was thriving in now, evidenced by the 96 percent the teacher had marked at the top of his test in big letters with two exclamation marks.

He looked around for his mother in the sea of parents. Not finding her, he began to look around for her car. Still, no sign of his mother. As the school buses filled up and pulled away one by one, and the sea of parents became a trickle, Deon grew annoyed by his mother's lateness. All of his friends had gone home already and he was still waiting.

His teacher exited the building and asked if he was still waiting for a ride. He thought about telling her the truth but remembered his mother's contentious relationship with his school administrators. Defending Deon's behavioral issues and making excuses for his tardiness and absences had not made Lenox a favorite among the staff.

"I'm okay," he told his teacher. "I forgot my mom said for me to walk home today. So, I'll see you tomorrow."

He rushed off before she could ask further questions. He walked toward the projects, looking around for his mother's car, wondering if she was just running late to pick him up. Maybe she was out doing some last-minute holiday shopping. He hoped she was at the mall buying him the Lazer Tag toy gun he wanted.

He went to his Aunt Mercy's apartment in the Harbor projects like he usually did with his mother after school each day. Maybe she was already there and had lost track of time. He knocked on his aunt's apartment door and waited. Mercy answered it smiling and ushered him inside.

"Hey, Deon. Where's your mama?"

He shrugged. "I thought she was here already. She never came to get me from school. So, I walked here."

Mercy frowned, trying to recall whether Lenox had told her about any appointments or plans she had for the day. She shook her head.

"I haven't spoken to her since this morning. She called to tell me Judah forgot his book at your house," Mercy said. Lenox had actually called it "Judah's encyclopedia." She chuckled at the thought.

Deon nodded, reached inside his backpack and held up a copy of *Rise to Rebellion*.

"It's heavy, too. I couldn't wait to get rid of it."

Mercy laughed.

"Judah's in his room."

Deon walked down the hall, and Mercy returned to the kitchen where she had been preparing dinner. She thought about Lenox and wondered if she was on a job interview or something. She had been coming by every day with Deon after school for close to a month. It wasn't like her to not at least call to say that she'd be late.

Still, Mercy didn't think too much of it. Lenox was, after all, unpredictable. Mercy got busy getting dinner ready while she watched an episode of *The Oprah Winfrey Show*. By the time they sat down to eat it was nearly 5:30. Mercy paged Lenox a few times, but her sister never called back. Then Mercy began to worry.

More hours passed and the boys spent the time watching TV while Mercy cleaned up the kitchen. She called Lenox's house, paged her, all to no avail. Finally, she decided to go over there to see what was going on.

She walked down the hall and asked Barbara if she would watch the boys for her while she dropped by her sister's house to check on her. Barbara agreed to hang out at Mercy's place until she came back. Just in case Lenox came over. She asked Deon for his house keys and walked to Lenox's place on foot. When she got there, she found the place seemingly empty, and all the lights were off. She knocked on the door and rang the bell several times before she used Deon's keys to enter the place.

Mercy stepped inside and found the place dead silent. She turned the lights on and walked through the house looking for signs of Lenox. The place seemed unchanged since the morning rush to school. Mercy found a cereal bowl in the sink and the coffee pot uncleaned. She washed those things, walked through the house looking for any clue of her sister's whereabouts. She paged her, hoping that Lenox would call back. Finally, Mercy dialed her own house. Barbara answered the phone and told her that Lenox had not come by and the boys were fast asleep.

Mercy waited a while longer before finally returning home. She would come back in the morning once she dropped the boys off at school. She brought some of Deon's clothes with her so that he would have a fresh outfit for the next day. She locked up the place and walked quickly home in the frigid December cold.

Along the way, she looked around for G's car. Something told her that he might have some idea where Lenox was. She saw no sign of him. So, she returned home, thanked Barbara for babysitting, and called it a night. Mercy barely slept. She couldn't imagine where her sister might be. Lenox would never leave Deon alone for this long without checking in. It just wasn't like her.

Mercy got up early the next morning and made breakfast for the boys. She put on a fake smile and pretended that nothing was out of the ordinary. Deon asked if she had heard from his mom and Lenox shook her head, smiling.

"She's probably gonna come in here today with some long and crazy story about where she went yesterday." She emptied some eggs into a bowl. "Y'all want some more?"

The boys finished their breakfast and Mercy ushered them off to school. First Judah, whose school day started earlier, then Deon. As soon as she watched him walk into the school, she rushed back to Lenox's place and waited. Still no sign of her sister.

By noon, Mercy was at the police station attempting to file a missing person's report. She was frantic, worrying about picking up the boys in time, wondering what she would tell them about Lenox's whereabouts. She could sense that something was horribly wrong, that Lenox was in danger, and they were in a race against time.

The officers at the precinct were rude and dismissive, and wouldn't allow her to file the report. They pointed out that Lenox was an adult and had not been missing for more than twenty-four hours yet. Mercy persisted, insisting that her sister would never abandon her son this way. Something had to be wrong. She got nowhere with the police. Just as she was about to exit the precinct, she overheard a conversation between a plainclothes cop and a uniformed one.

"Neighbors said they heard a gunshot early yesterday morning, but nobody called us. Wouldn't have found the body for weeks but the landlord stopped by unexpectedly."

"Tenant been living there long?"

"Just a few weeks. Used a fake ID and paid cash for the first month's rent and security. The owner lives in Brooklyn. Absentee landlord. He just collects the money and lets the tenants run the place. That was the reason he stopped by. He was supposed to pick up the next three months' rent in advance. He said she called and told him she was gonna be in and out of town for a while and wanted to make sure the rent was up-to-date while she was moving around. Which is strange because the place seems like a regular old crack house."

The hairs on the back of Mercy's neck stood up. She recalled Lenox paying Mr. Miller the first three months' rent on her restaurant. She kept listening, praying it was just a coincidence.

"Dead girl had a diamond tennis bracelet on, though. So, she can't be an addict. A crackhead would've sold that in a heartbeat."

"True. No clothes or ID at the scene. Just a dead girl in diamonds." .

With each word they uttered, Mercy's heart sank deeper in her chest. She felt a churning in the pit of her stomach as she stepped toward them. She cleared her throat.

"Excuse me. My name is Mercy Howard. Can you tell me was it a black woman that was found? I'm trying to find my sister. She never came home last night, didn't pick up her son from school, and hasn't called. It's not like her. I'm worried that she's hurt. But these people in here won't take me seriously."

The officers looked at each other.

"What's your sister's name and physical description?" the one in plainclothes asked.

Mercy described Lenox, down to the birthmark on her left hand that was shaped like a puzzle piece. The detectives scribbled notes down and told her to wait while they got more information. Mercy sat on a bench nearby as she waited. Her body was in knots, her mind racing. She could sense it, deep down in the pit of her stomach. As if Lenox was calling out to her in spirit. For reasons she couldn't put into words, Mercy began to cry silently.

Moments later, a stout man with red hair approached.

"Hello. I'm Detective Hockley. You can follow me."

Mercy went with him into a room at the end of the corridor. The detective got right down to business.

"Tell me about the last time you saw your sister."

Mercy recounted speaking to her sister on the phone the prior morning, seeing her on Wednesday night at her apartment after school. The detective took notes. Mercy reiterated that Lenox would never be gone this long without calling. Something had to be wrong. She cleared her throat.

"The cops outside said they found a dead girl . . . wearing a diamond tennis bracelet. My sister has one. So, you understand . . ." Her voice trailed off, too fearful to speak the words.

The detective nodded. "I'm going to show you some pictures. They're graphic, so I'll warn you ahead of time. They might be upsetting for you."

Mercy nodded, dread bubbling in the pit of her stomach.

The detective removed a manila folder from his drawer and slid two photos across the desk. Mercy's hands felt clammy as she reached for them. As she stared down at the pictures, her eyes flooded with tears. Her worst fears were laid out in front of her in cruel confirmation.

Her body trembled and she sobbed. She wailed gutturally, shaking her head and shouting, "Please, God! NO!"

The detective watched her sympathetically.

Mercy cried, her heart shattered. "That's my sister . . ." she sobbed. "They killed her!"

Mercy felt faint. She could hear people around her saying comforting words. She could feel hands on her, holding her as she flailed in despair. Through her tears, she could see the photos of Lenox spread out on the table. And all Mercy could do was weep.

WISHING ON A STAR

There was no solace in being right this time. No comfort in the knowledge that she had warned her sister about the dangers of the drug game. Losing Lenox was the cruelest twist of fate. Mercy felt a pain in her heart so powerful that she could hardly breathe.

Lenox's funeral service and repast at Fellowship Baptist Church was well attended. It was three days before Christmas and Mercy couldn't help noticing that it was as cold on the day of Lenox's funeral as it had been when they buried their mother not so long ago. Mercy was beside herself with grief. Xavier had dropped everything and rushed to New York to be with her. He sat by her side on the front pew of the church, holding her as she cried.

Deon sat staring at the closed coffin with tears streaming down his face. Judah was by his side, staring down at his hands, at a loss for words. There was barely an empty seat in the church, full of quite the cast of characters. Neighbors and friends, hustlers and even a few addicts, Deon's teachers and faculty from his school. G was noticeably absent.

The reverend invited those in attendance to share comments and remembrances about Lenox. Several people took to the podium to share charming recollections of Lenox's short but fun-filled life.

"She turned heads everywhere she went," her next-door neighbor said. "And she was generous. She knew that I was struggling to get back-to-school clothes for my daughter, and she brought me a bag full of brand new outfits for her."

"Lenox had a smile that made you forget all your problems," the bodega owner shared.

"One time she came into the salon and started a Soul Train line for no reason." Her stylist beamed at the memory. "My clients loved it. Especially the older ones. We still laugh about seeing Miss Carla doing the Cabbage Patch!"

Despite their attempts at highlighting the more joyous parts of Lenox's life, Deon never cracked a smile. He stared ahead at the casket wondering how he could be sure that his mother was really in there. Aunt Mercy had explained that Lenox's body was "traumatized" and he shouldn't see it. She had chosen a closed casket service for that reason. But Deon longed to see her one last time. He focused on the photo of his mother perched on an easel near the coffin. In the picture, Lenox wore that smile that everyone spoke of. He fixated on it, realizing that he would never see it in real time again.

He recalled his conversation with Judah months prior. He felt ashamed now for ever wishing Mercy was his mother instead of Lenox. He had longed for a life like the one Judah had. And now his own mother was gone for good. Even though she had never heard him express those thoughts, Deon was guilt-ridden for thinking them in the first place.

Benny arrived, and Mercy knew right away that it was him. Deon had described him perfectly. His clothes were flashy and expensive, and he walked in with two large, imposing-looking men who took seats in the back of the church. Benny stood nearby, surveying the room as the choir sang.

As the service concluded and people began to file down to the church's lower hall for the repast, Benny walked over to Deon, his thick gold chains rattling as he walked. He squatted down so that they were eye-to-eye, and took Deon's face in his big hand.

"Your mother loved you more than anything in this world. She believed in you. All she talked about was seeing you win. I promise you, she's always gonna be with you. Not in the physical. But her spirit will always be around you, watching over you. So will I. If you ever need anything, Uncle Benny is just a phone call away."

Deon nodded, his expression blank. Benny's heart sank. He wasn't the type to shed tears. But seeing Deon this broken made his eyes water.

Seated beside her nephew, Mercy stared at Benny. She knew that he was Lenox's friend, that he had been kind to Deon. But she wanted no part of anyone associated with that side of the life her sister lived. He caught her gaze and took her hand.

"You must be her sister, Mercy."

She nodded.

"She talked about you all the time, too. I knew Lenox loved you. And you're the only person she would ever admit to being scared of."

Mercy smiled, weakly, knowing that was true.

"Can I talk to you in private for a minute?" Benny asked.

Mercy nodded. She patted Deon's back reassuringly, and followed Benny to a secluded corner of the sanctuary. He looked sad and regretful, and he assured Mercy that her sister loved her deeply.

"Every time I saw her, Lenox was either on her way to see you or she just left you. You were her best friend. She trusted you and she wanted to make you proud."

Benny spoke with a thick Nuyorican accent and his tone was full of passion. Mercy believed him, even though she knew that he had come to see her with an agenda in mind.

He handed her a big envelope full of money.

"This is for you," he said as he handed the hefty package to her. "No amount of money can help you with Deon and all that you have to deal with raising him. This definitely won't bring your sister back. But this is my way of honoring her, honoring our friendship. Lenox was a special girl. She was fearless, and I'll never forget her."

Mercy thanked him for the money, aware that it was as much a condolence as it was hush money. The police were asking questions about what types of things Lenox had been into, who she had been hanging around. Benny needed to be sure that his name was kept out of it. He added one additional observation before he left.

"You know I never liked G. I'm speaking freely to you because Lenox said that you never liked him either." He shook his head in disgust. "He's the type of coward who runs from a beef with a man but can't stand to have a woman outsmart him."

Mercy stared at Benny as he spoke, hanging on his every word.

"Couple months ago, G had a problem with his cousin. He ran and hid and paid money rather than shedding blood. He brought heat on your sister with that situation, and she was smart enough to stop dealing with him. He was very upset about that. I haven't heard from him since Lenox passed. And that tells me everything that I need to know."

Benny sighed.

"Believe me when I tell you, Mercy, G's name is no good uptown. He comes up there to re-up, comes up there to shop, to party, or eat at a restaurant . . ." Benny slid his hand demonstratively across his throat. "I promise you that."

Mercy nodded. "She talked to me about you. She said you told her it was safe for her to come back to New York. But that was bad advice."

Benny heard the contempt in Mercy's voice and didn't fault her for it.

"I know he did this," Mercy said. "Even though she was hustling, everybody loved my sister. Except him. Deon told me that G's the reason why Lenox changed her phone number. That he was coming to her house and the police were called. I didn't know any of this before.

But now it makes sense. It had to be him. That's why he couldn't show his face here."

"I warned her. I promise you that. I told her that G was out of control. She was moving, trying to get away from him. But he caught up with her. I take this very personally. When I get my hands on him, he's finished. My word is bond."

Mercy wished that was some solace to her. Nothing—not even Gerard's head on a platter—could ease the pain of losing her sister so tragically. She dabbed at her eyes.

"I'm so sorry this happened," Benny said. He handed her a piece of paper. "Here's my number. If you need anything at all for you, Deon, your son, whatever—you don't hesitate to call me."

She took it and nodded.

"And if you hear about or see that coward, I need to know. I don't care what time of day or night it is. Call that number."

Mercy agreed. She watched as Benny returned to Deon, pulling the grieving boy into a hug. He whispered something to him before walking out of the church.

"I gave your aunt my number," Benny said to Deon. "I'm giving it to you, too. Keep in touch with me. Let me know if you ever need anything."

Deon nodded and watched as Benny gestured to his goons and they walked out of the church.

After the burial and repast had concluded, Mercy sat alone in a corner reminiscing. She reflected on all the times Lenox had held her together over the years. Fighting the bullies at school, financing her short-lived restaurant and picking her up at the end of each shift, paying Judah's school fees. Lenox had always been one to look on the bright side. Even at funerals, she always found a way to make Mercy laugh. She thought about the sight of Lenox dancing, snapping her fingers, winding her waist. She remembered the sound of her sister's voice, the gleam in her eyes. Mercy hung her head and cried.

Xavier was at her side in a flash. He pulled her close.

"What am I gonna do without my sister?" Mercy's voice was low and small.

Xavier rocked her. "You gotta keep going. Make her proud."

Mercy's neighbor Barbara approached, gingerly.

"I'm gonna take Judah and Deon home with me until you wrap things up here," she said. "I know today has been a lot for all of y'all. I figured the boys can hang out with Chanel and her brother and try to take their minds off things. And you can have some time to yourself. I know this is so hard for you." Barbara fought back tears. She and Mercy had grown quite close over the years. She knew that Lenox was not just Mercy's sister, but her best friend.

Mercy thanked her and watched as Barbara rounded up the kids and bundled them up for the journey. Xavier turned to face Mercy.

"I know you're hurt. On top of that, you have to comfort Deon and Judah. That's a lot to handle. I'm worried about you."

She sighed. "I have to do it. Got no choice."

Xavier squeezed her hand. "You keep saying that, but you do have a choice. You could leave here and come live with me."

Mercy looked away.

"I've been settled in DC for a while now," Xavier said. "I keep telling you how nice my place is. Good neighborhood. You would love it." He had spoken about it so much that Mercy could practically picture it. "New York is so wild right now. I think it's time for you to consider getting out of here."

"DC is wild, too," Mercy pointed out. "Crack is everywhere."

"That's true, but where I live it's not like that. We could do some research. Find good schools for the boys. Get you situated and start over."

Mercy shook her head. "I have so much going on right now, Xavier. I have to pack up Lenox's apartment and settle her affairs. I have to get through the holidays without my sister, try to get Deon through this. I have to stay here. At least until I can get custody of my nephew and get him and Judah through the school year. We're all dealing with enough change right now."

"Why don't you come spend New Year's with me? You and the boys. Come down for a day or two. You need a break, Mercy."

She shrugged. "Let me think about it." She closed her eyes, sensing a headache coming on.

They were interrupted by the reverend and his wife. They came with cards and envelopes some of the attendees had left for Mercy. She thanked them and went to collect the rest of her things. Xavier watched her. He knew that losing Lenox had rocked Mercy to her core. Some of the spark inside her had gone out when her sister died. He prayed that it wasn't enough to break her.

Xavier stayed in town for several days while Mercy wrapped up Lenox's affairs. He tried to comfort her as she mourned the loss of her sister and handled the complexity of assuming custody of her nephew. He asked her several times to come back to DC with him, suggesting it gently every chance he got. But Mercy wouldn't budge. And a week later, Xavier reluctantly left New York City without her.

Part Two

POST-TRAUMATIC STRESS

Bronx, 1991

The clock on the wall read 11:32.

Mercy and Judah waited patiently on metal chairs in Spofford Juvenile Detention Center in the Bronx. She grimaced as she looked around at the peeling paint on the walls and the filthy floors. It felt cold and clammy, dangerous. The thought of her nephew being housed in a place like this made her stomach turn. At the young age of fourteen, Deon had managed to amass a rap sheet that would impress some hardened criminals. He was being released today after serving twelve months of an eighteen-month sentence for firing five shots from a .25 caliber automatic into an open window in the projects where they lived. Mercy had taken custody of him after his mother's death, and it had not been an easy adjustment for any of them. Both Mercy and Judah sat reflecting silently on the journey their family had taken in the years since Lenox's murder.

"He's gonna be different this time," Judah said. "I can feel it. All the letters he wrote me in the beginning seemed defiant. Nothing was his fault. But lately when I talk to him, he sounds like he's finally ready to do the right thing."

Mercy prayed that was true. "He's still grieving," she said softly.

"I lost my sister, my best friend. You lost your aunt. But Deon lost his mother. As sad as I am about her death, I comfort myself with a lifetime of memories we had together. But Deon won't get that. And he's angry. I don't approve of his behavior. But I understand."

Mercy stared down at the dirty floor. She felt the same rage Deon felt. Only he had made a habit of taking that anger out on everyone around him. For nine years of his life, it had been him and his mom against the world. He adored her and couldn't accept that someone had put a gun to her chest and left her to die cold and alone on the floor of some run-down shack.

He had moved into his aunt's apartment, a place he had spent a great deal of his childhood in. So, it felt familiar. As close to home as he could feel without his mother. Deon withdrew into himself, the rage and frustration he felt turned inward at first. He wouldn't eat, had violent outbursts in school, and began drawing graphic and murderous sketches on his tests and quizzes rather than answering the questions. Judah tried to talk to him, hoping that their close bond would help him open up.

"You know you can talk to me, right?"

Deon would nod, staring off into space. He spent a lot of time alone, often sitting on the bench sulking while Judah and the other kids played in the park.

Then he seemed to shift his focus outward and began bullying other kids in school. He beat up classmates for their lunch money, even though Mercy was giving him everything she could financially. He disrespected his teachers, disrupted classes and school assemblies, crying out for attention of the most negative kind.

Mercy knew that much of Deon's behavior stemmed from his frustration over the fact that no one had been held accountable for his mother's murder. The police chased the few leads they had in the case. There was a .45 caliber gun used in the shooting. It was at close range, and Lenox had been raped. They recovered crack vials at the scene and "drug paraphernalia" as the local newspaper reported it in the last paragraph of the Crime Roundup section. But the police hadn't found the person who did it even though Mercy knew that G was involved.

The first clue had been his absence in the wake of Lenox's death. He hadn't stopped by to offer his condolences or sent any flowers. For someone who had been so entranced by Lenox when she was alive, once she was gone he had disappeared.

Then Benny had reached out to Mercy again. She still wasn't sure how he had found her. But Benny showed up at Mercy's apartment one afternoon. It was two months after Lenox's death. While the boys were in school, he knocked on Mercy's door with another burly guy in tow. The guy with him didn't speak, just nodded in Mercy's direction respectfully.

"I apologize for stopping by unannounced," he said. "I couldn't get hold of a phone number for you. So, I decided to come in person."

"It's okay," Mercy said, unsure why her pulse rate had sped up.

"I won't stay long," Benny said. "I came to tell you that I got a report about Gerard. He was found dead in a burnt-out car parked on a dead-end block in Harlem." Benny watched Mercy digest the information, a wave of emotions washing over her face. "They found the body on 147th and Lenox Ave." Benny winked at her as he said it. He handed her a small envelope. "This is for Deon. Give that to him for me. And I know you work hard and you have pride and all that, but please don't hesitate to call me if you ever need anything."

He hugged Mercy goodbye and hoped that she would be able to find some ounce of solace in the fact that G had faced street justice. But it had done little to ease her pain.

It had done absolutely nothing for Deon. He felt no closure. Instead, to him it felt like someone had stolen his life with his mother and gotten away with it. Nothing but having Lenox back would fill the void she had left.

Mercy was afraid to be too hard on him. She worried that if she doled out too much tough love, he would sink even further into despair. She let him know that she was angry at his behavior, but stopped just short of condemnation out of fear that he would run away from home. She felt that she owed Lenox that much. To keep her son close and do her best to get him on the right path. Mercy had tried reasoning with Deon. She sat down to talk with him on the first anniversary of Lenox's passing.

"Deon, I don't know what to do or say to get through to you. You go to school and start fights for no reason. Then you get in trouble and I have to leave work to come and get you. If I lose my job, how are we supposed to get by? And if you get sent to juvie, do you know what that's gonna be like?"

Deon had shrugged. He didn't care. "I feel dead inside, Aunt Mercy. I feel nothing."

Mercy shook her head. "That's not true, Deon. You feel something. Tell me what it is."

He stared at his hands and thought about it. "When she died, I did, too."

It was the best way he could express what he was going through. He didn't have the vocabulary or the strength to explain that the pain was too much for him to bear alone. That he wanted others to feel that pain, too. That he couldn't understand how everyone around him kept living life as usual when he was enduring so much trauma. His mother had been murdered and the world kept right on spinning. Teachers standing in front of his class trying to get him to focus on a curriculum while he was missing his mother's voice. Kids laughing together in the lunchroom or on the back of the bus while he felt like crying. Parents coming to the school for plays, conferences, and assemblies while he was an orphan. The words escaped him. But the emotions wouldn't stop tormenting him.

He had gone to the room he shared with Judah and returned to his aunt holding the envelope Benny had left for him. It had been weeks since that visit, and this was Deon's first time sharing its contents with Mercy. He handed it to her.

Inside was a picture of Lenox watching proudly as Deon blew

the candles out on the cake at his ninth birthday party. Lenox looked like a beautiful Afroed angel with her hair framing her face like a halo. On the back of the picture, Benny had written a note in what Mercy thought was surprisingly neat cursive.

> Deon, your mother was a queen. Queens raise kings. That's what you are. Don't ever forget that.

Mercy had held Deon in her arms as he clutched the picture and silently cried. That picture became his most valued possession.

As the years passed and he and Judah entered middle school, Mercy withdrew Judah from his private school. For one, she could no longer afford it without Lenox's help. She also hoped that having his cousin as a schoolmate might help Deon transition to a new normal. Mercy had worried at first that Judah was going to suffer as a result of switching schools. But it turned out that Lenox had been right. Judah thrived academically regardless of which school he was placed in. While they attended I.S. 61, Judah earned a spot on the honor roll.

Deon, however, sank deeper into despair. When he had been in elementary school, he knew all the kids from the neighborhood. The majority of the students lived within a twelve-block radius of the school. But in intermediate school, kids from a variety of neighborhoods were bused in each day. Deon made friends with all the bullies from areas he had never physically traveled to. But now he had cronies from all across the borough. And it only got him into worse trouble. By the age of twelve he was a familiar name to all the cops in the north shore. He stole cars, shoplifted, got caught bringing knives to school, and got caught skipping school and smoking weed.

He and a group of friends robbed a Puerto Rican kid after school, stealing his gold chain and his jacket. It wasn't long before the ghetto grapevine gave them up, and they got rounded up by the cops. Deon was brazenly wearing the kid's jacket when the cops arrested him.

They released him into his aunt's custody, and he was suspended from school. He waited a couple of days before following the kid home from school, chasing him at gunpoint in broad daylight. The kid made it to his building and fled up the stairs. Deon fired several shots into the open window of the kid's apartment, nearly striking the boy's grandmother as she sat watching television in the living room.

Mercy had pleaded with the court, explaining the turmoil Deon had been in since his mother's murder. She asked the judge to be lenient in his sentencing. But the judge pointed out that Mercy had been unable to corral her nephew in all the years she had been responsible for him.

"The Court believes a more forceful approach is called for. So, I'm sentencing Deon Howard to eighteen months in a juvenile detention facility for third degree criminal possession of a weapon, criminal possession of stolen property, and resisting arrest. He'll also have to pay a $250 fine."

Judah had taken it hard. He loved Deon and hated to see him punished, despite his rebellious behavior. He also understood that his mother was dealing with the weight of her own grief over Lenox's death. In an effort to lighten the load Mercy was bearing, Judah did his best to stay out of trouble. While Deon raised hell, Judah steered clear of drama. He focused on his schoolwork, spent time at the after-school center until his mother got off work, and did his best to avoid bullshit at all costs.

Now Judah glanced over at his mother as they sat waiting to welcome Deon home. He could see a noticeable change in her over the years. She laughed and smiled less than she used to. With her sister gone and her nephew struggling, it was no wonder she wore her pain like part of her daily wardrobe. Judah knew that she was under a lot of pressure, and he had no intention of adding to it. Judah had friends in the neighborhood, but not the same ones as his cousin's. Judah's crowd toed the line between fun and fuckery. Deon and his crew didn't give a damn about the line.

Deon had spent the past year housed in a detention center for juvenile offenders under the age of sixteen. While he was away, the tone in their home had been steadier and calmer than it had felt in years.

Xavier visited whenever his trucking route brought him to the tri-state area. Mercy still loved him, but the distance between them had taken its toll. Mercy had come up with one excuse after another for why she couldn't relocate. Judah was thriving in school, Deon needed her nearby during his incarceration, and she had gotten a promotion at work. Xavier had resigned himself to the reality that Mercy was stuck. Or at least she thought she was. So, he met her halfway, and as the years passed, they developed a long-distance relationship that worked. Judah looked forward to Xavier's visits. When he was around, Mercy seemed to brighten a little. And he gave Judah advice about girls, something his mother couldn't truly provide no matter how hard she tried.

Even when Xavier wasn't around, the climate at home had been peaceful. The chaos Deon wreaked with his violent and unpredictable behavior was gone. Mercy and Judah had been given a break from the madness. Though neither of them would admit it out loud, they weren't looking forward to Deon's return.

Mercy looked up and caught Judah staring at her. He smiled at her proudly.

"I don't think you know how strong you are," he said. "Dealing with all of this. I know it's not easy." He looked around at the cold and ugly surroundings and shook his head. "None of this is your fault. You did the best you could for Deon since Aunt Lenox died. I watched you shift from being a mother of one to having two boys to feed, two kids to look after. It's not your fault that he keeps getting in trouble, Ma. I don't want you to blame yourself."

Mercy smiled proudly. Hearing Judah speak, watching the way he moved through the world gave her so many reasons to count her blessings. He had the wisdom of a man twice his age and the courage to be himself. He didn't care who found his love of classic literature or his obsession with mathematic equations corny. He was confident and intelligent. She was so proud to be his mother.

"Thank you," she managed, choking back tears. It hadn't been easy. He was right about that.

Deon emerged then. He was tall and stocky. His face bore a few scars from the countless fights he had been in. His hair was uncombed and not well barbered. But he was still handsome underneath it all. He smiled at the sight of his cousin and gave him a hug once he reached his side.

"What up, Judah? You all grown up now," Deon said, smiling. He looked at his cousin, proudly.

Judah's handsome face, smooth dark skin, and athletic build made him a hit with all the girls around the way. He wasn't the best dressed in the hood, but he had a charm about him that made him popular nonetheless.

Judah laughed. "Hey, D. Missed you, man."

Mercy opened her arms and Deon rushed into them, hugging his aunt so tightly that he swept her off her feet. She squealed as he set her back down.

"Hey, Aunt Mercy. I'ma be good this time. I swear."

She looked at him, skeptically, and kissed him on his cheek.

"Let's get out of here. I hate this place."

"Who you telling?" Deon said, rhetorically.

Mercy hadn't visited Deon much during his time at Spofford. The trip was a long one coming from Staten Island all the way to the Hunts Point section of the Bronx. The place looked as unwelcoming from the outside as it was within. A vast, repulsive complex of white buildings surrounded by rugged barbed wire. The three times Mercy and Judah had made the trip to see Deon, she had reminded her nephew that they were trying to prepare him for a life behind bars.

"This place is gladiator school, Deon. They're teaching you how to be in prison, how to keep their system going and become another statistic."

Mercy kept Deon's commissary stocked and sent him packages constantly. But he had endured his sentence largely on his own. So, she listened carefully as he recounted his experience to Judah on the trip home.

"Were you scared?" Judah asked, gently. "At first, I mean."

Deon shrugged. "I wouldn't say I was scared. That's not a good word in there. Scared muthafuckas—" He caught himself and looked at Mercy apologetically. "Sorry, Auntie."

Mercy waved him off.

Deon continued. "Being scared in there will get you hurt. I was *nervous* at first."

Judah nodded, though he didn't really understand the difference.

"I got sentenced with three other n–three other guys. And I was the only one they sent to the B Dorm." Deon shook his head like he still couldn't believe his luck. Or lack thereof. "That's the toughest house in the whole spot. And there ain't a lot of dudes from Staten Island in there to begin with. Now I'm in B9 with thorough dudes from Brooklyn, the Bronx, and Queens. I got in a fight my first day."

Mercy couldn't help noticing the excitement in Deon's voice as he described getting jumped by a group of guys from Queens and holding his own. According to Deon, he had earned the respect of the other inmates and even a guard had told him, "You did your thing."

Mercy changed the subject, eager to hear what Deon thought about starting high school in a few weeks.

"You're a freshman now. You ready for a new start? It's a new school, new atmosphere. You can start over."

Deon smiled. "Sounds good!" He looked at Judah. "What's it like in there, cuz? You're a year older than me so you had a chance to feel it out already. Is high school as corny as it looks on TV?"

Judah laughed.

"Freshman year was cool. It's not too different from our last school, except there's more homework."

Deon groaned.

"This year will be better though. Now you'll be in school with me. Chanel, too. She's a freshman this year. So, the old crew's gonna be reunited."

Deon smiled at the mention of Chanel. He had spent many nights jerking off to thoughts of her pretty brown face.

"How's little 'Nelly' doing?" It was a nickname he had given her when they were kids. She hated it when he called her that, so he kept on doing it just to get her attention. "You know I'm gonna marry that girl someday."

Judah laughed.

"Yeah, right. Me and her already got our kids' names picked out."

Both boys erupted in laughter, teasing one another about who had the better chance of getting with their lovely neighbor down the hall.

Mercy laughed as she listened to them.

"I didn't know that both of y'all have a crush on Chanel."

"Judah has a crush," Deon clarified, smiling. "That's already my girlfriend, though. We just didn't make it official yet." He was joking, but he wished it was true.

"She forgot all about you," Judah said, grinning. "Out here playing Scarface and she wants a Romeo."

"You *think* she wants a Romeo. You probably be reciting poetry to her and all that."

All three of them laughed this time. Both boys came to a "may the best man win" style agreement and moved on to the topic of food.

"I know you kept me eating good while I was away, Aunt Mercy. Thank you. But can we please stop at Mickey D's on the way home? I thought about them fries every day while I was in there!"

Mercy smiled. "I'll give you all the Mickey D's you want, Deon. Just promise me you'll stay out of trouble. For real this time."

He nodded, perhaps a little too quickly for Mercy's taste.

"I will, Auntie. For real."

Deon did his best to keep his promise. During his time away, he had plenty of time to reflect on his behavior.

Through his counseling sessions, he learned that his rebellion was a by-product of the trauma he had been through. Mr. Shaw, in particular, had finally broken through the wall Deon had built up. Mr. Shaw was a dreadlocked brother from Queens who took no shit. He made it clear to Deon that his outbursts would not be tolerated. And as big and imposing as Mr. Shaw was, Deon believed him.

It had taken several sessions before Deon felt comfortable enough to speak. At first, he listened to what Mr. Shaw had to say about himself and gave one-word answers to the questions he was asked. But by their third session together, Deon began to unravel the knots in his heart.

"When you victimize someone, how do you benefit from it?" Mr. Shaw asked. "What do you profit?"

Deon thought long and hard about it. "I gain dominance. I have control."

Mr. Shaw had leaned forward, so close to Deon that for a moment he felt uncomfortable.

"Your mother was taken away from you. There was nothing you could do about it. You were just a kid. When you fight, when you commit a robbery or shoot a gun, you feel like you're taking back some of that power. Taking control. Dominating the situation like you wish you could have for your mom."

Deon felt like crying but held it together.

"But you're not controlling anything by doing that. In fact, the opposite is happening. You get kicked out of school, put under surveillance, incarcerated. In here, you have no control. In Rikers, if you go that route, it will only be worse."

Deon knew that he had to change his reactions to things, had to control his need to dominate situations. And he did his best to work on those things in the months after his release.

Judah talked to him, too. As they walked back home from the park one afternoon, Judah broached the topic of his outbursts.

"While you were gone, my mother prayed for you all the time. I did, too. But for Mom, all of this is even harder to deal with. Every time you mess up, she feels like she's letting Aunt Lenox down."

Deon stared straight ahead as they walked, but he heard every word Judah was saying.

"Now that you're back, I'm not gonna go easy on you. I can't have you stressing my mother out anymore. She's been doing her best to hold it together, and I want you to make it easier for her. No fighting, getting locked up, getting high, and all that shit. Just do what you gotta do to stay out of trouble. I'll help you in any way I can, D. Believe that."

Deon nodded. "I hear you, Judah. I love Aunt Mercy and I ain't trying to add to her problems. At this point, I'm sick of getting in trouble."

Deon had every intention of turning over a new leaf.

When school began that fall, he didn't anticipate the excitement he felt leading up to his first day. He woke up early that morning to make sure he got to take a shower and groom himself before Judah rose. He trimmed his light mustache and prayed that his little goatee would grow in. He combed his hair, got dressed, and checked himself out in the mirror. He wore a pair of jeans, some Jordans, a black long-sleeved T-shirt, and a zippered velour jacket. He put on the chain his mother had given him, and grabbed his new Nike backpack full of supplies his aunt had carefully selected for him.

"Hurry up!" He rushed Judah to get ready.

"Damn!" Judah said, stepping into his pants. "Somebody's excited."

Deon hated to admit it, but he was. He peered out of the bus windows as they approached the school. His eyes were wide as he absorbed it all. Seeing kids he hadn't seen in a year and marveling at how the girls had blossomed into young ladies in that timeframe was exciting for him.

Day by day, he began to mesh into the fabric of Port Richmond High School and he got into a flow that made Mercy breathe a sigh of relief.

A big part of Deon's ability to switch gears was having Judah and Chanel around. The three of them met up between classes and ate lunch together in the cafeteria while debating topics like which was the better R&B group—Jodeci or Boyz II Men. Deon and Chanel shared a couple of classes together as freshmen, and she often teased him about his performance during lunch.

"What was that answer you gave in earth science?" she pressed him as she leaned across the lunch table.

Deon smirked, but feigned innocence. "What you mean?"

Chanel sucked her teeth and turned to Judah, seated beside her.

"Mr. Shultz asked your cousin what he thinks meteorology is the study of. This fool said it's the study of meat-eaters."

Judah laughed. Deon shrugged his shoulders and shoved some French fries in his mouth.

"I thought he said 'meat-eater-ology.' He needs to speak clearly and shit."

Chanel shook her head at him. "Stop passing notes to me in class, too. I need to focus."

Deon noticed Judah laughing.

"What's so funny?"

Judah looked at him and winked. "Finally realized Scarface wasn't gonna cut it, huh?"

Deon laughed. "Whatever, fool."

Chanel looked confused. "Scarface? What y'all talking about?"

Judah waved it off as the bell rang. "Nothing. Let me walk you to your next class."

LESSONS LEARNED

Just the scent of her was enough to make him weak in the knees.

Chanel sat beside Judah on the bus headed to the Harbor after school. Deon had a longer schedule than they did because of all the classes he had to make up. So, he would join them later. For now the two of them sat huddled together in the back of the crowded S46 bus.

"You got an A in Mrs. Rivers' class? HOW?" she demanded.

Judah laughed. "It was easy. Everybody else in the class is trying to front like they read the book and they keep focusing on all the stuff in the CliffsNotes. She's smart enough to see through that. She wants to know that you really read the book. And the way to show her that is by talking about the stuff not covered in the study guides. Like the way Ogbuefi's facial expression changed from anger to a sinister smile, which symbolized his rage turning to bloodthirst."

Chanel stared at him speechlessly.

"I'm telling you, *Things Fall Apart* is a great book. You just gotta take your time with it."

Chanel wasn't sure she agreed. "It's like reading a fable but with grown-up themes."

"Exactly," Judah said. He saw the confused expression on her face and chuckled. "I'll help you. What chapter are you on?"

"One!" she admitted sadly. She held up the book in frustration.

Judah laughed and patted her reassuringly on her leg.

"Okay. Let's take it from the top."

Chanel opened it up to page one and began reading.

Two teenaged boys in baggy clothes got on the bus talking loudly. Their language was vulgar and they were unmoved by the stares of disapproval from the elders seated in the front. They moved to the back of the bus and seemed to set their sights on Judah and Chanel instantly.

"Look at this nerd trying to kick it to shorty!" One of them glared at Judah with a sinister smirk on his face. He looked at Chanel and licked his lips. "She fine, too. I should punch this corny muthafucka in his face and take his girl."

Judah avoided making eye contact with the guy. But he couldn't ignore the feeling of his heart pounding nervously in his chest. He was scared to death that he would get jumped, especially in front of Chanel. He hadn't been in a fight in years and wasn't sure if he could even hold his own. He battled hard to keep his hands from trembling.

The second guy stared at Judah, aware that he was frightened. He narrowed his gaze and took a closer look. "Ain't you Deon's cousin?"

Judah's heart kept thundering, but he managed a slight nod.

"I thought so. That's my man. We were in Spofford together. Word. Tell him Kadeem said 'what up.'" He looked at his friend. "Leave this kid alone. I know his family."

The first guy sucked his teeth in disappointment. He rolled his eyes at Judah and looked Chanel up and down one last time for good measure. Moments passed that felt like an eternity. Judah and Chanel rode in silence while the two guys loomed nearby. Two stops later the two guys got off the bus, much to Judah's relief. He felt embarrassed, though he wasn't sure why. He worried that Chanel had sensed his fear; that she was aware that it wasn't his own reputation that had spared him an ass whipping. It was his cousin's street credibility that had allowed him to escape unharmed. He stared at the floor, silently.

Chanel cleared her throat. "Don't let them idiots bother you, Judah."

He forced himself to look at her, painted on a grin, and shrugged. "Nah. I'm good," he lied. "Ain't nobody worried about them."

Chanel nodded, though it was clear Judah had been worried. She didn't hold it against him, though. She had known Judah and Deon their whole lives it seemed. She admired their bond and appreciated their differences. But she could tell in that moment that Judah wished he had more of the grit his cousin possessed. Although he tried to play it off, she knew the encounter had shaken him.

"Anyway," she said, shifting closer to him in the seat. "Let's keep reading."

An hour later, Deon waited alone at "The Shelter," a literal bus shelter that served as a mini transportation hub near the Staten Island Ferry terminal. He shifted his backpack to one shoulder and peered around the bend for his bus.

"What up, Deon?"

He turned to see a familiar face and smiled.

"Hey, what's up, Sha? How you been?"

Shakim was a kid Deon remembered from middle school. The two of them got into trouble together quite often, one of their most memorable incidents being the extortion of a frail classmate for five dollars a day in protection money.

"Chilling. Just came from a little punk-ass family court hearing." Shakim shrugged like it didn't mean anything.

"Everything good?"

"Yeah. Moms is tripping. Trying to emancipate me and shit. Fuck it."

Deon wasn't sure what that meant. But judging by the way Shakim looked down at the ground as he said it, it didn't sound good. He nodded.

"I'm out here getting money now. So, I ain't worried about none of that family shit no more anyway." He lit a blunt as he stood there, unconcerned about the looks he got from a few people nearby.

"Getting money how?" Deon asked, intrigued.

"Hustling for Theo and them. They getting money out here."

Deon nodded. The idea of selling crack had been tempting to Deon over the years. He still recalled the days when Benny had been his hero. Though he was just a kid when she died, Deon was old enough to remember the opulent life his mother had provided thanks to the proceeds of the crack trade. He knew that Benny was involved in it somehow and that if he wanted to, he could call him and get plugged in. There were lots of his peers making plenty of cash selling a drug that seemed to sell itself. But it was something Deon just couldn't bring himself to do. Not since the crack game had cost his mother her life.

"That's good," Deon said. "I can't fuck with that shit, but I'm glad you out here making moves." He slapped Shakim five.

"What you about to get into?" Shakim asked. He looked at the backpack on Deon's shoulder and frowned a little. "You coming from school?"

Deon didn't know why he felt a little embarrassed to admit it. He nodded, then shrugged like it didn't mean anything.

"I just got out of Spofford. You feel me? Early release for a gun charge. So, for six months at least, I gotta look the part."

Shakim laughed. "I forgot what a wild muthafucka you are!"

Deon smiled, proudly. His reputation for not giving a fuck served him well sometimes. It had earned him the respect of guys most people around them feared.

"Yo, take a walk with me real quick. I gotta get some more

weed from New Brighton. Then I'm headed out to the Harbor to get my hustle on."

Deon looked over Shakim's shoulder and saw that his bus was approaching. The S46 would take him home to Aunt Mercy and Judah. To a night of homework and dinner conversations about how the day went. Nights that made him long for his own mother and for her conversation. He looked at Shakim and nodded.

"Yeah, come on. I'll take that walk with you."

Back at their apartment, Mercy put away the last of the dishes and left Deon's plate wrapped in aluminum foil on the stove. She turned the kitchen light off and went into the living room to watch TV. Judah and Chanel had eaten dinner with her and then gone to Judah's room to read some book Chanel was having trouble with. Deon had never returned home from school.

It had been a month since his release from juvie, three weeks since school had started. She had been hopeful that Deon would get swept up in the newness of high school and the promise of a fresh start. But it seemed like he was bound to go back to his old ways, and she felt powerless to prevent it.

She thought about Lenox and the conversations they had about their sons. Lenox had never been too concerned about Deon's education. She treated his schooling like it was another system she was manipulating to fit her needs. School had been more of a babysitting service for Lenox than an opportunity for Deon to learn something. Mercy imagined that Lenox was alive, something she did quite often when she was alone this way.

What you think now, Len? You still think I'm uptight and I worry too much?

Mercy huffed and lit a cigarette. It was a habit she had picked up since her sister's death. When Lenox was alive, Mercy had indulged in one every now and then. Occasionally bumming one from her sister's pack when they were having one of their good

times together. Since Lenox's death, Mercy kept a pack of New-
ports on hand at all times. They reminded her of the old days. And
lately they helped ease the tension she increasingly felt raising two
boys.

She heard Deon's key in the door and looked at the clock. It was
7:30. Not bad, she thought. At least he had made the eight o'clock
curfew the juvenile courts had imposed. She was sick of taking time
off from work to go to hearings related to Deon's conduct. All she
wanted was some peace in her family, in her home, and in her life. She
reasoned that maybe Deon had just been hanging out with some of his
friends after school and lost track of time. She watched as he walked
through the door and waved at her.

"Hey, Auntie. Sorry I missed dinner. I ate already, though. I
stopped by my friend's house and had dinner over there. So, I'm good.
I don't need no food or nothing. I'm just gonna get something to
drink real quick. Then I'll get out of your way. Judah's here, right?"

Deon was talking fast and moving oddly. Mercy set her cigarette down in the ashtray and narrowed her eyes at him.

"Yeah," she said. "He's in his room. What's wrong with you,
Deon? Why you look like that? Why are you talking like that?"

He rubbed his head slowly like a dope fiend.

"I'm just tired, Auntie. I'ma go lay down."

He stopped in the kitchen and poured a tall cup of water before
stumbling down the hall to the room he shared with his cousin.

Mercy closed her eyes, took a deep breath, and shook her head.
She spoke to the spirit of her sister once again.

What you think now, girl?

Deon opened the door to the bedroom and found Judah and
Chanel engrossed in a deep conversation. He didn't seem to notice,
plopping down on his bed in a dead heap.

Chanel looked over at him.

"You alright?" she asked. "Why you look like that?"

Deon groaned, kicked his sneakers off, and lay there motionless.

Judah and Chanel exchanged glances.

"You high, Deon?" Judah couldn't hide his disgust as he asked the question.

Deon didn't respond.

Judah got up from his bed and walked over to Deon's.

"Yo. Answer me. Are you high, D?"

Deon sucked his teeth.

"Fuck outta here, Judah. I'm tired. That's it." Deon's voice was muffled as he spoke with his face half smushed into the pillow.

"Nah, you stink. Where did you go after school? My mother saw you like this?"

Chanel could tell Judah was growing increasingly angry.

"Judah," she said. "Give him a minute."

"Nah." Judah waved her off angrily. He shook Deon's leg roughly. "GET UP!"

Deon rolled over and faced his cousin. His eyes looked demonic and beet red.

"Muthafucka, I was with Sha. We smoked some dust and fucked some chicks from New Brighton. Damn." He rolled back over as if Judah should be satisfied with that answer.

Judah was anything but satisfied. Furious, he pulled Deon off the bed and dragged him onto the floor.

"JUDAH, WAIT!" Chanel yelled. "STOP!"

Deon scrambled to his feet angrily and got into fighting stance. He was visibly high and his movements disjointed. Judah punched him dead in his face, and Deon recoiled. He rushed at Judah, but Judah caught him again with another punch to the face. Deon stumbled back hard against the wall.

Chanel stepped between them, holding Judah at bay while Deon got his bearings.

"You must be out your mind!" Judah yelled. "After all the shit my mother went through, you think she needs to see you coming in here like this? I told you to get your shit together!"

Mercy burst into the room and her eyes widened when she saw the scene before her.

"What happened?"

"He's high!" Judah yelled. "I know you saw him when he walked in here. You're too scared to confront him. Scared he's gonna run away or go out there and try to shoot somebody else."

He shook his head. He was sick of seeing his mother tiptoeing around Deon out of guilt and fear. It wasn't her fault that his mother was gone.

"I'm sorry, Aunt Mercy." Deon sounded like it hurt him to speak.

Chanel looked at Judah, pleadingly.

"Let's take a walk and calm down," she said. "Come on."

Judah looked at his mother and she nodded.

"That's a good idea. Let me talk to Deon alone for a minute." She smiled at Judah weakly. "It's okay, baby."

Judah took a deep breath, put his shoes on, and followed Chanel out the door. His mother squeezed his hand as he passed her.

"We have to be patient with him," she said. "He'll get it to-gether."

Mercy took Deon into the bathroom and washed his face. She could see why Judah had reacted so angrily. When Deon had breezed past her in the living room, she hadn't gotten a good look at him. Now, in the bright glare of the fluorescent bathroom light she saw the crazed and distant look in his eyes. She could smell the stench of something unholy on him. She held his face in her hands and spoke to him as openly as she could.

"Your mother would whoop your ass! And you know it. If Lenox was alive, you wouldn't be doing this shit."

"She left me." Deon said it so matter-of-factly that it caught Mercy off guard.

"She . . . she didn't leave you, Deon."

"Where's she at, then?" He laughed sadly. "She left me here with nobody. Judah has you. Who I got, Auntie?"

She gripped his face tighter and spoke to him through clenched teeth.

"You have ME! I'm HERE! Every day."

Deon saw the tears pooling in her eyes and watched them cascade down her face.

"You're not alone. Judah and I are here. We have been here from the start. You gotta stop feeling sorry for yourself. We *all* lost Lenox. All of us. I lost my sister. I miss her every moment of every day, and she's never coming back. You think I don't hurt because of that? You think it's easy for me? Judah lost his aunt. The fun one who made the room light up whenever she walked in it. You think he doesn't miss her? You're not the only one hurting, Deon."

She let go of his face and took a step back. She exhaled.

"Lenox didn't leave you. Somebody took her from us. She was smart, beautiful, funny, lively, and she was fucking stubborn. That's where you get it from. But that stubbornness cost her dearly. And if you're not careful, it's gonna cost you, too."

Mercy handed him a fresh towel and washcloth.

"Take a shower. Then go to bed and sleep this shit off. Then we'll start over tomorrow."

Deon nodded, feeling guilty despite the haze he was in.

Mercy stepped out of the bathroom and walked down the hall. She walked into her room, plopped down on the bed, laid her head back, and cried harder than she had in years.

Outside, in the darkness of the Big Park, Chanel sat on the bench beside Judah, listening as he poured out his frustrations about everything.

"I feel like I lost my mother, too," he said. "I know that sounds selfish, but it's true."

Chanel shook her head. "I don't think it sounds selfish. It makes sense. He lost his mother and now you have to share yours."

Judah shook his head. "That wouldn't have even been hard for me. I love him like a brother. I would share anything with him.

My mother, my kidney, whatever he needed. But now he's not just sharing my moms, he's stressing her out. Keeping her up at night, making her sadder than she already is. I feel like she never got to fully mourn her sister's death because she had to focus on Deon. That muthafucka's selfish. He acts like all the trouble he's causing only affects him."

Chanel felt sorry for Judah as she listened to him. It was obvious that he loved his mother and his cousin deeply.

"He needs to get it together," she acknowledged. "Deon is smarter than this. I think he's just angry, and he doesn't know how to express that. So, he's doing dumb shit like smoking dust." She shook her head. "My brother, Dallas, used to smoke that shit, too. It's what got him kicked off the basketball team. Next thing you know he dropped out of high school. Now he's locked up. My mother says it's a cycle. And Deon don't seem to realize he's on the same path."

Judah was relieved to talk to someone who understood what he was dealing with. Chanel smiled at him and took his hand in hers.

"You're a good son. I like the way you stuck up for your mother. And Deon is lucky to have you as his cousin. You care about him and he's blind if he can't see that."

"Thank you," Judah said.

"But damn, Mike Tyson, you didn't have to punch him in his face like that." She laughed as she said it, recalling the two good blows Judah had landed. "Impressive!"

Judah laughed, too. He felt better now.

"Thank you for coming out here with me. Talking to you has me feeling a lot calmer now."

She smiled. Truth was she thought Judah was cute and had a little crush on him.

"No problem. That's what friends are for."

She leaned over and gave him a long hug. Judah prayed she

didn't notice his heartbeat racing as he held her. The crush he had on her was anything but little.

When she let him go, she stood up and held out her hand again.

"Come on. Let's get you home, Iron Mike."

THREE'S A CROWD

Like their mothers before them, Judah and Deon allowed crucial words to remain unspoken.

They never discussed the fight they had. The topic was too touchy. Acknowledging the fact that they had come to physical blows didn't sit well with either of them. Deon knew he had been wrong, though his ego wouldn't let him apologize. Judah never brought it up again. But he kept a close eye on his cousin, waiting to see if he would slip up again.

Life went on in their family, gingerly at first. The boys were careful to stay out of each other's way while Mercy went on working, cooking, and cleaning as a means of coping with the chaos in her home. Over time, the boys went on as if nothing ever happened, falling back into their old playful banter and their shared love of basketball. And Chanel.

One day after school, Judah walked into their shared bedroom and plopped down on the bean bag chair. He wore a smile so big that Deon couldn't look away.

"What you grinning so hard for?" Deon asked.

Judah linked his hands together behind his head and sat back. "Chanel gave me a little kiss on the cheek today."

Deon laughed. "You lying."

"No, I'm not. She walked me to my social studies class 'cause she was excited and wanted to tell me about making the National Honor Roll. Mr. Raganucci said that she's one of the top students in the country, and if she keeps it up she'll have her choice of colleges and they'll all be begging her to choose them. She was hyped! I congratulated her and said that I always knew she was one of the smartest girls in the world. She lit up! Threw her arms around my shoulders and kissed me on my cheek!"

"What happened after that?" Deon asked.

"She went to her next class."

"So, that's it? That's the whole story?" Deon stared at Judah like he was disappointed.

"Yeah," Judah said. "She kissed me. That's the story." He smiled again, still feeling the softness of her lips against his cheek.

"Judah, you buggin'!" Deon fell back against his mattress, laughing. "That wasn't a real kiss! That was a friendly peck on the cheek like she would give her brother. You ain't special."

Judah sucked his teeth. "Nah, D. Trust me. I felt a spark and shit."

Deon kept laughing. "Whatever! That was a 'thank you for kissing my ass and telling me what I want to hear' kiss. Not a 'I'm feeling you and I want to give you these drawers' kiss! You getting all excited over nothing."

Judah wasn't fazed by his cousin's teasing. "Here's what I know. Chanel came to tell me her good news. She could've told anybody in the school. But she ran to come and tell me. And she kissed me. She didn't kiss your jealous ass, did she?" Judah grinned at Deon teasingly.

Deon chuckled. "Nah. She hasn't kissed me. YET! But trust me, when she does, it's not gonna be innocent."

"Keep dreaming, Deon." Judah winked at him.

Each of the boys had bonded with her in their own unique way.

With Judah, Chanel enjoyed an easy and carefree friendship. They traveled to and from school together most days and did their homework together after school. They bonded over their frustration and concern over her incarcerated brother and Judah's cousin who seemed destined for the same fate.

"Dallas got sent to Rikers yesterday," she told him as she sat sadly in the back of the bus on the way home from school one afternoon.

Judah looked at her with concern, unsure at first what to say. "How do you feel?" he asked.

Chanel thought about it. She felt so many things.

"I'm scared for him," she said. "I think about my brother in there surrounded by guys bigger than him, stronger than him. Dudes with nothing to lose and nothing to live for. And it makes me want to cry." She paused to gather herself. "Plus, he's been smoking dust, too. So, he's in there messed up. He needs rehab, not prison. But the judge wasn't trying to hear that. Not after he got a look at my brother's rap sheet." She sighed. "I worry about him getting hurt. And it's hard watching my mother deal with all of this."

Judah knew exactly how she felt. "That's how it is in my house, too. Whenever Deon gets in trouble, I don't think he realizes that it affects all of us. Not just him. I used to lose sleep at night thinking about all the horrible things Deon was seeing and feeling when he was locked up. But worrying doesn't help."

"What does?" Chanel asked.

Judah looked at her sincerely. "Praying. That's what I learned to do. And you can write to him. Deon told me that when he used to get letters from me while he was away, it felt like he was home again. Even if it was just for a little while."

Chanel felt better after talking to Judah. She made it a habit. Whenever she felt stressed out or under pressure, she went to him for comfort and reassurance. Judah was happy she felt comfortable talking to him. He looked forward to their conversations and wasn't afraid to express his dreams, fears, and vulnerabilities with her.

With Deon, Chanel was surprised to discover that his penchant for trouble was only one aspect of his complex personality. Deon was often ejected from the classes they shared together over his refusal to submit to authority. If a teacher asked him to stop talking during a test, he would curse them out. He didn't bother to raise his hand if he had something to say, interrupted other students when they were talking, and gave substitute teachers hell. The result was constant detention, threats of suspension, and countless trips to the principal's office. Chanel watched in bewilderment as the warmhearted guy she saw at home became a terror in public.

She challenged him on it constantly.

"Why do you act like that?"

"I'm not acting. I *am* like that," he'd say.

"Why?" Chanel persisted.

"Because I just don't care, Chanel." He shrugged. "Like . . . sometimes I feel like I'm mad at the world."

"You mad at me?" she asked.

He shrugged. "Sometimes, yeah. I guess."

"Why?"

"Because you have times when you can laugh and forget about your problems. I can never forget about mine. Even when I'm in the middle of laughing at something or I'm having a good time. I'm always sad on the inside. That shit never leaves me. And I can't shake it, so it makes me mad. Then everything is downhill from there."

She accepted that answer for a while. He had lost his mother in such a devastating way that she decided it wasn't her place to judge his coping methods. But the more she watched Judah and his mother suffering under the weight of the pressure Deon was placing on their shoulders, the harder it was for her to keep silent. Chanel confronted him one Saturday afternoon in the Big Park.

It was December, and the park was empty. Chanel was walking home from the neighborhood flea market and took a shortcut through the park in order to get to her building quicker. She spotted a group of boys standing together near the handball courts. They wore bomber jackets and winter hats to shield them from the cold. A crackhead walked up to them and Chanel watched through the corner of her eye as one of the boys made a sale. She kept walking toward her building.

"What's up, shorty? Why you walking so fast? Let me holla at you," one of them called out.

Chanel kept walking. She heard a conversation happening between the guys, but didn't bother listening to the content of it. She just wanted to get home.

"Nelly, hold up!"

She stopped walking and turned around. *Nelly.* It was a name that only one person referred to her by. She saw Deon walking in her direction and shook her head.

"Why do you keep calling me that?" she asked.

"That's what I like to call you, that's why." He licked his lips as he approached, his eyes low and heavy looking.

Chanel sucked her teeth.

"You out here getting high with these niggas, Deon? I thought you were smarter than that."

Deon held up his hands in defense.

"No dust this time. Just a little weed. That's it."

"SO?" Chanel yelled. "Weed, dust, crack, all that shit is a waste of your time, Deon. For real . . . why do you hate your aunt and cousin so much?"

Deon looked hurt by the suggestion.

"I don't hate them."

"So, why are you out here fucking up like this? Every time you get in trouble at school, or the cops chase you, or you get in a fight with some idiot, it's your aunt that has to deal with that shit. Miss Mercy is like best friends with my mother. I hear the conversations they have in my kitchen about how much she worries about you. She feels like she's letting your mother down every time you fuck up."

Deon sucked his teeth and looked away. But what Chanel was saying had touched him. Guilt was written all over his face.

"And Judah loves you. He says you're the brother he always wanted. When you came to live with him, he tried so hard to make you feel at home. He probably never even told you how he folded all his clothes up and stacked them in plastic bins so that you would have enough room to hang up all of your fancy clothes in the closet. I know because I helped him do it. He was so worried about how you were feeling and what you must be going through. Sometimes I wonder if you ever think about him like that. Do you ever think about anybody but yourself?"

Deon looked at her, his eyes red and glazed over. He shook his head.

"Nah," he admitted, flatly. "And it's not because I don't care about them. It's that I'm the one whose mother got a bullet in her chest. Judah still has his mother. Aunt Mercy still has her son. The pain they feel ain't equal to mine. But I don't expect you to understand that," Deon said.

Chanel stared at him for a while, then nodded.

"Good," she said. "'Cause I don't."

She walked away and left him standing in the cold.

The next morning, he walked down the hall and knocked on her door with a peace offering.

She looked at the photograph he handed her, confused.

"What's this?" she asked.

"Read the back," Deon said.

Chanel did. She looked up at him, still not understanding what this was.

"When my moms got killed, one of her friends gave me this picture. He took it at my birthday party the year before she passed. The way she's smiling at me . . . I stared at it so much that the image is burned in my brain at this point."

Chanel held the picture in her hand tenderly.

"What he wrote on the back about my mother being a queen, that was true. She never finished raising me to be a king, though. So, sometimes I forget that I am one. I want you to hold on to that. For now. 'Cause I thought about what you said. It's not the first time you tried to talk some sense into me. But . . . I don't know. Today, for some reason, you made me understand that I'm disappointing my mother. And Judah and Aunt Mercy don't deserve the way I been treating them. I'm gonna start doing better. Acting right and shit. When you feel like I earned that back, you know where to find me."

He walked off down the hall and went back into his aunt's apartment. Chanel smiled and retreated into hers, hopeful that Deon had finally seen the light.

The holiday break was winding to a close, and Judah and Deon prepared to head back to school for the spring semester. They had been spending a lot of time together as a winter storm forced them to stay indoors. They played Monopoly with Aunt Mercy, Chanel, and her mother, Barbara, until close to midnight with Deon declaring victory over all of them. A peace had fallen over them that was so fragile none of them dared to even mention it.

As New Year's Eve approached, Barbara invited Mercy to a party a friend of hers was throwing at a Mason's lodge.

"You should come, Mercy. All these years I've known you all you do is work and take care of them kids. Mama needs a life, too!"

Mercy thought about it, worried that leaving Judah and Deon alone while she went out could be a disaster. It wasn't Judah's job to babysit his cousin. But she knew that Deon needed constant supervision. She pretended for a moment that Lenox was alive and imagined what her advice would be. She could hear her sister's sassy voice saying, "Go, bitch! You only live once." The thought made Mercy smile. Reluctantly, she agreed to go to the party with Barbara.

Judah was happy to see his mother going out for a much-deserved night on the town. He knew how much she needed this. He assured her that everything would be fine in her absence.

"Go have fun. Bring in the new year right."

Mercy felt her heart swell for him even more. Her precious Judah.

She put on makeup for the first time in years. Heels, too, which she second-guessed until the moment Barbara knocked on her apartment door. Mercy opened it wearing a black dress and heels and Barbara gasped.

"Yes, girl! This is what the fuck I'm talking about!"

With Mercy and Barbara gone, Chanel came over to hang out with the guys. They watched Dick Clark's New Year special on TV while Chanel painted her nails.

"That shit stinks!" Deon said, frowning. "Ugh!"

Chanel giggled. "It's not that bad. You're just dramatic."

Deon gagged, dramatically.

"Nah, that shit smells terrible. I'm about to go outside and get some air." He got up and grabbed his Timberlands. He began to slowly put them on, careful to avoid eye contact with Judah.

Judah stared at his cousin, watched him put his boots on and lace them up, then walk over to the closet and pull out his coat.

"D, you know it's past your curfew, my nigga. How you going outside?"

"I can't breathe in here," Deon protested. He meant that in more ways than one. He felt suffocated lately.

"Just crack a window." Judah's jaw clenched.

Chanel started putting the top back on her nail polish.

"I'll go home and finish this," she said, gathering her things.

"Nah!" Deon said, already out the door. "Stay. I'll be right back. I just gotta walk outside real quick."

Judah watched him go, thought about going after him. But he looked at Chanel. She shook her head.

"You can't fight for somebody that won't fight for themselves. Trust me. I watched my mother learn that the hard way."

Judah heard the door slam behind Deon and sighed.

"Shit is frustrating."

"I know it is," Chanel said. "My mother said the streets are as addicting as a crack pipe or a needle full of heroin. Watching my brother fuck his life up taught her that. She tried everything to keep Dallas out them streets. First, she tried buying him everything he wanted. But she couldn't keep up. All his friends were hustling and wearing a new pair of sneakers for every day of the week, had four or five pairs of $100 jeans. Dallas just kept wanting more. After that, she tried kicking him out. He just got worse. He wasn't gonna stop, no matter what she said or did."

Judah prayed that Deon wasn't destined for the same fate.

"Now that he's on Rikers, he said he would give anything for a do-over. He had to learn the hard way. I think Deon is like that, too. You talked to him. So has your mom, and so have I. Now it's up to Deon to do the right thing."

Judah nodded, still worried that letting Deon go had been a mistake.

"Well, now that he's gone, you might as well finish doing your nails. The smell ain't that bad to me."

Chanel smiled, sat back down, and resumed her masterpiece.

With his coat zipped up to the neck and his hood covering his head, Deon walked up the block toward the corner store. It was cold and windy. But there were still plenty of people outside. Some were dressed up, scuttling off to New Year's Eve parties, while others stood around getting their hustle on. Crackheads didn't care about holidays. If anything, they were more likely to get high in an attempt to escape the loneliness and isolation of addiction. Several of them scuttled by in search of their next fix. Deon recognized a few dudes he knew, and he greeted them as he walked.

He got to the store and ordered a turkey and cheese sandwich on hero bread.

"Mayonnaise, mustard, salt, and pepper," he added.

He walked around the store while the guy behind the counter prepared his sandwich. He grabbed a Sprite, some salt and vinegar chips, and a bag of Doritos. Then he headed back up front, placed his items on the counter, and fished around in his pocket for his money.

The door opened and two of his friends walked in. Phillip and Ronnell, two of the wildest guys in Deon and Judah's age group. Everywhere they went trouble followed. Tonight would be no exception.

They walked in conversing loudly about some girl and her oral skills. Deon laughed as they greeted him.

"Y'all talking about Gina? Yeeeaaaah."

All three of them laughed. Deon handed the clerk his money and waited for his change while Phillip and Ronnell rudely demanded two White Owl cigars.

"Let me get that shit!" Ronnell said, leaning over the counter so far that he could have easily grabbed it himself.

The clerk handed over the cigars and took the money they tossed at him.

"You should come up top with us," Phillip said.

Deon frowned. "Up top? What you talking about?"

Phillip held the cigars up, demonstratively. "We're about to go up on the roof of 150 and smoke some blunts. Then we gonna bust off a few shots."

He pulled a gun halfway out of his pocket and smiled.

"Cops will think it's firecrackers and shit."

Ronnell laughed. "More like M-80s!"

Deon felt his adrenaline rushing at the thought of squeezing a trigger again. The power he felt with a gun in his hand was unmatched. It made him feel stronger, tougher, and it gave him a satisfaction he couldn't explain. His eyes widened.

"You should come with us. Fuck it." Phillip shrugged.

Deon thought about it. Figured it couldn't hurt. Just a few shots fired off the roof on New Year's. Happened every year. If somebody did call the cops, by the time they got there Deon and his friends would be long gone. He nodded.

"Fuck it." Things like this always excited him. Breaking the rules, breaking the law, defying authority. He associated those things with his mother. With people like Benny and the hustlers he had grown up around. When he was committing crime, fighting, robbing, and stealing, it reminded him of the life he used to live. Reminded him of what he believed to be the good times. When his mother was alive and she was breaking all the rules. When his closet was full of every coveted label and he had every possession he desired. When he was the envy of all his friends and his mother was the queenpin overseeing an empire. With the cold and steely gun in his hand, he imagined himself the way he had always envisioned. A young man in control. His mother's heir apparent. He imagined the direction his life would have taken if Lenox's life had never been robbed from her. And in those visions, he was not forced to conform or to adhere to society's rule. His defiance of authority was his birthright.

They set off to 150 Brabant Street and hung out in the stairway. Phillip lived in the building, and just about everybody in his family had faced—or were currently facing—criminal charges. His grandfather was home on parole after serving more than ten years for bank robbery. Both of his parents had a pending drug case against them, and his older brother was serving time upstate for attempted murder. His family was wild, and Phillip fit right in.

"Where did you get the guns from?" Deon asked. He sat on a step eating his sandwich like it was his last meal.

"My cousin," Ronnell said. "He got a bunch of them. So, if you wanna buy one or if you know somebody who does, holla at me."

Deon nodded. "Let me see it." He finished the last of his sandwich and wrapped up the foil. He tossed it aside and took a long sip of his soda.

Phillip passed the gun to him, smiling like he had manufactured it himself.

"That shit is pretty, ain't it?"

Deon laughed.

"Yup. Unless you're on the wrong side of it. Then that shit look ugly as hell."

They laughed and headed up to the roof.

The air was icy and brutal up there. All three of them pulled their coats more securely around their bodies, pulled their hoods, on, and braced themselves against the cold.

Deon let off the first shot. It was loud and reverberated in a way that made Phillip squeal with delight.

"Let me see that shit," he urged.

Deon's face was lit up with excitement and adrenaline as he handed the gun over. "What kind of gun is that?"

Phillip smiled like a proud parent again. ".357!"

Phillip squeezed the trigger twice, squealing at the top of his lungs each time. The expression on his face was maniacal.

Deon turned to head home.

"Y'all niggas crazy."

Phillip and Ronnell laughed as they followed after him. All three of them rushed back into the stairwell and were met face-to-face by uniformed police officers rushing in their direction.

With nowhere to run, the boys held their hands up and surrendered.

The judge had no pity for Deon. Neither did Judah nor Aunt Mercy. Deon's parole was revoked and the judge returned him to Spofford to serve out the remainder of his sentence. This time, his aunt assured him, there would be no visits. His commissary would be whatever Mercy could afford. She was fed up.

"I've done everything I can for you, Deon. Everything I know how to do. Maybe that's not enough and you need some type of help that I can't give you. But I'm not gonna keep living my life like this. Scared to leave the house because you can't be trusted to act right unless someone is supervising you. Judah doesn't deserve it either. We can't help you succeed if you don't want to."

He sat now, back in a cell in the B Dorm—B3 this time—where they housed all the wildest juvenile inmates. He had learned a lot during his time back inside. A Spanish kid taught him how to start fires using a lead pencil and an electrical socket. That skill came in handy whenever he managed to bum a cigarette from a C.O. and needed to light it. He mastered the art of holding a razor in his mouth and spitting it out in the middle of a fight. He also learned a lot about his anatomy. The B Dorm was across the street from a house of ill repute. Whores and crack addicts hung out there twenty-four seven. Sometimes at night when the prostitutes were feeling charitable, they would flash the boys in B Dorm. Deon spent many nights jerking off while peering through a barricaded window at some scantily clad woman wiggling her titties in his direction.

Aunt Mercy and Judah kept their word and didn't visit him. But they did write him letters each week. He wrote back, apologizing for his bad decisions and promising that he would do better this time. He meant it, too. He was tired of living up to everyone's low expectations of him.

He received a letter from Chanel that came as a surprise. She explained that she had gotten his address from Judah, and she wanted to encourage him to stay strong in there. With the letter, she included the photograph Deon had given her of him with his mother. A Post-it note was stuck to the back of it. He peeled it off and read it. Tears flooded his eyes and he rushed off to avoid detection. He went back to his room, sat down on the bed, and read it again.

Deon,

Just because you can't see your crown doesn't mean it's not there.

☺ *Nelly*

MISSING PEACE

She wasn't sure how she had gotten here. But Mercy was tired. Exhausted, really. It had felt like one nonstop sad day that wouldn't end. One crisis after another. Once she recovered from one loss or tragedy, another was right behind it. She thought about Lenox every day, missing their laughter and easy conversations. Wishing she had fought harder to save her sister from herself. Maybe then she would be here to deal with her own son. Maybe then Mercy could have a life of her own.

Xavier called her one night in early winter and broke the news to her.

"I met somebody," he said.

Mercy waited for him to say more, but his silence signaled that he was unsure what more there was to say.

"I knew it would happen eventually," she said, honestly. "I kept you waiting too long. I knew it would only be a matter of time before some lucky woman stole your heart."

Xavier struggled to find the words. "I wish it was different."

Mercy did, too. "It's my fault," she said, softly. "I should have listened to you when you asked me to go with you in the first place. I told myself that I stayed because I was worried about Lenox. But

staying here didn't stop her from getting killed." She chuckled maniacally at the irony in that. "Then she was gone and I tried to keep
things stable for Deon. But that was another one of my little fan-
tasies that I let myself believe in for a while. Deon might never get
his act together. So, I've been stuck in one place for years, thinking
if I hold steady long enough then everything around me will stop
swirling like a tornado." She stopped talking, fearful that she had
been rambling. She cleared her throat. "Anyway, I'm happy for you,
Xavier," she lied. "What's her name?"

He hesitated before answering. "Her name is Jennifer." He
thought about everything she had just said and knew that this was
breaking her heart. "I'll love you for the rest of my life, Mercy. It
might not be right, but I don't want to lose what we have. The
friendship between us is more important to me than anything. Can
I still call you sometimes?"

Mercy felt her eyes watering, but pushed through it and smiled.
She hoped her voice sounded stronger than she felt. "Of course. You
can call me anytime."

He held the phone, wishing he had the words to tell her how
much she meant to him despite the fact that he had fallen for someone else. "So, this ain't goodbye?" he said.

"No," she said. "Not goodbye. Just 'see you later.'"

He felt a glimmer of hope that their friendship could survive
this. "Later."

The new year didn't make her feel optimistic or hopeful. Those
emotions had deserted her long ago. Instead, she felt anxious, thinking about Deon and Judah and the diverging roads they faced ahead.

While Deon was paying his debt to society, Judah was entering
his junior year of high school. His academic advisors were helping
him prepare for college, providing applications, editing his essays, and
writing letters of recommendation for him. He wanted to go away to
school rather than staying in the city. His literature teacher, Mrs. Bristow, had taken a special interest in Judah. She seldom saw young black

men as well-versed as he was in classic literature, and so passionate about debating different topics with his peers. She often marveled at him in class as he held court defending a character that the rest of her students found deplorable. His point of view was always fresh and well thought out. Mrs. Bristow urged Judah to apply to HBCUs, Morgan State in particular. As an alumnus herself, she knew that an atmosphere like that would nurture a bright and blossoming mind like his.

Mercy agreed, and she took Mrs. Bristow's advice and brought Judah to Baltimore, Maryland, to visit the school. They took an Amtrak train from Penn Station one weekend at the end of February. Along the way, they talked about Judah's plans for the future.

"I don't really know what I want to be," he shared, honestly. "Not because I don't have options, but 'cause I have so many. Mrs. Bristow said that's a nice problem to have. But I wish I could narrow it down. I could study law or medicine. That's where the money is."

Mercy liked the sound of both of those career options. But she could sense that there was more. There always was with Judah. He was a big dreamer, and she loved that about him.

"If money wasn't an option, what would you want to wake up every day and do for a living?"

He smiled.

"It's gonna sound corny, but I would do exactly what Mrs. Bristow does. I would teach. Maybe not a bunch of idiots in high school. But I would be a professor of literature . . . something prestigious like that."

Mercy smiled back at him.

"There's nothing corny about that. I can see it."

"Yeah?" he asked, wide-eyed.

She nodded. "Definitely. And there's not too many black men out here teaching. I bet you would have an impact on students from all over the country. That's exactly what you should do."

Judah thought about that, the possibilities ahead of him. He looked at her again.

"You gonna call Xavier while we're down here? He lives in Rockville, but that's not too far away. I'm sure if he knows we're down here he'll make the drive to come see you."

She laughed. "I thought about it," she admitted. "It's funny how all these years I made excuses for why I couldn't come down here to visit him. Always worried about leaving Deon unsupervised or taking time off from work. Now there's a chance you might be going to college down here. If things had been different, I might have been living down here, you'd be going to Morgan State, and me and Xavier would be together." She looked out the window wistfully. The cruel irony of the situation stung. "He's happy now. I'm gonna let him enjoy that."

"What about you? Are you happy?" Judah asked.

Mercy shrugged. "I will be. When I get to see you graduate and go off to college to start chasing your dreams I'll be the happiest woman on earth."

She looked out the window at the horse stables they passed along the way. It occurred to her that she had never ridden one. She thought about how free that might feel.

"You ever think about starting another restaurant?" Judah said it gently, hoping to remind her that she didn't have to keep postponing her happiness.

Mercy smiled. "Yeah. I think about it sometimes." She looked at him and came clean. "If I think about it too long, it makes me sad. It reminds me of Lenox. She used to come and entertain me while I cooked. She was always in there twirling around and making everybody laugh. Each night when I closed up, she was right there to drive me home. She wouldn't even wait till we pulled off to start eating the leftovers I brought for her. She was so greedy."

They both laughed at the thought.

"I miss her. And as much as I loved having my own soul food spot, I don't think it would be the same without her." Mercy smiled at Judah reassuringly. "Don't worry about me. I've still got plenty of living to do, God willing. I'll figure out where my happy place is. Eventually."

Judah grabbed his mother's hand.

"One day I'm gonna pay you back for everything you did for me. I know seeing Aunt Lenox making all that money back in the day had to be tempting. Now that I'm older and I think back to those days, I know you could have sold drugs, too, if you wanted to. I was jealous of all the stuff Deon had growing up. So I can imagine how you must have felt seeing Aunt Lenox making money while we were struggling. But you kept going to work, kept being the best mother I could ever ask for. You put me in that school I know you couldn't afford. And I swear, one day I'm gonna pay you back for all of that. You'll see. When I start stacking chips, I'm gonna make sure you find that happy place. No matter what."

Mercy shook her head at him, smiling.

"You already paid me back, Judah. You pay me back every single day by not getting in trouble. By listening to me. Most of the time, at least."

Judah laughed again.

"And you thank me by the way you show up in the world. Every time some mother from the neighborhood comes and tells me that you helped them carry groceries upstairs or that you held the door for them. Every time a teacher like Mrs. Bristow sees something special in you. It's the same thing I see in you. You can do anything you want in life, Judah. The world is yours."

They arrived in Baltimore and took a taxi to the Morgan State campus. From the moment they stepped out and Judah's feet met the soil at the university, Judah was sold. He felt like he was being welcomed into a world full of people like him. Brilliant black scholars who grew up in the nation's inner city, loving hip-hop and all aspects of black culture. Here, he wasn't one of the smart kids who stood out from the crowd. Here, he was just Judah exploring the possibilities of what his future might look like if he could spread his wings.

He looked at his mother, beaming.

"Ma . . . this feels like home!"

The whole train ride home was filled with Judah's animated recounting of all he had seen and heard. To him, Morgan State was the mecca of black excellence, and he wanted to be a part of it. He repeated things he learned on the tours they went on, as if Mercy hadn't been right by his side when he learned those things. She could tell that he was excited, though, so she didn't complain as he regaled her for three long hours.

They got back to New York and headed for the subway station. Mercy and Judah went over to the token booth and stood in line to get tokens. Thankfully, the line was a short one. They reached the window and Mercy did a double take at the clerk.

"Tommy?"

"Mercy?"

Both of them stared at each other in amazement, then erupted in laughter.

Judah watched, confused.

"Wow! I can't believe it's you. Where you been? Where you going? What you been up to?" Tommy asked all at once.

Mercy couldn't stop giggling. Judah was frowning now.

"I live in Staten Island now. I'm on my way back there now. This is my son, Judah. He's going to college next year. We just came back from a tour of Morgan State in Maryland."

Tommy smiled and said hello to Judah. He congratulated him and Judah nodded.

"You still in Harlem?" Mercy asked.

"Yeah," Tommy said. "Never left." He stared at Mercy longingly, as if he wished she hadn't either.

"How's Lenox doing?" he asked.

Mercy's smile faded. "She passed a few years ago."

Tommy looked stunned.

Judah cleared his throat as several agitated subway riders complained behind them.

"COME THE FUCK ON! I GOT SOMEWHERE TO BE!"
one lady shouted from the back of the line.

Tommy slid a handful of tokens through the slot and waved his
hand when Mercy tried to put her money through. He scribbled on
a piece of receipt paper and slid it back to her along with her money.
Mercy smiled, seeing his phone number written on it. She waved as
she walked away with Judah.

"Good seeing you!" Tommy called out as they passed through
the turnstile.

Mercy turned and waved, smiling brighter than Judah had seen
in years. They walked to the front of the platform to wait for the 1
train. Judah didn't waste any time asking questions.

"So, who was that?"

"That was Tommy. I went to school with him back in Harlem."

"He liked you?"

Mercy chuckled. "Yeah. Can you tell?"

Judah chuckled, too. "A blind man could tell."

The train roared loudly into the station and they boarded it.
They found two seats side by side and sat down.

"Did you like him?" Judah asked.

Mercy shook her head.

"No. I liked your father."

They rarely spoke about the man, but Judah knew that he had
bounced out of town the moment his mother's belly began to swell.

"Your father was older, more interesting to a young girl like I
was then. Tommy was a nice guy, but I didn't pay him too much
attention. We flirted a little. But mostly I liked him as a friend."

Judah nodded. He thought about it and realized his mother
could probably use a friend right now. Miss Barbara down the hall
was cool. But he had never seen his mother's face light up with Barbara the way it did when she laid eyes on Tommy again.

"You gonna call him?" Judah asked.

Mercy grinned. "I might."

She did. Tommy and Mercy began seeing each other regularly, getting reacquainted after so many years apart. They met in lower Manhattan at first, a midway point between Staten Island and Harlem. Mercy took the ferry over and met him at cafés for coffee. They walked through museums and sat in parks, reminiscing on the old days, and getting caught up on each other's lives. Mercy told him about losing Lenox and the chaos of raising her nephew. Tommy told her about his two children from two failed relationships, and how he was doing his best to co-parent in a sticky situation.

Soon, Mercy invited Tommy over to her apartment for dinner. It went so well that she invited him back again the week after. Eventually Tommy became a constant presence. He came over on weekends mostly, and called all the time, and before long they were in a full-blown relationship. Judah didn't mind. He even grew to like the guy. As long as his mother was happy, Judah was, too.

He had his own reasons to be happy, after all. He and Chanel had grown closer since they spent New Year's Eve together worrying about where the hell Deon was and what kind of trouble he had gotten himself into this time. When the clock struck midnight, Judah had kissed Chanel. That kiss grew so passionate that both of them were flustered (and a bit relieved) when Mercy came home early. She had been hoping to bring in the new year with the boys since the party she and Barbara went to turned out to be a dud. She found Judah and Chanel alone instead and soon discovered that Deon was locked up again.

In the months since then, Judah and Chanel began to acknowledge the feelings they had been developing for each other over the years. Feelings that went beyond friendship.

"I want to be able to call you my girl," he told her one day as they hung out in her room after school watching BET.

"So, ask me to be your girl, then," Chanel challenged him.

He felt awkward, afraid to sound corny. Finally, he shrugged and swallowed his pride. "You wanna be my girlfriend?"

She smiled and nodded emphatically. "Yes!"

They met between classes and made out in the school stairwells. They escaped into the solitude of Chanel's apartment and explored each other's bodies while her mother was at work. They didn't go all the way, though it took a great deal of restraint to avoid it. Chanel was a bit of a dreamer, too, it seemed. She wanted to wait and lose her virginity on prom night.

"It's how I always pictured it," she told Judah breathlessly after she abruptly ended one of their heated make-out sessions.

"Your prom night or mine?" he asked. He was a year older than she was, after all.

"I guess . . . it doesn't matter." She looked at him shyly. "You think it's dumb, don't you?"

He shook his head and lied.

"Nah. It's cool. I understand." He felt his erection going down and sighed. "That's a long time from now, though. That's all I'm saying. I won't be a senior until next year."

She grinned at him.

"Good things are worth waiting for, right?"

Judah smiled. He respected her decision to wait, aware that prom night for some girls was as close to a wedding night as they might ever get. He kissed her and got up slowly.

"I'm gonna go home and take a shower. Your moms will be home soon anyway."

She knew he was disappointed. Truthfully, she wanted him just as badly. But she wanted their first time to be special. Not just some ordinary day the way her friends described losing their virginity.

Chanel watched Judah as he looked at all the trinkets on her dresser. He picked up a teddy bear he had given her for Valentine's Day.

"You keep him right on top of your panty drawer."

She giggled and protested as he opened the top drawer and began pulling out her underwear.

"Don't go in there!" she shouted. "For real!"

He laughed and sniffed a pair, then fished around with his hand for more. He bumped something heavy and grabbed it. His eyes widened, expecting to find some type of sex toy. Instead, he pulled out a 9mm handgun. He looked at her in shock.

"My brother asked me to hold it for him," she said guiltily.

Judah frowned. "Didn't he just get out of jail?"

"Yes," she said. "And he's already back to his old bullshit. Mommy said he can't come back here. So, he's staying with some girl. But he asked me to hold that for him until he comes back for it."

Judah put the gun back in the drawer and shut it slowly.

"You should be careful," he warned. "If your mother finds out . . ."

"I know," Chanel said. "That's why I told him to come get it before I get rid of it."

He walked back over to the bed and reached down to get his shoes. He glanced at her, grinning.

"Let me find out you're a thug."

Chanel giggled. "If I'm a thug, what does that say about you?"

He shrugged. "I'm not sure."

She reached for his hand and pulled him back down on the bed. She straddled him, smothering him with kisses, tickling him playfully until he begged her to stop.

"We belong together. If you go away to Morgan State, I'm going, too," she said softly. The thought of being away from him filled her with dread.

Judah kissed her gently on the lips and grinned.

"You better. Or I'm coming back to get you."

HOMECOMING

Deon was released from Spofford in June 1992. This time his Aunt Mercy wasn't there to greet him. Judah wasn't either. Life, it seemed, had gone on without him. He made the long trip from the Bronx to Staten Island, grateful for every point in the journey. The smell of the hot dog carts and the vendor selling roasted nuts. The sound of car horns blaring, sirens, kids laughing, people talking shit. The sight of the Staten Island Ferry and the rush of being among the passengers as they boarded. He stood on the outside deck and stared at the Statue of Liberty as the ferry glided past. He had never felt happier to be home.

This time would be different. He had promised himself that countless times over the past several months. No more hanging around with knuckleheads and finding himself in situations he knew he had no business in. This time he was going to align himself with Judah and do his best to make his family proud.

Despite the solo journey home, Deon did arrive to a welcome party of sorts. When he knocked on his aunt's apartment door, she opened it with a party favor in her hand. It was a horn, and she blew it loudly in his direction.

"WELCOME HOME!" she yelled, leaping excitedly.

He hugged her and walked in smiling at the sight of his cousin,

taller now and with facial hair. The two of them embraced and patted each other hard on the back. Chanel and Barbara were there. So
was Tommy, and Mercy introduced them for the first time.

"What's up, Nelly?" Deon picked her up and spun her around
as she squealed.

Barbara came over and hugged him, welcoming him home.

"You look good!" she said as he took a seat on the couch.

Deon sat back and took it all in. Aunt Mercy had a man now.
He seemed like a nice guy, too. Judah seemed cool with him. Another
thing Deon observed was that Judah and Chanel were a lot more
than friends these days. With all the empty seats in the room, Chanel
was perched on Judah's lap, her arm draped affectionately around his
shoulder. Deon felt a twinge of jealousy, then reminded himself that
he had fumbled the ball when he got locked up. He had felt a real
chemistry with Chanel before he went away. And he had thought of
her constantly while he was gone. The Post-it note and the photo of
him and his mother had been taped to the wall above his bunk, making them the first things he saw each morning and the last things
he saw each night before he laid down. It was sad to see that she had
feelings for someone else. But if he had to lose her to somebody, he
reasoned, at least it was Judah.

"Mom and Miss Barbara have been in the kitchen all day making you a feast," Judah said, looking at Deon. "Welcome home."

"Thank you," Deon said. He looked around, noting the little
changes Aunt Mercy had made to the place while he was gone.
"I appreciate y'all for real. All the letters you wrote me kept me
going. I thought about everything you said. How I was letting
my mother down and you were right. I want to say that this time
I'm not coming back here to cause trouble. I want to try to finish
school, maybe get a job or something. Start figuring things out,
you know?"

Everyone responded affirmatively, encouraged to hear Deon
sounding like he was ready to start fresh.

"Well, I bet you missed my cooking while you were gone." Mercy stood up.

"Sure did!" Deon sat forward and rubbed his hands together. "I promise you I laid in that hard-ass bed every night thinking about your chicken and biscuits and that peach cobbler you make on Thanksgiving."

Mercy laughed.

"Let me go and serve up this food, then."

Barbara and Chanel stood to help her in the kitchen, leaving the men alone to chat in their absence.

"It's nice to meet you, Deon," Tommy said. "Mercy and I grew up together. I knew your mother, too."

Deon nodded. "Yeah. Judah said something about that in one of his letters. What was she like back then?"

Tommy smiled. "Lenox was a firecracker. She liked to sing and dance. Real outgoing. Mercy was always the quieter one."

Deon laughed. "That didn't change."

Judah agreed.

"I'm not trying to get in your business, but I know you're trying to get on track. If you graduate, or at least get your GED, I can help you get a job with transit. It ain't glamorous, but the pay is good. Benefits and all that. When you retire, they set you up nice."

Deon imagined himself in a transit uniform and shrugged.

"Aight. Thanks." He looked at Judah. "So, your Romeo shit worked out, huh? You didn't tell me about that in your letters."

Judah shifted in his seat. Deon was right. Judah hadn't wanted to rub it in his cousin's face. It was bad enough that Deon had been sent back to juvie. Telling him about his relationship with Chanel seemed like rubbing salt in an open wound.

"I mean . . . it ain't like we're getting married or nothing."

Deon smiled.

"Y'all look good together. Where her friends at? I need somebody to sit on my lap, too, shit."

Judah and Tommy laughed as the ladies reentered the room.

"Come and eat, y'all," Mercy said, smiling.

"Thank you, Aunt Mercy," Deon said. He hugged her. "I'm gonna make you proud this time."

After dinner, Barbara and Chanel went home. Mercy and Tommy sat in the living room watching TV while Deon and Judah hung out in the room they shared. They had the radio on and "Come and Talk to Me" by Jodeci was playing.

Deon sat on his bed and grinned at his cousin.

"You look good, nigga! And I'm glad you decided on Morgan State. It'll get you the fuck outta here."

Judah plopped down on his own bed and shrugged.

"I hope I can afford that tuition. If I don't get these scholarships and grants I applied for, I'll be right here going to one of the city colleges."

Deon sucked his teeth. "Smart as you are, you don't need to worry, Judah. They're about to start throwing money at you like a stripper."

Judah laughed.

"Yo, I missed your crazy ass!"

Deon laughed, too. "Nah, you ain't miss me. Looks like you had Chanel to keep you company."

Judah nodded.

"True. But she's on some 'wait for prom night to have sex' shit."

Deon sat up.

"She's still a virgin?"

"Yup!"

"Daaaamn," Deon said, sadly. "So, you ain't getting no ass?"

Judah laughed. "Not from Chanel. I mess around with Nia from back in the day. On the low. So, keep your mouth shut."

"Puerto Rican Nia you went to Catholic school with?" Deon was wide-eyed.

"Yeah. She let me hit it twice, but she keeps threatening to tell

Chanel. So, I got my hands full and shit." He chuckled a little. "I love Chanel. And I understand she wants to wait until the time is right before we go all the way. But I gotta get some satisfaction in the meantime."

Deon clapped dramatically. He was proud of Judah. He had a girlfriend and a chick on the side and was thriving academically. At their young age, that qualified as living the American dream.

Judah laughed.

"Don't clap for me yet. Nia's just something to keep me satisfied while I wait for what I really want." He thought about Chanel and the feelings he had for her. "Chanel's the one. I'm gonna marry her one day. Mark my words."

Deon smiled. He had believed the same thing once.

"She'll be a good wife, too. She be in the kitchen watching Aunt Mercy work her magic. I know she be in there taking notes."

Judah laughed.

"So, if you not really feeling Nia like that, pass her my way, nigga. Share the wealth."

Judah balked at the suggestion.

"Hell no! She got some freaky friends, though. Don't worry. I'm gonna hook you up."

Deon smiled. "Bet!"

They fell into an easy rhythm in the following weeks. Mercy's home was fuller now with Tommy over several days a week, Barbara stopping by constantly, and Chanel boo'd up with Judah. Deon spent his days at the Big Park, careful to steer clear of his old friends and his old habits. He played ball, went to visit girls in other neighborhoods, and did his best to stay out of trouble. Eventually, he got a job stocking shelves at a local supermarket. It earned him enough money to shop and gave him something useful to do with his time. He was home before Mercy's 10 P.M. curfew each night, and he helped around the house as much as he could. For a while, things fell into a welcome calm.

Judah had been true to his word and introduced Deon to some

of Nia's friends. Deon had established a quick chemistry with one in particular—Ayana. She lived in New Brighton, and he visited her often at her family's apartment on Jersey Street.

Visiting Ayana was never easy. Deon wasn't from New Brighton. Though Staten Island was small, each hood was protective of its territory and outsiders were often unwelcome. Deon had never lost his flair for fashion or his unapologetic demeanor. He stepped off the bus alone and walked boldly through the projects to Ayana's building like he belonged there. Some of the local guys didn't appreciate that. On several occasions he had words with them as he came and went.

"You ain't from around here, stranger. Who you here to see?"

"Your sister," he'd mumble, walking past them without further discussion.

Soon, there was a small army of goons waiting for him when he walked up. Ayana had to send her brothers downstairs to diffuse the situation, and Deon had left in a cab for his own protection. After that, he stopped going to see Ayana, although the whole situation left a bad taste in his mouth. They had backed him down. Even though he knew he was outnumbered and that fleeing the scene had been his only option, he didn't like the feeling of being conquered.

Still, he was determined to stay out of trouble this time. So, he focused his attention elsewhere. Judah helped with that. They became closer than ever as the summer went on. Deon confided in his cousin about his uncertainty about his future.

"I don't know where I'm gonna end up," he said one night as they sat together on a bench in the Big Park. "I think about starting school again in a couple of months. The thought of sitting in a classroom all day listening to some teacher talking about some shit I'm not interested in . . . I know I'm not gonna last for long. I want to get my GED. Get a job. Get the fuck out of here."

"You can't get your GED until you're sixteen. So, you gotta wait a little while for that."

Deon sighed.

"You gotta start looking at it differently," Judah said. "I never hear you talking about what you want to do."

"I want to get money."

"That's not a career. You know that's the type of mindset that got Aunt Lenox caught up."

Deon looked at Judah, both aware that those words had struck a nerve.

"Chasing money will get you in trouble sometimes. Mrs. Bristow told me that if you do what you're passionate about the money will chase you."

Deon thought about it.

"I think Mrs. Bristow is waiting for you to turn eighteen so she can push up on you."

Judah laughed.

Deon got serious, his cousin's advice taking root somewhere deep down inside of him.

"I don't know what I want to do. Honestly, I want to travel. Like . . . just moving all the time. Meeting new people and seeing new things."

Judah nodded.

"You could be a truck driver. Or a train conductor. Or a pilot."

Deon laughed.

"A pilot? Ain't no black pilots, Judah."

"Don't make me give you a list of books to read to prove you wrong."

Deon held his hands up in surrender.

"Okay, fine. Maybe there's black pilots. But I'm not about to be one."

"Why not? You gotta start imagining the impossible."

Deon scoffed.

"You a motivational speaker now?"

"You feel motivated?" Judah asked, staring back at him.

Deon thought about it.

"Yeah," he said. "Maybe."

Chanel invited Judah to a party her cousin was having at a catering hall on Forest Avenue. It was a Sweet Sixteen party, but it was really a who's who of Staten Island's teen set. Chanel's cousin Keisha knew everybody. She had invited a host of people to a party that promised to be unforgettable, all of it financed by her drug-dealing godfather. Judah invited Deon to come, too. He also made him promise to behave himself, and Deon agreed.

"I'm not looking for trouble, cousin. I swear."

Barbara was going to her niece's party, too, and had invited Mercy to tag along. Mercy had declined since she and Tommy had plans for a date night in Manhattan. It was mid-July and the city was under a heat advisory. With no air-conditioning in the apartment, everyone was grateful for the chance to get outside. All curfews had been set aside for the night.

Tommy and Mercy left first, eager for some alone time. Barbara left early, too, in order to help with the decorating and setup at the party. Judah and Deon waited for Chanel to get dressed, which took longer than they expected. By the time the trio arrived at the party, it was ten o'clock and the event was in full swing.

Hip-hop pumped from huge speakers as the deejay did his thing. The dance floor was crowded with teenagers and a few adults. Tables lined the perimeter with a buffet of food laid out for the taking. Chanel found her mom and went over to greet her. Judah stood next to Deon as they surveyed the crowd.

"Yo, everybody's in here!" Judah said, excitedly. He greeted several of his neighbors and classmates, many of them people he hadn't seen in years.

"What's up, La? I haven't seen you since summer camp in '89!" Judah greeted his friend.

Deon, too, saw many old familiar faces in the crowd. Not all of them friendly. He spotted two of the dudes he had bumped heads with weeks ago at Ayana's crib. He played it cool, not wanting to make a scene. He took note of their position in the room and did his best to stay on the opposite side. He sipped some punch a girl handed him and did a little two-step with her to a Redman song.

Chanel and Judah went over to the buffet for some food. Deon watched from where he stood, carefully keeping his eye on the goons from New Brighton partying wildly on their side of the room. They yelled at the deejay, ordering him to play the music they wanted to hear. The birthday girl seemed to be close to them. She kept patiently asking them to calm down and have fun while her parents looked on in silence. When she kissed the loudest one on the lips, Deon took it as confirmation that she was his girlfriend. He sipped his punch and kept watching the scene unfold as the party raged on.

The birthday girl danced with her boyfriend while his friend walked over to the buffet where Judah and Chanel were standing. Judah held a plate in his hand while Chanel piled it high with macaroni and cheese.

"Your mama made this, so I know it's good," she said, smiling wide.

Judah licked his lips in anticipation.

"She made the fried chicken, too. So, make sure I get two pieces of that."

Chanel did as instructed and was so preoccupied by it that she didn't notice the guy standing behind her eyeing her like a snack. She wore a curve-hugging black minidress like the ones En Vogue wore in the "Hold On" video. She had searched for it for weeks. She looked incredible in it, and the guy behind her couldn't hide his appreciation.

"Pardon me, Ma," he said, as he slid in behind her and grabbed a plate. As he leaned forward, he grabbed a good handful of her ass as well.

Chanel jumped, turned around, and glared at him.

"Yo, don't touch me!"

"Excuse me," he said, feigning innocence. "I'm just trying to get something to eat. I apologize."

"You grabbed my ass. The food ain't down there," Chanel yelled back defiantly.

Judah frowned and pulled her toward him protectively. "What happened?"

"He grabbed my butt!" Chanel pointed at her assailant.

Judah looked at the guy and he stared back at him, bemused. "Yeah, I grabbed it. What?"

The crowd around them gasped. Some people began backing up and muttering among themselves.

Judah was stuck for a moment that felt like an eternity. He wasn't sure what to do. He didn't have long to consider it, though. Deon appeared out of nowhere and hooked the guy in the jaw with a punch so hard the deejay stopped the music.

"THAT'S what, muthafucka!" Deon followed that punch up with a flurry of others, uppercuts and right hooks. All the maneuvers he had learned in juvie from the dudes from Brooklyn, Queens, and the Bronx. He swung until he stood over the guy crumpled on the floor.

Security and all of the adults present converged on the scene trying to break up the fight. The guy had gotten up and his friend was at his side. Together, they tried to grab Deon, both of them yelling threats as security held them back.

"Yo, that's that same muthafucka from a few weeks ago."

"I swear the next time I see you, you're dead. Word is bond."

Deon didn't respond, just kept glaring at them as bigger men than him tugged him toward the door.

The birthday girl was crying while her father, uncles, and godfather grabbed the two dudes from New Brighton and dragged them out the back. Chanel and Barbara rushed Judah and Deon to the exit. Somehow in the melee, Chanel had lost one of her shoes. Barbara got one of her brothers to drive them home. Soon the four of them were packed into a two-door car speeding back to Mariners Harbor.

Barbara looked at the three of them in the backseat. Chanel's makeup was ruined and she had never recovered her shoe. Deon was still huffing in the backseat high off adrenaline. Judah stared out the window in silence.

"Y'all alright?" Barbara asked.

Chanel was the only one who nodded in the affirmative.

When they got back to their building, Barbara watched as Chanel gave Judah a kiss on the cheek. She watched as Judah and Deon went into their apartment and locked the door. And she thanked God she had been there to get Mercy's boys home safe that night. She hugged Chanel and together they entered their own apartment, exhausted.

The boys were tired, too. Deon got in the shower and stayed in there longer than usual. He was furious, still operating off adrenaline and anxiety. Seeing his cousin disrespected like that in front of all those people had enraged him. He stood under the stream of hot water with his eyes closed, breathing deeply.

Judah lay on his back on top of his bed, staring up at the ceiling. He replayed the events of the night over and over again in his mind. The disrespect of having his girlfriend's ass grabbed right in front of him, the feeling in his chest when the guy bucked at him and dared him to do something. The moment he froze and tried to decide whether to fight or look like a pussy in front of his girl. It was a bigger decision than that, he realized. In that moment, what he faced was a choice between taking a stand or laying down.

But Deon had saved him from that decision. He came out of nowhere and defended Chanel. Defended Judah, too. He wasn't sure how to feel about it, wondered, too, what Chanel thought about it.

When Deon finally emerged from the shower and came into the room, Judah looked at him.

"Thank you for what you did. Good looking out." It was all he could manage. But within those words were so many more sentiments. *Thank you for stepping up and fighting my battle. Thank you for not being afraid like I was.*

Deon nodded, understanding the words unspoken.

"You ain't gotta thank me, Judah. We family."

He walked over and slapped five with his cousin. They held their hands clasped together for several poignant seconds before finally letting go and calling it a night.

CRUEL SUMMER

Judah wasn't sure why the situation unsettled him as much as it did. In the aftermath of the party, he had barely been able to think about much else. He felt like he had been emasculated and he was embarrassed by it.

Chanel seemed to sense Judah's uneasiness about what happened at the party. He avoided making eye contact when they met up the day after. She did her best to reassure him that she didn't hold it against him.

"I'm glad none of us got hurt last night. Guys like that just like to start shit for no reason. I would never give a fool like them the time of day."

Judah seemed to lighten up about it, though Chanel knew it was a sore spot for him. Deon didn't bring it up either. His discretion about it was more motivated by his desire not to disappoint Aunt Mercy.

Barbara had told Mercy about the incident at the party, though. While they shared some of Mercy's bread pudding and a bottle of wine, Barbara gave her the rundown. Mercy shook her head, frustrated. She was sick of something going wrong with Deon every time she tried to loosen the reins a little. She had been apprehensive about letting him go to the party in the first place. Now he had caused a scene and gotten ushered out of it. But hearing how the events had unfolded, she also couldn't help but feel relieved that Deon had been there. It sounded like Judah was in over his head and things could have gotten even uglier. Mercy just prayed the whole thing went away without further incident.

On the last Friday in July, Mercy left for work and said goodbye to Judah and Deon. She had a strange feeling in her gut that day that she couldn't shake. A sense of dread that she couldn't explain. She attributed it to the new supervisor she had at work and reminded herself that it was Friday, at least. The weekend would provide two solid days of rest and relaxation.

"Do me a favor please? Straighten up your room today so that tomorrow I can dust and mop in there. And don't leave dishes in the sink."

"We got it, Ma." Judah kissed her goodbye.

"See you later, Aunt Mercy." Deon waved at her as she walked out the door.

When she was gone, Judah scarfed down a bowl of cereal while watching a show about a man who tamed tigers. Deon watched a few minutes of it and shook his head.

"That muthafucka's crazy."

Judah laughed. He watched Deon put his shoes on.

"Where you off to? I thought you were off work today."

"'Bout to go to Keisha's house. She told me her mother leaves for work at eight." He grinned at Judah.

Judah set his cereal bowl down.

"Chanel's cousin Keisha? From the party?"

Deon nodded. "Turns out she liked what she saw that night. She was like, 'Not too many niggas stand up to Luv and Dre like that.'" Deon mimicked Keisha's voice as he recounted her words.

"You're crazy. Why would you even fuck around with her knowing she's cool with them fools? For all you know she could be setting you up."

The look on Deon's face let Judah know that the thought hadn't even occurred to him.

"I thought you said you were trying to stay out of trouble. Sounds like you're running right toward that shit to me."

Deon thought about it. He put his shoes down and sat back on the couch.

"Aight. You got a point. I don't know shorty like that. So, I'ma chill."

Judah nodded. "Ain't like she's the only chick out there."

Deon shrugged.

"I'm not even feeling her like that, to be honest with you. I just wanted to fuck her so I could laugh in that clown's face the next time I see him."

Judah laughed, and together they watched the crazy tiger tamer do his thing.

It was later that afternoon when all hell broke loose.

Deon decided to go to the Big Park to play some basketball. He had to get out of the house because of a combination of heat exhaustion and boredom. He asked Judah if he wanted to come along.

"Yeah," Judah said. "I'll whoop your ass on the court. I'm gonna stop by Chanel's real quick. Then I'll meet you out there."

They left the apartment together. Deon waited for the elevator while Judah walked down the hall to Chanel's place.

"Don't get lost in the pussy and forget about me," Deon joked as he boarded the elevator.

"Whatever." Judah laughed as Chanel opened the door and ushered him inside. She stuck her tongue in his mouth the second he crossed the threshold.

"Damn," he muttered, as he came up for air. "Somebody's happy to see me."

Downstairs, Deon walked out of the building dribbling his basketball. He squinted his eyes against the brightness of the sun as he walked toward the park. He had only taken a few steps before he ran into Keisha. She frowned as he approached.

"I thought you were coming over this morning," she said, getting right to the point.

"I got caught up," Deon said. "Had some shit I had to handle. My bad."

"Mm-hmm." She rolled her eyes. "You don't have time to come and see me, but you have time for basketball." She nodded toward the ball in his hand.

He grinned guiltily. "It ain't even like that. I'm telling you, I was on my way over there this morning and my cousin needed me to handle something for him." He looked her over from head to toe, his eyes lingering on her thick thighs accentuated by the tiny shorts she wore. "Where you going now? You should come upstairs with me. I got the crib to myself."

She looked toward the building then back at him. "Your cousin ain't home?"

Deon shook his head. "He's with *your* cousin. Doing all the nasty things me and you should be doing right now."

Keisha smiled. "Okay, let's go."

Deon turned around to lead the way.

"KEISHA!" a deep voice boomed behind them.

Deon and Keisha turned at the same time to see Luv and Dre—the two goons from New Brighton—charging in their direction.

"What you want, Luv? I told you to leave me alone," Keisha yelled, backing up toward the building in fear.

Deon could sense her nervousness and smiled at her reassuringly. "Relax, Ma. These muthafuckas are in *my* hood now. What's popping?"

Deon got into fighting stance ready to box it out with both

of them. A car screeched to a halt at the curb and three more New Brighton guys piled out of it. Deon spotted them charging in their direction with baseball bats. His heart raced in his chest.

"LUV, STOP! Leave him alone!" Keisha was pleading as the guys encircled Deon. He was outnumbered and none of them were backing down.

Deon laughed maniacally. "All of y'all against me? It's like that?"

Dre spit at him. "Where your people at?" he asked, looking around. "This is your hood, right?"

He punched Deon in the face, and the two of them began fighting viciously.

Keisha ran into the building frantically, and charged up the stairs two at a time headed for Chanel's apartment.

Deon tussled with Dre, but it wasn't long before he felt the force of blows coming from every direction as they piled on him. The first crack of the bat hit him in the jaw, and he felt several teeth come loose. The impact rocked him, sending him falling backwards onto the concrete. Then all he felt were feet, fists, and more ruthless blows from the bat as he cowered on the ground.

Judah had Chanel pressed against the wall in her living room with one leg up on the arm of the couch. He kissed her as his hands worked magic with her pussy. Chanel moaned, grinding her hips against him with her eyes closed. Judah's dick was hard as a rock.

The pounding on the front door snapped both of them out of the trance they were in. Chanel's eyes flew open and she rushed to answer it. Keisha was there crying and speaking desperately between gasps for air.

"JUDAH! YOUR COUSIN IS DOWNSTAIRS GETTING JUMPED . . . LUV AND DRE . . . THEY'RE CRAZY . . . THEY GOT BATS AND A WHOLE BUNCH OF GUYS FROM NEW BRIGHTON WITH THEM . . ."

Judah's heart thundered in his chest and he went into some type of autopilot. He rushed out the door then stopped dead in his tracks, frozen by fear. Trembling, he turned back around and rushed into Chanel's bedroom.

Chanel looked at Keisha, shaking now.

"They look like they're gonna kill him, Chanel."

Chanel was crying now, too. She hugged Keisha and watched in shock as Judah emerged from her bedroom holding the gun in his hand that he had retrieved from her dresser drawer.

"JUDAH!" she cried out as he rushed past her. "Don't do this!"

But Judah was already rushing down the stairs, scared to death of what he would find when he got down there. He got to the lobby and could hear the commotion before he even reached the door. A large crowd had gathered watching as Luv and Dre took turns beating Deon with bats while their friends held everyone at bay, daring anyone to intervene.

Judah emerged from the building and held the gun up. The crowd began to scatter.

His hands were shaking as he approached the fight. He felt the same nervousness he felt at the party. But this time he wasn't going to lay down. Not when Deon's life was on the line. He could feel the pounding of his heart in his chest, but he pushed himself forward.

"BACK UP OFF MY COUSIN!"

Luv was mid-swing with his bat. He dropped it as Judah approached with the gun.

"Oh, it's like that?" Luv smirked, aware that this kid was scared.

Judah fought to steady his hands.

Dre still stood over Deon, who was lying unconscious on the pavement. His face and clothes were bloody, and several witnesses were crying and asking if Deon was already dead. Judah felt like crying, screaming, running, fighting, all at the same time. He aimed the gun at Dre.

"Back up off of him," he repeated again.

Dre laughed. "You ain't gonna use that shit. With your bitch-ass." He remembered Judah from the party. Remembered the way he looked like a deer caught in headlights when Dre grabbed his girl's ass right in Judah's face. He looked Judah dead in his eye and spat on the ground, grinning. Dre swung the bat high up over his head and brought it down on Deon with all his might. But he never got to make that final deadly blow. Dre heard a loud crack that seemed to echo in his ears, and everything faded to black.

As the gunshot rang out, the crowd scattered, running and screaming in every direction as the bullet pierced Dre's body and he fell to the ground with a thud. All of Dre's friends deserted him, hauling ass back to their car as Judah stood with the smoking gun in his hand.

He felt sweat dripping down his face and thought for a moment that he might pass out. Chanel was at his side, pushing him back toward the building, urging him to run. He could feel himself moving, could hear commotion behind him. But all of the sounds were distorted. Screams, Chanel's voice, Keisha crying, sirens, and then he was running up the stairs, rushing into his apartment, hurrying to hide the gun in his closet.

Chanel was having a panic attack.

"Judah . . . oh, my God . . . they're gonna know. Everybody saw you."

Judah rushed back out the door. Chanel was hot on his trail.

"Where are you going?" she called, running after him.

"Deon!" was all Judah could say as he flew down the stairs, leaping in an effort to get to his cousin's side. He prayed that he was still alive as he ran out the lobby door and into a scene even more chaotic than the one he had just left.

One group of paramedics crouched around Deon's body, while another rushed Dre on a gurney to a nearby ambulance.

"Is he alive?" Judah called out. He heard people whispering that it was him, as he felt Chanel tugging at his arm. But his focus was on Dre's motionless body as the paramedics tried to revive him. "DEON!" Judah called out, fighting back tears.

Police were there now with their guns aimed at him. Judah felt the tears pour forth then. He raised his hands in the air, sadly aware that in that moment he was surrendering all hope.

FALLEN

Mercy was beside herself and inconsolable. Judah was under arrest, charged with second degree murder. Deon was hospitalized—brought into the emergency room at the hospital where she worked, strapped to a gurney surrounded by detectives. Chanel had called her mother and alerted Barbara to what happened. That Deon had gotten jumped, that Judah had shot one of the assailants in defense of Deon and was now facing fifteen years in jail.

Barbara held vigil at the hospital with Deon while Mercy rushed to the precinct to see about her son. Deon had been punched and beaten repeatedly in the face, head, and body with a bat. The doctors spoke of contusions, lacerations, and broken bones. Barbara was just grateful that Deon was going to survive. His recovery would be painful, but at least she could give Mercy some good news. Her nephew would be okay.

Judah was another story. The scene at the precinct was contentious. The D.A. had witnesses at the scene who had IDed Judah and who were willing to testify. They had searched Mercy's apartment—trashing it in the process—and found the gun stashed in a coat pocket in the back of Judah's closet. Judah was being charged as an adult with second degree murder.

Mercy asked to see her son, and the police stalled her at every turn. Frustrated, she sat in a hallway and cried. She had never felt so alone in her life.

Judah was emotionally and physically exhausted. The police had grilled him for hours about where he had gotten the gun. He told them he found it in the park weeks earlier and kept it for protection. It was a lie, of course. But there was no way he could tell them that he had swiped it from Chanel, who was holding it for her drug-dealing brother. As he sat now in the cold and dank bowels of the police precinct, he replayed that decision over and over in his head. Why had he gone to get that gun?

The moment he heard that Deon was in trouble, a switch had flipped in Judah's mind. His worst fear was feeling as helpless as he had the night of Keisha's party. When Dre had challenged him, weakened him, made him feel small. In that moment, he had imagined his cousin surrounded, feeling hopeless and outnumbered. And Judah had asked himself what he should do.

Go help him.

The voice in his mind had been clear. But, crippled by fear, he had frozen again. He knew he couldn't fight a gang of New Brighton dudes by himself.

Get that gun.

Again, his thoughts were so loud in his head. Seconds had ticked by, though it felt like it all happened so quickly. His feet were moving down the hall, he was in the room, grabbing the gun from the drawer. Even as he held it in his hand and headed back for the front door, he told himself that he would just wave it around. Scare them all off. He heard Chanel protest, felt himself push past her, saw the look of horror on Keisha's face. And still he had run down those stairs like he was the one whose life hung in the balance. As Deon took a physical beating in front of the building, Judah was getting an emotional beatdown as he rushed to his defense. All he wanted was to save Deon's life.

He thought about his mother as he stepped outside and waved the gun at the guys beating Deon. When Judah raised the gun, he saw the looks on the faces of the people who had gathered to watch the fight. People he had seen around the neighborhood countless times. They looked shocked, and disappointed, and afraid. He knew that if Mercy were there, she would have been disgusted.

But then Deon's attackers were laughing at him. Saying he wouldn't do anything. Until that second, Judah had no intention of hurting anyone. But then Dre had raised his arms again, threatened to hit Deon again, right in front of him. The smile on Dre's face as he prepared to bring the bat down one last time was what sent Judah over the edge. He squeezed the trigger without hesitation, catching Dre in the chest right before he could land the blow.

Judah knew he was in trouble now, though. He had asked for a lawyer and for a phone call and had been provided with neither so far. He was hungry and tired, and no one would give him an update on his cousin's condition. Quietly, alone in a room and at his wits' end, Judah prayed.

In the wee hours of the morning, Judah was given a court-appointed attorney. Mercy was allowed to see him for a few brief minutes before they told her to come back to court in the morning for his arraignment. She left the precinct in a daze. Tommy came to pick her up. He gave her the news that Deon was going to recover. She seemed only mildly relieved as he took her home and got her settled in. She lay in bed in the fetal position and cried herself to sleep while he held her.

The next morning, Mercy was the first one up. She hadn't slept much at all. She had been up thinking, planning, trying to figure out what to do next. As the sun rose that morning, she remembered the envelope full of money Benny had given her after Lenox died. Mercy had never spent a dime of that money. She had been saving it for Deon, thinking of it as some sort of inheritance Lenox's sacrifices had left behind. She grabbed that money now and held it tucked beneath her arm as she dialed a criminal attorney. She knew that a paid lawyer would do more for her son than one appointed by the state, who was likely friends with the prosecution.

She went to the attorney's office that morning and paid him a $10,000 retainer in cash. He went to see Judah right away.

Judah told his attorney everything he could. He stuck to his story about finding the gun in the park.

"It was in the bushes. I saw the handle sticking out of a plastic bag. I thought it was a toy at first until I picked it up."

"Why'd you take it home?"

"My cousin got in a fight a few weeks ago with the same guys. They had been threatening him. Threatening me. So, I just thought I should hold on to it just in case."

His attorney didn't seem to buy it. But Judah wasn't changing his story.

All the rest of what he told his lawyer and the detectives assigned to the case was true. He had acted in defense of his cousin's life.

In court the next day, Judah's lawyer argued that his client had no prior involvement with law enforcement of any kind.

"Judah Howard is an honor roll student headed for Morgan State University. Not a murderer as the prosecution would have you believe."

The prosecutor agreed. Judah had been a model citizen until July 31, 1992.

"On that date, Your Honor, the defendant grabbed an illegal high-powered handgun and fired it in broad daylight in full view of children and elderly people. On that date, Judah Howard killed a young man who was not posing a threat to the defendant in any way."

The judge set Judah's bail at a quarter of a million dollars and sent him to Rikers Island. Mercy cried so loudly in the courtroom that Judah had to fight back tears himself.

His lawyer explained that he was facing a Class A felony—

murder. But he was going to talk to the D.A. about getting the charge knocked down to manslaughter—a Class B felony with a lesser sentence. Judah asked what his chances were. His lawyer's face told him it was a long shot.

Arriving at Rikers for the first time was the scariest experience of Judah's life. Like all New Yorkers, he had heard horror stories about the place. And from the second he arrived there, he knew it would live up to its terrible reputation.

The place was filthy and smelled like mold, sweat, and a thousand grimy men. When the bus arrived, they were unloaded into a holding pen packed with men from all five boroughs. They waited to be processed, assigned a dorm, and moved to their new confines for the foreseeable future. When he was arrested, Judah had on a pair of basketball shorts, a T-shirt, and a pair of Nike sneakers. Now, standing in the pen with a rowdy group of criminals, he realized that the clothes he wore could make him a target.

He found a corner and got comfortable, squatting down on the floor since all the benches were filled up. A few dudes got into arguments that escalated into tussles over coveted seats on the benches. Judah looked around, careful to avoid making eye contact with anyone who might misinterpret it as aggression. Judah watched one kid in particular who was clearly as scared as he was. In fact, the kid looked so afraid that Judah checked himself, maybe overcompensating a bit just to ensure that he didn't appear as timid as that guy. The kid was tall and thin, with a cut on his face. His eyes darted around the room as he paced back and forth. He stood with his hands in his pockets now and shifted his weight from one foot to the other nervously. It wasn't long before one of the more seasoned inmates spotted him, as he stood out like a sore thumb.

"Yo, Slim! You got them new Tommy Hilfiger boxers on. Hand them shits over."

Bellows of laughter broke out along with shouts and taunts as the other inmates reacted to the demand.

The skinny kid shook his head, laughing. "Nah. I got 'em on right now. I know you don't want a pair of used drawers."

Oohs erupted, along with laughter and more banter among the inmates. The larger, more menacing inmate stepped closer to the skinny one.

"I look like I'm laughing, nigga? Take them shits off. They mine now."

Seconds ticked by like a time bomb. The skinny kid hesitated too long and was met with a loud smack to the face. It knocked him to the ground, where the beating continued. Judah looked around, waiting for the guards to come rushing in to break it up. The level of noise was surely enough to alert them that something was happening. But no guards came. The fight only ended when a few of the more seasoned inmates broke it up themselves.

The aggressor stripped the now bloody and beaten skinny dude down to his socks. He took his underwear, his sneakers, and his T-shirt, leaving him with nothing but his shorts balled up next to him as he groaned on the floor.

In another corner of the large room, a group of men shouted at a guy they had just robbed of his designer labels. The guy was stripped down to his boxers and crying as they forced him to stand in a piss-soaked toilet with his bare feet.

Judah was sickened by all of it. He stared down at the floor, praying that this was some type of nightmare that he would wake up from. It felt like the place was full of animals running around wildly with no consequences. He felt like he had been plunged into hell.

He dozed off for a while as he sat crouched in the corner for hours. He awoke to the awareness of a presence very close to him. He opened his eyes and found that a guy he had never seen before had squeezed himself into the corner next to Judah. He had his foot side by side with Judah's, sizing their feet up.

"What size are you? Ten or eleven?" The guy grinned. "Let me try 'em on."

Judah looked at him, aware that this would be his first test. He remembered the stories Deon told him about his days at Spofford. How dudes sized up each other's feet before robbing them for their sneakers. This guy questioning Judah's shoe size was demanding that Judah hand over his kicks or prepare to fight.

Judah got right on his feet. The guy was up, too, and it was on. Summoning all his strength, Judah hit him hard, aware that this was what Deon had described as "gladiator school." It was a place he never imagined he would find himself. But now that he was here, he knew that this was his dreaded moment in the center of the arena when he would have to fight for his life. With all the power he could muster, Judah fought for more than his sneakers. He fought to survive.

Meanwhile, for Mercy the time went by so slowly that she felt like she was being tortured. Deon was released from the hospital. But the family of the guy Judah killed was threatening to kill him when they saw him. Mercy lost weight, barely sleeping as she sat up at all hours of the night worrying that she would lose Judah and Deon for good.

Tommy was by her side as much as possible. He took days off work to go with her to Judah's court dates. He held her as she cried for her son and listened as she expressed her fears and even her resentment for Deon.

"I know it's not his fault," she said to Tommy one night in the darkness of her bedroom. "But I can't help thinking that there's no way Judah would have grabbed that gun and ran down there like that if . . ." She shook her head and closed her eyes. The "if" too unbearable to say out loud.

Mercy sobbed into her pillow. Sometimes the tears snuck up on her during the day, flooding her eyes as her heart broke over and over again for her son.

Deon heard her cries. During sleepless nights in the bedroom he once shared with Judah, he lay awake listening to Mercy's torment. He was wracked with guilt.

He found it difficult to remain under Aunt Mercy's roof. There was a tremendous gulf between them. Their conversations were brief and terse.

"Deon, come and eat dinner," she'd say. They would eat in silence with only the droning of the television to break the tension. After they ate, Deon dutifully washed dishes, took out the trash, and tried to assume the role Judah had once played. The role of a responsible "son" who would do anything to ease her pain.

Deon believed that all of it was his fault. If he hadn't gone to the party with Judah and Chanel, maybe he never would have fought with Luv and Dre. If he had never gone to New Brighton to mess around with Ayana, he never would have had beef with them dudes to begin with. If he had never become a burden on Judah and on his Aunt Mercy, none of them would be in the situation they found themselves in now.

Deon confided in Chanel. She stopped by on Fridays after school to bring him his schoolwork. He was still recovering from his injuries and wasn't attending class in person. She lingered there when she came, looking around at Judah's things.

"Can I have one of his T-shirts?" she asked sadly one Friday. "I want to sleep in it. I miss the smell of him." Her voice cracked as she spoke. "I know it sounds dumb."

Deon sat on the edge of his bed with his shoulders slumped. "Not dumb at all. It ain't the same without him here." He looked at her, watched her walk around touching Judah's things with sadness and longing. "This is my fault," he said. "He should have let them kill me."

Chanel shook her head. "He got the gun from my room," she pointed out. "If it wasn't there . . . if Dallas never brought that shit in our house in the first place! What if I had thrown myself in front of Judah? He wouldn't have pulled the trigger if he knew I could get hurt. I've been blaming myself, too."

They locked eyes, understanding their shared anguish and regret.

"It's not your fault," Deon said.

"It's not yours either. And it's not Judah's fault. It's this fucked-up place we live in."

Deon shrugged. "Judah was doing everything right. If I wasn't here and he didn't have to get involved in my bullshit, he would have never got in any trouble. I'm the problem in this family." He looked at her and shook his head. "I gotta get out of here. Get away from them so they can have some peace."

Chanel stared at him. "This ain't your fault," she said. "You went outside and got jumped by a bunch of animals that tried to kill you. You were unconscious and Judah tried to save your life. Blaming yourself is a waste of time." She folded Judah's T-shirt carefully and hugged it close to her chest. "But I understand what you mean about wanting to get out of here. I do, too. Nothing feels like it used to anymore. All the plans we made are ruined now. And I don't know how much more I can take."

He nodded. "Thanks for listening," he said.

"Thanks for the shirt."

Judah was housed in Rikers C-74 adolescent confinement unit. The place was a zoo, overcrowded and understaffed. Judah was confined in "the box," a solitary confinement cell that consisted of a bed, a sink, a toilet, and a metal door with a small window. That window was the slot his food came through at mealtime. It was also the passageway mice and roaches used to enter and exit the cell.

The walls were grimy and streaked with blood and caked-up shit. It got so hot in there sometimes that the floor and walls sweated and Judah lay on the floor in his underwear to cool down. He was in the box for thirty days before they released him into general population. He learned how to maneuver through the mess hall without provoking a problem. It had quickly become clear to him that the place was full of cliques. Brooklyn ran together. Queens, the Bronx, and Harlem were the same way. But Staten Island was grossly underrepresented on Rikers Island. The minute other inmates found out that's where he was from, he had a mark on his back. They considered him soft, or at the very least isolated. He had no clique, no crew. And for that reason, Judah had to fight all the time.

In late August, Mercy came to visit him. She brought Deon and a letter from Chanel with her. Chanel had wanted desperately to come along on this visit. But Judah had asked his mother not to bring her. Mercy wasn't sure why, but she honored his wishes.

Tommy had prepared for the visit, warning her that she had to be tough for her son. Her performance in the courtroom at his arraignment had obviously shaken him. Tommy explained to Mercy that it was hard enough to face incarceration without the added burden of hearing your mother wailing in the background.

So, Mercy steeled herself as she sat down in the visiting room and waited to see her son. She prayed silently that she would be able to handle whatever came her way. Those prayers came in handy when Judah finally emerged. She understood immediately why he hadn't wanted Chanel to come to see him today. One of his eyes was black and swollen and beet red inside. It looked like the left side of his face had been beaten by something or someone far more powerful than Judah could handle. Despite his disfigured face, Judah smiled at his mother and cousin as he sat down.

"Hey, family!"

Mercy stared back at him, her expression pained.

"Judah . . . are you okay?" Her eyes searched his face, lingering on each bruise, each scar and scratch.

He shrugged.

"I'll be better when they lower my bail. Any word on that?"

Mercy shook her head. She didn't have the money to pay his bail or the money to hire a decent lawyer. Judah was facing a minimum of fifteen years with a subpar attorney representing him. Mercy had never felt so powerless in her life.

Deon could barely look at his cousin. He had an overwhelming sense that it should be him in there fighting for his life instead of Judah.

Judah sensed his family's anguish and sat forward in his seat.

"It might not look like it. But I'm holding my own in here. All I need is for you to get in touch with my lawyer. Tell him to get the charges reduced and I'll plead to manslaughter."

Mercy balked. "Judah, are you crazy? If you plead guilty to manslaughter, you'll be facing a minimum of five years."

He nodded, having resigned himself to his fate by that point.

"I read up on it. Got a pass to the library and did all the research. Ma, I did it. People saw me. They got the gun. I'm going to jail regardless."

"Don't say that!" Mercy admonished him.

"If I take it to trial and lose, I'm finished. I don't have a good lawyer, don't have a good defense. We have to face reality. If I take a plea deal, I can be home in five years instead of fifteen."

Mercy forgot everything she promised Tommy and cried openly then. She had been in denial up until that point. Hopeful that somehow the judicial system would see that the whole incident had been a fluke. Some freak accident that happened as the result of a twisted set of circumstances that put her good son on the wrong side of the law.

Deon wanted to comfort this aunt, but worried that she wouldn't want him to touch her in that moment. He looked at Judah, finally.

"I should be in there. Not you. And if I gotta kill one of them muthafuckas to get locked up so I can fight it out with you in there, then so be it. I don't give a fuck no more."

Judah felt all the rage he had been suppressing bubble up to his throat. He gritted his teeth and glared at Deon.

"You better give a fuck! If both of us are in here, who's looking out for my mother?"

Deon felt more guilt wash over him, different this time. He hadn't thought about it like that.

"Stop trying to make yourself feel better about this shit, Deon. It is what it is. I did what I did. Even if I wanted him to, the judge isn't gonna let you do the time for me. And if you go to jail, what's the point of all these years my mother's been working her ass off for us? To keep us out of here."

Deon felt emotional and fought to keep control.

"I'm ready to face the penalty for what I did. I took somebody's life, whether it was justified or not. Everything that's happening to me is because of the decision I made to pull that trigger. So, both of y'all stop feeling sorry for yourselves. Stop feeling sorry for me. Just get my lawyer in here." He sat back, exasperated. He looked at Deon, gesturing with his hands as he spoke. "I need you to act right for the next few months, D. You'll be sixteen soon. Get your GED like we talked about. Remember that?"

Deon did remember. It was a conversation he replayed often in his head these days.

Judah continued. "Get your license and call Xavier. You remember when we were kids he used to talk to us all the time about his job. You could get in touch with him and he can help you get a job driving trucks from state to state. Live your life, Deon. And I'll catch up with you when I get out of here."

Deon stared down at the table, choked up. This was never how things were supposed to play out.

Judah looked at his mother, tenderly.

"And you can stop worrying about us. You did the best you could. None of this is your fault. If I keep my head down and keep some money on my books so I can maneuver in here, I'll be alright."

Mercy nodded. She asked him what items he needed, and he rattled off a short list of things she could send him right away. She made a mental note of all of it.

"Tell Chanel I'm gonna write to her. I have some things I want to say. And I don't want to say them over the phone."

Mercy and Deon nodded.

Judah looked at both of them sadly.

"You don't have to come back up here to see me. I know it's a long trip and you gotta go through a lot with the guards and all of that. Just write to me. I read your letters so many times I practically memorize them."

Mercy promised that she would.

"I love you, Judah," she said softly.

"I love you, too, Ma. I swear I do."

LETTING GO

November 3rd, 1992

Dear Chanel,

Thank you for all the letters you've sent me over the past few months. I'm not always good with writing back. A lot goes on in here and I don't always have the time to focus long enough to sit down and write all the things I need to say to you. But today I made time.

I want to start by saying that I miss you. I have your pictures up on my wall and I think about you every day. I picture you sitting in class, twirling your pencil like you do when you're focusing. I remember all the things we did when we were alone. I wish we had the chance to make it all happen like we planned. But I made a choice that fucked it all up. Now I have to pay the price.

By now I'm sure my mother told you that my lawyer was able to convince the D.A. to agree to a plea deal. They got a bunch of letters from my teachers like Mrs. Bristow, the deans, and all my counselors saying that I was one of the best students they ever had and that I made an error in judgment that shouldn't cost me my life. My lawyer brought up Dre's criminal history in court and highlighted my clean record before this incident. The D.A. knocked the charge down to manslaughter in the first degree and the judge sentenced me to eight and a third to fifteen years instead. That means that even with time served, I won't be eligible for parole until at least seven and a half years from now.

By the time I walk out of here we'll be in our mid-twenties. By then, you'll be finished with college, living the life you talked about as a sports journalist. Hopefully, Deon will be doing alright. Maybe he'll get to live the life I left behind.

My mother is taking it pretty hard. She's not sleeping, hardly eating, and the last time I saw her it made me want to cry. She looks older than she is. I want her to be happy, too. I need her to stay strong while I'm gone.

I'm writing this letter to tell you not to wait for me. Just because my life changed that day doesn't mean yours has to. Don't waste valuable time worrying about me. These last couple of years of high school should be the best for you. I wish I was there to enjoy it with you. I'm sorry I won't be able to take you to prom or to do all the things we planned on doing afterwards. Those promises we made keep me going in here, Chanel. Imagining what it would have been like to take your prom dress off and feel you for the first time. I meant every word I ever said to you. You're the only girl I ever loved. So, don't see this letter as me breaking up with you. I would never do that. I'm just setting you free.

I'm sorry I did what I did that day. I want you to know that there was nothing you could have done to stop me. I blacked out, and I would have grabbed whatever I could get my hands on. The only person responsible for what happened that day is me.

When I get home in a few years, I'll look you up. Maybe we

*can pick up where we left off. If some lucky guy hasn't snatched
you up by then.*

   Don't forget me, though.

Love Always,

Judah

Chanel read the letter three times in a row and cried each time.
Judah sounded so hopeless, so at peace with his fate that it made her
sad. She carried it with her to school for the rest of her junior year.
She didn't bother applying to Morgan State. She had no desire to go
if Judah wasn't going with her. Instead, she was accepted to Delaware
State University. Her mother was thrilled that she was getting out
of New York City and the war zone that the crack epidemic had cre-
ated. Chanel was excited, too. But it was bittersweet. Without Judah,
none of it felt right. She wrote to him a few times but got no reply.

11/8/92

*Judah, I'm not leaving you. No matter what you say. I know
you're dealing with a lot right now. But I'm your girl. Now and
forever. Don't shut me out. Please write me back.*

Love Always, Chanel

11/23/92

*Judah, I cried at school today when the teacher asked us to write an
essay about thankfulness. I know I have a lot to be grateful for. But
without you here, I can't think, eat, or breathe. Please write me back.*

   I love you.

Chanel

Every week, she sent letters to him. Some of them were half a page. Others were three or four pages with writing on the front and back of the page. Judah read them all, studied them really. He used them to remind himself that he wasn't forgotten. Several times he started to write her back.

Chanel,

I got your letters and I don't want you to think that I'm not writing you back because I don't love you. The truth is I love you too much to put you through this. I'm fighting every day for my life. That sounds dramatic, but it's the truth. Every day I have to wake up prepared to defend myself against any threat. It's hard in here. Harder than I want to describe—

Chanel,

I miss you so much. I miss taking the bus to school with you, looking forward to seeing what you put on that day or how you did your hair. I miss the way you looked at me when you were happy about something. Sometimes I wish I never went back inside your apartment that day—

Chanel,

I feel so alone in here. This is worse than anything I ever imagined. I heard a song today that made me think about you. Remember when we were in your room that time and the song "Pretty Brown Eyes" came on? When I heard it today, for a minute I wasn't locked up in here. I imagined myself with you—

But he never finished writing any of those letters. Each time, he tore the paper up and threw it away. Too afraid to cling to any hope whatsoever. If he was going to survive the next few years in the hell he was in, he had to accept that Chanel was not going to put her life on hold and wait for him. Even if she wanted to, he felt selfish asking her to. She was too big for a life like the one he had sentenced himself to when he made the decision he made.

Back in Staten Island, Deon struggled to find his way after Judah's sentencing. Aunt Mercy was a wreck. She was gaunt and frail, as if the light had gone out of her. Work became the only constant in her life. When she wasn't at work, she was a shell of her former self. No laughter, no joy, no positive energy. She stayed in her bedroom, writing to Judah or putting together packages for him. She barely spoke to anyone except Barbara. Tommy began to come around less, and she barely seemed to notice. Deon struggled himself to bear the weight of what happened. Judah's lawyer had called it a crime of passion. That Judah had an emotional reaction to seeing his cousin being bludgeoned in front of him. Deon thought often about the events that led up to that moment and how he had continuously placed himself in the path of anarchy. If he hadn't gone outside that day. If he had made a million different choices, things might have been altogether different.

Deon was never able to shake the feeling that it should have been him behind bars instead of Judah. Hearing Aunt Mercy cry herself to sleep at night affirmed it for him. Deon was wracked with guilt, and it drove him to put a plan in motion. For once, he took Judah's advice verbatim.

He went in to speak with his aunt one afternoon as she lay on the couch with a blanket over her, watching TV.

"Hey, Aunt Mercy. You got a minute?"

She sat up. "Yeah. What's going on?" Her face looked weathered, like she hadn't slept well in a long time.

"Do you think I could reach out to Xavier? I know you two broke up years ago. But he used to talk to me and Judah about driving trucks. When I was younger, I barely listened to him. But now . . . I need something to do with my life. I think if I talk to Xavier, he might help me figure it out."

Mercy sighed. She forced a weak smile and nodded. "I'll call him."

As she waited for him to answer the phone, Mercy tried to recall the last time she had spoken to Xavier. She wondered if he was still with "Jennifer" and tried to ignore the jealousy that bubbled up inside of her at the thought.

"Hello?"

"Hey, Xavier. It's Mercy."

He hesitated. "I've been thinking about you," he said. "Haven't heard from you since . . . damn it's been years."

She was embarrassed to admit it.

"I tried calling you a couple times, but I never got an answer," he said. "I figured you got married and rode off into the sunset with somebody."

Mercy laughed. As she did, she realized it was one of the few times she had done so since Judah went away.

"I did find somebody," she said. "For a little while at least. But when the going got tough, he got going." She shook her head, thinking about Tommy.

"Tough?" Xavier questioned. He knew things had been hard enough for Mercy most of her life. "What happened?"

Mercy sighed deeply. "Where do I begin?"

She told him about running into Tommy and finding romance again. She recounted the events leading up to the fateful day—the party, the fight Deon had gotten into. Then she told him about the day that had changed their lives forever. As she told him about Judah's arrest, his sentencing, and her family's current state of affairs, Xavier sat on his sofa transfixed. It took him a while to find any words at all.

"Mercy . . . my God! Why didn't you call me?"

"I didn't want to bother you. You have a new life—"

"Fuck that! I'm in another relationship but we're still friends. You should have called me. This is . . ." Xavier wasn't sure why he was angry. "Mercy, this is too much for you to deal with on your own. I don't care what I got going on, I would drop everything for you and those boys. And I thought you knew that." Xavier was heartbroken for her.

Mercy felt guilty for not reaching out sooner. "I should have called. But I figured we had both moved on. The last thing I wanted to do was burden you with more of my problems. The fire, Lenox, Deon getting in trouble. I felt like calling you for this would just make you think I was bad luck or something." She chuckled, though she didn't find it funny. She was starting to wonder whether she had been born under a bad star.

"I don't think that," he said. "I know this is killing you."

"It is," she admitted. "But I have to stay strong for my son." She cleared her throat. "He hasn't changed, you know? He's still trying to make sure me and Deon are okay even while he's dealing with his own problems every day. He told Deon that he should contact you to see if you can give him some advice about getting in the trucking business. He wants to do what you do. Driving those big monsters around the country."

"I'll do anything to help you," he said. "Tell me the truth, though. Just so I know what I'm getting myself into. Is Deon still acting up? He still got that wild streak in him?"

Mercy was honest. "He's my nephew and I love him. But I'd be lying if I said that he's a saint. But since this happened to Judah, he hardly leaves the house unless it's for work. He seems like he's just ready to get out of here and start his life over."

"What about you, Mercy?" he asked, though he knew the answer already.

"I can't leave now. Even if I wanted to. I'm all Judah has. He's all I have, too." She shrugged. "Besides, *Jennifer* wouldn't want me hanging around. I'm sure of that."

He smiled. "She wouldn't even be around if you had said 'yes' to me. You'll always have my heart, Mercy."

She melted. "I guess you're home alone," she quipped.

He laughed. "I am." He thought about everything Mercy was going through and his laughter faded quickly. "How can I help you with Deon?"

Xavier listened as Mercy explained. Then she put Deon on the phone.

With Xavier's guidance, Deon took his GED and failed it the first time. The second time he passed. Next, he got his driver's license, then his CDL. Xavier referred him to a colleague who had a trucking company in southern New Jersey, and by his seventeenth birthday, Deon was on his own. An emancipated minor making money driving eighteen-wheelers up and down I-95.

He went in to speak with his aunt before he left. He felt awkward doing so. After Judah went away, Deon and Mercy had existed in the apartment in an odd cadence. Their relationship was tepid, their conversations minimal. So much remained unspoken between them that they both felt nervous as they sat down together in the living room that day.

"Aunt Mercy, I want to tell you that I'm sorry for everything I put you through. Even for all the things my mom put you through. I know that had nothing to do with me. But she was my mother and I know you loved her. Because you loved her, you loved me. Just as if I was your own child. You fed me, bought me clothes, helped me with school. And none of it was enough for me. But that's not your fault. It's mine."

Mercy hung on every word, her heart breaking with each syllable.

"You did the best you could for me. I was never rebelling against you. I just couldn't find a way to express the way I was feeling. And I was feeling really messed up. None of that was your fault. And it damn sure wasn't Judah's fault. I got him caught up in the situation he's in. I'll always blame myself. But starting now, I swear I'm gonna do everything right. No more bullshit. I'm gonna make you proud."

Mercy smiled.

"Deon, I'm already proud of you. You didn't always do what I wanted you to do. But I understood that losing your mother nearly broke you. So, you needed time to heal. I understand that more than ever now. Because losing Judah almost broke me. I imagine the hell that he's enduring every day and the life he could have had if—" Mercy shook her head sadly. "I'm just saying that I know what it's like to lose someone you love and get stuck in how unfair it is."

Deon nodded.

"I want you to know that your mother would be proud of you. You made it out of here. Alive. You got your diploma, a job, and a second chance, Deon. Don't waste it."

He hugged his aunt tightly and rushed out of there before she saw him cry.

While life at home went on without him, Judah awoke each day in Greene Correctional Facility to a battle zone. Fights breaking out were such a frequent occurrence that the sight of blood barely fazed him anymore. Almost daily, inmates waited for the chance to pounce on one another with homemade shanks and other crude weapons they managed to pillage. C.O.s took their time breaking it up, so inmates learned to sew up each other's wounds after fights. The reasons for the skirmishes varied. Blacks versus whites one day. Blacks versus Hispanics another day. Muslims versus the Aryans. It was always something. A constant game of dominance that none of them were really winning.

Judah learned to keep to himself. He enrolled in school, aware that the parole board was more likely to grant release to inmates who obtained their diploma during their incarceration. He passed the test with flying colors, then enrolled in a prison college program.

He took courses in law, sociology, and literature while other inmates marveled at his intellect.

"Yo, Einstein. Can you read this paperwork my lawyer gave me? What's all this shit mean?"

As the months went slowly by, Judah learned how to make himself useful to the other inmates and began to barter his intelligence for protection and favors. He found a way to occupy his time and avoid altercations most days. And when it was unavoidable, he learned how to fight and how to stand on his own two feet like a man. He was only seventeen years old, but the state of New York had deemed him a man. Looking around the prison compound, all he saw most days were kids forced to grow up way too quickly.

He woke up one morning in March of 1993 and felt a sadness unlike any other. For the whole day, he walked around the prison in a fog, barely responding to attempts at conversation. He kept to himself even more than he usually did. It was a Monday, so there were no visits. He thought about making a phone call but didn't feel like going through the drama of trying to get phone time. Instead, he sat in the TV room staring at the wall.

His cellmate noticed. He kept his distance until it was time for the count. As they stood in their cell waiting for the guard to mark them present, his cellmate turned to him.

"What's up with you, Howard?" He called Judah by his last name, as was the custom behind bars. "You been looking like somebody died today."

Judah shook his head. "Somebody was born," he corrected. "Today's my eighteenth birthday."

Stunned, his cellmate looked at him and smiled. "Yeah? Happy birthday!"

Judah nodded. "Thanks."

When the count was over, Judah sat on his bunk and reread the letters his mother, Deon, and Chanel had written to him. His cellmate walked over and handed him a Hostess cupcake wrapped in plastic.

"Happy birthday. For real. Keep your head up."

Judah forced a smile, took the cupcake, and thanked him. He unwrapped it and imagined that it was one of his mother's home-made cakes, fresh out the oven. His eyes filled with tears that he quickly wiped away as he took a bite.

Back in Staten Island, Chanel was forced to accept a new nor-mal. Her two best friends were gone—Judah to prison and Deon to start a life on his own. By her graduation in June of 1995, Chanel had given up hope that Judah would write back. Still, she sent him her graduation photo and a letter with her new address at college. It came back marked RETURN TO SENDER. Apparently, Judah had been moved to a different prison farther up north.

Through Mercy, she got updates on his movements. She knew that he was in a prison way upstate and that Mercy had to leave her home in the middle of the night to get the bus that traveled there. She knew that Judah had been in some fights and that he had got-ten a job at the prison he was in now. Mercy said that he still asked about Chanel every now and then. And when she urged him to write back to her, Judah would say, "I don't want to waste her time."

Chanel cried as she boarded the bus for college and waved good-bye to her mother. The promise of going away to a new school, mak-ing new friends, and starting over was exciting. But a special part of her would always remain in Staten Island. As the bus rolled on to-ward Delaware, she thought about everyone she was leaving behind and how much she would miss them. Judah, most of all.

Judah slowly began to adapt to life behind bars. He learned how to maneuver in this new world. It required a combination of physical and mental strength and dexterity. He kept to himself for the most part, but was careful to make friends that would prove beneficial to him in a crunch. Big dudes who could fight with him. Hustlers who got their hands on contraband and sold it for things like Kool-Aid packets, cigarettes, and canned goods. Judah didn't have to go to the mess hall anymore. His mother sent so much money that his commissary was always at capacity. He cooked for himself, using the recipes he learned from her when he watched her in the kitchen all those years. He didn't always have access to the same ingredients she had. But he made do with what he had. Even though he didn't have to go to the mess hall with the other inmates, he still went from time to time. He learned that in prison it was good to keep a low profile. But not too low. It was necessary to show your face and make your presence known. It was a carefully choreographed dance. One misstep could cost an inmate their life.

He got visits and letters from Nia, the girl he lost his virginity to in high school. She started writing to him back when he was on Rikers Island, and he wrote back to pass the time. Over the years, she kept in touch with him sporadically. Nothing consistent, since she was in an on-again, off-again relationship and had a kid. But it was enough to let him know that the whole world hadn't forgotten about him. And that felt good.

Judah learned to exist inside of a fantasy world in his mind. In that world, he was in college at Morgan State with Chanel. Deon was driving eighteen-wheelers and would stop by DC from time to time to see them. Mercy and Xavier were back together, and Aunt Lenox was alive and well. His soul felt untethered in that alternate reality. Even though he was locked up, whenever Judah traveled in his mind to that fantasyland, he was free.

He wrote letters to Chanel that he never sent. But he stopped tearing them up and throwing them away. Now he kept them in a corner of his cell. He intended to give them to her someday after he was released and they were finally reunited.

Chanel,

Sometimes I dream about you. You're always smiling at me, telling me that you love me and how much you missed me. Then I wake up and I'm still here.

Deon shows up in my dreams a lot, too. I see us as kids playing basketball or video games together in my room. I never tell anybody about this. Not even my mother. But I hate thinking about Deon. It's not his fault that I'm in here. But I hate the years that he took away from me. The years before I came to prison. After Aunt Lenox died and he came to stay with us, he spent so much time making our lives miserable. Getting arrested, getting high, stressing everybody out. All that time is gone forever. And being in here taught me how valuable time is.

I just want peace in my life. For once. And I want that for my mother, too.

I really miss you. Hopefully tonight I'll see you in my dreams.

Love,

Judah

Every month or so, his mother came to visit him. Those visits gave him a chance to let his guard down for a while. With her, he never had to posture or pretend. He was her baby for those few hours, and it felt like a breath of fresh air.

She came to see him on Christmas Day in 1997. It was the fifth year of his incarceration. Five years of holidays spent in a visiting room. No more home-cooked meals and beautifully wrapped presents. By now, they had established a new tradition. Mercy and Judah would arrive at the visiting table each Thanksgiving with a list of things they were grateful for, big and small. At Christmas their lists were of things they wanted to give to each other, whether it was realistic or not.

That year, Mercy was ready. Judah could tell from the moment he stepped into the room and saw her face lit up like a Christmas tree that she was excited about the list she had prepared. He smiled at her, relieved to see that she was looking more upbeat than the last time he had seen her. They hugged and he noticed she had lost more weight. He didn't mention it. She had told him during one of their recent phone calls that she hardly cooked anymore since she was alone all the time. She ate leftovers or made a quick soup or sandwich when she got hungry. He knew her loss of appetite was the result of all the worrying she did. But it was Christmas, she was in good spirits, and he pushed it to the back of his mind as he sat down.

"Merry Christmas! You got your list?" she asked.

He laughed. "Merry Christmas, Mama. Yeah. I got it. Right here." He tapped the side of his head.

She looked him over. No new scars since the last time she had seen him. No new tattoos either, thankfully. "You look good," she said. "You walked out here like a bodybuilder."

He thanked her. "Pull-ups every morning. I do my dips, sit-ups, and I lift weights in the yard sometimes. Helps me keep my mind occupied."

She frowned. "It's winter, Judah. Up here it's even colder than it is in the city. It's thirty degrees outside today. I know you don't go out there when it's cold like that."

"Sometimes I do," he admitted. "Not every day." He winked at her and smiled so she would relax. "Okay, so ladies first. What you got for me this year?"

Mercy stared at him lovingly. "I wish I could give you everything you ever dreamed of, Judah. You have been the best son a mother could ever ask for. Always. You weren't perfect. Nobody is. But you were the perfect son for me. You became my friend after all the things we went through. I remember all the times you asked me how I was doing, if I was okay, whether I needed anything. Sometimes it felt like you were the only one who cared. You've been that way your whole life toward everybody you love. That's why you're here."

Judah bit his lip as he listened.

"I thought about what I want to give you this year. The first thing is freedom. And I mean that in the literal way. But I also mean freedom from worrying about everybody else—me, Deon, the people out in the world who will judge you because of this." She gestured at their surroundings. "I want you to have the freedom to focus on yourself and on living the rest of your life to the fullest." She paused to dab at her eyes with a tissue she held in her hand before continuing. "Next thing I want to give you is strength." She looked him over, dramatically. "Not the physical kind because you don't need that."

He laughed.

"I want to give you mental strength to withstand everything life throws at you. Don't crumble. Stand tall. Don't use the pain you've been through as an excuse to give up. And don't use it as a weapon against anybody. Be strong enough to know that what happened to you had to happen. And know that you can handle *anything,* Judah. Anything!"

He nodded, too choked up to respond.

Crying softly, Mercy wiped her eyes again and blew her nose.

"The last thing I'm giving you this year is peace. I know it's crazy in here, Judah. I love you because you're so brave. So strong. You put on a smile and walk out here like nothing's wrong. But I know you keep a lot to yourself. You deserve peace. When you go back in there, and even when you step out of here, protect your peace. It's yours. You earned it."

Judah sat silently for several moments. He nodded a few times, looked around the room, and took a few deep breaths. He looked at his mother through flooded eyes and shook his head.

"Thank you. But damn. Now I don't even want to give you my list."

They both laughed, lightening the mood a bit. Judah wiped his eyes discreetly and exhaled before he began.

"Okay. The first thing is gratitude. I thank you all the time for the things you've done for me. But until I came in here, I don't think I realized how blessed I was that you're my mother. Some of these guys had no chance in life because of the childhood they had. Those home-cooked meals every night, the way you got up and went to work every day, kept the house clean, and listened to me when I had something to say. All of that was more than a lot of dudes had. Even now. I can tell you're tired. You don't feel good sometimes and you still come all the way up here to see me. We don't talk about my father a lot. But I know he walked out before I was born. So, it's just been me and you since the beginning. Deon could say the same thing about him and Aunt Lenox. But she was gone a lot. You were always there. Always taking care of me, Deon, all our friends. I can never thank you enough. But if I could, I would give you all the gratitude in the world."

She squeezed his hand across the table.

He cleared his throat. "Aunt Lenox," he said. "That's the other gift I would give you if I could." He knew it was impossible. But she would be the only person that could possibly comfort his mother now. "When she was alive, you two held each other up. You grounded her and she loosened you up. You need her now. To make you laugh, make you dance."

Mercy smiled, remembering.

"And the last thing I would give you this year is Tommy's phone number."

Mercy sucked her teeth.

"Ma, come on. Y'all had a good thing before all of this. You said he got impatient in the beginning. But a lot of time has passed now. You should call him and see what's up."

Mercy rolled her eyes. "I'm gonna have to give you that gift back," she said. She pushed an imaginary package back across the table in his direction. She sat back and sighed. "I called him around Thanksgiving to see how he's doing. He's living with some woman in Brooklyn now. She works for transit, too. So, with all due respect, fuck Tommy."

Judah agreed. "Yeah. Fuck that bum. I'll take back that gift. I'm giving you the keys to a mansion instead. Go furnish the place and set up a wing for me when I get out."

Mercy smiled from ear to ear. "Yeeeeaaah! Now *that's* more like it!"

WONDER

Deon stared at his reflection and saw a man he never thought he'd meet.

Once considered least likely to succeed, he somehow managed to defy all the odds. He couldn't believe the turn his life had taken. When he left New York, he had set out at first like a leaf on a breeze, blowing whichever way his truck route took him. He eventually settled in Philadelphia. The city held special significance to him knowing that his mother had found refuge there at a crucial point in her life. He got an apartment there where he stayed for two or three days at a time before he hit the road again in search of his next adventure.

He had kept a safe distance from his family. In fact, he kept to himself in general. He had convinced himself that he was a magnet for bad luck. He believed that getting too close to him could be toxic, so he kept people at a safe emotional distance. He called to check in on Aunt Mercy from time to time. He wrote letters to Judah and kept in contact with Xavier by telephone. He dated a few women, but nothing serious. He made a few friends but found it hard to maintain any real relationships with his demanding schedule. His life had become a far cry from the one he had lived in New York.

He sat around on his days off watching TV and doing laundry. He called his Aunt Mercy a few times a month and he stopped by whenever his truck route took him to the five boroughs. He never stayed for more than an hour, certain that the sight of him must be bittersweet for her. He knew she loved him. But he was a constant reminder of the son she had lost. He always brought her some money and left her with a warm and meaningful embrace.

It was a Sunday in the spring of 1999 when Deon got a call from Judah that shook him up. Over the years, Deon kept in touch with his cousin through letters. Judah called him at home on occasion. But they hadn't seen each other face-to-face in three years, not since Deon's last visit to see Judah up north.

Judah greeted his cousin like no time had passed at all.

"What up, Scarface? You still out there breaking hearts?"

Deon laughed.

"Judah, what's up, cousin? Good to hear your voice."

Judah held the phone as he leaned against the wall, chewing on a toothpick. He looked calm and casual to the average observer. But his eyes discreetly surveyed the scene around him. Leaning against the wall was more about staying on point than an attempt at relaxation.

"I'm hanging in there. Finish line is in sight. If I keep my act together, the parole board should have no problem letting me out of here in nineteen months."

Deon was happy that his cousin sounded optimistic. He did the math in his head, realizing that nineteen months amounted to just under two years. His heart sank.

"I spoke to my mother today," Judah continued. "She don't sound so good."

Deon frowned. "Really? I called her about a week ago. We talked for a while and she sounded fine." Deon recalled the conversation and realized that it was probably more like two or three weeks ago. Time had gone by quicker than he thought.

"She's been sick. She won't tell me too much about it. Just that she's going to the doctor and Miss Barbara next door checks in on her. But I wonder if there's shit she's not saying because she knows I'm in a fucked-up position right now."

Deon listened, his mind rewinding to his last conversation with Aunt Mercy. He nodded.

"I'll call her," he offered.

"Nah," Judah said. "I need you to go there. Drive to New York and check on her for me. I know it's asking a lot. But please. Do that for me."

Deon didn't hesitate. "I'm on my way."

He got to New York three hours later. Traffic had been light since he had left home at around seven o'clock that evening. Plus, it was a Sunday night so there were no rush hour commuters to contend with. Arriving in Staten Island, he drove slowly through the borough, reminiscing on the memories he had of various locations. The first fight he ever got into at the ferry terminal; the school he had been attending the day his mother brought him to school for the last time; the precinct he and Judah had been brought to before being shipped off to juvie or prison. Finally, he arrived at the Big Park adjacent to Aunt Mercy's building. The place held so many memories for Deon and they all came flooding back. He had come of age in this neighborhood, in this park. Being back there now felt so surreal.

He parked his Suburban and hopped out. As he strolled up the walkway to his aunt's building, he looked around to see what had changed about the neighborhood. Not much, apparently. The place looked the same as the last time he had seen it. No growth, evolution, or variation whatsoever.

He knocked on Aunt Mercy's apartment door and waited. No response came, so he knocked again and waited. It took a long time before he heard any movement inside the apartment. But soon he could hear the sound of slippers shuffling slowly toward the front door. He waited as he heard the peephole slide open, saw Mercy's eye pressed against the hole, and then heard her slowly begin to unlatch the locks on the doors. Finally, the door opened, and Deon stepped back at the sight of his aunt.

Mercy had lost a considerable amount of weight. She looked small and fragile, definitely less than one hundred pounds. Her eyes appeared sunken, and her skin hung from her body due to the drastic weight loss. She smiled at Deon and he wondered if it hurt her to move her face.

He could hardly find the words to greet her.

"Aunt Mercy! How you doing, Auntie?"

She opened her arms for a hug and he rushed into them. Her body was so thin that he could feel her bones even through the thick bathrobe she wore. She shut and locked the front door, then led him into the living room.

"Well, this is a surprise," she said. "I didn't expect a visit from you. Especially so late."

He sat down on the recliner. Mercy sat across from him on the couch.

Deon cleared his throat.

"I'm sorry for coming by so late, and for coming without calling. The whole thing was kind of last minute. I spoke to Judah today. He's worried about you, so he asked me to come and check on you."

Mercy sighed. "Judah's behind this, huh?"

Deon nodded.

"Now that I'm seeing you face-to-face, I can see why he was worried. He said he hasn't seen you in a while. He mentioned that you've been sick, but he said you haven't told him any details. So, I'm here now. And I'm looking at you with my own two eyes. You don't look like the Aunt Mercy I know. So, tell me what's going on with you. How long have you been sick?"

Mercy stared down at her hands resting in her lap guiltily. She was aware that her appearance had declined along with her health. She hardly recognized her own reflection in the mirror anymore.

"I didn't want to put more stress on Judah than he already has," she began. "He's been dealing with so much these past few years. And I know he's doing everything he can to keep himself from losing his mind. He's reading all the time, taking classes, working out. Keeping himself occupied as much as he can. He's been feeling optimistic for the first time in years. I can hear it in his voice when we talk on the phone. After all this time, he's finally starting to see the light at the end of the tunnel. He has hope."

That was the part that made her prognosis hard to handle. They were so close to the promised land.

Deon nodded. Judah had sounded more upbeat and optimistic when he spoke to him earlier.

"I started feeling weak a few months ago. To be honest with you, I haven't felt like myself in years. It started around the time Lenox passed away. I never really had the chance to deal with that grief, you know? I had to keep going. Had to make funeral arrangements, figure out how to get custody of you. How to keep Judah from falling behind in school with everything that was happening. I cried sometimes. But I needed to scream! Do you understand what I mean?"

Deon had never heard Mercy speak this way. He nodded.

"I needed to holler from the rooftop so loud that the whole city could hear me! I had lost my sister. My best friend. You had lost your mother. But I never got the chance to scream or yell. I cried a little and rolled right on."

Deon watched her as she spoke. She sat with her shoulders slumped and a crestfallen expression on her face. He went over and sat next to her on the sofa. She reached for his hand and patted it affectionately.

"When Judah was arrested, I had my first health scare. You were in the hospital recovering from what those animals did to you. Judah had been sent to Rikers Island, and I was beside myself. Couldn't eat or sleep. Tommy was working that night, so I was home by myself.

I got up to go to the bathroom. I walked back to my bedroom afterwards. The next thing I knew I woke up on my bedroom floor. I had passed out. I'm not even sure how long I was down there before I regained consciousness. I didn't tell anybody about it."

"Why?" Deon asked, frowning.

"Because I figured I knew why it happened. I was dealing with a lot of stress. And I wasn't taking care of myself. So, I did better after that, and I felt fine for a while. Then when Judah was sentenced, I really felt like the world was ending. I started losing weight and my hair was falling out. I went to the doctor and he ran a bunch of tests. That's when they first warned me about my blood pressure. They said that I needed to talk to a therapist because I could be depressed. They put me on blood pressure medication. That worked for a while. But sometimes I forgot to take it."

"Aunt Mercy . . ."

"Don't lecture me. You of all people should know what it's like not to follow the rules all the time."

Deon grinned.

"Okay," he said, nodding. "You right."

"So, not taking my medication led to a whole bunch of other problems that I didn't need."

"Like what?" Deon pressed.

"My kidneys are failing."

She said it so flatly that Deon almost thought he'd heard wrong.

"I started dialysis three weeks ago."

Deon's heart sank. Instinctively, he pulled his hand away.

"Nah. I spoke to you a couple of weeks ago . . ."

"Three weeks ago," she clarified. "You called on a Sunday. I remember because I was scheduled to begin dialysis the next day. I had every intention of telling you during our call that day. I kid you not. But I changed my mind at the last second."

"Why?" Deon felt terrible. Judah had left his mother in Deon's care and he had allowed her struggles to go unnoticed.

"Because I knew you would tell Judah. Like I know you're going to tell him about this conversation the minute you speak to him."

Deon didn't deny it.

"Barbara has been helping me. I had to stop working. She went around with me and helped me apply for welfare and Social Security benefits. So, now I'm just getting into the swing of this whole dialysis thing."

"What about a kidney transplant?" Deon asked.

Mercy shrugged. "It's a long list. They said the best chance I had for a match was from Judah. But I'm not gonna give him another thing to worry about right now. When he gets home—"

"It could be too late by then, Aunt Mercy. I'm not trying to scare you."

"Nothing scares me anymore." She looked at him, smiling as she said it. "Deon, I have felt every kind of pain there is to feel. Every type of hurt. So, I'm ready for whatever comes next."

She grabbed his hand again. "I *want* to live, Deon. I want to be here to welcome my son home and help him get on his feet. I want to sit and laugh with him again, to touch him without guards telling me to keep my 'hands off the inmate.' I want to see better days than the ones I've had so far. But if that's not what God has in store for me, I'm fine with that. 'Cause I'm tired, Deon. My soul, my mind, and now my body is worn out. That's just what it is."

Deon wanted to cry but kept his composure for Mercy's sake.

"Aunt Mercy, I love you so much. You left out a big part of what contributed to your pain and your stress. And that was me. Getting arrested, sent away to juvie, all the problems I had at school. I never gave you a break." He shook his head, disgusted by his younger self. "I kept doing wrong, waiting for you to get fed up and put me out. That way I would have an excuse just to lose my mind and throw my life away completely. But you never did. Every time, you kept welcoming me back."

"You were grieving," Mercy said. She smiled again. "*All of that* was you screaming, hollering, yelling from the rooftop so that the whole city could hear you. You understand? That's how you managed to survive."

Deon felt one determined tear fall from his eye and wiped it away quickly.

"I'm sorry," he said.

"I know. I knew even then that it wasn't about me. Your rebellion wasn't directed at me or at Judah. We just felt the effects of it because we were the closest ones to you." She squeezed his hand. "I forgive you. And I want you to forgive me, too, for keeping secrets from you and Judah. Barbara has been in my ear for weeks about calling you. But I can tell that you finally found your path in life. You got all your frustration out and now you deserve to have peace."

Deon didn't feel like he deserved it. Right then all he felt was sorrow.

"So, what happens to you now? I can't just go back to work and leave you here with Miss Barbara going to dialysis."

Mercy shrugged.

"I don't know. We'll figure it out. But not tonight." She got up, painstakingly, and walked over to a shelf on the wall. She pulled down a photo album and brought it to Deon.

"Open it up. This is what I've been doing with my time lately. Scrapbooking." She laughed gleefully, and it was clear that the hobby had become a source of joy for her.

Deon opened it and his mouth hung open.

"WOW, Aunt Mercy!"

The first page was a collage of pictures of Mercy and Lenox as little girls. Polaroids of them wearing pretty dresses, posing on their stoop in Harlem, dressed up for Easter, and playing together. He turned the page and the next was filled with similar photos of him and Judah as kids. The third page was full of pictures and mementos from Mercy's and Lenox's lives as adults. Smoking cigarettes, dancing, laughing together. Deon stared at one shot of his mother reclining on the beach on her twenty-fifth birthday. He remembered that day vividly. There was a picture of Mercy, Judah, and Deon in front of a gorilla exhibit. Beside the picture was a receipt from that day at the Bronx Zoo. Deon smiled as all the memories came flooding back.

"I remember that day! In the car going there, you and Mom were talking to each other in some type of crazy language I never heard before."

Mercy laughed.

"Pig Latin. I'll teach it to you one day now that you're grown."

Deon hadn't stopped smiling.

"This is like a trip down Memory Lane," Deon said. He shook his head. "I like how you did this. Like history repeating itself. First you and Mom, now me and Judah."

"It's funny how life goes," Mercy said. She yawned, then apologized for her rudeness.

"Don't apologize. I know you're tired. I didn't mean to disturb your sleep. But now that I know what's going on with you, I can't just go back home like nothing's wrong. If I heard you right, tomorrow you have dialysis. Am I right?"

Mercy nodded. "Now you want to listen, huh?"

Deon smirked. "I'll sleep on the couch, if that's cool."

Mercy understood that sleeping in his and Judah's old room might be difficult for him. "No problem. Let me get you some pillows and blankets."

While she did that, Deon looked around at all the old familiar things in the apartment. The coffee table had been there since he was eight or nine years old. In fact he noticed that there wasn't much that had changed about the place at all. It was like Mercy had gotten stuck on pause when Lenox died. Deon hated himself for not noticing sooner.

Mercy returned and got the couch set up for him.

"Before you tell Judah anything, I want you to think about

what it's gonna do to him. You know how he is. He'll be in the prison library researching kidney failure and hypertension and he'll lose focus. He'll start getting into fights again and he'll get sent back to solitary. And the parole board will look at all of that when they consider whether or not to grant him early release. He can't afford a misstep at this point, Deon. He's too close now."

She kissed and hugged him before she retired to her room for the night.

He got comfortable on the couch while Mercy shuffled off to bed. It took him a long time to fall asleep. Not because the sofa was uncomfortable, but because he wasn't sure how to handle this complex situation. The knowledge of his mother's illness would no doubt cripple Judah emotionally. But Deon knew it would be impossible to keep a secret of that magnitude from his cousin. He decided that he would go with Aunt Mercy to her dialysis appointment in the morning. Then he would prepare to go and visit Judah so that he could break the news to him in person.

Deon dreamed more vividly that night than he had in years. In his dream, they were all together again. Lenox and Mercy, Judah and Deon. They were sitting on the beach and the boys were kids again. Their mothers both young, beautiful, and full of life. The sun was shining so brightly and the water behind them was so clear and still. His mother looked at him and her radiant smile widened. She took his chin in her hand, leaned in close to him, and whispered, "Good boy."

He woke up still feeling the sensation of her hand on his chin, her breath against his face. He sat upright on the couch, disoriented at first because he wasn't sure where he was. Once the events of the previous day flooded back into his recollection, he stood up and stretched. He saw sunshine flooding through the window curtains and was surprised Mercy wasn't up yet. She typically rose with the sun to make breakfast or clean something. Deon reminded himself that she was sick. Perhaps too weak to do all of the things she used to do. He went to the bathroom and relieved himself, washed his hands and splashed some water on his face. Then he walked down the familiar hallway and knocked on Aunt Mercy's door.

"Auntie, it's 8:30. What time is your dialysis?" He waited. He recalled how long it had taken her to answer the door the night prior and assumed that she was slowly getting out of bed.

A few moments later, he knocked again.

"Aunt Mercy."

Silence. Deon didn't want to barge into the room, so he knocked a little harder, called her name a little louder. Still nothing.

Panic set in as Deon turned the doorknob and rushed in.

"Oh, no. Aunt Mercy. No!" He grabbed the phone at her bedside and dialed 911.

"Send an ambulance right now please."

"What's your emergency?" the operator asked robotically.

"My aunt . . . I think she's dead."

Deon was right. Mercy had suffered a massive stroke in the middle of the night. By the time he discovered her, rigor mortis had already begun. So, the sight of his aunt's cold, stiff, and lifeless body would be seared into his memory for the rest of his life. The paramedics had been patient and polite. They offered Deon their condolences as the coroner arrived to remove the body. With all the chaos, Barbara emerged from her apartment and was shocked to see Deon standing in the hallway leaning against the wall.

"She's gone," he said. "She had a stroke during the night."

Barbara wept as Deon rubbed her back soothingly. She and Mercy had been friends for more than a decade and had weathered many storms together. Both had family members involved in the drug game, sons who had gone to prison, and lovers who let them down. Through it all, they had been each other's confidantes. Now Mercy was gone. Barbara told Deon to come by if he needed anything, then retreated back into her apartment to cry in private.

Deon leaned his head back against the wall and sighed. He

thought about the dream he'd had during the night. "Good boy" were the words his mother whispered to him, cryptically. But as he prepared to go and face Judah with this news, he felt like the complete opposite.

SECRETS

Judah sat stone-faced in the visiting room at Greene Correctional Facility feeling like the life had been sucked out of him. The noise and chatter in the room all seemed far away. He was deep in the corners of his mind trying to make sense of everything he had been told in the past twenty-four hours. His mother had been sick for a while, had hidden that from him, and now she was gone.

It was April and rain was typical during that month. But the downpour that occurred on the day Judah was called into the warden's office and notified of his mother's death seemed particularly poignant.

Judah looked a lot different now. Daily workouts had made his physique more toned and muscular than ever. His arms and neck were covered in prison tattoos. His face was harder, his tone of voice more serious. He looked like a completely different man than the one he once seemed destined to be.

Deon watched his cousin, aware that he was digesting a lot. He was also aware from his own experience that Judah was living in a place where showing emotion—even over something as heartbreaking as the unexpected death of your mother—could be seen as weakness. Judah didn't have the luxury of weeping openly. Instead, he sat silently, stoically, and locked eyes with his cousin.

"I know she kept it to herself to protect me. But it's hard to understand that now." In Judah's anger, he wished he could somehow tell his mother that her plan had backfired. Instead of protecting him, she had robbed him of the chance to say goodbye.

"She said she wanted you to focus on coming home. She didn't want you to be upset, get off track, and end up staying in here longer than you have to," Deon said.

Judah went silent again. Just days ago, nineteen months had seemed like the blink of an eye. It was nothing compared to the years he had spent in prison. Now, nineteen months felt like an eternity when he thought about the idea of his mother enduring dialysis for that long. Suffering alone without him. Judah thought about the apartment he had grown up in. It occurred to him that he might never get to step inside of it again. By the time he came home—*if* the parole board granted him early release—that apartment would be rented to a new tenant. Everything he left behind when he picked up the gun that fateful day in 1992 was gone now. The finality of it was a crushing blow.

"If I was home, this wouldn't have happened."

Deon didn't respond. He had known that Judah was thinking that, so hearing him say it was unsurprising.

"I would have fixed it. She'd still be here."

"She said that if you knew you would have researched the whole thing until you found a cure."

Judah grinned. It was true. Anything for his mother.

"You know this is the year I would have graduated college?"

Deon did the math in his head and nodded.

"She would have held on, just to watch me walk across the stage and get my diploma. If I was home, she'd be alive."

Deon stared at Judah, watching him beat himself up for being absent. Deon had been beating himself up the same way for years.

"I could say the same thing," Deon said. "What if I never left? I could have stayed in New York, checked in on her more often. I would have found out sooner that she was sick. What if my mother never got involved in the drug game and didn't die, and I never had to come and live with you? Then *none* of this shit would have happened."

Judah didn't respond.

"I looked at the pictures in that scrapbook and saw what Aunt Mercy made peace with. None of it was in our control."

Judah wasn't buying it. "We had choices. All of us could have done things differently."

"But we made the choices we made. And there's no going back to do it over again. So, now we have a new choice to make. Do we let it eat us alive?"

Deon sighed. He chose his next words carefully. "It should have been me in here. You were on your way to Morgan State. You did everything right, followed all the rules. I was the one who belonged in here. I studied to be here while you were studying for the SATs. You came outside that day to help me fight my battle. I was the one who had beef with them muthafuckas. Not you."

"I never blamed you," Judah said. "I came outside to help you. But I did what I did for my own reasons, too. I was proving to myself that I had heart. Standing up to them even though I was scared to death. I got clowned on the bus one time. I never told you about it. I was riding home after school with Chanel, and some dudes got on and started talking shit to me. I was scared then, too. Kept my head down and avoided eye contact while they disrespected me. Lucky for me one of them knew you. He recognized me as your cousin, and they left me alone. But that shit bothered me. Then the situation at the party happened, and it was you that came to my rescue again. So, when I heard that you were getting jumped, I knew it was my turn to man up and hold you down. I went too far, got in over my head. Now I'm paying a big price for it." He shrugged. "So, I guess you're right. Now I gotta decide if I'm gonna let it eat me alive."

"You're not," Deon said. "You can't because Aunt Mercy wanted you to come home. She was trying to live so she could see you walk out of here a free man."

Judah wanted to fall apart. But he knew his cousin was right. He owed it to his mother, who had died of a broken heart, to live what remained of his life to the fullest.

"I can't be there to make the arrangements. So, I need you to do it for me."

Deon agreed. "I called my job, told them I'll be out of town for a few weeks. I'll make sure everything gets taken care of."

Judah thanked him. "They said that I can attend the funeral. But they'll bring me there in shackles." The thought of it filled him with shame. But he could not pass up the opportunity to see his mother's face for the last time. He looked at Deon. "When Aunt Lenox passed, did you want to die, too?"

Deon smirked. "I did. For a long time. But you wouldn't let me. Aunt Mercy wouldn't let me. And I ain't gonna let you die, Judah. So, get that shit out of your head right now."

Deon returned to Mercy's apartment and wept. He sat on his old bed in the room he shared with Judah growing up and cried for the loss of their family. What remained was an apartment full of memories and broken dreams.

He heard a knock at the door and hesitated for a moment. He chided himself, unsure what made him pause, and went to answer the door. He opened it without checking to see who it was and he inhaled sharply when he saw her.

"Nelly!"

She smiled at him. "Hey, Deon."

"Wow . . ."

He rushed forward and hugged her. She squeezed him back tightly. He stepped back and she looked at him sadly.

"My mother called to tell me about Miss Mercy. She's pretty upset. Hasn't stopped crying for long. So, I came back to Staten Island for a few days to stay with her until the funeral."

Deon thought about the last time he had seen Chanel. Five years ago at least.

"Where do you live now?" he asked.

"Delaware. I go to college there. It's a small town, but I love it."

He nodded, his mood lightened suddenly. "You want to come in?"

Chanel glanced inside the apartment. "Sure."

She stepped in, expecting the place to feel eerie with Judah and Mercy gone. Instead, the whole scene came flooding back to her like an instant replay. The smell of Mercy's cooking, the sound of Lenox's laughter, the sight of them dancing together. It seemed like only yesterday. She smiled despite the sadness of the occasion.

"Remember the time I beat you and Judah at Connect Four so many times that you told Miss Mercy to send me home?"

Deon laughed, remembering the incident vividly.

"You were being a bitch that night. So, yeah, we wanted you out of here."

Chanel laughed, too. She caught herself after a moment. "How are you holding up? My mother told me that you found Mercy yourself."

"Yeah. I'm okay. I just have to figure out how to pack this place up, put all this stuff in boxes, and get Aunt Mercy's affairs in order."

"How's Judah doing?" Chanel asked. "Have you seen him?" She tried not to sound too eager, but she had thought about Judah for years. She still had the letter he had written her, still wondered what might have been.

Deon nodded. "He's having a hard time with it. Everything happened without warning and he's still in shock."

"He loved his mother so much. All he ever wanted to do was protect and provide for her." Chanel and Judah had confided in each other about their worst fears and their wildest dreams. She wished she could talk to him now.

"Will they let him come to the funeral?" she asked.

"Yeah. He'll be there. After that, he told me to give away all of the furniture and pack up everything else for him to go through when he gets out."

"I can help," Chanel offered. "My mother is taking a nap and she only has basic cable." Chanel rolled her eyes. "So, I have time."

Deon smiled, grateful for the offer. He pointed to the boxes he had brought up earlier from his truck. "Let's get busy, then."

Three hours later, they had made considerable progress. They started in Judah's room. Deon had taken everything he wanted when he left years earlier. So, what remained belonged mostly to Judah. Trinkets, clothes, and shoes from years earlier that Judah had probably forgotten about completely. They moved on to Mercy's room and found that she was as levelheaded and organized in death as she had been in life. Her life insurance policies and vital records were all placed together neatly in a large manila envelope at the top of her closet. With that information, Chanel helped Deon arrange a meeting with a funeral director that night to make arrangements for the funeral service. She and Barbara accompanied him. They helped him choose the casket, the prayer cards, and the date of Mercy's funeral service. As Mercy's best friend, Barbara knew which of the dresses in her closet had been her favorite. So, they brought the flowy lavender dress to the funeral home with them.

By the time Chanel went back to her mother's apartment that night, Deon felt relieved. Half of the task was completed. And he had help. He was more grateful to Barbara and Chanel than he could say.

Chanel came back the next morning with coffee and donuts. She wore jeans and an old T-shirt and her hair up in a ponytail.

"Ready to work!" she said as she came in.

They got busy in Mercy's room packing up the last of her belongings. Then they moved on to the kitchen. While packing up the pots and pans, Chanel chewed a glazed donut and leaned against the counter.

"How's life as a trucker?" she asked.

Deon laughed. "Something about the way you said it made it sound funny. But I love it! I hit the highway and turn some music on. Soon I'm lost in thought. Or sometimes there's no thoughts at all. Just me and the road. It's peaceful."

Chanel smiled. "I can tell it makes you happy. You seem different now. Happier than before."

He wrapped some plates in newspaper and set them inside one of the boxes.

"How about you?" he asked. "How's college?"

"I graduate next year. I got a job working at a local newspaper in the editorial department. After I graduate, I want to try and get a job at one of the major TV networks as a sportscaster. If not, maybe print journalism. I'll see how it goes."

Deon smiled. "Look at you doing big things."

She picked up some dishes and began helping him pack them.

"It's not how I pictured it though. When we were together, Judah and I would talk about going to Morgan State together. Being like Whitley Gilbert and Dwayne Wayne from *A Different World*. When I pictured my future, I always saw him in it."

Deon nodded. "Judah felt the same way. He told me he was gonna marry you someday."

"So, why did he push me away? I wrote him letters and sent him pictures of us together, trying to remind him that he had a life before all of this. And trying to show him that I would still be there for him. But he wouldn't let me."

Deon looked at her. "There's a lot you don't understand about what it's like to be in jail. They try to break you mentally and physically. So, every man has to figure out how to do certain things to survive. Some of them become food. They just roll over and play dead and let the other inmates run all over them. They pay for protection, allow themselves to get disrespected, and they get ridiculed, all for the sake of survival. Others decide that's not an option for them. And they're forced to fight all the time. To get up every day and prove that you're not the one who's gonna get walked over. That's what Judah is doing. He's in there fighting every day to maintain control of his body and his mind. I think he had to let you go so he could do that without distraction."

Chanel grabbed a mug and wrapped it carefully.

"I hate the thought of that, Deon. That's not who Judah is. Fighting, and trying to prove how tough he is. That's not the man he was becoming." It broke her heart every time she thought about Judah and what his life had turned into. "I knew when he took that plea deal that his life would never be the same. He missed out on so many milestones. He had just learned how to drive a car. Never got to go to prom or attend his graduation. Every time I do something for the first time—go to a concert or eat a new food they don't make in New York—I think about Judah." She began to cry. "He missed out on so much. And he doesn't deserve it. Now Miss Mercy died. And I know it's gonna crush him. And he's all by himself dealing with that. It breaks my heart."

Deon hugged her as she cried. He understood all too well just how helpless she felt. It took a few minutes, but she eventually composed herself.

"You okay?" Deon asked.

She nodded. "Yeah."

He sat down on one of the kitchen chairs. "I know how you feel," he admitted. "Truthfully I think about Judah all the time. Especially when I'm driving. Judah and my mother. How much I miss them. How much they taught me. The funny thing is it's easier for me to think about my mother. With her, the situation was completely out of my control. I wasn't there. I couldn't have helped her. I had no idea really what was going on with her. I was a kid, so it was out of my control. But when I think about Judah, I get mad. I feel ashamed of myself."

Deon's voice cracked, and Chanel watched him wrestle with his emotions. He fought back tears as he continued.

"That *was* in my control. And it was my fault. He's in there because of me. And his mother is gone and he never got to say goodbye. He left her in my care and I fucked up."

Deon shook his head, closed his eyes, and sat that way in silence. When he opened his eyes again, he took a deep breath, looked at Chanel and smiled.

"So, I know what you mean about having a broken heart. Join the club."

They spent another hour packing up a few more boxes before calling it a night. Deon grabbed his duffel bag and left the apartment with Chanel. She watched him lock up the place.

"You're not staying here?" she asked.

He shook his head. "Nah. Hard to sleep in there. Too many memories. I got a hotel room. I'm gonna stay there until after the funeral."

Chanel nodded.

Deon took her hand. "Thanks for helping me with all this, Nelly. Feels good to have somebody to talk to about it. Not too many people understand the history between me and my family. But you do."

"Judah loves you. You're more than his cousin. You're his brother. Your mother and Miss Mercy are at peace now. I picture them reunited in Heaven having a dance party in the kitchen."

Deon smiled. He hugged Chanel, said goodnight and watched her disappear inside her mother's apartment.

He left the projects that night and headed to the hotel, imagining that party in Heaven Chanel had described, and it made him smile.

The day of Mercy's funeral, a dark cloud hung over Staten Island. The sky looked as ominous as Deon had ever seen it. He felt like he was operating outside of himself. Some type of out-of-body experience. He dressed in his hotel room, the first time he had worn a suit since his own mother's funeral. He checked his reflection in the mirror and thought that his mother and Aunt Mercy would be gushing over him if they were alive. They always got excited whenever they had an opportunity to see him and Judah dressed up. Whistling and shouting compliments at them to boost their confidence. He knew that they would smile at the sight of him.

He got to the funeral home and greeted the small crowd gathered. Xavier had gotten there early. He sat in the front, closest to Mercy's casket. He stood and greeted Deon as he entered and Deon could tell that he had been crying. Xavier sat back down with his pocket square in his hand, staring solemnly ahead. He had driven through their old neighborhood that morning, reminiscing on the good old days. As he looked at Mercy's lifeless body in front of him, he couldn't stop crying. It seemed so unfair for a woman with such inner and outer beauty to have lived a life filled with so much loss and pain.

Deon made his way around the room greeting everyone gathered. Chanel, her brother, Dallas, and their mother, Barbara. A few of Mercy's coworkers were there. And Tommy.

Deon went over to him and they shook hands. The expression on Tommy's face was full of regret as they sat down in two seats side by side. He shook his head to fight back tears as he looked at Mercy's body in the casket.

"I couldn't reach her after Judah went to jail," Tommy said. "I tried. I really did. But she died the day he got sentenced. She stopped living. After that she was just existing."

Deon nodded.

"I loved her. We were talking marriage. But when Judah got in trouble, she changed. Shut down. I couldn't get her to talk to me. Instead of hanging in there and being patient with her, I got fed up and walked away. She deserved better than that."

Deon wasn't sure what to say. He didn't have long to think

about it before a commotion occurred near the door. The state police arrived with Judah. He was flanked on all sides by heavily armed law enforcement. He wore a green prison uniform and was shackled like a slave. They led him in and escorted him to the front of the room. A row of seats had been reserved for them there and they sat as the service began.

The minister spoke about Mercy and about the life she'd lived. But all eyes were on Judah. He sat staring at his mother's remains. His hands were folded in his lap, and he sat with his shoulders squared. The expression on his face was pained.

Chanel sat behind him, wanting desperately to reach forward and touch him. She knew that if she did the officers would admonish her. She couldn't take her eyes off him. He looked so different now. Still as handsome as he ever was. But there was a hardness to him now. He looked like a man who had lived much longer than his twenty-two years.

Deon stared at Judah also. He couldn't tell whether Judah was listening to the reverend as he spoke about Mercy. Judah didn't react to anything that was said. He never took his eyes off his mother lying before him for the final time.

Judah thought all the way back to his earliest memory of life. He was about three years old and it was his birthday. He didn't remember much, but he could vividly recall a chocolate cake with three little candles in it. He saw his mother's smiling face, and he remembered how he felt inside. Like he had everything in the world that day. He had all he wanted and needed.

Their bond had been a close one with him being the only child. For so many years it had been just the two of them. He remembered telling her about the books he read and she would give him her full attention. He listened to her stories about work as they ate dinner together. He realized as he sat there staring at her lifeless body that those had been what he would call the good old days. Those were the sweet moments that would define his lifetime. He wished he had known it then. That those were the good times. He would have reveled in them more.

Memories came flooding back to him in waves. Watching his mother and Aunt Lenox in the kitchen together laughing and talking. His mother taking him to libraries and museums all over the city when he was a kid. Always so willing to feed his hunger for books and knowledge. Their trip together to visit Morgan State and the things they discussed during that train ride. The countless visits over the years where they spent hours pretending that they were anywhere else but in a cold prison building surrounded by guards. He remembered the days when she had her restaurant, when she and Xavier first got together, and he realized that was the happiest he had ever seen her.

The congregants all around him rose, and Judah did, too. He wasn't sure what part of the service this was since he had been so lost in thought that he hadn't been listening. He soon realized that the small gathering of people was filing past the coffin one by one. He saw some people he didn't recognize. Two white women and a Hispanic man who he assumed were coworkers of Mercy's. They looked at him as they passed. Judah felt ashamed, knowing that this was not the way she would want to be remembered. The mother of a felon who had to attend her funeral in shackles.

He swallowed past the lump in his throat and straightened his posture. He reminded himself that Mercy had told him to stand tall like a man, even when he felt like falling apart.

Barbara and Chanel were next to file past. Chanel wore a simple black dress but still managed to look like a supermodel to Judah. He looked at her and they locked eyes. She walked over to him while her mother stood at Mercy's casket crying softly.

Chanel looked at the guards. "Can I hug him?"

One guard shook his head no, his expression stone-cold.

Chanel looked at Judah.

"Judah, I'm so sorry. Miss Mercy loved you so much. And she

knew you loved her, too, Judah. She knew it. She was so proud of you."

He nodded.

Chanel stared at him, waiting for him to say something. He just looked at her, his expression blank. She cleared her throat, slightly embarrassed.

His hands were clasped together in front of him. He pressed them tighter together, willing himself not to weep. Chanel was the only person on earth besides Deon who knew how deeply Judah loved his mother. Seeing her again, hearing her speak about that love was enough to make him want to crumble.

Again, he nodded. This time, Chanel walked away.

Tommy was at Mercy's coffin now. Judah tried to keep his temper in check. He wanted to fight Tommy. Standing up there crying now, openly expressing regret for abandoning her when she needed him most. As far as Judah was concerned, Tommy was a coward. He knew that their breakup had only made it harder for his mother to weather the storm. Thankfully, Tommy only nodded in Judah's direction before he exited. Judah breathed a sigh of relief.

Xavier lingered for a while. He leaned down and whispered to Mercy one last time.

"I'll miss you, Quiet Storm." He touched his fingers to his lips then touched her cold cheek.

He walked over to Judah and could see him trembling as he fought to keep himself from falling apart. Xavier hadn't seen Judah in years. Though a hardened and battle-worn man stood in front of him, Xavier could see the little boy who wanted so badly to run to his mother. With his eyes full of tears, Xavier touched his heart and bowed in front of Judah. He stood inches from Judah and looked him in the eyes as he spoke.

"You are her pride and joy. Don't you ever forget it."

Judah bit his lip and nodded quickly. Xavier exited briskly, overcome with emotion.

Deon walked over to where Judah stood. He spoke to one of the guards.

"Can I walk with my cousin to see her for the last time?"

The guard nodded. He escorted Judah to the casket, walking on one side of him while Deon walked on the other. The three of them stood at Mercy's casket peering down.

Deon rested his hand on his aunt's shoulder.

"Aunt Mercy, I'm glad that we got the chance to talk the night before you went to Heaven. I told Judah everything you said. Including the part about you being sorry for keeping secrets. And I'm glad I got to say sorry to you. I'm sorry for so many things." Deon cried. "I love you, Aunt Mercy."

He sniffed and wiped his face with the back of his hand.

Judah reached forward with both of his shackled hands and touched his mother's hand. The chains on his wrist rattled as he moved, but the guard didn't stop him. Mercy's hand felt so cold in his own, and Judah opened his mouth to speak.

"Ma . . ." Tears fell from his eyes. "Ma . . ."

Judah let it all go then. His body quaked as he cried gutturally. The guard graciously stepped back and gave him space to weep. Deon held on to his cousin as the sound of his cries filled the room.

"MA!"

BROTHER'S KEEPER

Deon wanted to get the fuck out of town.

He was emotionally drained following Mercy's funeral. Everything of value from Mercy's apartment had been packed into the back of his Chevy Suburban. He had given Barbara the furniture she wanted from the apartment and tossed the rest out for the sanitation trucks to collect. Now he wanted to leave Staten Island behind for good. He had found nothing but pain and turmoil in that place.

He walked through the apartment for the last time. He stood in Mercy's room where she had died. He thought about the nights she spent in there praying for all of them and wondered if those prayers had fallen on deaf ears. He lingered in Judah's room the longest. The room they had grown up in together. They talked about sports, girls, Judah's books, and all of his dreams. They had fought in this room, argued, and given each other the silent treatment. They had gone from boys to men within those four walls. He touched the spot where Judah's Michael Jordan poster once hung. Then he went into the kitchen. He could still smell the scent of Mercy's cooking even though the place was empty now. He remembered seeing his mother standing in there snapping her fingers and singing. He smiled, shook his head sadly, and walked out the door.

He went down the hall and knocked on Barbara's door. Chanel answered and held the door ajar for him to come inside.

"Hey," Deon said. "I can't stay long. I just came to see your mother so I could drop off the keys to Aunt Mercy's apartment before I leave. Miss Barbara said she would bring the keys to the rent office for me." He handed her the keys.

Chanel took them, frowning. "You're leaving?"

Deon nodded. "I was gonna stay until tomorrow, but I gotta get out of here. Today was too much."

Chanel understood. "I feel the same way. I'm catching a bus back to school in the morning."

Deon thought about it. "If you want to leave tonight, I can drive you back. I'm leaving soon, though."

She thought about it. She looked around and shrugged.

"Are you sure?"

Deon nodded.

"Are you packed?"

She chuckled. "Yeah. Just let me grab my stuff."

Fifteen minutes later, they had piled into Deon's truck with Chanel's suitcase and Deon's duffel bag in the backseat. The trunk was full of the contents of Mercy's and Judah's lives all packed up in boxes.

Deon put the radio on and took one last look at the projects before he started the car and pulled away.

"Is it just me, or does this place feel smaller now?" Chanel asked.

"It ain't just you. I noticed it, too. It seemed so much bigger when we were kids. Like these four or five blocks was the whole world. But once you leave and come back you realize it's just a tiny piece of the puzzle."

"Nothing ever changes either. I told my mother that. I want her to get out of here. There's so much happening, so many people to meet and things to do. But in Staten Island, everybody's stuck in a time warp. Every day feels like the day before it."

"I'm never coming back," Deon said, flatly. "No reason to now."

Chanel sat back and got comfortable. For a while they rode along without talking, each of them lost in thought. The music on the radio filled the void as Deon drove and Chanel stared out the passenger window. The sun began to set as they crossed the Goethals Bridge and Chanel smiled.

"Remember that time you dared Judah to run through that swarm of mosquitoes?"

A slow smile spread across Deon's face and he nodded.

"Yeeeah, I remember that dumb shit. We were in the third grade. Judah was in fourth."

Chanel laughed and pointed at him.

"Judah wouldn't do it and you kept calling him a sissy. So, I dared *you* to do it."

"My dumb ass did it, too," Deon said. "I got attacked while you stood there laughing."

"Judah felt so bad for you. He thought you were gonna explode because you got all puffy and swollen." Chanel couldn't stop laughing.

Deon chuckled. "I was suffering. Every part of my body itched. I was scratching so hard that I started bleeding. Judah got some calamine lotion from Aunt Mercy and I plastered that shit all over myself for days."

"Judah was always so caring," Chanel said. "When I got chicken pox, he did the same thing. And he brought me books to read so I wouldn't be bored."

"He had a dark side, too, though," Deon said, grinning. "He ever tell you about the time he tied my sneaker laces together while I was asleep on the park bench?"

"No," Chanel said.

"He woke me up all of a sudden and told me to run. 'THEY'RE SHOOTING, D!' So, I got up in a panic and took off running. Bust my whole knee open when I fell." Deon laughed at the memory.

Chanel did, too.

"Do you go upstate to see him often?" she asked.

"Not as often as I should," Deon admitted. "I left New York for good when I was seventeen. Started working, moving around a lot. I write him letters all the time. Send him money, packages, and shit. But I didn't make it my business to see him more than once or twice a year. I guess I figured Aunt Mercy was going up there to see him . . . it's no excuse. After everything we been through, I should have visited him more. And I will. Now that Aunt Mercy's gone. I'm all he got."

Chanel stared out the window.

"It killed me seeing Judah like that today," she said. "I'm not just talking about the shackles and the uniform either. He's just . . . different now."

"He's adapted to his environment," Deon said.

Chanel thought about that.

"When he went away, he wrote to me and told me not to wait for him. I loved him, you know? I thought we would get married someday. So, when I got that letter it crushed me. All this time I told myself that he didn't really mean it. That he was just saying that to protect me and maybe to protect himself from getting hurt. But today when I saw him, it felt like he looked right through me. He didn't look at me like . . . like he used to. It hurt."

"He's a zombie right now," Deon said. "I'm sure he was glad to see you. It's just that losing his mother is the one thing that could probably destroy him if he lets it. When my mother died, I acted a fool for years. Judah can't afford to do that right now. He's trying to hold it together. That's all."

She nodded, wishing she believed him. She looked at Deon.

"How about you? How have you been holding it together?"

He laughed. "Who said I am? For all you know, I could be falling apart, too."

She smiled. "No. I watched how you swooped into town and got your aunt's affairs in order. That's not how people act when they're falling apart. I'm proud of you, Deon."

He glanced at her and smiled. "Thanks." He drove on silently for a moment, lost in thought. After a few minutes he spoke again.

"I thought about what you said the other night. That thing about my mother and Aunt Mercy having a dance party in Heaven. I had a dream about her the night Aunt Mercy died."

Chanel looked at him, curiously. "Your mom?"

He nodded. "First time I've dreamed about her since she passed. In the dream, me and Judah were little. She grabbed my face and she leaned in close to me and said, 'Good boy.' I woke up and Aunt Mercy was gone."

Chanel turned it around in her mind over and over.

"What do you think it means?"

Deon shrugged. "I have no idea. But I needed to hear it." He got choked up.

Chanel sensed his emotions were at their height. She watched him and listened as he chose his words carefully.

"You ever had somebody say something to you . . . and until that moment you didn't realize how much you *needed* to hear that?"

Chanel nodded.

"It was like that." He shrugged. "I was never the 'good boy.' Judah was. He got the good grades, held the door open for old ladies, always played fair. That's not who I was. Not ever. From preschool, I was challenging authority. Breaking the rules. Then I fucked up so bad that Judah got sent away and . . . I just thought the best thing for me to do was to get away from everybody. I disappointed them, so why stick around? But then this happened."

He sniffled, and Chanel handed him a tissue. He thanked her.

"I went back to New York and that conversation I had with Aunt Mercy the night before she died is something I'll never forget. She forgave me. And she gave me a chance to step up and be a good boy for once. I got to honor her, and by doing that I honored Judah and I made my moms proud. So, that dream . . . and what you said about that dance party in Heaven has me feeling optimistic. Maybe I'm not such a piece of shit after all."

Chanel smiled. "I've been trying to tell you that for years."

Two hours later, they arrived at her apartment complex and Deon pulled into the parking lot.

"Thank you for the ride," Chanel said, unbuckling her seat belt. "This beats Greyhound any day!"

He climbed out of the car and grabbed her duffel bag from the backseat. He walked around to the passenger side where she stood and set the bag down. He opened his arms for a hug.

"Good seeing you again, Nelly."

He hugged her tightly.

She looked up at him, sadly. "I guess this is the last time I'll see you," she said.

He nodded. "Guess so."

They stared at each other, still embracing. Then he kissed her, lightly at first. She parted her lips and their tongues intertwined. Their kiss deepened and moments passed before they breathlessly pulled apart.

"Don't leave," she whispered. "Stay."

Deon nodded. He picked up her bag and followed her inside.

The second the door shut behind them, she gripped his face and kissed him again. There were no words, only sounds as they explored each other in her darkened apartment. The intensity of Deon's touch told her that he had wanted her for years. The passion in her kisses showed his desire for her was mutual. Stripped down to nothing, she led him to her bedroom. Their lovemaking was loud, raw, and uninhibited. They came undone together, each of them seeking to heal wounds deep inside themselves that only they knew existed.

They went at it all through the night. As the sun began peeking its head up, Deon lay across Chanel's queen-sized bed trying to make sense of it. In the light of day, the taboo things that happened between them felt exposed. He watched her sleeping and told himself that it was only physical, it would only be a onetime thing.

But the moment her eyes fluttered open and she smiled at him, he knew he had been lying to himself. Chanel was, and had always been, special to him. There was no way he could pretend that what happened the night before hadn't been significant.

"Hey," she said, propping herself up on one elbow.

"Hey," he said back. He pinched her nose, playfully.

"I was scared you would be gone when I woke up."

"I thought about it," he said, honestly. "That would be the easiest thing to do."

Chanel knew it was true. "We would have never seen each other again. Like you said. Nothing left for you in Staten Island anymore."

He nodded.

"So, why'd you stay?" she asked.

He wasn't sure what the answer was.

"'Cause you're cute when you sleep," he said. "I was enjoying watching you so much that I forgot to sneak out."

She laughed. "Makes sense."

Chanel stretched her body and laid back flatly, staring up at the ceiling.

"For real," she said after a minute. "What was this?" She gestured at the crumpled sheets and their clothes flung all over the room.

Deon had been trying to figure that out since he woke up. Chanel watched him fumbling for words. She sat up and faced him.

"Be honest. I can take it."

"I'm not sure," he admitted. "I know Judah wouldn't approve."

Chanel wasn't sure she agreed. "Judah forgot all about me."

Deon sighed. "It's different for men. Women wear their hearts on their sleeves. Men are better at hiding what we're feeling. Even though a lot of years passed, in his heart I'm sure he still considers you his girl."

Chanel shook her head. "Well, let's get that straight," she stated. "I don't belong to him or to you. I belong to me."

Deon felt like he had been put in his place.

"I learned that the hard way when Judah left, then you left, and all I had was myself." She knew where Deon was coming from, but she wanted him to view it from her perspective.

"Growing up, the three of us were so close. You and Judah were my best friends. We played ball together, liked the same music and TV shows, and hung out together all the time. I was closer to you in a way because we're the same age, went to the same school, and a lot of times we had the same classes. I was close to Judah, too, because he was so smart and he had a way of making me think outside the box. He read a million books and he would get so excited to talk to me about them. When we got to junior high school, I had a crush on you."

Deon grinned. "You did? You never told me that."

"Because you started acting up. Your mother had passed and you were in trouble all the time. Everybody was saying that you had a bad attitude and you were headed down the wrong path. But I knew the real you. Even when we got to high school and you would say stupid shit in class to get kicked out or get in fights and get suspended. I could tell that you were just playing a part. You were *acting* like an idiot. But you were never really dumb. You needed attention. Maybe you needed a hug. But you didn't need to be locked up."

Deon thought about high school and the times Chanel tried to talk some sense into him.

"When you came to my house that day and gave me that picture of you and your mother, I wanted to cry. No guy had ever given me something so special and so sweet before. I loved you from that day."

Deon recalled the butterflies he had felt in his stomach as he knocked on Chanel's apartment door that day. He had been crazy about her then. In fact, that hadn't changed.

"So, why didn't you say something?" he asked.

"I was fourteen! I was shy, didn't know how to say it. Plus, I wanted to see if you were gonna change. You were getting high all the time, getting in trouble. As much as I liked you, that's not the kind of guy I wanted as my boyfriend. You know me. I wanted to go to school dances and pep rallies, go to the movies and to the mall. You were more interested in posting up in the stairwell and smoking weed."

Deon laughed. "That's true."

"Then you got sent back to juvie. Judah took it really hard and so did I. We bonded over that. We talked about you all the time, and how frustrated he was that you wouldn't act right. He talked to me about his desire to be a good son, to get out of the hood, and to be great. I talked to him about things I never shared with anybody. Like how I felt about my brother going back and forth to jail, and how I wanted my mother to pay as much attention to me for doing the right thing as she paid him for doing wrong. Me and Judah were dreamers together. We had a game where we would add things we wanted in life to a list we kept in our heads. He would come up to me in the hallway at school and go, 'Surfing in Hawaii!' and he'd rush off. I would see him in the lunchroom, and I would go over and say, 'Eating croissants in Paris.' And nobody else knew what we were talking about. It was our little language that only we understood."

She smiled at the memory. She closed her eyes and the tears came then. She looked at Deon.

"I did love him. I thought we would get married one day and have kids and live the life of our dreams. But he went to prison, and he shut me out of his life. I wanted to wait for him. I would have waited. But he pushed me away. That was the loneliest time of my life. Judah was gone. Then you were gone. Nothing was the same anymore. I went to prom with my friends and it sucked because all I could do all night was think about Judah and what our plans had been. At graduation, I wanted you to be there so we could drink a forty-ounce like we joked about since freshman year."

Deon smiled and wiped away Chanel's tears. He remembered joking with her about smuggling in forty-ounce bottles of malt liquor underneath their graduation gowns. He pulled her close to him.

"Since I came to Delaware, I've started fresh. Made new friends, established a new routine, and moved on. Then Miss Mercy died. My mom called me crying hysterically. I rushed home and there you were. All grown up and living the life I always knew you were capable of. And I saw Judah. And he looked right through me. I finally gave up hope that he would be the guy I loved once. That guy is gone. And that's not Judah's fault. But it's still true. I don't meet too many guys who spark a fire inside of me. The ones I've dated are not from where I'm from. They haven't seen what I've seen. But these past few days with you I've felt understood. And it confirmed the fact that I understand you, too. I always have. I was right when we were younger and I suspected that you weren't really a coldhearted asshole. I knew that you were just acting out your pain. I believed that you could be a good man if you chose to be. And seeing you now is proof that I was right. When I heard you say that you were leaving Staten Island and I realized I might never see you again, it scared me. I wasn't ready to see you go. I'm still not. So, for me this . . ." Chanel gestured again at the disheveled bed. "Is a sign that maybe you and I could start over."

Deon sighed. She had given him a lot to digest. The light in the room brightened slightly as the sun rose higher in the sky. He looked at her.

"You asked me earlier why I was still here when you woke up. The reason is everything you just said. When I'm with you, I feel understood. You always made me feel like that. Like you could see right through me. When I left New York and started trucking, one of the things I liked about it was I could be whoever I wanted to be when I was on the road. I've made up so many stories about where I'm from and who I am. It felt good to be somebody else for a while, knowing that I would never see these people again and they would take whatever I was saying at face value. Nobody knew the real me and I could forget all the ways I fucked up for a while. But seeing you and talking to you this week, I felt more like myself than I have in years. Talking to you about the old days . . . it's the first time I've allowed myself to talk about it in years. Because I would get emotional and start regretting the shit I did. And there's no way for me to go back and fix it now. So, I'd rather just forget it."

He looked at her, his expression at once sad and full of love.

"But I can't forget you. And I don't want to."

Deon stayed with her for three days before he reluctantly got in his truck and headed up I-95 to Philadelphia. He thought about the events of those three days as he drove home. He and Chanel had tucked themselves away in the sanctity and solitude of her apartment. Their time together had been sweet, soul-stirring, and passionate. They talked for hours about their childhood, reminiscing on shared experiences and reveling in their commonality. She cooked for him, fed him with her fork, her fingers, and with her body. He devoured every inch of her and she returned the favor. Their heated lovemaking was only matched by their intense conversations. Deon spoke to her about things he had never shared with anyone. Like how the loss of his mother, his cousin, and now his aunt made him feel more alone in the world than ever.

They were careful in those conversations not to mention Judah directly. They spoke of their childhood, of Deon's family and their shared history in broad terms. They tiptoed around the elephant in the room until the day he left. Chanel had come up to him in the bathroom that morning and wrapped her arms around his waist while he was brushing his teeth. She looked at his reflection in the mirror and spoke to it.

"I know you want to run from this because it's the easy thing to do," she said. "Maybe it's even the right thing to do. Run from this so Judah won't be upset. But I don't want you to run, Deon. Don't disappear on me. This is the first time I've felt like this. I don't want to lose you."

He had kissed her and promised that he wouldn't run. Now, as his foot mashed the gas pedal in his truck, he wondered if that was a promise that he could keep. There was no doubt that he cared about her. They understood each other deeply and she was one of the few people able to see through his façade. Since they were kids, she had always challenged him in ways no one else dared to. She knew he was smart even when he played dumb. Chanel had always brought the best out of him. She made him want to be a better person.

But he knew that there was no way Judah would ever understand this. No matter how much time had passed, Judah wouldn't accept that Deon had fallen in love with the girl he had left behind.

Deon busied himself with work for a couple of days. His mind drifted back to her again and again and he found ways to distract himself. He wrote a letter to Judah telling him about returning to Philadelphia and putting Mercy's belongings in storage. He left out the part about the three-day layover in Delaware with Chanel. He pushed thoughts of her to the back of his mind and kept moving. Then she called him and he lost all willpower.

"I miss you," she said. "Come hold me."

He was back in her arms hours later.

They established a rhythm. When Deon wasn't on the road for work, he was at her place. When school let out at the end of May, she began traveling to Philadelphia by train on the weekends. Deon picked her up at the station and they spent days together holed up in his apartment. For both of them, it was their first real adult relationship. Without giving voice to it, they fell in love.

Chanel changed that as they lay together in bed one summer night.

"What would your mother think about us?"

Deon smiled. "She would love you," he said. Chanel reminded

him of his mother in some ways. Her free-spiritedness and determination to go after what she wanted at all costs. Lenox would approve, he imagined.

"Do you love me?" Chanel had asked it so sweetly.

Deon was silent.

"I love you," she said. "You don't have to say it back. I just want you to know that's how I feel."

She touched his face, tracing the line of his sideburns and goatee gently.

He had stared at her for a moment before climbing on top of her and smothering her with kisses.

"I love you, too," he admitted. "Now, what are we gonna do about it?"

She didn't answer him. They made love instead. Now eighteen months had passed and they still didn't have an answer to that question.

Deon felt like a traitor. He was living a double life, having a full-blown relationship with Chanel while keeping Judah in the dark about it.

Chanel was keeping their relationship a secret as well. Her mother and brother knew that she was seeing someone and that it was serious. She spoke of him only in the broadest terms, wouldn't give them a name. But at her graduation in May of 1999, Deon arrived with a big bouquet of flowers. Barbara was surprised at first, then appalled when Chanel greeted him with a kiss on the lips that made it clear that they were far more than friends. Deon sat with Barbara and her son, Dallas, during the graduation ceremony. It was awkward and confusing for her. She was preoccupied the whole time trying to come to grips with the thought of Deon and Chanel together. She pulled her daughter aside the second they found her in the crowd after the ceremony had concluded.

"The guy you've been seeing all this time is DEON?" Barbara

hissed. She stared at her daughter in disgust. "Mercy must be turning over in her grave!"

"Ma! You're making a scene." Chanel looked around, embarrassed.

"Are you that selfish, Chanel? Don't you think Judah has been through enough already? You want him to find out that his cousin betrayed him, too?" she asked.

"Me and Judah were kids when he went away. You read the letter he wrote to me and saw the ones I wrote to him that came back marked return to sender. Why are you acting like we're stabbing him in his back?"

"'Cause that's exactly what you're doing. And I'm not gonna fake like I think it's okay."

Barbara was true to her word. She didn't address Deon directly for the rest of the day. He felt the change in her energy around him and kept his distance. He tried to shrug it off, but it got under his skin. Barbara was treating him like some new guy she was meeting for the first time rather than a young man she had practically watched grow up.

It began to wear on Deon's conscience more than ever. He thought back to the question Chanel had asked him when they professed their love for each other. What would his mother think of all this? Suddenly, he wasn't so sure.

He occupied himself with more work than usual, taking longer trips in an effort to put some distance between him and Chanel. He hoped that the absence of her would quell the longing he felt. But the opposite was true. Each time he returned home, he felt lonely without her. He could picture her in the kitchen making them dinner or sprawled out across his sofa watching TV. He felt the emptiness on her side of the bed and found himself dialing her number against the advice of all the voices in his head. She would come to him or he would go to her, and it felt like time stood still. As wrong as he knew it was, Deon loved her deeply.

Another year passed before he knew it. Chanel had been offered a job at CNN headquarters in Washington, DC, and was considering moving to Philadelphia. As excited as he was by the prospect of moving in together, Deon realized that it meant having the inevitable conversation with his cousin that he had been avoiding. Reluctantly, he decided to go and visit Judah in New York.

"I'm gonna tell him." Deon and Chanel were out to dinner to celebrate her twenty-third birthday in early August. He looked at her and nodded as if to convince himself.

Chanel stopped chewing.

"Now? While he's still in there? I thought you were gonna wait until he came home."

Deon had said that. All the times they discussed telling Judah the truth, Deon had argued that it would be better to tell him when he was home and on solid ground.

"I'm gonna tell him now. I feel like a snake keeping secrets from him like this. Every time he calls me or I write to him and he asks me what I'm up to. I want to tell him. But I need to do it man-to-man. Face-to-face."

Chanel could see that he meant it. She sipped her drink and set the glass down on the table.

"Should I come with you?"

Deon's eyes widened. He shook his head, perhaps a little too quickly for Chanel's liking.

"No," he said, emphatically. "I need to do this by myself."

Three days later, Deon made the trip to upstate New York.

Judah stared at his cousin intently. He sat forward with his arms resting on the table in front of him.

"Did you hear what I just said?" Judah asked, frowning. "I'm coming home!"

Deon was speechless.

It infuriated Judah. He leaned in even closer.

"Yo, why you don't seem happy to hear that shit?"

Deon shook his head, tried to fix his face.

"I'm happy, Judah. I'm just . . . you didn't even go to the board yet . . ."

"My counselor called me down and said that my hearing is coming up in November. I told you I did the research on cases like mine. I read my file and I talked to dudes in here who went through this process before. Until this case, I had no run-ins with the law, no prior convictions. I've been an unproblematic inmate for years. I got my diploma since I've been in here, and I'm three credits away from my degree. I'm gonna go in there and express remorse for the crime. And I'm walking out of here, Deon."

Deon forced a smile, hoping it was convincing. But Judah saw right through it.

"Yo, D. I'm gonna ask you one more time what's up with you?"

"I'm happy to hear this," Deon said. "I just don't want you to get your hopes up based off some shit a couple of niggas in there told you."

Judah banged on the table in frustration.

"What the fuck else do I have if I don't have some hope, Deon? Tell me that."

Deon knew that he couldn't tell him then. Not when hope was the last thing Judah was clinging to for dear life.

"I'm sorry," Deon said. "I'm not trying to put any doubt in your mind. I remember what it was like to—"

"Nah," Judah said. He smiled and turned his head away. He looked at his cousin again. "You went to juvie for a minute. I'm not saying that shit wasn't bad. But it wasn't this."

Judah stared at him meaningfully.

"Trust me."

After the visit, Deon made the long drive back to Chanel's place in a daze. He didn't turn on the radio, riding in silence as the reality of the situation sunk in at last.

She opened the door, smiling. She opened her arms and he

melted into them. They stood there embracing silently for several moments. She stepped back and looked at him. Noticing the look on his face, her smile faded.

"Are you okay?"

Deon shook his head. "No."

"What happened?"

He shook his head again. "Nelly, I have to go."

She frowned.

"I can't do this. Not to him. Not with you."

Chanel stared at him, her heart racing. She saw a series of emotions play out in his facial expressions and his body language. His posture was slumped. He looked drained, defeated.

"He was happy to see me. First time since Aunt Mercy died that I've seen him smile. All these years of sadness and he was finally happy for the first time. And I almost took that away from him."

"Deon—"

"He knows me. So, he could tell I had something on my mind. But I couldn't tell him. Sitting there with him, I realized I can never tell him. He would never forgive me." Deon looked at her, pleadingly. "I'm all he got. That's it. Just me. I've let him down my whole life. I can't do it this time."

She wanted to scream and yell and offer a million reasons why Deon didn't need to walk away from her. But the look in his eyes let her know that his decision was final. She fought past the lump in her throat.

"So, this is it?"

He stared at her. Finally, slowly, he nodded.

He wanted to tell her that he would never stop loving her. That this was the hardest thing he'd ever had to do. That she had been the only girl who made him feel like the king that his mother wanted him to be. But he allowed the tears that fell from his eyes speak for him. He pulled her close as she cried, too. He kissed her deeply as she clung to him, wanting desperately to change his mind.

He could feel his resolve weakening. Deon groaned in agony, pulled himself away, and walked out of the door without looking back.

Chanel watched the door swing shut behind him and wept.

COLD WORLD

November 2000

Freedom felt bittersweet.

Judah walked toward his cousin and had to resist the urge to run. He hadn't stepped outside of a correctional environment unshackled and in civilian clothes since he was a teenager. At twenty-four years old and newly paroled, he felt like a new man in every sense of the word. Having Deon there to greet him was the icing on the cake.

Deon rushed toward him and hugged him tightly. He patted Judah's back enthusiastically, aware that this moment was incredibly powerful for his cousin. He stepped back and looked at Judah.

"Welcome home," he said. "How's it feel to be a free man?"

Judah smiled wide. "I can't even describe it, D. I want to get the fuck out of here though."

Deon laughed and they climbed into his truck.

Judah tossed his modest belongings into the backseat and looked at Deon.

"I want to thank you again for letting me parole to your place. It's enough that you're doing that for me. You didn't have to drive all this way to come and get me, too. I could have taken a bus to Philly and saved you the trip."

Deon started the car and waved him off.

"Please! There's no way I was letting you walk out of there without seeing my face."

"I have to check in with the parole board out there within forty-eight hours."

Deon nodded. "I took some time off work so we can take care of all of that. I figured we'll go to the DMV and get you an ID card. Aunt Mercy left a little life insurance policy. It wasn't much, like I told you. Just $30,000. I used some of it for her funeral expenses. The rest is in a bank account I set up for you."

Judah nodded. "Thank you, D. I know you handled everything with the funeral, packed up that apartment, and got all my mother's affairs in order. I appreciate that, cousin. I can never repay you."

"You would've did the same for me," Deon said. "One other thing. I got you a job lined up."

Judah's eyes went wide. "What?"

Deon nodded. "There's a guy I deliver to on one of my routes needs some help. Stocking shelves, loading and unloading the truck, sweeping up. That type of thing. The pay won't be great, but it's something to get you started."

Judah grabbed his cousin's arm excitedly. "Yo, Deon, THANK YOU! As happy as I am to be home, I was stressing about the job thing. I want to stand on my own two feet, not depend on you for everything. This means a lot, D. For real."

Deon smiled, grabbed Judah's hand, and reminded him, "We're family."

They rode most of the way to Philadelphia in silence. Judah seemed lost in thought as he stared out the window at the changing landscape. Deon had plenty on his mind as well and was grateful for the silence. Three months had passed since his breakup with Chanel. He had resisted every urge to call her, but still thought about her every day. He wondered whether she had taken the job in DC and found himself looking for her as he drove through the streets there on his work route. Glancing at his cousin from time to time, Deon knew that he had made the right decision. Judah stared out the window looking like his younger self. Carefree and full of optimism for what his future held.

Judah turned to him as they rode along.

"Nothing turned out the way I planned it," he said. "I thought by now I'd have my degree from Morgan State and I'd be teaching literature somewhere. I saw myself being a role model for young black boys like us." He laughed at the thought now. "Instead, I'm a felon who has to report to a parole officer every week and adhere to an eight o'clock curfew."

"But you're free," Deon said. "And you know who you are. Regardless of what the government labels you as. You're a man. Aunt Mercy would be proud of you. Just remember that."

Judah smiled at that. He thought back to their last visit and how she voiced a similar sentiment. He sat back and reminded himself to look on the bright side.

They stopped and had dinner at a seafood restaurant. Judah ate so much that Deon marveled at it.

"I used to be the one throwing back three heaping plates at dinnertime. Now it's you!"

Judah patted his stomach, guiltily. "Word. Prison made me appreciate a decent meal. I haven't had food this good in a very long time." He thanked Deon for the dinner and they headed home for the night.

When they got there, Judah complimented Deon on his apartment.

"I shared a room with you. So, I thought you were still a slob. I walked in here expecting the worst. But this place is actually nice!"

Deon laughed. "Fuck you, cuz. Come see your room."

He led Judah down the hall and walked him into his new living space. Deon had been using the spare room as a walk-in closet for all his sneakers and clothes. He had packed it all up and squeezed it into his bedroom in order to make room for Judah. He thought about a story Chanel told him once. How Judah had once cleared out his own closet to make room for Deon after Lenox was killed. Deon felt grateful for the chance to return the favor. Especially as he watched Judah gleefully open up the closet and see all the clothes and shoes with tags still on them, all in Judah's size. He looked at Deon.

"These are your clothes?" he asked, confused.

Deon shook his head. "Nah. They're yours. Welcome home, cousin!"

Judah's joy had bubbled over then. He started snatching shirts off hangers and stripped down so that he could try everything on.

Deon watched, gleefully.

They spent the next few days getting Judah established. They went to the parole office and met his assigned officer. He was instructed to check in weekly with his parole officer and was told that he would be subject to surprise visits to ensure that he was adhering to the curfew. Deon brought him to the convenience store in Germantown where Judah would be working six days a week. Judah and the store owner hit it off easily, and all the pieces slowly began to fall in place in his life. Some mornings, Deon drove Judah to work on his way to start his local truck routes. When Deon's routes took him out of town, Judah caught the train to work. He took his job seriously and enjoyed interacting with the customers. All the little things he had once easily taken for granted now brought him tremendous joy. Simple things like a "thank you" from an old lady or a smile from a child. For Judah those occurrences became as special as seeing a shooting star.

On weekends, Judah and Deon watched football on the large screen TV in the living room and drank Hennessy. As the year drew to a close, they reminisced on the holidays they spent with their mothers in years gone by. Judah sat slouched on the sofa with a glass of brown liquor in his hand, grinning as he retold a story Deon had heard a thousand times.

"Aunt Lenox was like, 'Judah, you've read so many books that you should write an encyclopedia. Call it Judah's Jewels of Wisdom.'" Judah laughed. "I should do that shit for real. Dedicate it to Aunt Lenox."

Deon laughed. "She said that shit hoping you would go and start writing it then and there. That way you would stop talking her ear off about some fuckin' Sherlock Holmes and Watson bullshit."

Judah laughed. "Hater!"

Deon laughed, too. "Encyclopedia. You wish!"

Judah sighed. "You ever miss it?"

Deon frowned. "What? New York?"

Judah nodded. "You been back to Staten Island since my mother's funeral?"

Deon shook his head. "Nope. Once I packed up the apartment and loaded up my car, I never looked back. Nothing but bad memories in that place for me."

Judah shrugged.

"I feel you." He sipped his drink. "I think about it sometimes. Maybe because when I left I never thought it would be for the last time. I still feel like I have unfinished business there."

Deon looked at him and noted the pensive look in Judah's eyes. Deon knew that he was referring to Chanel before he even said her name.

"I know she moved away. Last time my mother mentioned her, she told me she was living in Delaware. But I can't think of Staten Island without thinking of Chanel."

Deon was silent, watching, waiting for Judah to say more.

"Sometimes I wonder if she still thinks about me." He glanced at Deon and caught his eye. "Silly, right?"

Deon shook his head. "Nah. I don't think it's silly."

Judah swallowed the last of his drink and closed his eyes.

Deon was out of town for work the week leading up to Christmas. It was an adjustment for Judah at first, having the apartment to himself. He realized that he had never lived alone his entire life and had become so used to the noise of a correctional facility that he needed the TV on just for background noise as he slept. He checked in with his parole officer as scheduled, went to work, and came home each night with fast food in hand. With his first paycheck, he had gone to the bookstore and purchased a bunch of hardcovers as a reward for himself. He had devoured several already and started reading a new one as he sat on the couch with ESPN playing in the background. The author of the book—a woman named Zane—had written some wildly erotic sex scenes that got Judah aroused. He set the book down and tugged at his erection.

He thought of Nia. Since coming home, he hadn't reached out to her. Too preoccupied with establishing a new routine in this new city. While he had been locked up, Nia had given him a much needed distraction from the madness. He wondered what it would be like to see her in the flesh.

He picked up the phone and dialed her phone number. He waited, half expecting her on-again, off-again boyfriend to pick up. But to Judah's relief, Nia's voice filled his ear.

"Hello?"

"Nia?"

"Who's this?"

"It's Judah."

She paused. "Judah? You're out?"

He chuckled. "Yeah. I got released in November. I'm staying with my cousin Deon in Philadelphia."

"Ohhh," Nia sang. "I was wondering who was calling me from a 215 area code! I almost didn't pick up. Thought you were a tele-marketer or a bill collector."

"Nah, you can relax," Judah said. "It's just me."

"How does it feel being out?" she asked. "You like it in Phila-delphia?"

"Feels great! I got a little job, got me a little routine going. I'm figuring it out."

"That's what's up," Nia said. "But since you're in Philly, does that mean you can't come and see me?"

He sighed. "Yeah, unfortunately. Unless I sneak out of town real quick. But I can't take chances like that yet." Judah's freedom was so precious to him that he wouldn't risk it. Not even for the promise of Nia's wetness and warmth. "You could come and see me, though."

She thought about that and smiled. "That could work. Maybe I'll get a babysitter and come and visit you for New Year's."

Judah smiled. "That sounds nice. I'd like that."

Nia propped the phone against her shoulder. "I ran into your ex today at ShopRite. She was in there with her mother looking at turkeys, probably for Christmas dinner."

Judah's heart skipped a beat. "My ex? Chanel?"

"Yeah," Nia said. "I heard she moved out of New York, but she must be back to visit her family for the holidays."

"How did she look?" Judah asked it without thinking.

Nia frowned, sucked her teeth, and looked at the phone like it was a foreign object. "What type of question is that? I don't know. Same as she did the last time you seen her."

Judah recalled the last time he had seen Chanel, at his mother's funeral. He had been so devastated and crushed by his loss that he could barely recall how Chanel had looked that day. He remembered her standing in front of him talking about how much his mother loved him. But his eyes had been flooded with tears, blurring Chanel from his view.

"You got a lot of nerve, Judah. Asking me to come and see you in one breath then in the next you wanna know how your ex is looking."

Judah apologized. "I didn't mean it like that. It's just that I haven't seen her in years. It was just a question."

Nia rolled her eyes. "She looks the same," she answered. "You want to know how I look?"

Judah sighed. He had forgotten how complicated women were. "Yeah," he said, trying to sound as sincere as he could. "I definitely want to see you, Nia. It's been a long time."

She lightened up then and began talking about getting a day off from her job so that she could come to town on a Friday.

Deon walked in the apartment while Judah was on the phone. He entered carrying the big duffel bag he brought with him on the road and a bag of food that smelled so good it made Judah sit up on the sofa. Judah waved and gestured at the phone in his hand as he continued his conversation.

"Yeah. That sounds like a plan. Let me know when you find out the Amtrak schedule and all that. I'll make sure I'm there to meet you." He talked for another minute or so before hanging up and greeting his cousin.

"What's up, D. What did you bring in here? That smells amazing!"

They greeted each other with a pound and Deon began unpacking the bag of steaming hot food.

"I stopped at that soul food spot in Takoma Park. Hooked us up!"

Judah rubbed his hands together excitedly and dug right in.

"Who was that on the phone?" Deon asked.

"Nia. I gave her a call. She's gonna come and see me for New Year's."

Deon smiled wide. "That's what the fuck I'm talking about, Judah. You ain't wasting no time, huh?"

Judah laughed. "After eight years, I hope she knows what she's in for."

Deon laughed, too. He set the last of the containers on the stove and wiped his hands on a paper towel.

"I gotta get in the shower before I eat," he said. "I feel disgusting after being in that rig for two days. I'll eat when I get out."

Judah nodded while Deon went to his room to unwind.

Judah sat down at the kitchen table with a plate of food. He heard the shower go on and then the distant sound of Deon singing along off-key to a Carl Thomas song.

Judah replayed his conversation with Nia. As happy as he was about the prospect of seeing her again and having sex for the first time in his adult life, it was the other part of their conversation that got him the most excited. Nia had seen Chanel.

He set his fork down and went into the living room and picked up the phone. He sat down on the couch and dialed the phone number to Barbara's house. He still remembered it by heart. It rang only twice before someone picked up. Judah's heart leapt as he recognized the voice instantly.

She started talking the second she picked up. She sounded so breathless and anxious that it caught Judah off guard.

"Oh, my God," she gushed. "I thought you'd never call again. I miss you so much."

Judah could tell that she was crying. He frowned, wondering how she knew it was him calling. He opened his mouth to speak but she kept on talking.

"I know it's complicated and it's messy and everybody thinks we're crazy. But I love you. I know you love me, too. We can figure it out."

Judah's heart raced as he listened to her, frowning. None of it made sense.

"Hello . . . Chanel?"

She stopped talking immediately. She began to sweat. *Chanel.* Not Nelly. She knew instantly that she had fucked up.

"Is this . . ."

"This is Judah," he said.

"Judah? Oh, my God. You're home?"

He didn't respond. He was too busy trying to piece it all together. Slowly, painfully, he began to unravel it. Deon walked into the room with a towel and a bathrobe on, fresh out of the shower. He smiled at Judah and nodded his chin in his direction.

"Romeo's back at it, huh?"

Judah didn't smile. He gripped the phone tighter as Chanel spoke into his ear again.

"Judah, is that you?"

"You thought it was Deon. Didn't you?" Judah stared at his cousin as he asked it.

Deon frowned. "Who you talking to on the phone?"

Chanel's heart sank. "Judah . . ."

"Huh, Chanel? You thought Deon was calling you, right?"

Deon felt his world crashing down around him. Aware now who was on the other end of the phone call, he knew that their secret was out. He felt his adrenaline rushing as Judah stared at him hatefully.

Judah pulled the phone away from his face, set it down beside him on the sofa. He looked at Deon as he stood up slowly.

"You fucking her?"

Deon shook his head. "Nah. Nah, Judah. It's not like that."

"She thought it was you calling." Judah took deliberate steps in Deon's direction. "She said she loves you. Said y'all can figure this out. So, what the fuck is going on, D?"

Deon held his hands up in front of him defensively. "Judah, that shit is over—"

Judah punched him in the mouth with so much force that Deon's teeth chattered. He tasted blood in his mouth then felt another punch, this one knocking teeth loose. Deon, still wet from the shower, fought to get his bearings. But Judah didn't let up. He rocked him with a blow to the eye. Deon pushed him back with all the force he could muster. Judah fell back, knocking a picture off the wall, and the frame fell to the floor loudly.

Deon backed up, eager to put some distance between them.

His eye began swelling up immediately. Through blurry vision, he held his arms out between them defensively.

"Judah, I swear to God that's finished. I ended that shit because I knew it would hurt you."

"YOU KNEW THAT SHIT WOULD HURT ME FROM
THE BEGINNING!"

Judah's voice thundered through the whole building. He rushed
Deon again, this time scooping him up off his feet MMA style and
slamming him hard on the floor. Stacks of CDs and DVDs fell from
the entertainment center as they fought. Judah was on top of Deon
beating him with a flurry of blows so powerful that Deon worried he
might get knocked out. He hit Judah back, more in an effort to stop
him than as an attempt to hurt him. One blow connected with Judah's mouth, enraging him even more. He got up and grabbed a bottle of Hennessy from the table and cracked it hard over Deon's head.

The intensity of the blow rocked Deon. He felt a ringing in his
ears as Judah hit him again.

Deon got up and rushed his cousin. Both of them fell into
the glass coffee table, shattering it into a million little pieces. They
grunted and gritted their teeth ferally as they fought.

Deon got to his feet, wincing from the pain of the glass on the
floor cutting into his flesh. He finally managed to put enough distance between them for a conversation. Breathlessly, he stood behind
the sofa that had been moved to the center of the room during the
fight. He looked at Judah, his eyes pleading.

"Judah, let me explain. It wasn't like that." Even as he said it, he
knew he was lying. It had been exactly like that. He shook his head,
wishing he could take it all back now. "It's done. That shit is over. I
swear to God. I haven't seen her in months."

Judah's chest heaved and he felt like screaming from the pit of
his gut. He shook his head, glaring at Deon and fighting back tears.

"All the women out here and you had to fuck with *her*?" He
shook his head, so deeply hurt that he began to cry. He didn't have
the energy to fight it anymore. He cried furiously as he spoke. "After
all I did for you! I went to jail for you, D. I gave up eight years of
my life trying to defend you. I lost my mother! You hear what I'm
saying? I lost *my moms* while I was in there. I can never get that time

back. I will never see her again. And I did that shit for you. The whole time . . . year after year I kept telling myself that you would have done the same thing for me. That you were my brother." Judah's voice cracked. He shook his head. "I should've let them muthafuckas kill you that day."

"Judah—"

"I should have let Dre bash you in the head with that bat and scatter your brains all over the fucking concrete that day. If I had, my mother would still be here. I wouldn't have spent the past eight years of my life in hell. The whole time I was in there fighting for my life you were out here fucking Chanel."

Deon shook his head. "Judah, nah. You're wrong. I came out here and started over. I never even thought about Chanel until I went back for the funeral."

"You had EVERYTHING!" Judah spun around in the apartment gesturing at all of it. The large screen TV, the clothes, food, the apartment itself. He looked at Deon, incredulously. "You had your freedom. While I was living in a cell listening to rats rustling through my food at night, praying to God that He would get me out of there, you were here living like a king. You could have had any chick you wanted. But you had to fuck with mine." Judah laughed maniacally. "You stole my life from me. I was the one with the promising future and the girl. I had my mother and I had hope. You took all that shit. I went to prison and you stepped into my shoes and took the life I left behind."

Judah vaulted over the couch so quickly that Deon barely had a chance to react. Judah grabbed him by the throat and pushed him back against the wall so hard that Deon felt the bones in his back crack.

Someone pounded loudly on the door. Unswayed, Judah squeezed Deon's throat, wanting to kill him. The person at the door banged again. Louder this time.

"Montgomery County Police Department! Open up!"

Judah's chest heaved as he stared at his cousin, his hands still wrapped around Deon's thick neck. He knew that the presence of law enforcement meant that he could be going back to prison. But he didn't give a fuck.

"Judah . . ." Deon struggled for air. "Let me get that. Come on." Deon didn't want to see his cousin go back to jail. And he knew that if the police kicked that door down and found them in this position that's exactly what the outcome would be. "Let me get the door."

Judah let go of Deon's throat and slapped him so hard across the face that his own hand stung afterwards. Deon recoiled, resisting the instinctive urge to hit Judah back, and stood up tall. He pulled his robe around his body, aching all over now from the effects of the battle. He opened the door and found three police officers and several of his neighbors standing there.

"We got a call about a disturbance," one of the officers said. He peered inside the apartment and saw Judah pacing the floor angrily. "Is everything alright?"

Deon nodded. "Everything is fine. My cousin and I just had an argument. That's all."

The cop looked at Deon skeptically. It was clear that he had gotten the worst of the fight, evidenced by his swollen eye and bloody mouth. His robe had blood on it, too, and he had a cut on his right hand.

"You sure about that?" the officer asked. "Your neighbors said they heard what sounded like a murder going on in here."

Judah huffed when he heard that. If only the cops had been a little longer getting there. He could have made that happen. He walked down the hallway as Deon spoke with the officers. He threw a bunch of clothes into a bag and grabbed his coat out of the closet. As he gathered those items, it occurred to him that Deon had purchased all of it for him. Judah thought it was a generous gesture at the time. That his cousin had lovingly supplied him with a wardrobe to welcome him home. Now it felt like a guilt offering for the betrayal Deon had inflicted on him. Judah snatched it all up angrily and barreled back down the hall.

Deon was still speaking with the police, assuring them that everything was fine. Judah charged back into the room, snatched the keys to Deon's truck off the table, and picked up his wallet. Deon watched Judah remove all the cash from his wallet and stuff it into his own pocket. Judah looked at Deon and the police as he walked toward the door.

"It's all good, officers. I'm leaving." He looked at two of Deon's neighbors as he left. "Sorry about the noise."

Judah got into Deon's Suburban, started it up, and peeled out of there, daring the cops to stop him.

One of the officers looked at Deon. "You want to file a report?"

Deon shook his head. "No, thank you." He watched as the truck disappeared from sight.

Judah was so blinded by rage that he could barely see. He hadn't driven a car in years and his right leg trembled nervously as he pressed it on the gas pedal. He swerved a bit now as he barreled down the highway, enraged.

He kept hearing Chanel's voice in his head.

I love you. I know you love me, too. We can figure it out.

His mind was reeling, overloaded as he tried to wrap his mind around the truth. Chanel and Deon had crossed the line. They had betrayed him. Judah's emotions mingled together in a toxic mixture. Rage, jealousy, and a thirst for vengeance had him thinking unimaginable thoughts. He considered going back to that apartment, waiting until the police were gone, then going inside and murdering Deon with his bare hands. He could commit suicide afterwards maybe. Or perhaps he would just wait for the cops to come and put him back in prison. Either way, he knew that if he did what he wanted to do and killed his cousin, Judah's life would be over.

And it wouldn't undo the damage that was already done. Deon and Chanel were in love.

He exhaled angrily, floored the gas, and continued on his journey. He wouldn't give Deon the satisfaction of ruining what remained of his own life. He wondered how long it had been going on. Had it started before his mother's passing or afterwards? He thought back to her funeral, trying to remember if there had been any signs he may have missed that his own cousin was doing him dirty. He thought about the past few weeks since his release. The way Deon had lavished him with clothes and a job and welcomed him with open arms into his home. All of it, Judah realized now, had been a guilt offering. He recalled the visit Deon made to see him at Greene. How lackluster his reaction had been to the news that Judah would be coming home soon. It all made sense now. Of course Deon hadn't been excited by the fact that his little party with Chanel was coming to an end.

Judah hadn't felt so unhinged in years. Not since he was on Rikers Island at the age of sixteen. Back then he had gotten jumped by a gang of Harlem dudes who had stabbed him, kicked and punched him until he lay leaking on the floor. The C.O.s had stood by and let it happen, then locked Judah in solitary confinement "for his own safety." He remembered it well. Lying on his bunk feeling the physical and emotional effects of being beaten mercilessly and the embarrassment of knowing dozens of people had witnessed it. Being taunted, laughed at, and powerless to do anything about it had made him feel frustrated to the point of being violently angry. He spent two days screaming at the top of his lungs out of sheer exasperation. He felt the same way now. But this time, he had no intention of yelling until he lost his voice. He floored the gas, gripped the steering wheel, and focused on the road ahead.

Two hours later, Barbara looked through the peephole and gasped.

"Oh, my God!"

Frantically, she unbolted both of the locks and slid the chain from its latch. She threw the door open and froze.

"JUDAH!"

"Hi, Miss Barbara."

"Come in!" She stood aside as he entered. She locked the door and turned to him.

"Judah! My goodness, how long have you been out?"

"Couple months," he said.

She stared at him in awe. She noted how handsome he still was, though the light had gone out of his eyes. "God, I wish your mother was here to see you."

He nodded. "Me, too."

Barbara threw her arms around him and pulled him into a tight hug. She began to cry softly. She apologized.

"I'm sorry. I know you don't need this right now. I'm just so happy to see you free. And I know Mercy was praying for this. Every day and night she prayed for you."

Judah smiled weakly. "I miss her," he said.

"Me, too." Barbara wiped her eyes. "She was the best friend I ever had in my life."

Chanel stood at the door of her childhood bedroom, trembling. She listened to the murmur of their voices down the hall and her body shook with fear and dread. Deon had called her hours ago after Judah had taken the keys to his truck and disappeared. Deon worried that his cousin might hurt himself. Now, hearing his voice down the hall, she worried that he intended to hurt her instead.

"She would be so proud of you," Barbara said. "I'm proud of you." Absentmindedly, she glanced down the hall toward Chanel's room. She looked at Judah again. "I want you to know that I'm so sorry for everything."

"Thank you," he said, flatly. "Is Chanel here?"

Barbara nodded. She looked at him and could sense his anger by the set of his jaw. His hands were fisted and he stood staring back at her expectantly.

Chanel emerged from her room and saw Judah standing with her mother near the front door. He turned and locked eyes with her as she approached.

"Hello," she said, faintly.

Judah didn't respond.

Barbara cleared her throat. "I'm gonna let you two talk. There's a lot that you both need to say to each other. I just want you to know that Chanel is my daughter and I love her. But I don't agree with everything that she does. I know your mother wouldn't agree with a lot of things either. But Mercy would tell you to remember what's at stake here. You've been through so much already." She looked at him, meaningfully.

Judah nodded.

Barbara rubbed his arm warmly.

"Come in and sit down. You want anything to eat?"

Judah thanked her and shook his head. "No, thank you." He sat down on the couch, his gaze fixed on Chanel.

Barbara looked at her daughter and sighed. Chanel had been crying for hours and finally seemed to grasp the severity of Judah's pain. Barbara had given her all the advice she could muster. Now it was Chanel's turn to face the music like a grown woman. Barbara gave a slight nod in her direction and retreated to her bedroom.

Chanel walked over and sat across from Judah on the love seat.

His eyes bore into her. He noticed her trembling and could tell by the way she sat gingerly on the edge of her seat that she was scared of him. It only made him angrier. He hadn't come there to hurt her. Although he felt that he had every right to.

"I never thought I could feel any worse than I did the day they sent me to Rikers Island. But it got a lot worse. The day I got sentenced and heard the judge say eight and a third to fifteen years. The day they called me down to the warden's office to tell me my mother was dead. The day they brought me to her funeral in shackles and I had to stand there and accept that I would never get to talk to her again."

Chanel dabbed at her eyes and his face twitched. He wanted to wring her neck. She stared down at her hands.

"I really thought I must have seen the worst of it by now. But today I found out that you and my cousin . . . y'all betrayed me. And I just needed to come here and look you in the face and find out why you would do that to me. After all the shit I already went through."

She took a deep breath, steeled herself, and looked at him. The expression on his face was so pained that she felt it like a stab in her own heart.

"Judah, I'm not sure where to start."

"Start at the beginning. Did you ever love me, Chanel?"

She nodded and squeezed her face tightly, fighting back tears. "I did."

"But now you love my cousin." Judah said it sarcastically, pain dripping from every word.

"I didn't mean to." Chanel felt ashamed of it. But there was no denying the truth.

Judah glared at her contemptuously.

"After you went away, I wrote to you and I swore that I would be here when you came home. That I would wait for you and I would look after your mom. You wrote me back and you said—"

"I know what I said!"

"Then you know that you pushed me away. I didn't just accept it. I wrote back to you. I begged Miss Mercy to convince you to let me come and see you. I kept trying—"

"Did you try, Chanel? Did you try to put yourself in my shoes and imagine what it was like for me in there by myself?"

She nodded and he looked away, disgusted.

"I thought about you every day," she said. "I missed you and I cried for you."

"When did that stop?"

She stared back at him.

"Answer that. When did you stop missing me and start fucking my cousin?"

She looked away then.

"Judah, you keep talking to me like you gave me a chance to be there for you. You cut me off. You didn't write me back, never called me. When I left here and went away to college, I felt more alone than I ever felt in my life. I had lost touch with you and Deon. My family wasn't around anymore. It was just me. It was nothing like we planned. We talked about going to Morgan State and I really envisioned it being that way. Me and you. But it was just me. And I was lonely. Your mother passed and I came home, praying that I would get the chance to see you. That maybe you had changed your mind about us. I helped Deon make the arrangements for the funeral. And we talked about you and about the old days with the three of us."

"And you fucked him."

"It didn't happen like that. I saw you at the service and you hardly said a word to me. I asked the cops if I could hug you and you didn't seem like you even wanted me there."

Judah sat forward, glowering at her angrily.

"Chanel, I had just lost my mother. I was ready to self-destruct in that room. When you walked over to me and started talking to me about my mother and how much she loved me, I damn near fell apart." He shook his head. "So, you took that as an excuse to go running to Deon?"

She knew it sounded bad.

"After the funeral we were both upset."

"How do you think I was feeling?" Judah asked.

She sat speechlessly and realized that nothing she could say would make this digestible for him.

"You could have picked anybody else. But Deon? I don't see how you could ever think that was okay. Or how he could be with you knowing how I felt about you."

Chanel's heart sank lower.

"I didn't know if you still felt that way," she said. "I didn't know, Judah."

"Yes, you did," Judah said. "Deon did, too. Aside from my mother, there was nobody I was closer to than you and D. I talked to you about him. Told you all the things I wanted for him when he didn't have enough sense to want it for himself. I talked to D about you. Told him all my plans for us and everything I was feeling for you." Judah smirked. "Y'all must have had a good laugh at my expense. Silly fucking Judah thinking we love him."

"No!" Chanel cried. "I'm telling you it wasn't easy. We love you. Especially Deon."

Judah laughed. "If this shit y'all did to me is love, you can keep it."

"Deon is the one who ended it between us. I was willing to face you and tell you that even though I'm sorry it turned out this way, I still care about him. I wanted to try to make it work. But he loves you more than he will ever love me. So, please don't be mad at him."

Judah stared at her. Somehow, he felt worse than he had when he arrived. Hearing Chanel beg him to forgive Deon showed how much she was in love with him. Judah knew in that moment there was nothing left to say.

He stood up and looked down at her.

"When a person goes to jail, it's like time freezes at that moment. In a way, you expect to come home and find things the same way you left them. But nothing stays the same. Things change. People change. I can deal with that. What I can't accept is that after everything I shared with you, you and Deon crossed a line as big as this. That will never sit right with me."

He reached inside of his jacket and pulled out a small stack of envelopes. He handed them to her unceremoniously. She accepted them with a confused expression on her face.

"These are letters I wrote to you when I was gone. I never sent them. I guess you took my silence to mean that I was done with you.

But I think when you read these, you'll understand a little better. I wasn't trying to cut you off. I was trying to spare you the weight of what I was going through in there."

Judah shrugged as if it didn't matter now.

Chanel stood up and faced him eye to eye.

"I'm sorry. I swear, Judah. I never wanted to hurt you."

He looked her up and down, shook his head, and huffed, realizing that she and Deon deserved each other.

"You probably didn't want to. But you did."

He walked to the door without further conversation and left. He walked down the hallway to his old apartment. He started to knock, hoping the new tenants might let him take a peek inside for old times' sake. But he stood at the door and heard a mother yelling profanities at a bunch of kids playing noisily inside. He opted not to knock. Instead, he held his hand up to the door and touched it one last time. Then he turned and walked down the stairs.

As he descended, he recalled all the memories he had of this stairwell. Him and Chanel pressed against the wall kissing. Him and Deon jumping down the steps two at a time as they rushed out to the Big Park. Each memory bittersweet.

"Judah," Chanel called after him down the stairs.

He paused his descent, looked up, and saw her leaning over the railing with tears in her eyes.

A sob escaped her.

"I did love you. Very much."

He stared up at her and nodded. "Good to know."

He kept descending the stairs as she watched him. He walked out of the building and glanced up at his old apartment windows one last time. He got in the truck and drove to the cemetery where his mother and Aunt Lenox were laid to rest. It was past 9 P.M., so the cemetery gate was closed. He decided that it was for the best. Staring down at a cold slab of dirt in the ground wouldn't comfort him anyway. He parked the truck and sat there thinking about his next move.

He pondered the thought of hitting the highway, heading west and never looking back, but he knew that the parole board would be after him. He wondered if Deon had reported his truck stolen or notified his parole officer that he'd left town. As tempting as it was to leave everything behind and never look back, he knew that he had to go back to Philadelphia and close this chapter of his life.

Judah took a deep breath, put the key in the ignition, and left Staten Island for good.

RECKONING

He took his time driving back. One reason he stuck to the speed limit was an abundance of caution. Now that his fury had waned somewhat, he realized what a risk he had taken by coming to New York. He was a parolee who had left the state without authorization. He also had no driver's license and had technically stolen Deon's truck—along with the cash from his wallet. As he drove, he thought about Mercy and what she would say about all of this.

"Judah," he imagined her saying. "You're smarter than this."

He pulled into a rest stop and used the pay phone to call Xavier. To his relief, he answered right away

"Hey. This is Judah."

Xavier was ecstatic. "Judah! My God, it's good to hear your voice. How you doing, son?"

Judah sighed. "This is gonna sound crazy, but I'm out of jail. I paroled to my cousin's place in Philly. But I had to leave. If I go back there, I'm going back to jail. Because I'll kill him."

Judah gave Xavier the rundown—that his cousin and Chanel had broken his heart. "I can't be anywhere near him. So, I need your help."

Xavier was already out of bed gathering his things. "Tell me where you are. I'm on my way."

Judah gave Xavier Deon's address in Philadelphia. He climbed back into his cousin's truck and started it up.

He glanced at the dashboard clock as he drove carefully to his cousin's apartment complex. Judah realized that it was slightly past midnight. Christmas Day. He smiled, recalling the tradition he and his mother had established during his incarceration of listing the gifts they wished to give each other. This would be his second Christmas without her. And his first one as a free man in eight years. He thought about the list of gifts she had given him during that final visit.

Freedom, strength, and peace. He allowed his mind to linger on each one. He had his freedom now. But Mercy had been careful to point out that she wanted Judah to be free not just in the physical sense. But in spirit. Free from worrying about others. He was starting to realize what a valuable gift that would be going forward. He felt alone in the world. His mother was gone. Aunt Lenox was, too. His relationships with Deon and Chanel would never be the same. He felt as alone as he had in solitary confinement. Only this time he wasn't confined. He was free. Relief washed over him like a wave.

Mercy had also gifted him strength of mind and spirit. Strength of character. He had summoned every bit he had in order to prevent himself from going back to prison for killing Deon. His mother's final gift had been peace. Judah knew that if he was ever going to have a chance at receiving that precious gift, it would mean cutting his cousin off completely.

He drove to the convenience store in Germantown where he worked. He parked the truck behind the store, reclined the driver's seat, and went to sleep for a couple of hours. He was exhausted after driving to and from New York City, and after the emotionally draining day he had endured. On top of that, he was in no rush to see Deon again, though he knew it was inevitable.

Judah woke up at 6:20 A.M. and put the car in drive. He stopped at McDonald's on the way and got some breakfast. He sat in the car and ate it, plotting his next move. It was time to take the gifts that Mercy had given him and live what remained of his life to the fullest.

He could feel the tension in his body begin to build up as he pulled up to the front of Deon's building that Christmas morning. He had received as much closure as he could possibly get from Chanel. Now he was eager to do the same with his cousin.

Judah walked into the apartment and noticed Deon's attempts to clean up the place. A pile of glass had been swept into a corner. CDs and DVDs were stacked on the floor. The sofa had been pushed back to its usual position at the far end of the room.

Deon sat in the leather recliner, staring at the TV even though it wasn't turned on. He had been sitting in silence that way for more than an hour, wondering if Judah had any intention of coming back there. As he walked in, Deon sat forward in his seat and opened his mouth to speak. Judah walked past him, though, and went straight to the kitchen. He grabbed a handful of Hefty bags and went into the bedroom. He began tossing his clothes and shoes into the garbage bags. When he was done, he carried them all down the hall and stacked them by the front door.

Deon watched in silence. Then Xavier appeared in the doorway, and Deon understood what was happening. He stood up to face the man.

Xavier nodded in his direction. "Hey." He wasn't sure what else to say.

"Hey," Deon said. He walked over and greeted him with a hug and a handshake. "I'm sorry you had to come out here." He was sorry for so many things.

Xavier could tell that this was weighing heavily on Deon. He patted him on the arm reassuringly. On the way to pick up Judah, he had thought about what Mercy would say about all of this. He knew that it would break her heart knowing the two boys she raised into men were at each other's throats.

Judah emerged from the room with another bag of belongings, and he greeted Xavier.

Judah turned his attention to his cousin and smiled. For a brief moment, Deon felt encouraged. Then he noticed the look in Judah's eyes. Despite the smile on his lips, Judah's gaze was full of contempt.

"The only reason I came back here was to get my shit, to bring you back your car." Judah tossed the keys on Deon's couch for emphasis. "And to get in touch with my parole officer so I don't get violated and sent back to prison. I'm gonna move down to Maryland with Xavier until I get a place of my own."

"You don't have to do this, Judah."

Judah looked at Deon sadly. They had been closer than brothers. Now Judah wanted to spit in his face. His expression was flat and unemotional.

"I could have killed you last night. With my bare hands. That's how mad I was. If I don't get away from you, I'm gonna wind up back in jail. So, I'm out."

Xavier cleared his throat and looked at both of them.

"Y'all come in here and sit down for a minute," Xavier said. He gestured toward the sofa and looked at both of them seriously. Noticing Judah's hesitation, he looked him in the eyes. "Do this for me."

Reluctantly, Judah sat down. Xavier sat beside him on the sofa. Deon sat on the edge of the love seat.

Xavier wasn't sure where to begin. He sighed. "Y'all are all you have left. Both of your mothers are gone. Both of you have lost so much. Time, family, life experiences. And it's time for us to talk about that. Because none of what's happening between the two of you is really about Chanel."

"That's exactly what it's about," Judah disagreed.

"No," Xavier insisted. "She might be the catalyst for this situation. But it's not really about her. It's about you two, and it's about your mothers. You've been living in your mothers' shadows for too long."

Judah rolled his eyes and looked away. Xavier glanced at Deon and saw the hopeful expression on his face. It was clear that he wanted to resolve things with his cousin. Judah sat defiantly staring down at the floor. Xavier noted how their roles had reversed. Judah had once been the focused and more reasonable one. Deon had always been the rebel who couldn't be reached. But years of incarceration had changed Judah into someone Xavier barely recognized. He wished for the millionth time that Mercy was still alive to help her son heal from his trauma.

"Xavier's right," Judah said at last. He looked at Deon. "You're a lot like your mother. And I'm a lot like mine. Funny how that happens. Aunt Lenox was selfish, too. Just like you."

Deon winced a little, hearing his mother described that way. But he didn't argue.

"Aunt Len wanted it all," Judah continued. "No matter what she had to do to get it. No matter who got hurt."

Deon didn't respond.

"You're like that. Gotta get what you want. Fuck everybody else. My mother was a giver. A caretaker. That's where I get it from. But whenever you put a caretaker next to a selfish person, the same thing happens. The selfish one always takes advantage of the caretaker."

Deon could sense Judah's quiet rage. Though he spoke in an even voice and his demeanor was calm, there was fury bubbling just beneath the surface. He realized as he listened that Judah's anger was not just for the things he had sacrificed. But for the things Mercy had sacrificed as well.

"Aunt Lenox died because of her selfishness."

"Watch your mouth," Deon warned, fed up now.

"When she died, she left my mother burdened with you."

Deon felt the power of Judah's words like a punch to the gut. He grimaced.

Judah didn't care.

"Instead of being grateful that she took you in, you tortured her for years with your bullshit. Then I was dumb enough to try to help you fight your demons. And those demons came and tore me apart. And while that was happening, you turned your back and walked away with everything that was supposed to be mine."

Deon cleared his throat. "I know you're upset. But I'm not gonna sit here and let you talk about my mother like that. I know she wasn't perfect. Neither am I. You're right about that. But you act like I plotted on you, Judah. Like I meant for this shit to happen. None of it was supposed to go like this. I didn't ask you to come outside that day to save me."

"Me and my mother were always saving you," Judah shot back.

"That's 'cause we're family," Deon said.

"Not anymore," Judah insisted. "You're not my cousin. Not my brother. I don't fuck with you at all."

"Hold on!" Xavier protested. He frowned at Judah. "Your mother wouldn't want that. And you know it."

"My mother ain' here no more. So, fuck it!"

Xavier heard the pain in Judah's voice and sighed. He shook his head.

"Mercy was a special lady. I never met anybody like her. She was funny and caring, and she loved being a mother." Xavier glanced at Deon. "Mercy loved you. She would be so proud of the way your life has turned out. She spent a lot of nights praying for you and it paid off."

Deon nodded. Judah huffed.

"I always liked Lenox, too," Xavier continued. "She was a star without trying to be. They loved each other. But they held each other back. Mercy didn't have to be tough. Because Lenox was the tough one. Lenox didn't have to think too hard about the choices she made. Because Mercy was supposed to be the sensible one."

He sighed. "The same thing was starting to happen with you two. Growing up, one of y'all was wild and unpredictable. The other one was levelheaded and responsible. You played those roles for years. And if things didn't turn out the way they have, you might have played those roles for the rest of your lives. That's what this is about."

He sat back like he had just solved the toughest equation. But he found both men staring back at him with confused expressions on their faces.

"Some things become clearer to you as you get older," he said. He looked at Deon. "You were always acting up as a kid. Even before your mother passed. But I recognized it for what it was. A cry for attention. It got worse after Lenox was gone. Mercy knew what it was, too. But it wasn't just about the attention. You were doing what everybody expected you to do. It was easy to act up because that was the role you were assigned. You got comfortable with it. Until Judah got caught up in the act. That changed you. Made you grow up. I heard it in your voice when you and Mercy called me to ask about getting your trucking license. You were forced to switch roles. Now you had to be the responsible one. Had to start planning for the future. Fun time was over."

Xavier looked at Judah next. "Your role was the dependable one. Always following the rules, staying out of trouble. Always so mature for your age. Getting love from all the neighbors and teachers. You were familiar with that role. Then this thing happened, and your scripts got flipped. Judah had to learn how to fight, how to make noise. Deon had to learn how to calm down, how to be responsible. And in the midst of all of that, Mercy passed away. Nobody predicted that and nobody expected it. But you were forced to deal with it."

Xavier leaned forward in his seat. "This shit with Chanel ain't much different. It happened. Nobody predicted it. But now we're all forced to deal with it."

Judah shook his head, still crushed by the thought of it.

"You can let it tear you apart for good or you can find a way to move past it. But no matter what you decide to do, you need to understand that it's not about a woman who came between y'all. It's about years of history, of loss and pain. And anger." He looked at Judah as he said it. "You have a right to be mad. You lost eight years of your life. You lost your mother. Your heart is broken. And you gotta start over from scratch. Anybody in your shoes would be furious. But don't let that anger eat you alive. Don't let it convince you that any one person is to blame for it."

He looked from one cousin to another. "All we can do is play the hand we got dealt. Ain't no do-overs in life. The only choice we have is to keep going. Y'all are still family. Whether you like it or not."

When he was done, Judah and Deon sat in silence for a while.

Finally, Deon spoke up.

"Judah, I fucked up. I know you feel betrayed. But I want to apologize."

Judah stared back at him.

Deon continued. "I know you don't want to hear nothing I have to say. But I owe you that. I'm sorry. You're more than my cousin. No matter how you feel about me. I'll always see you as my brother. You're the last person in the world I ever wanted to disappoint." He held Judah's gaze. "I honestly wish you never came downstairs to help me that day. I wish you had them guys beat me to death. I think about that all the time. Everybody would have been better off."

"That's not true," Xavier said.

Deon shrugged. He wasn't so sure. He looked at Judah again. "When you got locked up, I just wanted to get away from everybody. Seeing Aunt Mercy so sad every day was too much. I was so glad to leave New York. I stayed to myself for years. Me, that big rig, and the road. That was all I needed. I did a lot of thinking while I was out there driving. About my mother and how much I missed her. About Aunt Mercy and how I let her down. But mostly about you and how I wanted to be like you. You were always gonna be great. Everybody saw it. That's why Aunt Mercy robbed Peter to pay Paul so she could send you to that Catholic school. Everybody could tell there was something special about you. I wanted to be like that. If I could turn my life around, it could be my way of paying you back for saving my life that day."

Judah watched his cousin closely as he spoke.

"I worked, came home, and stayed to myself. Visited you when I could, called and checked on Aunt Mercy. And I tried not to get in the way anymore. Tried not to be a burden to y'all. And then she died." Deon looked down at his hand and shook his head sadly. "I wanted to take care of everything just like you would if you were home. And Chanel was there trying to console her mother who had just lost her best friend. And we started talking. About you, about growing up, life, and how much things changed. And that shit just . . . happened."

Judah stared at him, deciding whether or not he believed it. "It 'just happened' more than once." He said it facetiously.

Deon stared back at Judah. "I fell in love with her," he admitted. "I'm not proud of that. And I wish I could change it. I swear to God I would if I could. That's why I put an end to it. Because my relationship with you is more important to me than anything else. Judah, I'm sorry."

Judah felt a flood of emotions. He was so angry. But also incredibly hurt. A lone tear fell from his eye, and he wiped it away quickly, embarrassed.

Xavier noticed him wrestling with his emotions and spoke again. "Black men have it hard. Most of us don't grow up with our fathers in the house. I know mine wasn't around. When my daughter was born, I had to learn how to be a father without having one to copy. It was on-the-job training like a muthafucka!"

Both of the cousins chuckled a little at that, easing the tension in the room a bit.

"I learned how to be a man by watching my uncles and the OGs in the neighborhood. I was taught that men are supposed to be strong all the time. Men don't get weak or tired. We're not supposed to cry. A little girl falls down and the adults pick her up, comfort her. A little boy falls down and what happens? Everybody says, 'Don't cry'; 'Be a big boy.' Men never unlearn that shit. We suck it up and keep pushing. But that shit ain't healthy. Crying doesn't make you weak. It's a natural response to all the things you two have been dealing with for years. Grief, guilt, fear, frustration, loneliness, and anger."

Xavier shrugged. "Like I said, the older you get the clearer you see things. For most of your lives, you two have been on a seesaw. One up, one down. But now, for the first time in your lives, you're on the same level. Both of you have lost your mothers. Both of you have spent time behind bars. You've experienced love and loss. And you both survived."

Judah and Deon exchanged glances, each processing Xavier's statement.

Judah looked at Xavier and nodded, gratefully. It occurred to him that his mother had been blessed to have Xavier in her life. He was full of wisdom and had a way of looking at things from a fresh perspective. He wished his mother had been brave enough to move to Maryland with Xavier before it was too late.

Xavier softened his tone as he delved into troubled waters. "This thing between y'all has very little to do with Chanel. One of you loved her as a teenager. One of you loves her as a woman. But she's not what's standing between you. Nothing is anymore. You can start over from here."

Judah sat still and silent for several long moments. He was dealing with so many thoughts and feelings that he felt overwhelmed by it all. He had a choice to make. Accept Deon's actions with Chanel and remain a family or walk away from his cousin for good. He thought about what his mother would say, his Aunt Lenox, and all the wisdom Xavier had just shared with him. He knew what he had to do. Judah exhaled. Then he nodded his head slowly. He pressed his lips together, stood up, and walked to the door where his belongings were piled in plastic garbage bags. Deon and Xavier watched in silence as Judah loaded the bags one by one into Xavier's truck.

Deon felt a lump in his throat as he watched his cousin. There were so many things he wanted to say to him. So much he wanted to try his best to explain. That he had never intended to fall in love with Chanel. That he would do it all differently if given a second chance.

Judah loaded the last of his things into Xavier's truck and came back inside. He looked at Xavier.

"You ready?"

Xavier nodded. "Yeah," he said, standing. He walked over to Judah and placed a hand on his shoulder. "I'm gonna go wait in the truck. You take your time in here with your cousin." Xavier gave Deon a hug and walked outside.

The cousins stood face-to-face. Deon's heart roared in his chest.

"I won't see her again," he said. "I swear."

Judah shrugged. "What's done is done. Y'all fell in love. Leaving her now ain't gonna change that." He nodded his head in the direction of the door. "Xavier's right. This ain't about Chanel. Not really. It's about me feeling like you robbed me of my future. I was mad at you for years. I didn't realize how mad I was until this happened. I blamed you for making me share my mother with you. But I forgot about the ways you had my back, too. The way you were there for my mother in the end when I couldn't be."

A tear slid down Judah's cheek, and this time he didn't bother to try to hide it.

"Like Xavier said, we're all we got." He squared his shoulders and stood tall. "The two people I love the most love each other. It's hard to stay mad at that."

Deon welled up as he listened to Judah being the bigger man for the umpteenth time in his life.

"I'm sorry."

Judah nodded. "So am I."

They embraced, patting each other on the back forcefully as they did so. All of the unspoken words that had lingered between them for years came pouring forth soundlessly. Those words were expressed in the intensity of their hug, in the tears that flowed from both their eyes, and in the palms of their hands as they gripped each other tightly.

Deon's embrace said, "I'm sorry I let you down. I never meant to hurt you. I don't want to lose you as my brother." Judah's embrace said, "I forgive you. You'll always be my brother. But it's time for me to walk away."

Wrought with emotion, Judah pulled himself away. Sniffling, he wiped his face, turned around, and walked toward the door.

"I'll holla at you soon, D." He yelled it over his shoulder without breaking stride.

Holding back a flood of tears, he climbed into the passenger seat of the truck and stared straight ahead as Xavier put the car in drive and headed for Maryland.

Deon stood watching them drive away. He thought about everything Xavier had said about boys being told to stay strong. And Deon finally allowed the child inside of himself to cry as the truck rounded the corner and disappeared from sight.

ACKNOWLEDGMENTS

Monique Patterson, you are a gift from above. Thank you from the bottom of my heart for your raw, honest, insightful feedback, your guidance, and for being patient with me. You are incredible!

Sara Camilli, I am so blessed to have you in my life. Not only are we a great team, but you are an amazing person. You make me believe anything is possible. And I thank you so much.

ABOUT THE AUTHOR

Ashley Williams

TRACY BROWN is the *Essence* bestselling author of *Single Black Female; Boss; White Lines III: All Falls Down; White Lines II: Sunny; Aftermath; Snapped; Twisted; White Lines: Lost Diamond; Criminal Minded; Black;* and *Dime Piece*. She lives in Staten Island, New York.